I0726475

Wind Chimes, War and Consequence
A novel of the Vietnam War Era

Richard Alan Schwartz

Village Drummer Fiction
www.villagedrummerfiction.com

Dedication

This novel is dedicated to the following:

Mickey Krueger, of blessed memory, who sent me a paperback every month I was soldiering in Vietnam. The books provided an opportunity to escape the horror of war and was sorely needed by myself and the many platoon mates who read the books after I did.

My mom, Sonya Schwartz, of blessed memory, who sent thoughtful letters weekly and Scientific American each month, and was the first person to realize I could become a writer.

My father, Gerald Schwartz, of blessed memory. A crew chief in World War II, he prepared me for my service with his memories of that war, and helped me transition back to civilian life after the war.

My uncle, Mike Schwartz, of blessed memory. An infantry soldier during World War II. When I returned home, our discussions of the mental toll of combat, helped me understand the trauma of all who engage in combat against our fellow man.

Carolynn, my beloved wife and partner. Without her encouragement and patience, my novels wouldn't have been created. Many people ask what the key to happiness is. For me, the key is named Carolynn.

Mike, Craig, and Ben. Professional soldiers all. If I had to go into combat again, I'd want these three at my side. Thanks for staying in touch since our tour in 1970.

Lastly the novel is dedicated to all our nation's combat soldiers and their families. Especially those who still suffer due to PTSD and/or physical injuries.

"I would say two contrary laws seem to be wrestling with each other these days. The one, a law of blood and death, ever imagining new means of destruction and forcing nations to be constantly ready for the battlefield-the other a law of peace, work, and health, ever evolving new means of delivering man from the scourges that beset him. Which of these two laws will prevail, God only knows."
Louis Pasteur (1888)

Contents

Wind Chimes, War and Consequence
A novel of the Vietnam War Era

Prologue

"However horrible the incidents of war may be, the soldier who is called upon to offer and give his life for his country is the noblest development of mankind."
Douglas MacArthur

Private Brian Levin's contribution to the Vietnam War, began as a member of the infantry, under a star-filled but cold, moonless night in early January of 1970. He and his squad mates lay in a rain and mud filled rice-paddy. His body shivered enough, he thought, to generate seismic waves. Finding sleep impossible and trying to pass the time, Levin reviewed surgeries he'd performed prior to enlisting. Like a bad dream, the harder he tried to speed up time, the slower it became.

Word was whispered down the line that there was enemy movement in the stand of bamboo opposite them, which stretched for a mile in either direction then sloped up and away into the distant mountains. The whoosh of a rocket propelled grenade was heard. Levin reached for his M16, slipped it off safe. The RPG exploded to the former surgeon's left.

***

At the same time as Brian's first night of the war, but in the countryside northeast of Adelaide SA, Australia, twenty-two-year-old, Andrea Campbell, drove her Ute like a woman possessed. On the dirt and gravel backroads surrounding her parent's sheep station, she'd perfected tail-out drifts and slides. Ten-foot high rooster tails of dust and dirt announced her passage, as did the roar of the potent small block V8 which she and her brother installed to replace the Ute's anemic in-line-six.

Born into a family of sheep ranchers, Andrea had a few more months of study and she would complete the requirements for a degree in psychology at the University in Sydney. The future psychologist was home for Christmas break. On the way to town with her seven-years-older sister-in-law and the sister-in-law's infant son, Andrea was in heaven to be back in her two-door pickup. She demonstrating this by hanging the tail out on a number of dirt-road switchbacks and tight turns.

"Must you?" her sister-in-law complained.

"Makes me feel free…and competent…and glad to be home." She hung the back of the car out with a combination of steering and throttle, held the angle throughout the turn with the same, all the while looking out the side windows…because that's where the vehicle was headed. When the road straightened, the car did as well…much to her sister-in-law's relief.

"I'm going to vomit if you don't stop it."

"Near to town. Solid roads begin at the intersection."

She brought the car to an abrupt halt at a four-way-stop. Andrea glanced to the left and shaded her eyes as the setting sun blinded her. A car approached from the right. She assumed it would stop at the sign. Andrea proceeded left but halfway into the turn, sensed mortal danger. The sickening crunch of steel on steel, breaking glass, her sister's scream, and the squeal of tires forced to slide sideways, provided an auditory soundtrack which terrorized her as the Ute spun like a carnival ride. She jammed her eyes shut. Lastly, a sickening thud as the side of the car impacted a tree. Silence enveloped Andrea while the scent of gasoline and antifreeze filled the air. The lack of sound eventually yielding to moans as she felt the pain from cuts and bruises, a gash on her scalp throbbed, her hips, feet ached. Andrea opened her eyes, discovered her sister-in-law and child no longer in the car. Briefly pinned by the twisted wreck, which was once her Ute, she smelled smoke. With much effort she dragged herself out of the wreck as flames began licking at the engine compartment. She had difficulty moving her legs so pulled herself along the ground to her sister and nephew. Her sister-in-law's lifeless body was twisted. Upper body one-way. Lower body the other. There were tire marks on her hips where she'd been run over. The woman's face turned toward the sky, wide-eyed but no longer seeing; her body surrounded by a pool of her own blood.

Andrea dragged her nephew onto her lap, his eyes pleaded for help. He coughed up blood and the infant's eyes rolled back in his head as he exhaled his final breath.

Her wail rent the air, accompanied by thunder as a torrential rainstorm began.

***

Half a world away, twenty-six-year-old Rachel Moskowitz, entered her Manhattan townhome after a grueling thirteen-hour recording session.

The voice coming from the second floor sent chills down her spine.

"Where's the bitch? She put my brothers in jail where one of them died. When's she returning? Tell me or...when I find the little whore I'll gut and kill her right before I kill you," the voice growled.

Rachel, four weeks pregnant, slipped out of her shoes, pulled a survival knife from her purse, climbed the stairs to the second floor. She peeked into her bedroom. A slovenly man in a gray sweatshirt and jeans, his back to the doorway, pointed a gun at her husband. Dov, his military service having ended six weeks previous, was tied to a chair. There were bloody wounds and bruises on his face and neck. He cursed his attacker through bloody lips, his face beaten such that it was barely recognizable. The intruder used the butt of his pistol to slam the side of his victim's head. Blood oozed from a laceration caused by the pistol.

While the intruder continued to rage at her husband, Rachel padded into the room, survival knife at the ready. When she was an arm's length from him, the intruder noted her approach in the reflection of a small mirror on a nightstand. His eyes widened. As she had trained to do, the musician shoved the five-inch blade into the intruder's kidney. The gun fired. Rachel withdrew the knife, prepared for another thrust. The intruder's body convulsed, losing his grip on the gun which clunked to the floor. He arched his back, one hand straining to reach over his shoulder, the other reaching behind, as if reaching would end the pain; so severe it silenced its victim. He half turned toward her. The intruder stared at Rachel, mouthed a profanity. Hatred in his eyes, he took a step toward her. The hatred replaced by terror, his face turning pale, likely sensing now, the wound he'd received was fatal. A hand, like a claw, reached for her. She prepared for another strike, but he collapsed, a pool of blood spreading across the carpet. Eyes wide, his body convulsed twice. Rachel heard his last exhalation. She turned to her husband.

With a look of shock, Dov mouthed her name, the last gunshot having left a hole in his chest. His eyes pleaded for help.

She ran to his side putting her arms around him. He turned to her then his body went limp. Rachel held him tighter as if her embrace could keep him alive. She checked for a pulse but didn't find one. Rachel shouted his name, shook his lifeless body, pressing his head against her chest. His blood transferred to her hands, arms, face, and neck. She pleaded with God to awaken her from this nightmare and find Dov alive and well. After several minutes sobbing, Rachel struggled to her feet, picked up the bedside phone, dialed the police, and gave her location. She viewed the two bloodied bodies, dropped the phone and vomited, retching numerous times then staggered out of the bedroom, down the stairs, and out the front door. She alternated sobbing and apologizing to her husband then gazed skyward.

"I was so lonely Lord then you gave me Dov. We enjoyed a little time before he became a soldier, a lousy week during his R&R. You let him survive Vietnam then in such cruel fashion take him from us. How will I raise my child without its father?"

Rachel doubled over as a sharp pain invaded her belly.

PART ONE: BRIAN

Chapter 1

*The solider understands there are times when all others have failed, and
then he must "pay the butcher's bill" and fight, suffer, and die to undo
the errors of the politicians and to fulfill "the will of the people."*
Douglas MacArthur

1970 January

Halfway between Hue and Da Nang, they'd come up a dusty,
rut filled road, off Highway 1 that paralleled the Troi River.
The ride in the back of the stiffly sprung deuce-and-a-half
truck bounced the three men silly but they didn't notice; their
prime concern being survival during the next twelve months.
The heat was mid-nineties and humid as a wet sponge; and
this was early January. They arrived at a former Catholic
church. Its gray exterior pock-marked from bullet strikes, plus

its windows and doors were blown out long ago. The trio jumped to the ground, pulled their rifles and gear off the end of the deuce-and-a-half. The last item barely clear of the truck, the driver put it in gear and roared down the road to ensure he made it back to base camp before dark.

A shirtless soldier on perimeter duty pointed at the church. "Head inside. Ask for Staff Sergeant Touhy."

The Michelin Man shaped staff sergeant lined them up then lectured in a grim voice, "You don't use your training, then you step on your pecker; you Momma gonna be crying at your grave." He used his index finger to emphasize his message to the three new men. "Do shit like your leaders tell you, work as a team then you go home in one piece in twelve months. The lieutenant will talk to you shortly. I'll work out your squad assignments."

Private Brian Levin, slightly less than average height, big boned, wide at the shoulders and hips, and muscular arms revealed by his rolled-up sleeves, said, "Yes, Sergeant," in unison with the others then briefly remembered his mother's expression of worry and trepidation when she dropped him off at the airport for his flight to Vietnam. "All Levin soldiers make it home," she yelled in a trembling voice as he got out of the car. She was referring to his father and father's two brothers who survived World War Two.

Assigned to second squad, two of the newbies dropped their gear against the wall where most of that squad's men were sitting.

"Where y'all from?" Brian asked the other newbie in a thick southern drawl.

Arnie responded, "Brooklyn. Yourself?"

"Dallas, Texas." Sliding his helmet off to run a hand over his military short hair, Brian chuckled. "We sound like where we come from."

Arnie grinned and said, "Yea. You and John Wayne; me and Bugs Bunny."

Those within earshot laughed.

"Have some distant relatives in Dallas," Arnie said. "What did you do before the Army?"

"I was a student. Studied biology," Brian said, looking away from Arnie, folding his arms across his chest. "You?"

"Education major, although, if I had the talent, I'd play pro-baseball. Love that game, also love basketball. There was a YMCA near my home. When not studying or attending classes, I just about lived there." He stopped to sigh as he replayed memories of his hours engaged in sport. "The crack of a bat solidly connecting with a well thrown baseball on a bright spring morning, the glare of the lights at Yankee stadium, the rumble of the elevated trains while throngs of fans were moved to silence while the pitcher gets the sign and nods. He goes into the wind-up, anxiety in the stands rising, hotdogs no longer chewed, beer no longer sipped. People leaning forward, as if decreasing the distance between themselves and the field by a few inches, will make them feel closer to the drama on the field. The pitcher checks the runner on first base, then unwinds like a clock spring. The white sphere leaving his hand at ninety-miles an hour. The batter swings, the umpire yells strike, and the fans erupt."

"Great description," Brian said.

Arnie, grinning and staring at nothing but memories added, "I love the squeak of gym shoes on hardwood floors as multiple players try to stop or change direction while fighting for possession of a basketball...heck," he chuckled, "even like the smell of the locker room..."

The two newbies sat on the floor, leaning back against their rucksacks.

"You? Play any sports?" the Brooklynite asked.

"Weights, occasional hike, but no sports. I love vehicles," the Texan said, then thought to himself, *"In truth, I live for my biology-based career."* He glanced at his new friend and wondered if he should say more about his career then decided not to.

The dull church interior held some thirty soldiers, roughly grouped by squad assignment. Card playing, cleaning rifles, writing to family, reading and re-reading letters from home or fitful attempts at sleeping occupied most. The staff sergeant introduced the new arrivals to members of their squads. Most shook hands and returned to whatever they were doing. Inexperienced soldiers, and their possible screw-ups, endangered the experienced men so for the first few weeks, the new soldiers were expected to do what they were told and keep quiet.

As Brian scanned around the room, he noticed Lt. Moss who stood at the front of the Church.

"Y'all listen up," Lt. Moss yelled to the men of his platoon, his expression one of distress.

Everyone stopped what they were doing and turned to face their platoon leader.

He waved a handwritten letter. "Just got this. Most of us remember Alex Dunn." Many nodded. "He really had his shit together. Became an excellent squad leader. Everyone's friend. He rotated home a few months ago. This letter is from his parents. Seems he drove a car into a concrete silo at high speed. They believe he killed himself." Many men shook their heads in disbelief. The Lt. studied the letter. "Says here, the rest of us need to be wary when we go home cause we ain't the same after we been through this shit, and the world we goin' back to ain't the same." He looked around at his men, "Y'all watch your asses when you go home." The Lt. held up the letter. "Don't want no more damn letters like this."

The platoon leader's expression one of disgust, he then turned to the three new arrivals and yelled for them to report to him. They approached and saluted. He looked them up and down and returned their salute. "Do what you're told, remember you are part of a team, and make sure your buddies can rely on you." With a sloppy salute, he dismissed them. They heard the Lieutenant take a deep breath and let it out slowly while looking over his platoon. He sat on his folded poncho liner and studied a map.

An hour after eating dinner, second squad gathered their combat gear and headed to a night ambush position. Just out the door from the church, with an hour hike ahead of them, several of the men cursed as cold raindrops the size of walnuts pelted them.

***

Levin thought, *"I can't believe my first night in-country and I'm lying in three inches of water with my head on a rice paddy dike. And my damn poncho leaks. If I shiver any harder, I'll generate a tsunami…hell, my teeth are chattering so loud, I'll give our position away."* He stared into the inky darkness. *"At least the damn rain stopped."*

Brian chuckled to himself while he remembered complaining about the operating theatre in Dallas being too cool and he asked the temperature be raised three degrees. He mumbled, "Wouldn't mind trading this for that mild chill."

He'd wrapped his poncho and poncho-liner around himself thinking if he stayed still enough, the water trapped between his skin and the poncho combination would warm the water. It did but if he moved, the cold water entering sent a shock wave through his body.

Brian turned to Arnie. The Brooklynite tried to smile but only one corner of his mouth lifted.

The clouds separated around 0200, revealing glimpses of a star-filled sky with a prominent half-moon on display. The soldiers ignored the myriad of sparkling, diamond-like, points of light above them to concentrate on their surroundings. They watched for any sight or sound which indicated enemy activity.

A long line of bamboo stood at a right angle, fifty meters to the twelve-man squad's front. A trail between themselves and the tall green plants was used by the enemy to infiltrate villages in the area. Their assignment was to ambush enemy soldiers using the trail.

An hour before sunrise, the sky finally clear, any thought of Brian's own comfort became irrelevant as automatic gunfire erupted from the line of bamboo. The whooshing sound of a rocket propelled grenade, called an RPG, was followed by an explosion twenty meters to his left. His heart pounding enough to cause seismic waves, Brian reached for his M16, emptied two magazines while firing three round bursts then sent single shots toward the winking lights.

A man screamed. Someone next to the wounded man yelled, "Doc!"

Martin Evans, the platoon's medic, slithered through the mud and water like a salamander. Brian considered joining him but remembered why he volunteered for infantry and kept shooting. A good thing as they were obviously outnumbered.

The former surgeon realized the M60 machine gun to his left was silent. He saw all four members of the gun team were injured by the RPG.

SSgt. Touhy, the platoon sergeant, yelled at Brian and Arnie, "You two, get on the damn gun."

The twosome mirrored Doc Evans' salamander-like movements as they belly-crawled through the mud while rounds went over and between them like angry bees. They moved two wounded soldiers then the Texan moved behind the gun and the Brooklynite guided the belts of ammunition.

"Gotta get this right," Brian thought, his mind racing, filled with a mixture of fear and determination. *"They're depending on me."* As if back home on his drums, Brian began firing a repeated rhythm of six, six, and fourteen rounds at the enemy's winking lights. Arnie guided the belts with one hand, then linked the next belt from the next ammo box, allowing smooth feeding of the gun. Another swoosh of an RPG sounded then an explosion occurred behind them.

An illumination round announced its presence with a loud pop over the bamboo. Supported by a parachute, its million-candle-power brightness, powered by a burning chemical reaction, bathed the line of bamboo and the enemy soldiers in it. Now second squad's shots would be aimed at people, not just the area of winking lights. As one illumination round burned out, another arrived to achieve the same purpose.

Fifteen enemy soldiers assaulted their position from the right end of the enemy's line. Bent forward and firing from the hip, they advanced toward the Americans.

"Levin, left. Left. Give 'em hell!" SSgt. Touhy yelled over the sound of gunfire.

Arnie saw him pointing, looked left then yelled, "We're being flanked. Left side, left side."

Brian, moved to his knees, repositioned the machine gun, lay flat again then returned his right hand to the pistol grip. Pulling the gun into his shoulder, his left hand over the butt stock, his cheek welded to that hand. Arnie lined up the ammo belts in the new direction. Levin fired a short burst, watched to see where the tracers were hitting; adjusted his aim then opened-up on the attacking soldiers. Five were bunched together at the center of the line. They fell to Brian's machine gun like a scythe going through wheat, the balance continuing toward them. Rifle fire took out a few more. The machine gun decapitated one, his head exploding into a red mist. The last five turned to head back to the bamboo stand but a round from a grenade launcher dispatched one to meet his maker while the two men at his side fell with severe wounds to their lower bodies. On the ground and using their hands and arms, they clawed their way in the direction of the bamboo stand.

Levin turned the gun back to the center of the bamboo, where most of the rounds were coming from.

Since the firefight began, their squad leader was on the radio with artillery command.

Dirt, ripped bamboo, and torn bodies flew skyward as the first high-explosive artillery shell slammed into the enemy position. Screams of the dead and dying pierced the air. The ground shook as six additional shells arrived in unison. In the light of the illumination rounds, they could see the handful of remaining enemy soldiers disappearing through the bamboo, back toward the mountains. Another six-round blast. Smoke and debris obscured the enemy's retreat.

"Cease fire," SSgt. Touhy yelled a minute later after the last of the enemy soldiers had melted back into the jungle.

Others repeated the order. All became quiet except for the hissing of a still burning illumination round; the smell of cordite hung in the unmoving, dense air. The first glimmer of daylight appeared in the eastern sky.

"We got the range on 'em," SSgt. Touhy said. "They's buggin' out. Nice work, second squad. Be alert. They may come back. Reload your magazines with whatever you have left. He turned to Arnie and Brian. "You two, stay on the gun until sunup then bring it back to day position. Trout, radio for a medivac."

The two newbies exchanged nervous grins.

"Nice Shootin', Tex," Arnie said, trying to imitate Brian's southern drawl.

The Texan engaged in nervous laughter. He held up his trembling hands. "Shaking all of a sudden," he said.

Arnie held up his. "Me too."

The Texan smiled and nodded then watched the platoon's medic, Martin Evans, work on one of the men who'd initially manned the M60 machine gun. Referred to by the troops as Doc Evans, the medic held a bandage against an oozing wound. He said, "This is deep. Mo's losing a lot of blood. Pressure doesn't seem to stop it."

"Let me see," Brian said.

Lifting the bandage to examine the wound, Brian shook his head, pushed the bandage back down and said to Evans,

"This has to be sutured. I've done it before. I'll do it if you want. You should start an IV."

Doc Evans briefly stared at the new arrival, tossed him a package of suturing materials and latex gloves then inserted an IV in Mo's arm.

Brian asked for an injectable pain killer. He administered it, cleaned dirt from the wound then rapidly sutured and covered it.

"Hey, Levin," Doc Evans said. "Pretty fast with sutures. Where'd you learn?"

"I completed a course in Mountaineering Medicine," Levin said without looking at him. "For experience, I also volunteered to work with EMTs in an Emergency Room."

"Looks like you been practicing," the medic muttered while holding up the bottle with the IV fluid, all the while appraising Brian with a questioning expression.

"Nothing like practice," Levin said. He examined Mo's other wounds then took the IV bottle from Evans. "You put a row in here." He pointed to a small laceration in the man's thigh then guided the medic while he worked.

"Nice work. Good hands. Stitches evenly spaced," the former surgeon shouted to Evans over the raucous sound of the medivac chopper as it approached. They turned away from the downwash until it touched down.

With the chopper on its way with the wounded, Levin said to Doc Evans, "Is that a Texas accent I hear?"

Evans nodded and said, "So I'm not the only Lone Star. I'm from Houston. You?"

"Celina, north of Dallas."

"At the Red River?"

Brian replied, "I live a short drive south of there."

With the wounded evacuated, second squad formed up and headed back to their day position. They plodded in silence for a distance, steam coming off their uniforms as it dried from the intense heat of the sun. By the time they arrived at the old church, the uniforms would be soaked again; this time by sweat.

"We took out a number of them. Were you…?" Arnie asked Brian in a subdued voice.

Nodding, Brian stated while shifting the machine gun from one shoulder to the other, "Scared as hell, adrenaline pumping, my heart pounding, but too damn busy shooting to think about it, also worried…"

"About?"

"First time in combat. Didn't want to let anyone down," the Texan said.

"When the shooting started and when we got on the gun, my primary feeling was, don't screw up, the squad depending on us, you depending on me," Arnie said. "Shit I was scared. We were way out numbered. Good thing you can play an angry song on that gun."

"You did well," Brian said, "and yes there were a lot of them. Lucky we could bring in the arty or that angry song might have become a tragic song."

The squad waded through a shallow, wide stream.

Arnie sighed and said, "Played a tragic song for those we were shooting at."

Brian noticed Arnie had bowed his head and was mumbling. *"Likely, a prayer,"* he thought.

Nearly back at the abandoned Catholic Church, Brian felt worn as the adrenaline which kept him alert was wearing off. As they walked, the Texan thought he heard a sound like the wind chimes he'd hung just before he left for Vietnam. He glanced around as if he expected to see them then asked Arnie if he heard the sound.

The Brooklynite chuckled and said, "Don't hear a thing, but we just did a hell of a lot of shooting so maybe your ears are ringing."

Doc Evans suggested Brian heard the distant gongs of a Buddhist Temple. "They're all around here," the medic said.

Brian smiled while he remembered hanging the gleaming crystals on his front porch, now half a world away, seeing a sunrise refracted through them.

Back at the church, although his hands still trembled, he made some notes on the firefight, Arnie's reaction, then stuffed them in an envelope, and placed the envelope in a pocket of his rucksack to be mailed later.

He silently recited a brief prayer of thanks that he survived his first firefight and asked that he'd make it home to hear the sonorous sounds of his wind chimes again; finally prayed that his secret be kept and his fellow soldiers not find out they were the unwitting subjects of his research project.

Chapter 2

The morning after the firefight, members of second squad were occupied with eating canned or freeze-dried breakfast, cleaning their rifles, and reloading magazines.

"Where's home?" Arnie asked a barrel-chested six-footer who arrived in the same deuce-and-a-half as he and Brian.

"Butte, Montana," James Ware said.

"Mining country," Brian stated.

The tall man nodded. "Mr. Cunningham, he's the mine owner, took my truck and stored it until I come home. Truck has two kinds of power," James continued, pride in his voice. "Kind of like a locomotive. Big diesel, around nine-hundred horsepower, connected to a generator and electric motors that drive the wheels."

"Love machinery," Brian said. "Own a John Deere tractor; all seventy horsepower of it." The others laughed. He disassembled the machine gun then ran a series of patches down the barrel.

James removed a picture from his pocket and showed it around. "That little man standing on the platform in front of the driver's windshield? That's me."

"Damn that thing's big," Arnie said.

"'Bout twenty feet tall, almost that wide. Hell, one tire weighs nearly a ton."

"What's it like, driving it?" Arnie asked.

"Took a few months to get used to it. Takes lots of planning. Had a trainer with me full time until I got a feel for backing up." He grinned and said, "With all that weight, if you'd hit something, you'd likely go through it before you knew what happened."

The others chuckled.

"You get bored?" Brian asked while he oiled another patch and attached it to the cleaning rod, "I mean, driving the same thing every day?"

"Hell no. Takes skill to get it from one place to another. I love the sounds it makes and the paycheck takes good care of the family." He displayed another photo. "My high school sweet-heart and our two boys,"

"Nice looking family." Arnie said.

"Truly, my pride and joy."

"You volunteer?" Brian asked.

"Hell yes," Ware said. "Gotta stop them damn Commies. Better doing it here than back in the States. My pa served in WWII so I thought I should do my duty as well."

"I joined for the education benefit," Arnie said. "Started college but ran out of money."

They looked at Brian.

"Quite a firefight last night," he said.

Doc Evans approached Brian. "I'm ordering medical supplies. I never know which squad I'll go out with. You want anything…in case I'm not there?"

"Suturing kits, gauze, latex gloves, and non-alcohol wipes," the Texan replied.

"That's it?"

"Scalpels, hemostats, anti-septic soap…just in case."

The medic eyed Brian for a bit then said, "I'll ask. I don't always get what I request." He walked to a radio operator to call in his order.

Brian disassembled and cleaned the machine gun.

The second squad leader, Sgt. Jason Wabash, pulled Levin and Zalman aside.

"Mo and Henry won't be back for a while," the sergeant said. "The other two on the gun team should be back in a couple weeks. You guys performed well last night. Mind being responsible for the gun?"

"Fine with me," Brian said, "but are the other guys ok with us new guys taking over?"

"SSgt. Touhy saw your shooting last night. Something about accurate fire stopping a flanking movement. It was his recommendation."

Brian looked at Arnie who nodded.

"Sounds good, Sergeant," the Texan said.

After lunch, Arnie and Brian sat on the floor and leaned back against their rucksacks. The Brooklynite remarked,

"You, well really, we, mowed down a number of 'em last night."

"True." Brian turned to his new friend. "How do you feel about that?"

Arnie shrugged then said, "That's what we're here to do, I guess." He thought for a while staring out the door of the church. "Actually, I felt exhilarated for a moment then witnessed one man's head…like exploded. What an awful sight."

"Bad alright but he died quickly," Brian replied.

The Brooklynite was quiet for a while, glanced at Brian a few times then said, "The fact that it was bloody as hell last night…that bloody wound you closed, doesn't seem to bother you."

"Blood and guts haven't bothered me since I was a kid."

Arnie closed his eyes for a while leaning back against his ruck. "But—"

"Arnie," Brian interrupted, "I feel sorry he died, sorry for all of them, but this is war, and this is what happens."

"Course it does," a soldier said in a thick Southern Louisiana accent. Brian looked up and saw that it was Paul Slidell. Average height and chubby, the Baton Rouge native shuffled over and sat down. "The government sent us here to do just that. Stop them commies."

"So how do you feel when you kill someone?" Brian asked his fellow Southerner.

"Hell. Don't feel anything. Besides, those gooks was trying to kill us. Why should I feel anything except glad we're all alive and did what the country sent us here to do?"

"No idea," the new machine gunner said while shaking his head. "Just asking..."

"Gooks," Brian thought. *"Likely a word invented by soldiers. Demeaning originally, but I notice most say it with respect...like you'd refer to a worthy adversary."* He put his head back on his ruck and thought, *"Likely using the word in place of anything which would make the enemy soldiers seem human. Does calling them that make it easier to kill? Have to listen to its use; then I'll have a better idea. I'll bet soldiers from all wars made up names like that. Remember reading that Brits referred to the Germans as Huns. Should write a note about that."*

Arnie mumbled, "His head...like exploded." He turned pale, ran a few meters away from the church, retched a few times then, after wiping his mouth and catching his breath, grabbed his entrenching shovel and covered the mess.

"He'll get used to it," Paul said, then heard poor Arnie retching a few more times. "Or not."

"You okay?" Brian asked Arnie as the Brooklynite drank from his canteen.

"Yea." He sat on the floor, leaning back against his rucksack. "I was raised an Orthodox Jew. What we did last night; I know the Talmud says we have a duty to defend ourselves. Even so, feel sad for those we killed, guilty really. Satisfied initially as those we killed wouldn't be able to kill us, but then guilt...lots of guilt."

"But you volunteered for the Army," Brian said.

Arnie shook his head, cursed. "I desperately need the education benefit. Hell, I hope I live long enough to use it."

A jeep towing a trailer arrived mid-day. Arnie and Brian helped a few others remove insulated food containers from the trailer. They placed them in a row as their platoon mates took out their eating gear and formed a line. The newbies served the men.

At the end of the line, a few Vietnamese children, who stayed around the troops during the day, lined up and were served whatever was left.

"Nothing like a hot meal," Arnie said as he and Brian placed the empty containers back in the jeep's trailer.

Later that day, a helicopter came out with supplies for the platoon.

"Got the medical supplies you asked for," Doc Evans said, handing a package to Brian. "They wanted to know who was going to use the stuff."

"You replied?"

"Someone who knows what do to with 'em."

They laughed.

Evans gave Brian a questioning expression then said, "They call me Doc but I'm just a medic. I'm guessing you know more than me about medical stuff. If there is a technique you can teach me…you'll do that right?"

"Of course."

Evans grinned and said, "Also sent these out." He held up two small plastic bottles. "Looks like a clear liquid. Funny name...cyan...something."

Brian's face lit up. "Holy crap. This is fantastic. Read about this stuff but never saw it."

"It is..."

"Skin adhesive. Used instead of sutures in appropriate circumstances."

"You'll teach me?"

"Shit yea." Levin fitted the supplies into a medic's pack he'd acquired from one of the medics who was headed home that week then asked Evans, "How long you been in-country?"

"Arrived here one week before you. Nice to know there's another guy who knows about medical stuff."

Levin asked, "After the Army, you thought of going into medicine?"

"Not sure what I'll do. Maybe medicine, but really, no clue."

"You've got the hands," Levin said.

Evans shrugged. "Wouldn't know about that."

"Get some paper for notes. I'll make some diagrams then show you how and when to use the new stuff."

***

A week later, Brian, Arnie, James, David Trout, and Doc Evans and the company's sniper, Eddie O'Connell, left their day position, each carrying their rifle and a couple magazines. It was mid-morning as they walked one-hundred yards along Highway One then crossed to the middle of a bridge over the wide, slow moving, Troi River. A half mile further downstream, the Troi emptied into the South China Sea. The sea's blue-green surface appearing dark where fresh water from the Troi emptied into it.

Three meters above the water and at the center of the bridge, a two-foot wide by four-foot long board stuck out from the side of the bridge. It was used by the locals and occasionally soldiers to dive into the river. A ladder extended down to the water's surface.

"I was a competitive diver in high school," Eddie said then handed his sniper rifle to Brian. He stripped down to his shorts, went over the wood railing and out to the end of the board.

"Swan Dive," he announced with a grin. Hands at side and standing straight, he took a deep breath, his last. Eddie's body went limp as he fell off the board. A fraction of a second later the crack and thump of a single shot reached their ears.

"Down," Arnie yelled. They flattened themselves to the roadway. Clicks of rifles going off safe were heard, each man checking their surroundings to determine where the shot had come from. Arnie and Brian peaked over the edge of the roadway, saw Eddie face-down, his blood coloring the water around his body, the sniper began moving his arms.

"Eddie's still alive," Arnie yelled. James leaped to his feet, jumped the railing and plunged into the river. A second shot rang out.

After radioing the Lieutenant, describing their location and situation, David Trout checked on James. "Ware is swimming Eddie to shore."

Brian, trying to show as little of himself above a row of two-high sandbags, used the sniper rifle's optic to study the wood line which bordered the southern side of the river.

"Where would I hide?" Brian thought. *"Long time from crack to thump. At least a two, maybe three football-field shot."* He noticed a group of three trees with bushes around their base which he judged to be two-hundred-fifty yards distant. Brian imagined

he'd hide in the right-hand tree which was slightly closer to the river and had thicker foliage than the others.

He adjusted the optic for distance then aimed two mil-dots to the right, allowing for the steady breeze coming off the South China Sea. He squeezed the trigger; his effort rewarded as he watched a man pinwheel out of the tree.

"You got that fucker," Doc Evans said, rising to his knees.

Brian grabbed his shoulder, pushed him down, growling at the medic, "Fuckin' stay down. He might not be alone."

"Third squad is on the way," radioman David Trout said.

Brian leaned over the edge of the bridge to view the bank of the river where James had pulled Eddie out of the water. They were behind a stacked-sandbag barrier so couldn't be seen from the bridge.

"How's Eddie?" Brian yelled.

"Gone," yelled James.

"Shit," Brian said, then continued to glass the southern bank for more enemy soldiers.

Third squad approached with Lt. Moss who was briefed on what happened. He told those not part of third squad to head back to day position, gather their gear and be ready to assist if needed.

"Levin, Slidell," SSgt. Touhy called out. They hurried to his side. "Lost our sniper today." He turned to Brian. "Heard you used his rifle to take out the shooter. Three-hundred-meter shot?"

"About that far, Staff Sargent."

"Adjust for distance?"

"Two clicks."

"Wind?"

"Two mil-dots."

"You learned to shoot…"

"I'm from Texas. Had a rifle in my hands at a young age; scoped rifle used for hunting from age thirteen."

"You hunted…"

"Deer, wild hogs, ducks and geese."

"I thought Jews don't hunt."

"My Dad, a WWII vet believed, if Hitler's National Socialists come again, we'd best be armed and practiced."

The staff sergeant grinned and said. "Tom White is going to sniper school. Until he returns, you fill that slot. Slidell will be your spotter."

***

As darkness approached, the sniper team made themselves appear like the fauna surrounding them by wearing camo skin-paint on their face and hands plus inserting branches and plants in their ghillie suits. They crawled into position, taking over an hour to move thirty yards so as not to be noticed. The duo, on a ridge overlooking a small valley which was crisscrossed with trails, alternately drank water and ate a freeze-dried dinner.

An hour later, the area illuminated by a full moon, Levin whispered, "Something moving across my legs."

Slidell slowly turned his head then whispered a reply, "Don't move. It's a damn snake."

"Poisonous?"

The Louisianan replied with a smirk. "Shit. I'd ask but I don't speak snake."

The snake slithered on its way and the duo settled in for the night. Every two hours, one stayed awake on watch while the other slept.

Near sunup, Slidell, using binoculars, sighted then pointed to an eight-man squad as it made its way from their right to left on one of the trails one-hundred yards distant. Based on his uniform, Levin recognized the fourth man was the leader. He adjusted his scope and squeezed off a round. The leader collapsed. The others made for a low berm. Having no clue where the round came from, they decided to shoot in random directions for a few seconds to see if there was return fire. With an occasional round landing near them, Levin and Slidell remained motionless. Having received no return rounds the enemy soldiers apparently decided to fire again and make a run in the direction they came from. The minute they did Levin dropped two more before they disappeared into the jungle.

Slidell moaned.

"You hit?"

"Fuck. Feels like a bad bee sting in my hip. Right Side. Shit that burns."

"You'll have a scar to show your folks."

"No folks. I'm an orphan. Raised by a foster family, who I hated. You guys in the platoon more family then they ever were."

"That lady you write to…" Levin began examining his wound.

"Savanah. A pen pal…but writes real thoughtful letters. Hope to meet her when I get back to the world…so you gotta make sure I'm okay."

Brian removed a bullet fragment then used the new adhesive to close the wound.

"I know it hurts but you're lucky, the bullet hit something and fragmented before it hit you. Should be good in a few weeks."

Brian repacked his medical supplies. They moved to a clearing where Slidell radioed for a chopper to pick them up.

He got on the radio and was told to move to a location a few miles away where they would be picked up the following morning.

"Damn," Brian whispered, "Have to wait twenty-four hours before they can get a chopper out here."

Paul shook his head.

The duo waited until dusk before moving. Brian checked his map and compass. Used hand signals to indicate the path they would take.

Having walked roughly a half mile, they heard noise from their flank, a number of soldiers were approaching. They lay down in two-foot-high grass, Levin having to twist his body around a rock. The sniper team remained motionless. A patrol was searching for them. The enemy soldiers stopped to take a break, sat on the trail and chattered among themselves, a few lighting cigarettes. One stood, walked within two feet of Levin and Slidell, opened his fly and relieved himself. Brian held his breath initially but then decided it would be wiser to breathe slowly. The enemy soldier gave it a good shake and buttoned his fly. He spit once, his spittle landing near Brian's face, then returned to his patrol. Ten minutes later the squad moved on. The sniper team waited another ten minutes then, with joint's aching from remaining frozen in an awkward position for so long, slowly stood and continued moving. After another twenty minutes, they heard noises again. The duo lowered themselves to the earth a second time. Most nighttime insects became quiet; a sure sign of fellow humans moving nearby. Brian's anxiety was increasing by the second. They remained motionless except for an occasional rotation of their head to survey their surroundings. It was so quiet, the former surgeon was worried the sound of his breathing might give away their position. They waited another half-hour without hearing additional movement. Even the insects began their usual cacophony of buzzes, clicks, and squeaks. Brian checked his map and compass by moonlight, pointed in the direction they needed to head. The duo resumed hiking. Slidell's injury bothering him, evidenced by a slight limp, Brian whispered that the Louisianan should tell him when he needed to rest. His spotter used hand motions to signal they should continue.

Dawn found the duo at the edge of a clearing in the jungle. Slidell talked a helicopter toward them then popped a colored smoke grenade.

"I've got you Loud Mouth Lime," the chopper pilot said, identifying the green smoke. He used the name of a popular children's drink-flavoring product, to communicate the color of the smoke.

Slidell radioed confirmation then watched as the pilot lowered his machine to the earth a handful of yards away, the door gunners staring into the jungle at the edges of the clearing their machine occupied. As the machine lifted out of the jungle, the sniper team high fived. Brian recited a brief prayer. He was thankful his first sniper mission was complete.

***

Four weeks went by with no additional combat, although the sniper team was sent out regularly but had little contact with enemy soldiers.

Mid-morning, a group of eight Americans decided to walk to the local market. A smelly place, butchered meat and fish on display in the open while those hawking the animal flesh tried to entice buyers while keeping the flies away. Other vendors sold produce and still others, dry goods.

"You buy, my grandmother," a ten-year-old girl insisted. Her poor English indicated they should buy bread from her Grandmother's small bakery stand; their home and bakery behind it.

Levin bought two, six-inch, loaves which he put in the map pocket of his shirt. "One for lunch and one for dinner," he told the young girl.

"Yes, you like," she said with a huge grin, handing his coins to her grandmother.

Brian pulled out a box of hard candy, gave her two raspberry flavored treats. She gave one to her Grandmother then unwrapped the other and popped it in her mouth. The young one smiled.

He asked what her Vietnamese name was. He couldn't understand what she'd said. She had a quarter-inch dark red, circular birthmark on the left side of her jaw.

Brian said, "Dot. I'll call you Dot."

She turned to her Grandmother, said something in Vietnamese, and then said to him. "Linda." It was common for Vietnamese girls to call themselves, Linda or Sally.

Shaking his head, he pointed to her and said, "Dot."

The young girl laughed. Pronounced her new name, which came out with a long letter 'o' sound.

"You name?" Dot asked.

"Brian," he replied.

She repeated what she believed he said but it came out, "Dying," which his buddies thought was hysterical.

The Americans wandered the market, little Dot following close to Brian. She began singing. Ironically, it was the Animal's, *"We Gotta Get Outta This Place."* She'd likely heard it on Armed Forces Radio. Fortunately, Dot had no clue what the words meant.

The soldiers looked over the goods in the market, not noticing the three young men who, separately, slipped into the crowd after they arrived. They were the only young men, other than the Americans, in the market. The balance of males present were children or seniors.

Brian, SSgt. Touhy, and radioman David Trout, were discussing a combat mission which occurred before Levin arrived in-country. The balance of the eight men were on the other side of the marketplace.

Touhy said, "Six of them surrendered when the fighting ended. Not one of them over fifteen. One couldn't have been more than twelve. All firing AKs." The Staff Sergeant shook his head. "Kids. A bunch of damn kids."

Levin stopped to make a note. Pulling paper out of a pocket, he secured his rifle between his knees, and began writing. From across the market, a voice shouted, "Grenade!"

An explosion occurred at the edge of the crowd. Screams were heard.

At the same time as the shout about the grenade, Brian noticed the, short in stature, young man next to him had pulled a grenade out of his pocket, and was reaching to pull the pin. His reflex reaction was to jam his pen into and through the man's eye and into his brain. The man collapsed, one-third of the pen sticking out of his eye socket. His body quaked a few times then quit moving. The grenade rolled out of his hand.

"Pin still in place," SSgt. Touhy said, retrieving the grenade.

A second grenade exploded at the corner of the market. Civilians, took cover or ran, except a few who began helping the injured.

Brian retrieved his pen, wiped it on his pant leg.

SSgt. Touhy eyed him with disdain.

"My last pen," Brian said with a shrug. He remembered Dot, turned to her. "You okay?"

She didn't reply. Breathing rapidly, she stared at the body then the pen. Brian moved between her and the dead soldier. He kneeled on one knee, she leaned her head against his shoulder, sniffling. He put his hand behind her head briefly, said, "It's over." She stood straight, her gaze moving from his face to the pen. Her eyes widened. She slowly backed up, yelled something in Vietnamese. Brian reached for her hand. Dot screamed, turned, then while crying hysterically, ran to the bread stand and disappeared into the house behind it.

Brian glanced at his kill. "Little shit. Couldn't be more than fourteen."

"If you knew that beforehand, would you have done anything different?" SSgt. Touhy said.

He shook his head. "Guess not."

South Vietnamese soldiers arrived.

David Trout began yelling, "Lt. radioed. We need to return to day position. Going on a mission."

SSgt. Touhy yelled to the others. They formed up and returned to their day position.

"Sad we had to leave the civilian casualties," Trout said. He and the others ate a quick meal then assembled their gear for the move to a new location.

"The two grenades that exploded in the marketplace?" Arnie said as he finished a can of meatballs and spaghetti. "Remember?"

Brian nodded.

"One came flying at us. I batted it away with my rifle. The frag exploded near the edge of the market."

"The other?" Brian asked.

Arnie said, "Blew up the instant the pin was pulled. Split the guy who held it, wounded a bunch of locals."

"I heard their screams," David Trout said.

"If I didn't bat the frag, we'd been the ones torn up." Arnie said. He shook his head. "Should have hit it harder."

"Them or us," Trout said. "Glad it was them."

"Still, those poor civilians," Arnie said. "The guy whose frag blew up in his hand turned into a bloody mess. Just torn in half."

Trout nodded toward Brian. "He took one of 'em out or another frag would have gone off."

"Nice," Arnie said.

"Wasn't nice," Trout said, shaking his head while he eyed Brian with contempt then turned to Arnie. "Should have seen the kid's body quaking from the pen. Levin jammed it through his eye and into his brain. Disgusting sight, especially with that damn pen still sticking out of his eye."

Arnie appeared as if he was in shock. He sputtered, "A kid. P-Pen. Sticking out of..."

"Ask your buddy," Trout said. He gave Brian a look of contempt. "Hell, he's still got the damn pen."

The Brooklynite turned pale, walked outside, and began vomiting.

Brian ignored them, hoisted his rucksack, and buckled the straps together. As Tom White had returned from sniper school, Levin was again responsible for the M60. He lifted the machine gun onto his shoulder, and followed his squad members out to the area where the helicopters would land and take them deep into the jungle.

Chapter 3

Private Mark Acorn woke in the middle of the night and began shooting. Every one checked their surroundings but no one found signs of enemy activity. A few soldiers yelled at him to cease firing then asked what he saw.

"Thought sure I saw lots of soldiers coming toward us," Acorn said.

The others turned to Brian who was on watch at the time. "I was checking the area with the Starlight scope. I didn't see or hear anything until Acorn starting shooting."

"The lieutenant said to his radio man, "Call for a chopper at first light."

Brian volunteered to stay awake with Acorn the balance of the night. The following morning while waiting for a medivac helicopter to take him to the rear, Acorn talked to Brian about himself and a recent experience.

"I'm from a small town in Northern Wisconsin," Acorn said. "I've been hunting most of my life. Mostly deer and moose." He chuckled. "Never people." He pulled the magazine from his M16, checked to ensure there wasn't a round in the chamber then slammed the bolt closed and stuffed the magazine into a carrier on his belt.

He pulled out his canteen and took a long drink. "Fired up a Viet Cong a few weeks ago when we were on patrol. He came out of nowhere holding an AK rifle and suddenly opened up on us. Yelled some shit while firing. Little guy was really pissed." Acorn stared at his boots, picked up a twig to pry dried mud off the sole then took another long drink from his canteen. "I can still see the fury in his eyes as he fired, then my bullets slammed into him. He slowly collapsed, but kept trying to bring the AK up to fire again but didn't have the strength. He gave me one last look. Poor guy. He might have been asking for help. But...those eyes...that expression. Still angry or scared or I don't fucking know." He shook his head, then stuffed his canteen in the side pocket of his ruck sack. "Still see that damn expression..."

The chopper arrived and carried him to the medivac station.

Later that day, SSgt. Touhy, with rolled-up papers in his shirt pocket, stopped by second squad to report what he knew about Acorn. "They'll have Acorn talk to a shrink. If he's okay, spend the rest of his time in supply."

"If not?"

"Hospital ship or medical treatment at one of our bases in Japan, then home."

He eyed Brian then asked that he step away from the other soldiers.

"Sgt. Wabash is heading back to the world this week. You've been in his squad for six months. Your squad mates, including him, came to me, and asked that you be their new squad leader." The staff sergeant stared at him, shook his head. "Are you good enough to lead them in a way that accomplishes the squad's mission, and gets them back to the world without stepping on their peckers?"

"Yes, Sergeant," he said with a serious expression but was immediately joyous internally.

"Arnie and you are good friends. Gonna be a problem giving him orders?"

"No, Sergeant."

"He didn't think it would be a problem either. If it becomes one, you tell me, and I'll move him to another squad."

"Thanks, Sergeant."

The Staff Sergeant's face turned grim. "Damn it. Don't thank me. They asked for you. I didn't. Rather have you in charge of a squad you haven't served with. I have my doubts, but know this, you let them down and you'll know what a frog feels like that's been flattened by an eighteen-wheeler. Is that clear?"

"Yes, Sergeant," Levin said, no longer joyous as he felt the weight of his new responsibility hit him like a punch in the gut.

"Trout will be your radio man. You talk to Sgt. Wabash. Get his feel for team cohesiveness. You'll also have three new men later this week. And you train the hell out of whoever you decide to put on the gun. We hit the shit and that damn gun better sound like you're still behind it." He removed the papers from his shirt pocket, handed them to Brian. "Congratulations, Sergeant Levin. You've been promoted." SSgt. Touhy shook Brian's hand.

"An honor, Staff Sergeant."

Brian read the orders promoting him. To his amazement, he noted they were dated a week earlier.

***

Having endured a forty-five-minute chopper ride out to the A Shau Valley, Sgt. Levin took his seven-man recon patrol on a mission as directed by Tactical Operations Command. Their team also included an Air Force Forward Air Controller who humped his own radio. They plodded along a muddy trail which ran horizontal and half-way up a mountainside in a light mist. The jungle canopy letting scant light through.

Arnie, walking point, claimed to see movement on the mountainside opposite them, roughly a half mile away, a deep valley, separating them.

Sgt. Levin halted the squad, radioed tactical operations command to see if there were friendly units at that location. None were. He used binoculars to view the canopy covered area opposite them. The Sergeant thought he might have seen movement but wasn't sure.

He radioed the artillery controller, reported the coordinates of their current position, and the position of the opposite mountainside. A marker smoke round was fired. It exploded above the opposite mountainside; a cloud of white smoke indicating its position. Two more soldiers said they saw movement. Vietnamese voices echoed across the valley.

"Battery One," Brian radioed to the Fire Direction Controller.

"Shot," the FDC announced.

"Splash," the FDC said a few seconds later.

"Splash," Brian said. For the benefit of the newbies he reminded them, "That means impact in ten seconds."

A high-pitched whistling sound occurred briefly, followed by the gut shaking sound of six artillery shells exploding among the thick jungle canopy. Screams and yelling could be heard. Movement was occurring all over the opposite mountainside.

"Up fifty. Repeat!" Brian yelled into the radio. Every cannon the artillery base possessed responded. On the opposite mountain side, small arms fire broke out in random directions. The squad flattened themselves. The ground under them trembled as the shells exploded.

The Air Force FAC lying next to Brian, on his own radio, directed three Phantom aircraft to their location. He nodded to James Ware who popped a purple smoke grenade indicating their position. The lead pilot reported, "I've got you Goofy Grape." The FAC confirmed the color. The trio rolled in and dropped napalm bombs. Each shell tumbling to earth then creating a hundred-yard-long swath across the mountainside, consisting of yellow and orange flame topped with black smoke which billowed into the air. Screams echoed across the valley.

The recon patrol was told to regroup to a location further up the mountain. When a company of South Vietnamese troops began arriving, the recon patrol was ordered to a Landing Zone where a helicopter would take them to their platoon's new day position.

In the middle of the chopper ride, one door gunner was wounded by a random bullet fired at their airborne conveyance. While in the air, the man bleeding profusely, Sgt. Levin removed the round and repaired the damage to the soldier's intestine. Their chopper headed to the medivac station to drop off the wounded soldier. Brian and James assisted the wounded man off the chopper and lay him on a stretcher.

Brian explained to the staff that ran out to meet the chopper, "Bullet to the abdomen. Not deep. The round was removed, his gut repaired and closed."

"Who did this?" one of the doctors yelled over the noise of the chopper.

"Sorry, No time." Brian yelled.

He and James returned to the chopper and slid on. Leaning back on their rucks, the blades thrashing the air, small brush and grass leaned away from the rotors' down-wash as it lifted off. Their lower legs dangling, Brian gave a brief wave to the medical personnel as the Huey banked away, its blades clawing for altitude.

****

Back at their day position near the old church, Lt. Moss said, "I was told you performed surgery on a door gunner during a chopper ride, Sergeant Levin."

"Minor repair. Important to stop the bleeding, Sir. He would have bled out or had a belly full of blood before we got to the medical facility if I hadn't."

Lieutenant Moss put his hands on his hips. "Do I want to know how you are so familiar with surgical procedures?"

"It's better if you don't ask, sir."

He regarded the second squad leader with a look of disdain for a moment, then said, "You do your job as squad leader, keep patching 'em up if needed, and I won't ask."

The platoon spent three weeks hiking up and down mountain trails, and just returned to the flat lowlands. A supply truck stopped at the abandoned church then dropped off food and ammo. The driver spoke to Lt. Moss. "Sgt. Levin around? Supposed to take him back to the rear to start his R&R."

Lt. Moss got on the radio to TOC, Tactical Operations Command, and confirmed then yelled at someone for not telling him sooner. He informed Brian then suggested he take his squad's M79 grenade launcher to the rear to have an armorer inspect it as the weapon misfired a few times in the previous two weeks. Brian gathered his gear, the M79 and his M16, secured his ruck then climbed up to the passenger seat of the deuce-and-a-half.

"Where you going on your R&R?" the driver asked.

"Sydney, Australia. I know it's winter down there but I hope it'll be more like home than Hong Kong or Thailand."

As they roared and bounced up Highway 1 to Camp Eagle, every small bump in the road seemed to jar the truck. Brian commented, "Miserable ride in this thing."

The driver snorted. "Beats walking."

Brian shrugged then managed to sleep.

An hour later, he was dropped off inside Camp Eagle, one mile from his company HQ. He shouted a hurried thanks to the driver, hoisted his rucksack onto his shoulders, pulled the straps tight and began walking.

A hot, humid day, *"Likely 110 or warmer,"* Brian thought as he plodded along the edge of a wide dirt road. His temples began to throb. *"Fucking migraine coming on. Feel nauseous."* His sweat-soaked shirt stuck to his back and chest and his joints felt achy, the sweat running down his forehead stung his eyes. He stopped, slid his seventy-pound ruck off his shoulders and removed his eleven-pound helmet, dropping it to the ground. Brian straightened, arched backward then rotated his shoulders a few times. The wind in his hair felt as good as getting the heavy ruck off his shoulders. He placed his rifle against his ruck, the M79, breach open, in the bend of his right arm. The soldier pulled his canteen off the side of his ruck. Brian took a long swig, head back, not paying attention to anything else. A jeep drove past, locked its wheels, and slid to a stop on the dusty road just past him.

A short, pudgy Captain, wearing supply insignia, a pressed uniform and spit-shined boots, jumped out the passenger side then stormed over to Brian.

In a winy, feminine, high pitched voice, he screamed, "Don't you salute officers?"

"Yes, sir. Sorry sir, didn't see you." He waved a, too casual, salute.

"You're supposed to be wearing your helmet at all times."

"Yes, sir." He bent over to pick up his helmet, in so doing, the breach on the M79 snapped closed, the grenade launcher pointing directly at the Captain.

"Open that thing. Open that thing," the now hysterical captain screeched, He performed a little sideways dance on his tiptoes to avoid where the grenade launcher pointed. The Captain kept his hands in front of him as if a shell from the M79 could be warded off by bone and flesh.

"Only needs a tutu to complete the ballerina image," Brian thought. In full voice he said, "Opening the breach, sir." He would have laughed at the Captain's little minuet but was too damn hot and sore plus his head felt like it was in a vice. He flipped the lever, opening the breach, the M79 still in the bend of his right arm.

The captain began a tirade about grunts having no respect for discipline, and that he looked like hell, his uniform was missing a button, it had a tear in the sleeve, and numerous other items Brian couldn't have cared less about.

"My God," the Captain yelled. "Your shoelaces are loose on your right boot."

His sore back and leg muscles aching in protest, Brian kneeled to tighten the laces, the motion causing the barrel on the M79 to close so again was pointing at the captain, who once more daintily hopped to the side.

"Open that breach. Open that thing," the hysterical captain's dainty, high-pitched voice pleaded.

He opened the breach then strained to stand.

The captain approached, "Stand at God-damned attention when I'm talking to you! And don't wobble like that."

A rumble from deep in Brian's belly, like a water buffalo lowing, should have been a warning. His partially digested meatball and spaghetti last meal formed a projectile hurl; the Captain's next hop not quick enough, the stinky mass landed on the Captain's boots.

He raved, "You damn grunts are fucking lunatics. When the Army's done with you, every one of you assholes should be locked up." He stormed back to his jeep, alternating stamping and shaking his boots.

"Yes, sir," Brian replied, waving another sloppy salute as the jeep sped away. With a groan, he hoisted his ruck onto sore shoulders, tightened the straps, took a deep breath, and continued walking to his company HQ.

"When I get to Sydney," Brian thought, *"all I'm going to do is fucking sleep."* He smiled. *"What a treat, sleeping on clean sheets."* The grunt wiped his runny nose on his shoulder, detected a foul odor then chuckled. *"Best I shower first."*

***

As was Army typical, Levin had hurried to the rear to begin his R&R only to find he'd have to wait two days. He found Paul Slidell who was also waiting two days. At lunch they were introduced to three young women who worked for the Red Cross, one from Shreveport, La.

"I live in a small town west of Baton Rouge," Slidell said with shy smile.

"A pleasure to hear a Louisiana accent," a girl named Candice said.

Slidell nodded, could barely look in the lovely lady's eyes, and said, "Sound of home."

For the next hour, Brian and the two Louisianan's talked about their life back in the States, church, and southern cooking.

"Nothing reminds me of home," Brian said, "like the taste of my father's sixteen-hour smoked brisket."

"My momma's gumbo," Candice said, "fills the house with such a rich, savory scent, my mouth waters just thinking about her cooking."

"Sorry, Sgt. Levin," Paul said. "But I'd have to agree with Candice. A bowl of gumbo and the sound Zydeco music fill my soul with memories of dinner and dances on the bayou. That's the feeling of home for me."

Following dinner, the men and women were assigned separate sleeping quarters in the 2/327 Battalion's section of Camp Eagle. The small ten-by-eighteen-foot buildings were protected on their sides by shoulder high stacks of sand bags. The soldiers called it a hooch. The floor of the little building was three feet above the ground and just big enough for sleeping quarters for six people and their gear.

Around midnight, Brian heard the swishing sound of an approaching rocket. "Incoming!" he yelled, rolling off his cot and onto the floor of the hooch. The Texan folded his arms around his head, and crossed his legs.

A nearby explosion rattled the tin-roofed, wood structure he and five others slept in.

Brian grabbed his medic's pack and ran outside. The end of a similar building, had collapsed and was burning. Two Red Cross girls ran up to them screaming that their friend was still in the building. Slidell took off toward the fire at a dead run. Levin began treating one of the girls who had metal fragments in her arm and back.

Slidell disappeared into the burning building. Mere moments later, he returned, coughing and hacking, his uniform singed and smoking in places but with the girl in his arms.

"She was trapped under debris," he said while placing the coughing young lady on a stretcher. Her face was contorted and bruised, one eye swollen shut, the other a tiny slit.

"Trouble seeing," she said, her body trembling.

"You have swelling and bruises around your eyes," Levin said as he finished working on the first girl. "I'm going to bandage them, so you won't be able to see for a while."

"Don't you worry, Candice," Slidell said. "Sgt. Levin knows all kinds of medical stuff. He done patched up lots of the guys in our platoon. And he's a southern boy from Texas, so's you're gonna be fine."

"I'm sorry to cause you more pain," Sgt. Levin said as he assessed her wounds, "but I have to work on your legs which are going to hurt like hell."

"Hold my hands, Candice," Slidell said.

She did and jammed her jaw shut. Candice moaned and grimaced.

Brian saw her knuckles turning white as she squeezed Paul's hands like a vice. The pain, likely worse than she had ever experienced, seemed to punish her body with each of the Sergeant's movements.

"Hold this clamp," Levin said to Slidell.

Slidell tried to pull his hands from Candice's grip. She only released one hand, said, "Don't leave me, please."

He moved her hand to his shirt. "Candice, you hold on to my shirt 'cuz I need to help Sgt. Levin. Don't you worry none, I'm right here."

The two men continually tried to reassure her. Slidell continued to assist Levin who worked at a rapid pace. A soldier gave him a poncho liner, a type of thin blanket, which he tucked around the young lady, but left her arm free so the slim lady could keep herself attached to Slidell's shirt.

A deuce-and-a-half pulled up. The duo put her on a stretcher and moved her into the truck.

"Slidell," Levin said. "Accompany her to the medivac station and have someone treat your burns."

"Yes, Sergeant," the man from Baton Rouge replied then hauled himself into the back of the truck, again gripped Candice's trembling hand.

"See you in Sydney," Sgt. Levin yelled to his buddy.

PART TWO: ANDREA

Chapter 4

"If you know any Vietnam vets, give them a hug. They probably need it and certainly deserve it."
Aussie lady wearing pink skirt and a warm smile, selling clothing in a small shop, Sydney, Australia
(July 1970)

Brian ate a typical Aussie breakfast of eggs, beans, smoky bacon, and toast, washed down with Billy tea, then walked to a small shop for civilian clothing. Everywhere they walked, he and his fellow soldiers were shown a warm Aussie welcome.

That evening, Brain leaned against a long bar at a dance hall, located a couple blocks from his hotel in Kings Cross, Sydney. A hundred-plus US military personnel in civvies, just as many Aussie girls, drank and danced to an excellent sound system. Guys who'd visited Sydney on R&R before Brian, told him this was the best place to meet a girl who'd be willing to accompany him back to his room. He sat at the bar for a while, chatting with a couple guys from the 101st Airborne Division but a different battalion, each with a lady on their arm. Brian smiled at a few girls, said, "Hi," to a few more but none of them seemed interested. He downed his second Scotch.

He noted a cute lady, about five-feet-tall, with lovely auburn hair, a slim waist, muscular legs, and a modest dress. Brian asked her to dance. The unsmiling lady looked him up and down then nodded. Two dances later, he offered to buy her a drink.

"Girls who come here know what you guys want," she said after turning down the drink. "Only reason I'm here is my friend didn't want to come alone." She smiled then patted his shoulder. "You're nice looking and a good dancer. You'll find someone."

"Your voice," Brian said, "reminds me of home."

She turned and said over her shoulder as she walked away, "Find someone else."

"The hell with it," he thought. *"I'm still anxious...combat at any moment anxious. Need a day to relax."* Brian walked back to his hotel. Giggles and grunts from the rooms on either side of his, indicated his fellow soldiers weren't alone.

He perused brochures left on the nightstand. One described a beautiful beach at a place called Bondi Junction. *"Might be pleasant to be alone,"* he thought. *"A day of reading at the beach might be perfect for a little peace of mind."*

***

The following morning, Brian stopped at a news stand, purchased a paperback which went into his jacket pocket then walked to a bus stop. "Looking for a bus to Bondi Beach," he said to an older man waiting there.

A large bus hissed to a stop in front of them. "Not this one," the man said. Two passengers boarded; the door slammed shut. The bus's engine emitted a deep moan as it moved away from the curb.

"You enjoying Sydney?" the man asked.

"All the Aussies I've met, make me feel happy I'm visiting Oz."

"Good. You lads deserve a break."

A second bus stopped. A few people got on.

The man called to the driver. "This here Yank's looking to get out to Bondi Junction, visit the beach."

"Hop on, lad." A gray-haired driver with an infectious grin waved him on, then pointed to a nearby seat. "Sit there, Yank." He tromped on the throttle; the engine groaned as he spun the large steering wheel. The bus moved away from the curb and swung into traffic. The driver gave him a brief grin. "Met a lot of Yanks during World War II. Maybe your Dad?"

"He spent his time with the Air Corp in North Africa."

"Myself, I never left the Pacific."

Brian stared out the window, hoping the driver wouldn't ask about Vietnam.

"Been in combat?" he asked while making a turn.

Not wanting to discuss the battles he'd been in, Brian said, "No combat. Just a clerk."

The driver gave him a brief glance, checked his mirrors, then said, "That bad, hey?"

Brian didn't reply, stared out the window for two stops then asked him, "How'd you know?"

The old man's eye's filled with sadness. "A combat veteran myself. Know the look. Distress in the expression. A person what knows…he can peer into a soldier's eyes and see the wounds in his soul."

Brian wondered what the old man had experienced. They pulled up at a bus stop. A short woman with a full bust and a wide rump accompanied by five young, chubby, children climbed on. She greeted the driver in a cheery voice, paid their fare then waddled to the back of the bus, her brood chasing after. He chuckled as they appeared like ducklings following their mother.

The driver waited until they were seated, then studied approaching vehicles in his mirror, the turn signal clacking away. He guided the behemoth into traffic. "You try and get some peace this week. Find yourself a lass to spend time with."

The old man nodded as he spoke, honked at the cabbie who cut in front of the bus causing him to make a brief stab at the bus's brakes. A satisfied smile appeared on his lips, "Been together with my Gracie since I returned from the war. She kept me on an even keel in those tough months after I first came home." He nodded. "Take it from someone who's been there, that'll help."

A few more stops and Bondi Beach came into view.

"Here you are," the driver said pointing to the horseshoe shaped, white sand covered, shoreline.

Brian stood, held out his hand to the driver, "Take care. Good talking to…a fellow combat veteran."

After descending from the bus, he heard the driver yell at his receding form, "Give 'em hell when you have to."

Glancing back over his shoulder, Brian grinned and nodded as he gave him a brief, shoulder high wave.

***

Brian sat cross-legged on the sand, his butt sinking into the tiny grains. He wished he'd brought a towel to sit on. Brian breathed in the salty air, enjoyed the sounds of the surf, the gulls and giddy children's laughter as they played along the water's edge. A sunny but cool day in early July, a group of college aged men were huddled together, busy ogling the various lassies.

The combat vet closed his eyes and smiled, remembering his sex-starved college buddies who lived in the same apartment complex near Austin, Texas. Gathered in a pack at a party or dance club, with tongues hanging out, trying to consume enough alcohol to find the nerve to ask for a dance; then did so while panting and eyes riveted on some sweet young lady's chest. They were shocked and deflated when turned down. Thick-witted, they couldn't figure out why they couldn't pick up girls. Brian tried to avoid their never-ending, mindless, discussions of how to get a girl turned-on by grabbing at her various parts.

"If you want a girl's body," Brian tried to explain once, "She has to welcome you into her head. Once you have the head, the body comes with."

Their laughter and hoots of derision embarrassed him. The regularly made fun of his old, four door sedan, even though it was all he could afford.

A pack member, who's most intellectual achievement was knowing the exact number of breweries in Milwaukee, declared, "That's an old man's car. Never gonna pick up a babe with that thing."

"Hell, you don't even drink beer," another member of the pack stated, the others laughing. "And you're always studying, even on weekends. No babes for you!"

If only he had a camera to record the incredulous expressions of the pack members when he brought home various comely ladies who generally stayed the weekend. Dying to know how the short, wide, plain looking young man achieved his success, they were too macho to ask and therefore admit they had no clue.

In an attempt to be social, he joined them one weekend evening, all gathered around a beer keg. After an hour of mind numbing, pointless, conversation, Brian stated, "If belching and farting become an Olympic sport, you'd all be gold medal winners." The pack cheered.

The pack members tried to be friends, but only on Friday or Saturday evenings, hoping, hell, downright praying, to be invited on Brian's occasional prowl for a lady. He chuckled to himself and shook his head. Gathered in the common area, beer-besotted and unsteady by seven in the evening, waiting for him to leave his apartment; he'd disappear out the back.

Brian smiled as he watched children squeal with delight as the Bondi surf brushed their legs.

Enjoying the warmth of the sun on that cool but windless day in Oz, he checked his surroundings. A slim girl, wearing a yellow sweatshirt, lay belly-down on a pink beach towel. A plaid scarf casually wrapped around her neck and a gray jacket rolled up at her side. She was ten feet away and closer to the ocean such that he couldn't see her face. Concentrating on her reading; she displayed a cute butt wrapped in black denim jeans. Her auburn hair pulled into a neat bun; her unease evidenced by constant tugging at a few curls which escaped the bun and fell half-way to her shoulders. He noted ugly scars on the backs of her hands.

"Likely burns," he mumbled.

Brian put her out of his mind. He scooped up a handful of the sun-warmed grains, let them run out between his fingers, and remembered doing the same thing on Eagle Beach in Vietnam when his platoon was given a few days respite from the war. In-country R&R, they called it. Eating, drinking, sleeping, and flirting with the few Vietnamese women employed there. Live bands at night, sleeping-in allowed; it was a pleasant break.

He pulled a paperback out of his jacket pocket, thumbed through it, found where he left off. He'd come to the beach to lose himself in reading but glanced at the auburn-haired lady one more time.

Young men tried conversation but, without removing her gaze from her book and with a wave of her hand, she dismissed them.

Two hours went by while Brian concentrated on his reading.

"Good book?" a woman with a husky voice asked while standing in front of him. He could only see a dark form; the bright sun just over her shoulder blinding him.

He held up the book's cover. "First fifty pages slow but an interesting tapestry of well-developed characters and mystery. Takes place in Europe." He squinted, shaded his eyes with his hand, and discovered the yellow sweat-shirted girl, peering down at him through bug-eyed sunglasses, her beach towel draped over her shoulder.

"You chose that title because?" she asked.

"Wanted something to take my mind somewhere else."

She giggled. "Oz is a long way from anywhere else."

"Not far enough." He nodded to a news stand. "Headlines about Vietnam. For a lousy week, I'd hoped to forget."

"Hungry?"

"Sure." He stood, held out his hand, and shook hers. "Brian."

"Andrea." She pointed to a tiny, red-sided food stand. "Fish and chips?"

"Not big on fish but I'll try 'em."

"She gets hers from the boats every morning."

As they crossed the sand, he thought she looked familiar. He asked, "Didn't we dance last night?"

The auburn-haired lady smiled and said, "Didn't know your taste in literature, or we'd have danced more."

They took their newspaper-coned meals to a small table.

"Vinegar?" he questioned, as she sprinkled the acid on his fish.

"Try it, Yank."

He tried a small bite.

"Not bad…tasty actually." He tried another bite. "Downright delicious."

In between mouthfuls of battered fish and potato, they engaged in a lengthy discussion on the book he was reading. She'd read it the summer before.

Brian asked, "Is that why you decided to talk…"

"Guessed you might be interesting." Her eyes sparkled as she smiled. "Might have guessed right."

He returned her warm smile in kind. "Back at you."

"When did you arrive in Sydney?" she asked.

"Yesterday."

"So, you've got six more days. Where's home?"

"Texas. Small town named Celina, friendliest people in North Texas. Established in 1876 along routes of the old Chisolm cattle trail…north of Dallas."

"Therefore…" She giggled, then asked, "You own oil wells, cattle, horses…?"

He laughed. "Own a small home on decent acreage which I inherited from my folks. Before I was drafted, I bought a summer home, made from logs, near Whitefish, Montana." He smiled as if reliving a pleasant memory. "Can see the peaks of Glacier National Park from the deck…that's where I'll avoid the heat of Texas summers."

"Because…"

"Love the mountains. Great views, great hiking, a quiet area, and the entire Northwest to camp in. But my main residence is in Texas."

"A year Waltzing Mathilda in Vietnam then home to more? Thought you'd of had your fill of living rough."

He laughed again. "I have a motorhome waiting for me. Converted bus. Dad bought the forty-footer but didn't like driving it. I intend to go camping in a manner which includes indoor plumbing and a daily shower."

She burst into laughter. Andrea's eyes sparkled. Her voice reminded him of the sonorous tones produced by the long crystal wind-chimes which graced the front deck of his Texas home.

"Your laughter reminds me of home. You sound like my wind chimes."

Andrea imagined he was teasing her. "My deep voice? Has all the charm of sounds emanating from a rain barrel. Wind chimes…unlikely."

"Sonorous they are, and yes, their tone sounds like you."

She tilted her head, still not sure if he was teasing. Her expression warmed, showing she was pleased with his complement. "Thank you. Never heard the word sonorous used to describe my voice."

"The last thing I did before I left for Vietnam was hang them." Watching her eat, he noticed her face seemed not quite symmetric. She wasn't pretty, but her eyes sparkled, and when she smiled, warmed him. The lady from Oz made him feel, he wasn't sure what. Did she make his mind relax or was he willing to feel anything to get her in bed?

Andrea noticed his stare. "Car accident. Couldn't put my face back together like before."

"Sorry, didn't mean to…"

"Tell me more about those wind chimes."

"Long clear crystals that ring with deep tones." He leaned back, briefly closed his eyes. His memory filled with their graceful appearance and melodic sound. "Imagine, early on a cool, clear morning, seated in a rocker on my front porch sipping a mug of steaming coffee, the sunrise refracting through the crystals painting rainbows across the floor and walls, a sylvan breeze and their sonorous tones giving voice to the day's first sunlight as it pours across the North Texas plains."

Andrea's jaw dropped. "Your description..." She stared at him. "Articulate you are, Yank..."

Not sure of her reaction, he sighed and shrugged. "I forgot to take them down before I left. Strong winds probably destroyed them by now."

"Sad, if true."

He stared at his lap then in a quiet voice said, "But…there are times when I think I can hear them…"

She tilted her head again then asked, "When?"

"You'll think I'm nuts but…happens when I'm emotionally stressed. Even influences how they sound."

"Such as..."

"They reflect my mood, sad if I am, happy if things are going well."

She turned to stare at the surf, then asked, "Hear them during combat?"

He shook his head. "Afterward."

Andrea considered his reply while finishing her fish. She wiped her lips with a paper napkin. "Tell me, Yank. First trip when you get home?"

"My folks in Plano, Texas then Yellowstone National Park. Never seen it but read lots about it. Afterward, finish fixing up my house."

"Close to your family?"

"Yes. Dad and Mom both." He stared at her, wondered how much to tell her. "Lots of arguments before I left between Mom and me. I love her dearly but we have a different view of the world."

She raised her eyebrows. "Know the feeling but my Mom died when I was sixteen."

"Sorry to hear that."

They finished their meals. Brian collected their waste and dumped it.

"How about a walk?" she said.

Brian nodded. They followed a walkway which curved a couple miles around the beach, occasionally stopping to sit on benches then spent a couple hours talking about life in Australia versus the States. She insisted the States were too violent. The lady from Oz pulled her jacket on when a large cloud blocked the sun.

"Any college?" Andrea asked.

"Biology major," he replied. "You?"

"What you'd call Liberal Arts. Learning psychology."

Andrea perused a few store fronts, noted their reflection in one. "Nice couple," she mumbled then giggled. "Tell me about college life in the States."

Brian yawned. "Another time. Sorry but I'm exhausted. Couldn't sleep on the plane…or last night for that matter."

"Find a lass to take home?"

"My body was screaming for a girl, but my mind was depressed over something that happened the day before I left but couldn't get it out of my head which resulted in no sleep."

"Can I help? Maybe if you tell me?"

He took a deep breath, sighed then looked her up and down. "I'm enjoying your company but, I was hoping to go dancing again tonight so I should head back to my hotel and get some shuteye."

"Your lack of sleep. Because?"

"War crap. Cruel memories." Brian shrugged his shoulders, stared at her for a bit. "In truth, memories of having to make cruel decisions." He thought for a while, shook his head. "No. That's not right either." They continued to walk in silence. He stopped.

She turned partially toward him.

"Decisions," he said while nodding, "which are cruel to the decision maker as he knows their implementation will result in a human being's pain, suffering or death."

"Describe a cruel decision."

"I'm here to get away from...I'm not really comfortable talking about my decisions. I hardly know you. Why? What do you want to know?"

"Just one, please."

They walked in silence for half a block then, after a rapid sigh, he stopped walking, turned to face her and said,

"We agree. Just one."

"Yes."

"Our squad of eleven soldiers, out on reconnaissance, stopped to rest along a path on the edge of a small village. Vietnamese, two young women and an older man, were planting twelve-inch rice plants in a flooded paddy, fifty meters ahead of us. Two kids, a boy and a girl roughly three-years-old, were playing on the trail. When we stopped for a break, we sat on the trail leaning against rucksacks. The little ones approached. I dug in my ruck and gave each of them a hard candy…remember giving the girl a yellow lemon drop. She removed the wrapper, slipped the treat into her mouth, gave me a great smile, pointed at me, and, in a heavily accented voice, said, 'You number one.' One of the guys called me over to look at a rash. Another soldier pointed out the workers were no longer in the rice paddy. The female worker yelled something in Vietnamese at the children. They'd run a few steps when a mortar shell landed near us. Gunfire broke out. We'd been ambushed, the children injured by the blast. I emptied four or five magazines then low crawled to a point roughly halfway between them. Both sustained terrible wounds…both bleeding profusely. I was forced to choose, the boy or the girl. I'm right-handed and the boy was on my right so maybe that's why I chose him…truthfully, I'm not sure why…I began closing a huge laceration, bullets flying around us like angry bees. I looked over at the girl about halfway through my repair on the little guy. Flat on her back, she raised her head, turned to me with tears in her eyes, anguish in her expression. I knew she must have been in terrible pain. She beckoned with her little hand…asking…no…begging, for my help. I concentrated on the boy for a few more minutes, finished covering his wounds then low-crawled to the girl and, even now it hurts to say, she was gone. Eyes still open. Still full of tears. I slid my hand across her eyes, closing them. I watched a tear run down her rosy cheek. By now we'd called in cannon fire and the shooting was over. We got the little boy helicoptered to an Evac station…but the little girl's eyes haunt me. Her little hand beckoning. I've been racking my mind. What else could

I have done? Everyone else was busy shooting. There must have been something…"

He used a shoulder to wipe a tear off his cheek.

Teary eyed, Andrea turned him toward her, embraced him and kissed his cheek, then rested her head on his shoulder. "Such a pain-filled memory."

He lifted her chin and briefly kissed her lips.

The twosome began walking again.

She sighed. "Likely nothing you could have done."

Brian stared at her briefly, shrugged then studied a few dark clouds in a mostly blue sky. "Not sure."

"No one else could help?" Andrea said, using both hands to wipe away her own tears.

"One medic per platoon of three or four squads. He was out with another squad that day. Everyone else was busy shooting. Perhaps I should have been shooting as well…"

"You seem to be the kind of person who runs toward a fire…not away."

"I've been told that, but when a person decides to run toward a fire, what decisions will he or she make when arriving at the fire. My choice killed the little girl."

Andrea stopped him and said, "You did not kill her. The war did. I imagine decisions like that happen in all wars. Not like you can plan for them."

"Enough talk about that…depressing crap."

"Time to jolly-up Yank." She put her hands on his upper arms, kissed his cheek, and put on a warm smile.

He returned her smile in kind. "I'll try."

"My place is around the corner and down the block. Two small rooms; tiny but cozy. You can relax there instead of heading back to your hotel. And I'd love to go dancing."

"Uh…like to spend time with you but…I come with lots of anger, desires, and crazy expectations."

Andrea displayed a knowing smile. "I understand. You Yanks come here hoping to, as you say, get your rocks off. I get it." She bowed her head while they walked and without looking at him said, "I'm willing to be your girlfriend for the week, if you like, because…I've never met anyone who expresses himself, such as, the way you referred to your wind chimes, 'On clear mornings, the sunrise refracting through them painting rainbows…giving voice to the sunlight as it poured across the plains.' You created a perfect picture in my mind."

"Just a description…"

"And we communicate well…you tell me about your experience, and I can learn from you."

"Learn what…about war?" He shook his head. "Right now you'll only get sleep from me."

Under her breath she whispered, "You'll help me understand how soldiers manage after traumatic events."

"I'll what?"

She wrapped her arms around his left arm. Gave him a broad smile. "Home with me, Yank. How much have you slept recently?"

"Every night's sleep in the Army is interrupted by guard duty. Some guys adjust…I have to a degree but the last few weeks were rough. Lots of new guys. We don't know how they'll react when in combat. I always worried about newbies falling asleep on guard or screwing up such that others get killed."

They walked in silence for ten minutes then entered her little apartment. There were books, magazines, and newspapers, on numerous shelves and piled on every horizontal surface except one counter in the kitchen.

As they removed their jackets, which she hung on a peg board near the entrance, Andrea said, "We've had similar experiences and you're going to help me with memories from an event…which, as yet, I'm unable to talk about…to anyone."

"I'm not a therapist…and didn't come to Sydney to talk about Vietnam."

She nodded to the overstuffed, leather-covered couch while spreading her beach towel over the back of a chair. "Sit there. I'll put the kettle on."

He sighed as he sunk into the deep cushions. Brian mumbled, "This is comfy. Just need a moment to rest." He put his head back and sighed. He saw Andrea return with two mugs of tea. She placed the mugs on a glass-topped coffee table then grabbed a blanket, unfolded it and covered him. The Aussie lady whispered, "We'll take care of each other this week and you…will help me get over the deaths I caused." With gentle movements, Andrea sat at his side, spread the blanket over both then cuddled against him. He kissed the top of her head, put an arm around her and pulled her against him.

Andrea used her finger tips to caress his cheek, then rested her head on his chest. She whispered, "Six days. For the rest of the week, you're mine. I'll be so kind to you; you'll tell me what I want, and you're going to lean on me…use me to get rid of that turmoil."

"I'll try," he said then kissed her lips.

The soldier imagined he'd briefly close his eyelids then talk to her; but once closed, this girl and her apartment caused his mind to relax, for the first time in the last six months, and as a result, he was out like a light.

***

"Might help if you talk about combat," Andrea said as they entered a disco that evening then headed for the bar.

He shook his head, said, "Forget that," and ordered drinks.

Andrea's friend, Mary, called to her. They walked over, joined her at a small round table.

The music filling their spirit, Andrea shouted in a glee-filled voice, "Come on Yank. Dance with me."

They returned to the table thirty minutes later. He went to the bar to buy them drinks.

Around midnight, Andrea took a long sip of her drink then slid her hand onto his crotch, caressing his member until she felt it swelling. She leaned toward him and whispered, "Back to my place?"

He nodded.

At her apartment, he gave her a long kiss. Andrea removed his shirt, tossed it onto the chair next to the bed. She noted the silver chain and tiny, abstract, six-pointed star which hung from it.

"You're…"

"Jewish."

"Don't meet many in Oz."

She slipped out of her clothing then held his naked body tight against her. They engaged in another long kiss then Andrea pulled him into bed.

The following morning, Andrea was cuddled tight against him. Brian gave her a long kiss and they made love again.

"I'm going to shower," he said.

She nodded toward the bathroom.

Brian adjusted the water, stepped in, then to his surprise, Andrea entered.

Although blushing, she said, "Only have six days. No time to waste on modesty or inhibition." She soaped a washcloth. "Let me scrub your back."

He turned away from her. "Andrea, that's..." He moaned. "Oh my God that's wonderful."

"Brian, you have a body like..."

"A fire plug or a brick outhouse?"

She laughed, gripped his butt, which he flexed for her. Andrea said, "And well-defined musculature."

"Worked out with weights since I was young."

"My turn." Andrea turned her back to him.

A thought made him chuckle as he ran the soapy cloth over her smooth back side. "There's this tribe in…the Amazon, if memory serves. When a couple bathes together they're married…stop bathing together then divorced."

"Wow," she said then giggled. "A water contract."

"So, we're married."

"For this week," she said with a level of sadness in her voice, which surprised him. Andrea rinsed off, stepped out of the shower, threw him a towel, wrapped her hair in one towel then used another to dry her body. "You Yanks treat us like goddesses for a week; we give you what you want then we never hear from you again."

"Perhaps we'll be the ones to break that pattern."

She sighed while shaking her head. "Unlikely…"

"Andrea, I'm enjoying the hell out of our time together." He raised he chin and kissed her. "It's only been one day, but spending time with you…our conversations…we fit up here." He tapped her forehead.

"And in bed?"

"Last night was all a guy could ask for."

"We fit…you're right." She kissed his lips. "What would you like to do today?"

"See more of Sydney…with you, of course."

"There are ferry boats to take us all over the place. Might be fun to explore using them as a stepping off point."

They dressed in light jackets. Andrea wrapped her plaid scarf around her neck.

"Special plaid?" he asked

"Campbell tartan," she said with pride.

"Scottish Ancestry?"

"Of course. Just like Jackie Stewart."

"Oh yes. World Driver's champion. One of the great ones."

"Your ancestors?" Andrea asked.

"Russian and Spanish."

"Fiery mix. Have to keep an eye on you," she said.

On the street, Brian asked, "What is that delightful smell?"

"Bakery up ahead. How about breakfast there?"

They sat at a small round outdoor table and dined on flakey, just out of the oven, apple, cherry and banana fruit tarts, washed down with tea, then rode a bus to a wharf near Lynne Park.

Alighting from the bus at New South Wales and Kent Road, a horn wailed. Tire squeal from a delivery van assaulted their ears like fingernails on a blackboard. The small truck strained to stop then a sickening thud was heard as the van struck a small sedan; broken glass and metal parts clattering to the pavement.

Andrea sucked in her breath, put a hand up to her mouth then spun away from the scene.

Brian put an arm around her. "Aussie lady, what's wrong?"

She pushed his arm away. "You check them. Soldiers know what to do. Be sure they're okay, if not, help them."

First taking stock of their condition, he helped the occupants out of their crumpled vehicles and away from the traffic.

"All okay, just minor bumps and bruises," he yelled to Andrea over the din of the approaching emergency vehicles.

Trembling and whimpering, she nodded.

He returned to her side and held in a warm embrace. Brian guided her to a bench then held her tight against him.

"What happened lady?"

Andrea shook her head.

"Will you tell me?"

"Not yet."

"So painful?"

She nodded, buried her face in his chest and sobbed.

Chapter 5

On a cool but sunny, Saturday morning, they bought tickets at the wharf, proceeded across a ramp to board the ferry, purchased tea then sat together on an indoor, upper deck.

She took a long sip of her tea then appeared to gather her courage, and said, "I'd like to hear more about combat."

"In some bloody fights."

"Describe them."

"You had to eat cold food if you didn't fight your way to the head of the chow line."

She giggled. "Seriously please, I know you were in combat but how would I describe it to someone who knew nothing about it."

His previous upbeat mood left him; his brow furrowed. "Look! I'm not here to talk about combat. I like spending time with you but…" He took a moment to try and calm down. "Andrea, if I think about that crap, I relive it. The memories take my mood down a rat-hole. I feel guilt, then anger. Lots of it." He stared out a window.

"Talking won't help?"

He looked at Andrea then yelled, "Hell no!" Brian glared at her, stood then walked around the deck for some minutes. He returned to his seat, folded his arms across his chest.

"Okay, okay," she said. She waited a few minutes then pulled his arm around her. "I hurt you. I apologize."

More time passed…the only sound the rumble of the ferry's engine.

Brian sighed, squeezed her against him. "I get it. We don't have much time." He put his hand under her chin, kissed her lips. "Sometimes my emotions get the best of me."

She nodded.

He took a deep breath, let it out slowly, "I'm combat infantry and, in my case, when needed, a sniper."

Brian was surprised as her expression turned to one of satisfaction.

She said, "If you will, I'm not pushing you, please give me an excellent description of combat."

He looked around then faced her, spoke in a serious tone, "One description…"

Andrea nodded, "Won't ask again."

For a few minutes, Brian stared out the windows at passing sailboats rounding a mark, their crews then hoisting spinnakers which billowed to life, all the while considering what he would say. He took a deep breath, stared in her eyes. "Imagine you and your best friend Mary; the two of you are soldiers on patrol. A shot rings out. You begin shooting. Your friend no longer has her lower jaw, she utters a guttural sound then another round rips a painful hole in her belly. She collapses, bleeding profusely, grabs at you, makes ugly noises but can't form words. From her gestures, you know she's in terrible pain. You see she is choking on her own blood. You try to support her but you know there's nothing you can do, so you return to shooting. She grips your clothing, looks at you, her eyes pleading with you to stop the pain, prevent her death. But your mind knows it's hopeless. Your best friend is going to die. You are about to witness her last breath. No matter what you think of doing, she will die."

Andrea's eyes filled with tears, she turned away from him.

"Andrea," he said.

She shook her head then cried.

"What did he do to you?" an older man, seated nearby, asked. He glared at Brian.

Andrea turned to the old man and tried to smile. "He told me a sad story." Andrea twisted toward Brian, wrapped herself around him as much as she could.

He held her in a tight embrace. "Sorry," he said then kissed her cheek. "I didn't mean to be so graphic…"

"My fault. I asked. It's all so damn cruel. I assume you witnessed what you just described."

He nodded. "Left out the part where it became clear the soldier was begging for his mother to help him."

"His mother?"

"I heard pleading for help from their mothers, from our soldiers, Korean soldiers, and Vietnamese soldiers. If they were torn up, believed they are going to die, many plead for maternal help." He kissed her cheek. "Some years ago I read an article written by a mercenary soldier in Africa. He said he heard soldiers, on death's doorstep, pleading for their mothers in seven different languages."

Andrea took a deep breath, rested her head against his shoulder. "Thank you but…I'm curious about one thing concerning combat…how did you manage afterwards?"

"Don't know."

"But…surely you…"

"It's not afterwards yet."

She appeared puzzled.

His shoulders drooped, he stared out a window, his eyes exploring the verdure which spread from the houses on the cliffs down to the water's edge; all the while sensing the ferry's bow rising and falling as it crossed the wake of a larger vessel. Brian sighed. "One week from today, my nostrils will again fill with the sweet scent of mature rice, the rotting vegetation smell of the jungle, and the acrid odor of cordite. Combat won't be over for another six months."

Andrea wiped a tear away, smiled at him, grabbed his hand, turned his face toward her and kissed his lips. "But you're here today."

Cuddled tight against each other, they didn't talk for the next half-hour. The rumble of the ferry's diesel engines the only sound.

"Your descriptions," Andrea said, "were…down-right painful. I could sense what it must have been like. The suffering from events you were forced to witness."

"And events I caused," Brian said, "Most people don't know who they are or what they're made of until they find themselves in impossible situations."

"But what about the resulting emotional pain? How'd you deal with it?"

He looked at her with a quizzical expression. "I'm not sure what you're asking."

"Like after you…you've killed someone…isn't there emotional pain?"

"Not exactly pain." He thought for a while. "More like a combination of guilt, anger, and happiness."

Andrea took some minutes to consider his response. She repeated his statement in a whisper then said, "Doesn't make sense."

"Little about killing makes…Auburn lady, you expect logic when we're talking about war?"

"But happiness?"

He nodded. "Happy I was still alive and fought in a way which supported my squad members and accomplished our mission."

"I'm not sure…"

Brian leaned away from her, stared outside and remained silent so she didn't inquire further.

They left the ferry, walked along a row of three- and four-story buildings, most with shops on their lower floors and apartments above.

"Sun's out. Warming up," he said, unzipping his jacket.

At a street corner, a sign pointed in the direction of the Royal Botanic Gardens.

"Take me there?" she asked. "It's not far."

"Why?"

"Plants are peaceful."

"Which is good for?"

"Tortured souls."

They quickly covered the distance to the Gardens.

Andrea said, "A shame but little color this time of year."

They walked in silence until Andrea asked, "What is the difference between killing someone with a rifle and killing someone with a car?"

"One is intentional and the other is an accident...assuming the driver didn't intentionally aim for the other person who died."

"Is it different if the soldier is being attacked as opposed to his attacking someone?"

He considered her question for a bit and shrugged. "I suspect little difference in a soldier's mind, although, I remember a guy in close combat having a feeling of wondering why the enemy soldier was trying to kill him when they didn't know each other."

She wrapped her arms around his arm, then said, "You mentioned being a sniper."

"Worlds apart from fighting in a squad or platoon."

"From what I've read, snipers were hated throughout history."

Brian nodded. "My understanding as well. Most armies are desperate to use them then try to forget them as soon as an armed conflict ends."

"Is killing mentally more difficult on snipers because it's a more personal type of killing?"

"Personal?"

Andrea said, "You carefully select a target. It's unlike spraying bullets or dropping an artillery shell on an area."

He thought for a while as they walked, stopped to buy them tea, sipped his then said, "I didn't feel it was more personal. A sniper doesn't always carefully select, generally just aiming at a body." Brian sipped his tea again, pointed out perennials which were just pushing through their previous year's growth. "Maybe after the war, looking back on what I've done, I may feel differently but now, dropping an enemy is dropping an enemy whether at a distance or up close, although, as a sniper, I do it through a scope. Somehow that and the physical distance helps mentally separate me from the target. I also have a teammate with me. Not sure what, if any, his presence makes, although we are a team. Never want to let down a team member."

"Do you hate the enemy?"

"Not really, although one guy in another platoon lost his brother. He was full of hate. Willing to do crazy, dangerous stunts. The Army got him out of combat. They put him to work unloading airplanes till the end of his tour."

"You mentioned distance..."

"I have to think about that to give you a good answer." They walked in silence for a while.

She pointed out a row of bushes. Their dark, leathery, green leaves just beginning to emerge.

Brian vigorously shook his head. "I was wrong. Dropping an enemy is not just dropping an enemy. Surely it is more difficult the closer you are, especially if you see their eyes."

They wandered the gardens for a number of hours, then found a photography studio where they posed for photos, both serious and silly.

"A week to develop so I won't see them," he said as he paid.

"You give me your address in the states and I'll send copies. Back to my place?"

He nodded.

***

After a brief walk, the entered her apartment. Andrea said, "A bit chilly out there today. Favor a Brandy?"

He nodded. "Sounds good."

She poured Brandy into two snifters.

The duo held up their drinks, said, "Cheers."

They snuggled together on her couch. She pulled his arm around her then asked, "Did you worry about dying?"

"Not really. Worried about being captured and tortured. If I died, that would be the end. Over quickly one would hope."

"If you don't fear death, what kept you from engaging in irresponsible acts which might result in your death?"

"Imagining what my parents would suffer if I came home in a box. Also, doing something crazy might result in my squad mates getting hurt."

"Different topic?" Andrea asked.

"Thank you."

"I'm a country girl who doesn't fall for big city fellas. Why do I feel close to you?"

"I know but you may not like what I have to say."

"Even if I don't, please tell me."

He put his hands on either side of her face, kissed the tip of her nose. "We're both inquisitive and share strong intellect and, I suspect, similar emotional experiences. Mentally, we combine like two metals slamming into each other at high velocity and high energy with such force they meld together, become one, as if inside each other."

She frowned. "So close, we're inside of each other. I'm not sure if I like that."

"But being so close," he continued, "we feel each other's pain, and if not careful, can easily cause the other pain."

Andrea thought for a bit, looked up at him, smiled, nuzzled his cheek, "If we are, as you say, inside each other, then until you leave, our mental balance is in each other's hands."

His expression became one of concern. "Then we each have a huge responsibility to tread lightly, without leaving footprints."

Andrea pulled his arm around her. Brian pulled her close. Lost in thought, the duo were silent for a while then continued reading, then both slept in each other's arms.

Late in the afternoon, the phone ringing awakened them. Andrea received a call from best friend Mary. She asked Brian if he minded having dinner with another couple.

"No problem," he said.

Back on the street and after a brief walk, Andrea nodded to a set of double swinging doors. Brian opened a door for her and followed into a building where an elevator took the couple to a rooftop restaurant.

Checking out the sixth story view and queued near the bar with fellow patrons waiting for a table, Andrea called to Mary.

Her friend introduced her new acquaintance, Michael Cooper. He was a combat soldier from the 1ˢᵗ Air Cavalry Division, whose home was in Boston. The men moved to the bar, ordered drinks for themselves and their dates.

"You heard what it's like when we get home?" Michael asked Brian during dinner.

"Protests and stuff," Brian said. "You heard different?"

"Seems lots of guys having problems readjusting to the world."

"The world?" Mary asked.

"That's how we refer to back home," Brian said.

"My older brother," Michael said, "after his tour in Vietnam, withdrew from the family. We think he's living someplace in Boston, but no one knows where. His plan was to finish college and teach High School English. Came home, started drinking, moved out and no one's heard from him in…I guess, three years now."

"Was he a combat soldier?" Andrea asked.

"No. Army journalist. They'd be out in the field for a few days, then back to an office to write stories about the soldiers they met. He did see combat a number of times. He told some stuff to our father but not me. Dad told him he needed help."

"We've had Army journalists out with us a few times when we hit the shit," Brian said. "They acquitted themselves well…became disciplined riflemen until the shooting stopped. They experienced the same horrors we did. One guy helped me repair a bloody injury without flinching…" He added with a grin, "but puked his guts out afterwards."

The others laughed.

They were guided to a table with a marvelous view of Sydney harbor and the Opera House.

"I wonder," Mary speculated, "if it was harder on them…mentally speaking…coming from a peaceful rear area where they typed up their stories, to the hell of combat then back to the quiet rear again."

Brian, while considering Mary's comment, stared out a window. Sydney transitioned from day into night. Lights in buildings winked on while gaudy neon signs glared. In the distance, it was still light enough to make out the Sydney Opera House whose design made it appear like a group of intermingled sails. He held up his glass of Chardonnay, swirled the contents, peered through the golden liquid then took another sip. Brian let it rest on his tongue before swallowing. "Excellent," he pronounced then reached for the bottle and read the label. "From the Piccadilly Valley."

"Near Adelaide," Andrea said with pride in her voice. "A few hours from my family's sheep station."

Mary turned to Michael. "How was your twice-cooked Bangalow Pork Belly?"

"Sin full," Michael replied. The others laughed.

"Your spatchcock?" Andrea asked Brian.

"Crispy skin, moist interior plus the pomegranate sauce was the right note to accompany the dish. Not too sweet, not too sour. A perfect balance."

Michael asked, "And ladies, the lamb you shared?"

"Perfection," Mary said while Andrea nodded agreement.

"Mary," Brian said. "As to your thoughts on alternating between a peaceful area and combat, I've read that pilots in WWII experienced mental problems for that reason…peaceful airfield then an hour of doing your best to kill your fellow human beings while they did their best to kill you, then back to a quiet rear area as opposed to constantly in combat. It was a huge struggle for many."

"Wonder if it was that way for your brother?" Andrea asked Michael.

"If we find him, I'll ask."

***

Once the bill was paid, they left the restaurant where, three American soldiers accosted them, trying to entice their dates away.

"Leaving so early?" one of them queried.

"You ladies need to join some real men," another said.

Michael told the obviously tipsy trio, "We're both 11B10, so you're outnumbered. Walk away."

The man closest to Brian said, "Ain't afraid of you, little shit." A fist the size of a ham flew at Brian's face. The Texan leaned back, simultaneously slamming a foot between the guy's legs with enough force to lift him off the ground, the would-be assailant dropped to his knees then rolled onto his side while moaning and using both hands to grip his crotch. The second spun Brian to face him. For his trouble, the second assailant received an elbow to the face which broke his nose then a chop to his neck which left him choking. Brian followed with a fist in his belly, knocking the wind out of him. The second assailant slowly collapsed to the sidewalk, hands on face, blood spurting between his fingers while choking on his own blood and gasping for air. Brian's new acquaintance, having avoided the pipe the third man held briefly, used combinations to keep him against a wall. The man cursed at Michael. The 1st Air Cav soldier replied with a viscous kick which, based on the volume and intensity of his assailant's screams, shattered a knee cap. Andrea retrieved the pipe, gripped it like a cricket bat, fury in her expression, ready to assist. As the third man hit the ground, she cursed the three men, dropping the pipe.

The combat vets nodded to each other, took their dates by the hand and walked away from the groaning trio.

"Shites," Mary said, then asked, "You said, 11B10."

"The Army's designation of combat soldiers," Michael said.

Andrea glanced over her shoulder at their assailants, then asked, "What if those guys had been in combat?"

"No chance," Brian said, shaking his head. "Combat vets don't go looking for fights."

Michael nodded agreement.

"You picked up the pipe," Brian said to Andrea. "Would you have used it?"

"Hell yes. I'm a country girl. Tough as a mother croc protecting her nest, if need be. Wouldn't hesitate busting a couple skulls." She smiled at Brian, pulled him close, and kissed his cheek. "Our six days aren't over yet. Have to take care of you."

"Where'd you learn to fight?" Michael asked.

"Neighbor was a karate expert. Spent hundreds of hours working out and practicing together. You?"

"Grew up in a rough neighborhood, learned to box."

Continuing down the street, they stopped at a neighborhood pub with an area for dancing, Andrea watched Mary and Michael spin around the polished, wood grained, surface then shouted to Brian over the din of the dance hall, "Great couple. They're expressions sparkle at each other." She intertwined her fingers in his then stood. "Let's dance."

After enough dancing to develop a thirst, the foursome slid into a round booth. Michael took drink orders then he and Brian headed to the bar.

Upon their return, Mary shouted to be heard over the music, "Andrea said she's confident enough in your relationship to let me dance with you. Come on Yank."

Brian looked at Andrea who smiled and nodded. They headed to the dance floor.

Andrea shouted, "Come on, Michael."

The foursome spent the next hour dancing and laughing, occasionally changing partners.

They returned to the booth. Andrea cuddled against Brian.

He whispered, "Maybe you'll go home with Michael."

"No chance." With a mischievous smile, she poked a finger in his ribs then whispered in his ear, "He might not be as good in bed as you."

He burst into laughter and Andrea kissed his cheek.

Returning to her apartment, they slipped out of their clothing and slid into bed.

"An angel found me on Bondi beach," he said while caressing her chest.

"No angel here."

He kissed her lips. "Aussie lady, you are so much more than you realize. Kind, caring, intelligent…"

She interrupted, shaking her head. "Thank you, but not bloody likely."

***

The following day, after breakfast at the same bakery, they walked along the Bondi to Bronte coastal walk, stopping to sit on a bench and watch the ocean's waves crashing on the rocks at Mackenzie's Point. A cool breeze coming off the ocean that morning, they cuddled tight together. Andrea said, "Last night you said some kind words."

"I meant what I said. Spending time with you…nearly have my sanity back. You have a way of making me choose my words with care…no partial logic with you. Need clear, complete and concise reasoning when I voice a thought. I love that about you."

Andrea smiled. "Could be why the sex is so good. Doing…no…sharing…our bodies makes us closer." She kissed his cheek. "I have to admit, I love our talks, and yes, sharing our bodies, we were made for each other like bees and pollen."

"Which makes honey." He turned her face toward him and kissed her lips. "A beautiful simile."

Gazing out to sea at the gathering black clouds, Andrea said, "A bit cool and thunderstorms on the way." She shuddered when a distant flash of lightening was followed by a report of thunder which rumbled across the sky. "How about a day of reading at my place?"

"Love to."

As they walked to her apartment, a light mist began falling.

Brian watched her shudder after another deep boom reached them. "You seem anxious."

"I don't like noisy storms. Out on our sheep station, lightening can cause an endless variety of problems, and I'm anxious because I feel like we have limited time together, no matter the outcome of this week. We need savor every moment."

"I agree. We continue to build a relationship then who knows how long we might be together?"

"Still feel like we have a short time. I don't know where the feeling is coming from."

He put an arm around her, pulled her close. "One day at a time, lady from Oz."

Cuddling at her place while reading, the phone rang. "Hi Dad…doing well…Haven't forgotten."

She listened briefly then put her hand over the phone. "My father wants to know if I'm coming out to the Seasonal Fair the end of this week."

He nodded.

With sparkling eyes and a voice again reminding him of his crystal chimes, she said, "We'll be there. Have someone I want you to meet." Andrea listened for a while, laughed, grinned at Brian while saying, "He knows nothing about sheep." She listened again then said, "Serious enough we'll be staying in my room."

That evening, Brian and Andrea met Mary and Michael for a second dinner date. While the foursome waited for a table, they talked to a Marine pilot and his date. He was stationed at the airbase in Da Nang.

"Thanks for the support on a number of occasions," Brian said.

"If it was me," the Marine said with a laugh, "You're welcome."

"Brian, did you ever see the damage caused by the bombs?" Andria asked.

Brian nodded. "Yes I did. We patrolled a village that was napalmed. An hour earlier, we were taking fire from it. Bullets buzzing around and between us so we called in Arty. They said two Marine jets were nearby then directed them to our location. Each dropped two shells which flamed an area as long as a couple football fields, yellow-orange flames at the base, billowing, black smoke above." He sipped his drink while contemplating how much detail to tell them. "An hour after the airstrike, we recon'd the village. Small fires still burned in the remains of a number of buildings, everything black and soot covered. A deceased little boy, flat on his back, most of his clothing burned off, charred skin on his face and anywhere flesh was exposed, eyelids burned off, eyes in a permanent, sightless, stare. His arms extended heavenward, frozen in death, reaching out like he wanted one of us to pick him up and take away his pain, a woman's body nearby, also scorched, possibly his mother. The smell of burned flesh assaulted our noses. Other adults and children scattered across the ground in twisted poses indicating they'd been writhing in pain during their last moments. One of the worst scenes I'd witnessed."

The pilot stared at the floor. "I didn't know, never imagined, I just sit up there and flip a switch, can't see what happens under the fire and smoke...in an instant I'm miles away." He wiped a tear off his cheek with the back of his hand. He glared at Brian, said, "I wish I still didn't fucking know." The pilot took his date's hand and walked away.

Brian was surprised at the pilot's reaction. He looked at the others and said, "He asked."

"Never mind him," Andrea said to Brian. "We can spend another day exploring Sydney tomorrow then we'll be at my family's sheep station the day after. Nothing but good times ahead."

Chapter 6

After a ninety-minute jet flight from Sydney to Adelaide, a small plane flew them from there to Lameroo. On the last leg of the flight, Brian could see sheep grazing on distant rolling hills, the landscape dotted with occasional medium sized trees. Local transportation took Brian and Andrea to her father's sheep station. They arrived at the ranch mid-morning.

"So this is sheep country," Brian said as he paid their driver and walked their bags up to the porch. He turned and gazed at the handful of outbuildings then nodded at a pen holding a few dozen sheep. "Their bleating seems a proper greeting to a sheep station."

"This is also a grain producing area...formerly mining in some areas," Andrea said. She led him to her room where they unpacked.

Andrea handed him a six by eighteen-inch box which he carefully opened. "I bought these in Sydney. They're a bit fragile."

Brian's eyebrows lifted. "Wind chimes."

"Hang them outside my window, please."

"I'll have to make a hook to support them. Need flat stock and tools."

"Out to the wood and metal shop," she said, grabbing his hand.

He looked around the shop. Andrea sat on a stool. Brian cut a two-foot long section off one-inch by one-sixteenth steel flat stock. Using a vice, pliers, files, a drill press and drills, Brian fashioned a decorative hanger.

"Know your way around tools," she said while he sanded oxidation off the hanger.

"My father could repair anything. I learned from him," he said without looking at her and while boring two holes with the help of a drill press.

"What color?" he asked, pointing to a row of spray-paint containers.

"Blue," she said. "Light blue, please."

Brian pointed to the cap of a spray paint can.

"Yes. Perfect."

He suspended the hanger from a bent wire which he hung from a ceiling rafter, then sprayed all sides.

"Second coat in an hour should do it," he said.

"Good timing," Andrea said. "We can have lunch while the paint dries."

Following lunch and a second coat of paint, Andrea took him on a tour of the ranch. She asked Brian to drive them in a small pickup.

"Describe ranch life," Brian asked.

She stared out the side window for a bit then took a deep breath and replied, "Always work to do…from tending the sheep, working the crops, to fence, building, and vehicle repair. More to do than can be finished in a day."

"How do you decide when the day is over?"

Andrea rubbed her chin then smiled and said, "When you think you are so tired you can't lift your arms one more time, can't possibly take one more step, you finish one more task."

He smiled and thought, *Sounds like New Year's Eve in the Emergency Room.*

Brian drove them for another hour, visiting pasture land dotted with small ponds and the high point of the local terrain which Andrea said was called Campbell's Point.

Back at the house, he switched off the engine. They heard then watched a Ute roar up the drive. It parked adjacent to them.

"That's my dad." She hurried over to a tall, barrel-chested man, who gave her a bear-sized hug then extended a hand toward the soldier, greeting him with a firm handshake.

"Charles Campbell," he said. "Welcome."

"Brian Levin. Happy to be here."

"I've been showing him around," Andrea said. "About to saddle a couple horses. We'll head out to see parts of the ranch only accessible by horseback."

"The plants you asked for are in the back of my pickup," the big man said with a wide grin. "I've got some calls to make. You two have fun. Talk at dinner."

They rode for an hour then stopped at a pond to let the horses drink.

"You're comfortable in the saddle," Andrea said.

"Been riding since I was young," he said. He gazed at the pleasant surroundings. "Seems odd though. So peaceful out here. Meanwhile, my friends are fearing for their lives and committing acts which may cause them lifelong mental scars."

"Dare I ask that you let those feeling go for now and enjoy being here."

He smiled. "For you, Aussie lady, I'll try."

She pulled his lips down to hers for a long kiss.

Returning to the ranch, the sun low in the sky, they unsaddled the horses and put them in a corral.

Andrea asked, "Help me plant flowers?"

"Sure," Brian said with a shrug.

With shovel and hoe, he broke up the soil in a flower bed which fronted the porch. Together, they planted three-inch annuals.

"You don't mind doing this kind of work?" she asked.

He thought for a bit. "Not something I could do all day long. Kind of mindless, shouldn't take too long, but let's me think about other things while I work."

"I agree," she said.

"And like you said at the Royal Gardens, when grown, they might bring peace to tortured souls."

She kissed his cheek. "Is it a cliché to say you complete me?"

"Andrea…"

"I've never felt this close to anyone in my life."

His gaze moved from her eyes to the setting sun. "I feel the same way."

She continued, "I find myself considering what a future for us might look like."

"We're together for six days. Not enough time to know each other…know what it's like to live together and solve problems together. Talking about a future is foolish. I'll head back to the states, get involved in my old life…you'll find a man who understands sheep."

"That's shite." Hands on hips, she pouted. "I want a man who understands me; not the damn sheep…someone who loves me for who I am…makes me feel proud to be who I am, just like my Texan does."

He kneeled at the edge of the garden. While bedding a few plants, Brian said, "On my way to looking up something else, I've learned a word in the Maori language. Kairangi - someone held in high esteem. My six-day partner is kairangi."

Andrea lifted his face and kissed his lips then whispered, "Thank you."

***

Late-afternoon the following day, Brian sipped tea on the porch with Andrea's father. They each sat in a drift rope chair, the chair's open weave allowing the gentle breeze to help keep them cool on that sunny morning. A small, square, tile-topped, table between them, a broad lawn before them, sheep grazed on a distant hill. The old man scratched the gray stubble on his cheek, raised his hat with one hand, ran the fingers of his other hand through his hair then snugged the hat down. He turned to Brian then commented, "You're a little fella' for combat."

Brian laughed. "Just a bit taller than the minimum to qualify for the Army."

A steady breeze wafted across the rolling hills of the ranch; enough to cool sweat on that sunny day but not enough to raise dust. Twenty-meters in front of the porch, Andrea pulled damp clothing from an overflowing, meter-wide, rattan laundry basket then clothes-pinned items to a line. As the articles of varied shapes, sizes, and colors waved, they added a cheery visual note to the sylvan scene.

"Me daughter is filled with rainbows when she's around you. Haven't seen her like that since the accident." His expression turned dark. "But you'll head back to the war…you gonna take those rainbows with you?"

Brian sighed. "I'll try not to but…"

"Don't you hurt my girl."

Brian took a sip of tea then shook his head. He turned to Charles. "She belongs out here. In wide open spaces. I've lived near a big city all my life. The sound, grittiness, and velocity of a big city are in my blood." Brian sighed then nodded toward Andrea. "Her rough, ranch girl exterior conceals a woman with a giving heart and huge intellect…each as big as…as the outback. Hurt her? Couldn't do it." He rolled his shoulders.

"Andrea says you're full of tension."

"From the war." The Yank sipped his tea, then nodded. "At least tension."

"Back in the States, how did you get rid of it?"

"I have a drum set." He grinned and said. "Works well."

Charles nodded toward a small building. "That tan shed has an axe on the wall, gloves on the work bench...wood pile behind the shed."

"Wood pile? Oh…um…Thanks."

For the next hour, the staccato report of an axe splitting wood into quarters, accompanied by an occasional grunt, indicated Brian's location.

Shirtless, his sweat-covered upper body glistened in the sun.

There was a rhythm to the work. Place a round of wood on the stump, the fluid motion of his arms and upper body resulting in a silvery flash as the ax head arced into the round, splitting it in half, the same motion split each half into quarters, throw quarters into a pile, and begin again.

Place, swing, place, swing, place, swing, throw quarters.

Andrea approached carrying a pitcher of water.

He glanced at her then stopped swinging the ax, resting the handle against his thigh. Brian used his forearm to wipe rivulets of sweat from his forehead then smiled at Andrea.

"Feel better?" she asked.

He smiled. "Yea. How'd you know?"

"After my mom died…I found Dad out here plenty."

He raised the pitcher to his lips, drank most then poured the balance over his head.

"More?" she asked.

"No, but thanks."

"Reassuring," she said, "to see my partner-for-the-week working on our ranch…creating a primal sound heard as long as men have worked this land."

He laughed.

"Could you live out here?"

Brian hesitated then wiped his hands on his pants, and shook his head. "Not a country boy."

"How do you know?"

"Lots of repetitive, tedious work on a ranch. Don't do well with that."

"You'd said you inherited land in a rural area from your folks."

"The arable portions are rented to local farmers. My involvement is limited to upkeep on the house and vehicles."

"You'd adjust to life out here," Andrea insisted.

"Doesn't work. I've tried. After a short time, I begin messing up as I can't keep my mind on my work. Also miss the music clubs, symphony, and museums. I'm a city boy, through and through."

Andria waved a hand at the setting sun. "Sunsets like these…"

"Even sunsets become boring…for me."

"Will you become bored with me?"

He considered her question for a while, then nodded toward the shed. They walked over and entered the small building. Brian pulled off his gloves and tossed then onto the work bench. He put the ax in a vice, picked up a sharpening stone, ran it across the blade a few times, checked that the edge was in good condition then returned the axe to its wall mounted holder. Buttoning his shirt, the Texan turned to her and said, "Life is different when I'm around you. My mind relaxes when we're together. I'm able to free up some of my anxiety." They left the shed and walked a few paces. He stopped and turned her toward him. "Chopping wood helped, like a burden lifted from my shoulders, but that also happened when I awoke from my nap at your place last Friday. You were leaning against me, my state of mind, normally angry and anxious, but you, you and your little apartment, dare I say, felt like home. I don't see how I could ever become bored with you."

"I could do that for you out here." Andrea's eyes began tearing.

"Why sad?"

"I lived most of my life on this land. Always wanted to end up a rancher's wife...raise my children out here."

"During our handful of days, Aussie lady, you've seen into my soul. You understand, I'm as opposite from a rancher as a man can get."

In little more than a whisper, she said, "I know."

"So, it's for the best if we don't stay in touch after this week."

"That's cruel." Teary eyed, still facing him, Andrea used her shoulder to wipe a tear of her cheek then tugged on the belt loops at the front of his jeans, thought for a while, and pulled him close.

She kissed his cheek and embraced him.

"Andrea, I'm covered in sweat."

The auburn-haired lady rested her head on his shoulder, kissed him then said in a quiet tone, "Don't care."

Wrapping his arms around her, he kissed the top of her head then said, "I understand not staying in touch is cruel but it would be crueler still if one of us accepts a life they dislike to please the other." Brian hesitated then added, "I wouldn't do that to you and I know you wouldn't do that to me."

She gazed in his eyes. "You're a part of me. Like the combined metals...remember? How do I separate us?"

Brian put his hands on her cheeks, kissed her lips. "Remember what you want from life. Could you see yourself living in or near a big city in the States?"

"Never. The States...too much violence. Unlikely I'd even visit. And big cities, the tall buildings, the crowds, they close in on me like they're trying to crush my spirit."

"And yet you live in Sydney."

Her eyes filled with tears. She pushed out of his embrace and said in a trembling voice, "I caused a car accident not far from here. I killed two people and hoped that living and taking college classes in Sidney, would help me heal."

In an anger-tinged voice, he said, "We could have talked about this. Why didn't you tell me sooner?"

She replied in an angry tone. "You think it's easy to tell someone you caused the deaths of a mother and her infant son?" She turned away from him and sobbed.

Brian turned her to face him and wrapped his arms around her trembling body.

Andrea calmed after a bit and smiled at him. "So reassuring to have someone holding me when my world feels like it's heading over a cliff."

"I'm glad I'm here," he said, kissed her, then asked, "Did the time in Sydney help?"

She wiped her eyes then took his hand. They started walking back to the house. "My time away from here did nothing to help...until this articulate Texan arrived to turn my life on its head. Instead of all my mental energy being consumed by guilt, our relationship forced me to use it in other directions."

"Such as?"

"Please don't laugh, but, taking care of you."

His voice incredulous, he said, "You have to be kidding."

"I know, I know. A tough combat soldier, what's to take care of? But when you'd laugh at something I said, the way you looked at me when we danced and when I held you. I knew some of the crap from the war was erased. That made me happy. Satisfied really, and wanting to get over my guilt."

Brian shrugged. "And late tomorrow I fly back to Sydney then back to Vietnam the following day."

"I've never told anyone the crushing guilt I feel over killing those two."

"I'm glad you told me." He lifted her chin and kissed her.

Sounding apprehensive she stated quiet voice, "If I didn't tell you, I may not have told anyone."

"We need to finish talking about our future. Which I believe we don't have."

She sighed then kissed his cheek. "I understand. I fantasized about a life together but realized after we came out here we had little chance at a future. I wanted to write but, I'm not a city girl so...tomorrow is goodbye."

Heads drooping, sorrow in their hearts, they covered the distance to the house like mourners walking to a grave.

***

They arrived at the Seasonal Fair early the following morning. "As I mentioned previously, this area was originally perceived as mining country, yet for more than a century, it's an important regional support center for the pastoral industry," Andrea explained as they arrived at the Seasonal Fair. "We have an annual get together. Had it since World War II. Dad was here before sunup to get the steam-powered sawmill running. That's his project every year."

They wandered past many vendors; homemade goods available as far as the eye could see. The duo talked and laughed as they walked while sampling many of the goods on display.

"About the accident." Brian said. "I've been thinking, you should tell me specifics, before I leave."

Andrea shuddered then avoided looking at him, "Not sure."

"If you can't tell me…as close as we've become…and today is our last day together."

Pain was written on her face, her shoulders drooped as she stared at the ground. "I know."

"So, Andrea, who did you kill?"

She stopped walking, jammed her eyes shut, tightened her grip on his hand. "This is so difficult…members of my own family…my sister-in-law and her infant son."

A pressure wave rocked them, immediately followed by the sound of an explosion.

"What the fuck was that?" Brian asked. They heard screaming and yells for help.

She replied in a trembling voice. "Came from the direction of the steam engine."

"I'm going for supplies from the aid station we saw near the entrance." He took off at a dead run with Andrea close on his heels.

Upon return to the area where the steam engine once stood, they found a man with a sucking chest wound. Brian showed Andrea where to place the proper bandage so the man could breathe. "Keep that in place until EMTs arrive," Brian told her. "I'm going to check on others."

"I don't see my father."

"I'll keep an eye out for him but lots of folks need help."

He bandaged two wounds then moved to an older woman with a one-inch wound in her right side, which bled profusely.

"What are you doing?" said a slim young man wearing a white jacket with medical insignia.

"Using my finger to plug this wound to prevent her bleeding out. Who are you?"

"Dr. John Ronald."

"Experience?"

He replied in an anxious tone. "One year out of medical school. The more experienced doctor from our clinic was rushed to hospital in Adelaide with chest pains yesterday."

Sounding like a Sergeant, Brian said, "This woman is going to need surgery to repair her wound. Find an ambulance crew and I need two hemostats to stem her bleeding before we move her."

"Yes, Doctor…ah..."

"Levin. You need to perform triage and get patients sent to the clinic. We'll need surgical staff."

"They've been notified." He hesitated then said. "You sound like an American. You're not authorized to perform medical duties."

"If anyone asks, we'll tell them I'm assisting you."

EMTs approached providing the clamps Brian needed then consulted with him on a few other patients. He gave instruction to Dr. Ronald on a few more. Heavy rain began. Walnut sized drops. Brian grumbled, "Damn rain must have followed me from Phu Bai."

The EMTs secured the injured woman to a stretcher.

Brian rechecked her condition then said to the EMT's. "She needs immediate surgery." He turned and shouted, "Andrea. I'm heading to the hospital with the EMT's."

She nodded and waved.

They raced to the town's medical clinic. Rain and thunder accompanied them.

***

"I'm an anesthesiologist," an out of breath middle-aged woman said, while Brian changed into scrubs. The old woman was wheeled in as a nurse helped him into a mask, gown and gloves. Brian found the rivet which had pierced the left side of her belly, removed it, and began repairing the damage it had caused.

"Dr. Levin," Dr. Ronald called out. "The next patient is in terrible shape."

"I need a couple more minutes."

"Can you finish closing?" Brian asked the surgical nurse. She nodded. He watched her for a bit then ripped off his gown and gloves, burst into the other surgical theatre. A nurse helped him into a clean gown and gloves.

"Debris struck his face and sternum," Dr. Ronald said. "May have injured his heart."

Brian checked the monitor for vital signs. As a nurse cleaned dirt and blood off the old man's battered face, he noted the patient was Andrea's father. "You need to treat these burns," he said to Dr. Ronald who complied with the assistance of a nurse.

"Charles, it's me, Brian. Don't try to talk." He reached for the man's hand. "Squeeze my hand if you can hear me…excellent. We're going to put you to sleep and do some repair." Charles gave Brian's hand another squeeze. Dr. Levin nodded to the anesthesiologist.

As they investigated the injuries, Dr. Ronald said in a nervous voice, "These injuries require a vascular specialist."

"Fortunately for the patient, a surgeon with that specialty is across the table from you. Secure this, please."

"Yes, Dr. Levin."

A nurse said, "The patient's blood pressure is dropping."

Brian swore. "Where the hell is all this blood coming…? Shit. His spleen is torn to shreds. It needs to be removed."

Young Dr. Ronald appeared panic stricken. "I've never…"

"Not asking you to. You'll assist."

***

Three hours later, on a break but still wearing surgical scrubs and examining a man on a gurney, Doctors Ronald and

Levin plus the surgical nurse discussed a surgical plan for the next patient.

Andrea stormed into the hospital, looked around then made a bee-line for Brian.

"My father?" she asked.

"In recovery after a few hours of surgery," Brian said.

"We had to open his chest," Dr. Ronald said. "Lucky for your father, a surgeon with vascular experience was available."

The surgical nurse laughed and said, "He's a bit short in stature, but with amazing dexterity and, many years' experience. Typical Yank. He barks at the staff." She elbowed Brian and giggled. "Must think he's Ben Casey."

"What?" Andrea asked. "Who?"

A radiologist approached and handed two X-rays to Brian. "Are these the views you were expecting, Dr. Levin?"

"Perfect," Brian said while examining them. He turned to Dr. Ronald and the surgical nurse. "Let's go."

Andrea's voice incredulous, she asked, "Dr. Levin?"

He winked at her and nodded then disappeared into the operating theatre.

An hour later, a four-day old infant was brought in and placed on the operating table. Half of her left ear was torn off. She suffered torn ligaments in her ankle and a gash across the little one's scalp. Brian worked at a rapid, consistent pace. He directed Dr. Ronald and the other staff members who carefully followed his directions. They alternated operating theatres for the next few hours.

Brian found Andrea sitting in the waiting area, teary-eyed and trembling. She jumped as a flash of lightening was followed by a clap of thunder. The sound rattled the windows and was accompanied by an increase in the torrential rain. High winds whipped litter past the clinic's windows.

"Your father," Brian said, giving her a brief hug, "is stable, but needs to be flown to Adelaide when the weather breaks. You can visit him now. This way."

She nodded and followed him.

Brian reviewed his chart then observed the numbers on the equipment Charles was attached to.

Andrea sat at her father's bedside. Appearing tired and worn, Charles turned to Brian, pulled his oxygen mask aside then asked, "So, this is what you're good at?"

Brian smiled and shrugged, "Something like that."

The old man took a few deep breaths then said, "That there Dr. Ronald said I'd wouldn't a made it if you wasn't here. Said I'd a died before they could a moved me to a hospital with an experienced surgeon." He closed his eyes, grimaced, twisted a few times then relaxed.

"You in pain?"

He turned to Brian. "No. Just stiff. One of the nurses said lots of folks woulda' died if Andrea hadn't brought you out."

"The entire staff worked well together. It was a team effort. I couldn't have done what I did without them. You're headed to a fully equipped hospital."

"You and Andrea?"

"Were an incredible couple for a week."

Charles took a few more deep breaths. "My Andrea, deserves someone she can talk with, understands her, at her level."

"We've discussed our future," Andrea said. "We decided we don't have one."

"You need to rest," Brian said to his patient as he replaced the oxygen mask.

***

Brian moved to a hallway, talked to an injured man waiting on a gurney. Andrea followed and stood at his side. The minute he turned to her she wrapped her arms around him. "So, Surgeon Levin, you've kept a secret from me."

"Nothing influencing our relationship."

"My father?"

"Should be fine. You go with him to Adelaide. The docs there will tell you how to take care of him."

"You?"

Brian sighed. "Heading back to the war tomorrow. I'll fly to Sydney tonight."

"Then this is goodbye."

He nodded. "Sadly, yes it is." Brian put his hands on her cheeks and kissed her. "But please know, for six days, I've had the honor of loving and being loved by an angel. Thank you, my caring and intelligent, Aussie lady."

"Thank you…" She tightened her arms around him for a number of minutes. Andrea cried quietly, her head against his chest, then abruptly pushed away from him. She wiped her eyes with the backs of her hands, and, in a tone of disbelief asked, "Before you leave, explain why you're in infantry when you could be a surgeon, saving lives...why would you do that? Why?"

"A long story. Briefly, research on the stress of combat."

A nurse approached and interrupted them. "Excuse me, Dr. Levin, two people injured in a car accident have arrived. Dr. Ronald is asking for you."

He briefly kissed Andrea's lips. "Goodbye, wind chime lady."

Andrea stood there...disbelief and confusion written in her expression. "Thought I knew you…"

He smiled, turned to leave, hesitated then said over his shoulder, "You know me better than anyone else." Brian turned to the nurse, "Let's go."

Late the same day, a police constable, hat in hand, met him in the hall way and said, "Want to shake your hand. Whatever future my neighbor's four-day-old girl has, she owes to you. You gonna be around? A reporter would like to ask a few questions."

"No time. Need a ride to Campbell's ranch for my gear then to the airport."

"Honor to drive you, Doctor Levin."

***

Back in Sydney and the following morning, Brian met up with a couple platoon buddies who were lined up waiting to board the jet back to Vietnam.

"Where have you been?" Paul Slidell asked.

"Sheep station."

"No shit. Get laid?"

"Nah," Brian said. "Damn sheep run too fast."

The buddies laughed.

"What else you do out there?"

113

With a wistful expression, gazing into the distance, Brian replied, "Chopped wood, watched amazing sunsets…and filled my soul with the sound of a wind chime…a five-foot-tall, auburn-haired, wind chime."

"Yeah, sure." Paul chuckled, glanced at the man on the side away from Brian and shrugged, "Oh, well. Back to the war."

PART THREE: BACK TO THE WAR

Chapter 7

Most of Brian's platoon worked shirtless on yet another, steamy, humid day. They'd arrived for two weeks security duty at a small mountain whose top had been leveled for artillery and supporting staff. The platoon was working in front of and below bunkers which ringed Fire Support Base Hatchet like a string of olive drab pearls. The ends of the barrels of the 105mm and 155mm cannon, not far above the sandbag covered roof of the bunkers they would live in. The muzzles' closeness would keep them awake the first few nights but somehow their bodies adjusted and the soldiers managed to sleep through fire missions. The front of the bunker was protected by a wall of sandbags. Each bunker was cut into the side of the hill, had a waist high row of sandbags on either side where soldiers could observe down the hill. The bunker itself contained bunks for four soldiers and wood cases filled with fragmentation grenades and ammo. The area in front of and below the bunkers was clear of brush and trees to a distance of seventy-five meters down the hill but was interrupted by coils of razor wire.

"Monsoon season in a week or so," SSgt. Touhy said. "Been through that shit last time I was here. Rains for weeks. Heavy sometimes, light at others, but continuous fucking rain." He looked at the gathering clouds and shook his head.

Making those around him laugh, James added, "Something to look forward to."

"Make sure the razor wire is tight, second squad," the staff sergeant said. "Set the flares on a hair edge trigger so any enemy soldier moving the wire will trigger a flare."

Third squad was burying fifty-five gallons drums which were filled with napalm; a claymore mine set underneath it. An electrical wire ran from the claymore up to a bunker where the wire was connected to an igniter. When fired, the claymore would flame the napalm and force the burning, plasticized fuel up and out, raining down the hill in a fifty-yard semi-circle. Additional claymore mines were set near the front of the bunkers and their deadly shot aimed down the hill.

"Why is the napalm called foo gas," a newbie named Hadley asked.

"Comes from the name Fougasse which was developed by the Brits in 1940. It consists of a mixture of flaming material with an explosive device like a Claymore," Levin said. "Aside from the heat generated, which can sear lungs, it sticks to and burns anything it touches. Only thing worse is white-phosphorous which burns at a much higher temperature. Willy Pete can melt its way through an engine block and is almost impossible to extinguish."

Accompanied by, new platoon leader Lt. Senna, a group of three Red Cross girls walked by the bunker, introduced themselves to the guys. They made small talk with the men, who adored the ladies' attention.

"Are your Claymores set up?" Lt. Senna asked.

"Yes, sir," Sgt. Levin said. He held up one of the shoe-box-lid sized directional explosives. "Have a few left if another bunker needs more."

"What's inside a Claymore mine?" one of them asked.

"C4 plastic explosive with rows of ball bearings across the front so the direction it fires is controllable," Levin said.

"Wonder where they got the name Claymore," Lt. Senna asked.

"The inventor," Levin said, "a guy named Zimmerman, named it after a Scottish medieval sword."

"Regular encyclopedia aren't ya?" SSgt. Touhy teased. The girls laughed.

"Read a lot," embarrassed Levin mumbled.

The Red Cross girls moved on to the next bunker.

Hadley, the new arrival, was asked to steady a fifty-five-gallon drum, filled with foo gas, as his squad mates set a Claymore into the pit dug for the drum. Deciding he needed a cigarette, he let go of the drum and used two hands to light the tobacco, turned out of the light breeze and away from the drum which then proceeded to roll down the hill, only stopping when it ran into a small growth of bamboo, thirty meters distant.

SSgt. Touhy ran over, put his face an inch from the FNG's face and bellowed, "Hadley, you stupid shit. If these guys think you're a fuck up, one of them gonna flatten you." He shook his head and cursed. "Hell, another dumb stunt like this and I'll do it myself."

Red faced Hadley, said, "Sorry Sergeant."

"Sgt. Greenleaf," SSgt. Touhy said to the third squad leader, "Get up to the Arty guys and request a tracked vehicle with a winch to retrieve that drum."

The staff sergeant turned back to Hadley, eyed him with disgust. "Shit burning detail until we leave this damn hill."

A thoroughly chastised Hadley, staring at his boots and blushing, replied. "Yes, Staff Sergeant."

***

Just after dinner that day, in the lookout position of their bunker, Arnie, David and Brian scanned the mountains around them. Glassing to the east as the sky dimmed, Sgt. Levin thought he saw a reflection at the same level on a distant mountain side.

"Probably wood cutters," David Trout said.

"Wood cutters would be out of the mountains by now. More like a reflection from binoculars," Brian said.

Trout said, "According to SSgt. Touhy, locals are reporting North Vietnamese Army soldiers in the villages below us. Could be prepping to hit this hill."

"How many nights in a row have you heard that?" Arnie said dismissively.

Brian shrugged, "A number. We should be aware anyway."

"Arnie take first watch. Then me, then David."

Two hours after dark, Arnie was on guard duty next to the bunker. David and Brian were inside reading paperbacks when they all heard the hissing of a burning flare. Arnie's head spun in the direction of the sound. The flare's red flame illuminated an enemy soldier who was in the wire watching him not more than ten feet away. He fired at the man with his M16. More flares went off.

Arnie yelled, "We're being hit! We're being hit."

The enemy soldiers began yelling and advancing up the hill. An explosive device ripped into the razor wire, attempting to open a path to the bunkers and artillery beyond.

Brian and David ran out of the bunker and commenced throwing fragmentation grenades down the hill. An RPG slammed into their bunker causing a loud noise, briefly knocking them off their feet, but causing no damage. Sgt. Levin called the command post, "Bunker Seven. Gooks in the wire. Gooks in the wire!"

"Where?" the command post asked.

More flares were tripped. Arnie fired an illumination round.

Levin yelled into the radio handset, "Every fuckin' where. Looks like the hill below is covered with ants in black pajamas and firing AKs. Where's the fucking arty?? I want to hear some of those fucking cluster bombs they brag about."

In the background, he could hear the company commander yelling, "Give 'em hell, God damn it! Give 'em hell!" Another voice was yelling at Artillery Command. The bunkers on either side of them came alive with gunfire and men throwing grenades down the hill.

"Trout!" Levin yelled over the mounting small arms fire coming at them, "Foo gas." They each squeezed a detonator. Brian's heart was in his throat as the flames from one of the barrels arced up and nearly back on them. On their faces, they could feel the heat generated by the napalm as it burned. Screams could be heard from below. They saw a number of men, covered in flame running then tumbling down the hill.

"Poor bastards," Levin said under his breath as he emptied a magazine and slammed another into his rifle.

They heard a scream and calls for a medic after the bunker next to them triggered a Claymore which had been turned around; therefore emptied its deadly contents into a couple of the men at the bunker who tried to fire it and simultaneously watch its effect.

"Stay down when firing the Claymores," Sgt. Levin yelled. "They may be reversed."

Arnie and Trout yelled acknowledgement, detonated a few Claymores from a hunkered down position below the sand bags. One of the mines had indeed been reversed. Its deadly steel going over their heads and harmlessly striking the hill behind them. They exchanged sheepish grins then continued throwing grenades and shooting down the hill.

They heard a whoosh, a boom, then a sound like popcorn but deeper and louder. The cluster bombs went to work on the enemy force. Screams from the injured and dying echoed up the hill. Additional cluster bombs were fired.

Every couple minutes a mortar round hit the American base along with an occasional RPG.

"Where are those fuckin' mortar shells coming from?" Levin said.

"I'd use that deep saddle we saw a few weeks ago," Trout yelled in a shaky voice, "About three-quarters of a mile from here, down that ridge over to the southeast." He and Arnie emptied another case of grenades then ripped open a new one, continued throwing them down the hill. A mortar-fired illumination round from an Army mortar position popped open and began burning. The enemy soldiers began looking for cover as the illumination seemed like daylight over their position. Arnie used his M16 to fire down the hill while Trout dragged another two wood cases of frags out of the bunker and ripped the top off. David and Arnie continued tossing frags. Brian sat on the ground, back against sandbags, searched a map using a flashlight. Another enemy mortar round exploded among the motorized 155s. They could hear calls for a medic.

Levin rotated the map. "Where the fuck is that damn saddle...got it!" He called Artillery Command with the coordinates, requested High Explosive rounds. In less than two minutes, the mortar was silent.

Hadley stopped by their bunker, asked if they needed more ammo. They yelled yes. Staying low he headed toward the ammo bunker. He returned then ran to the next bunker to resupply them.

The combat continued for another hour then gradually died out. The only sounds now, the hissing of still burning illumination rounds.

Exhausted from the adrenaline coursing through their veins, rifles at the ready, the trio stared down the hill, watching for signs of a renewed attack. They looked at each other and, too emotionally and physically drained to smile, simply nodded.

SSgt. Touhy stopped by. "Anyone hurt?"

"Cut the side of my hand opening a case of grenades," Trout said, holding up his bandaged hand. "Not a bad cut. Sgt. Levin put a couple sutures in and wrapped it."

"Other casualties?" Arnie asked.

"Hadley," SSgt. Touhy said. "Tail fin from a, mortar launched illumination round buried itself in his head. Killed instantly. Also Ben Appleton in the bunker over there. Reversed Claymore. Poor guy. Damn device tore his head off. Wilson hurt but his bleeding is under control. Got him over to the helipad. Just waiting for the medivac now."

"Anyone else?" Levin asked.

"Two arty guys killed, six arty guys wounded, all from mortar rounds. Their medic and our medic, Doc Evans, are taking care of them. Sgt. Levin, head to the other bunkers and check your men. Make sure they're getting resupplied. Nobody sleeps until proper watches are re-established. This shit could start up again at any moment."

Mercifully, it didn't.

Next morning, relays of helicopters began arriving bringing fresh supplies. Everyone exhausted, there was little talking at breakfast. Following the meal, the squads were divided up. Some men assigned to perimeter repair and installing new Claymores and foo gas, others, the gruesome task of recovering enemy bodies.

Nervous but tension relieving laughter was heard from those performing the grim task when Brian referred to the burned bodies as "Crispy Critters," a popular breakfast cereal at the time. He was glad he'd made his fellow soldiers laugh, but immediately felt guilty as he reminded himself, each of the Crispy Critters was someone's son or brother. In a respectful manner, each enemy soldier was placed on a poncho then carried to a common grave. Brian kept count. One hundred nine soldiers were laid to rest. He and Arnie, and a few others recited a prayer for them.

Once covered with earth, a Buddhist Monk placed and burned incense over the grave.

"That was some shit," Arnie said. "Hope it doesn't happen again tonight."

Chapter 8

After completing their assignment at the fire support base, the platoon returned to the abandoned Catholic church. Brian and Arnie read quietly in a corner of the old building, away from the others.

After a brief glance at Levin's name tape, a tall journalist from Australia extended a hand. "I'm Cleburne. First name Malcolm. From Adelaide in Oz."

"Howdy," Brian said, stood then shook the big man's hand.

"Your first name?"

"Brian."

"Where from?"

"Texas."

The Aussie stared at him for a good thirty seconds as if considering what to say. "Heard a story about this Texan named Levin, on leave from the war, at the scene of an explosion out near Lameroo, saved a crowd of folks. He performed First Aid at the scene then performed surgery on a mess of 'em at a small medical facility. Disappeared before folks could give him a thanks. A proper hero that man."

"Sorry," Brian said, shaking his head. "Wouldn't know about that."

The journalist stared at him, put his hands on his hips. "Don't think there's many Texans named Levin out in sheep country."

Brian turned to walk away but the big man grabbed his elbow.

"Got family out that way. This doc, he saved a four-day-old. If it was you, thanks."

Brian gave him a brief smile, sat down and opened a paperback then read while leaning against his ruck.

Arnie, sitting near his friend, checked around to ensure no one else was within earshot. "So, it's true. You're a real doc. A damn surgeon. What the fuck you doing with us grunts?"

"I want to write a book about the war, stressing the impact of killing on soldier's mental condition. Like...why some manage and other's fall apart."

"Big topic."

"Believe me. We're talking Texas big."

"The frequent letters home?"

"Notes for the book. Going to be research that, God willing, is understood and utilized."

"Lofty goal. Like to meet up with you when we're back in the world." He leaned closer. "Attend *Shacharit*...you know, morning prayers."

"I know, and we'll do that buddy." Brian smiled then glanced around. "Ah…I don't want the guys to know that I'm using their experiences as research on my book."

"No sweat."

"Thanks, Man."

***

Two weeks later, Lt. Senna, with second squad had helicoptered into the mountains to perform reconnaissance duties. Arnie wiped sweat from his face, then cursed the blazing mid-day sun. The squad was following a well-used trail into the mountains. Arnie walked point. A small explosion then a baseball sized object popped out of the ground. He caught it in his left hand and froze.

Everyone else hit the ground.

"What the fuck was that?" James Ware asked.

"It's a fucking Bouncing Betty," Brian explained. "When triggered, a damn grenade comes up and explodes waist high...trying to blow you in half or at least tear up your manhood. A gift from the French when they were here back in the fifties."

"But he caught it."

"And he's not moving, likely praying it doesn't explode."

"Fuck," James said. "Somebody's got to help him."

"I'll go," Brian announced. "Second squad, stay here and keep your heads down. He stood, slowly walked up to Arnie who was covered in sweat, then said, "Don't move. Don't talk."

Brian eyed the rusted object now resting in the palm of his buddy's hand.

"With as little movement as possible and keeping your hand under it, lower your hand to the ground. I'll take it from your hand, you pull your hand out and I'll set it on the ground."

Arnie slowly bent his knees. His body trembling. When near the ground, Brian put his hands on either side of the device. Arnie pulled his hand out, rapidly backed away. Levin slowly lowered it to the earth then walked a few steps then ran to cover. After fifteen minutes, James Ware placed a Claymore mine, aimed it at the device then backed off and detonated the Claymore.

Arnie looked at Brian, said, "Bless the Lord, we're still in one piece." He closed his eyes. They recited a brief prayer, the *Shehecheyanu*, which thanked the Lord for allowing them to remain alive.

"Amen," they said.

A few others mumbled Amen as well.

"Likely more mines around here," the Lt. said.

Arnie, still trembling, turned pale then walked to the side of the trail. He dropped to his knees and vomited. The Lt. decided to avoid trails so they hacked their way through the jungle.

***

A few days later, still in the jungle covered mountains, the platoon walked down a ten-foot-wide, six-inch-deep stream which coursed its way out of the mountains following a series of valleys. Brian felt heat sickness coming on. He cursed, his head throbbing, feeling like it was trapped in a vice, the damn vice compressing with each heartbeat.

"Accompanied by a fucking migraine, of course," he mumbled.

This was the fourth time since basic training that it happened. He tried to drink more water. When the column stopped to rest, he sat in the stream to try to cool off, poured water over his head, and rubbed his temples. Walking down the stream for another thirty minutes, the heat sickness caused him to drop to his knees, his stomach muscles tightened, and he suffered from a couple minutes of dry heaves. Arnie and James helped him out of the water, got his ruck off his back. Brian mouthed a thanks to them. The lieutenant ordered pickets out. Came back to check on Brian.

"I'll be okay," Brian said, forcing a smile.

"Our night position is fifty meters up this hill," the Lieutenant said.

"I'll take his gear," James said.

Arnie helped Brian set up a place to sleep. They ate a bit then Brian slept until dawn. His squad mates didn't bother asking him to take a shift pulling guard duty during the night. The following morning, he felt guilty as hell for letting them down, having someone else carry his gear and not performing his share of guard duty.

***

"Hey, Sgt. Levin," Doc Evans shouted, early one evening. "Check this out."

Brian walked over. Grimacing and moaning, Tom White, lying flat on his back, tried to smile then lifted his shirt.

A quick examination and Brian said, "Call for a medivac. His appendix is inflamed."

Twenty minutes later, and sundown occurring in another thirty minutes, they heard a chopper following the Troi River to their position. They watched in disbelief as it wobbled for a bit then slowly slid sideways and into the ground. An explosion, followed by billowing orange flames topped by roiling black smoke indicated where it came to rest; three-hundred yards from the old church.

"Did anyone see or hear hostile fire?" the Lt. yelled. No one did. "Can't be sure," he said. "Third squad, set up a perimeter around the chopper. First squad, search for survivors. Find any, bring 'em back here. Second squad, take over security around the church. Trout, call for another chopper."

Brian gave out assignments to his squad.

David Trout spoke into the radio for a while then said, "They won't send one until we determine if the chopper went down because of hostile action."

"Shit," the Lt. said. He looked at Brian. "Won't know enough to get another chopper out here until morning."

"He needs surgery in the next hour or his appendix could burst."

"Can you do it?"

Brian cursed. "Need flashlights, sir."

Levin cleaned his hands with anti-septic soap while Doc Evans cleaned White's belly. David Trout held the flashlights and tried mightily to keep insects away.

Brian, tense because of the unsanitary conditions, worked as quickly as possible to remove the diseased tissue, closed, then bandaged the incision. "That will do but he still needs to be flown to a medivac station for antibiotics."

Chapter 9

"Good work, Sgt. Levin," the Lt. said the next day after radioing the medivac station. "Tom White is in great condition."

"Thank you, Sir," Brian replied.

He motioned Brian away from the others then said in a quiet voice, "Do me a favor. Keep an eye on Ware. Some of the guys think he's talking to some kids who were killed last week. Whatever you hear, let me know."

"Will do, Lieutenant," Sgt. Levin replied.

Brian mentioned the Lt.'s concern to Arnie, who said, "Mumbles sometimes but not sure about what. I'll sit with him. See if there's a problem."

A week later, no one with medical knowledge beyond first aid, accompanied third squad when on overnight ambush duty. When they returned to day position the following morning, Paul Slidell was carrying Dave McDonald on his back. David's left pant leg raised to the knee, a tourniquet tied at mid-calf. Paul looked around, yelled for Sgt. Levin and medic Martin Evans.

Paul's face and arms covered in sweat, his uniform shirt dark with moisture, his expression twisted in worry and concern, he forced his words through his panting. "Some crazy gook ran at us. We shot him. Thought he was dead, laying on the ground but that bastard grabbed a metal pipe then swung it into Trout's leg. Swelled up like a golf ball a few inches above his ankle. It burst when I tried to bandage it and bled like hell so I wrapped it tight like a tourniquet...that's what it took to stop the bleeding."

Brian examined Dave who let out an occasional moan. He uncovered the wound. Blood spurted across his face and chest. Levin swore a few times then said, "Likely a fucking arterial aneurism. Evans, you're going to assist. This needs surgery."

"Do something, man," Paul said to Brian. "McDonald and me, good buddies, come in-country together. We got plans."

Brian took stock of the injured man. His foot was a dark shade of blue, almost black. "When did you apply the tourniquet?"

"About forty minutes ago. C'mon, Man. Everyone knows you ain't just a grunt," Slidell continued to plead. "Do that medical shit or he's fucked."

Lt. Senna requested a medivac chopper.

Brian shook his head. "No pulse in his ankle. Can't wait. Have to repair this now."

"Can't it wait for the medivac chopper?" Doc Evans asked.

Brian shook his head. "Wait for a chopper and he loses that foot." He turned to Slidell, "I'll get my gear, but you and Doc Evans are going to help."

Paul, visibly shaking, said, "Anything man. You just tell me."

"Hold his leg so it doesn't move...absolutely doesn't move. Doc, start an IV then move across from me."

With minimal conversation, assisted by medic Evans while Lt. Senna held the IV bag, Brian clamped a severed artery, used another artery to provide temporary blood flow to the man's lower leg and foot.

"You gonna puke?" Brian asked Paul, as he pulled up an artery and clamped it, nodding to Doc Evans to hold the clamp.

Slidell was turning pale but said, "Can hold it until you're done."

"You're doing great, Paul," Brian said to the trembling soldier. "Just keep his leg steady and I'll be finished in a couple more minutes. Close your eyes if you need to."

A few minutes' additional feverish work and Levin covered the injury.

"His foot is getting its color back," Doc Evans said.

Brian nodded. "Good sign. Can feel a pulse in his foot as well. I hear the chopper. Let's get him moved. I'll radio his condition to the medivac station so they know what to expect."

***

That night, they were kept awake by combat five kilometers away, in the village where the market grenade incident took place.

In the morning, second squad was sent to go through the village and make sure no further enemy soldiers were hiding there. The village had suffered napalm and artillery shelling in addition to a hail storm of small arms fire.

"Not much left," radioman Arnie said in a sympathetic voice to squad leader Levin.

Most of the soot covered buildings were partially or completely flattened. Many small fires burned; charred remains of wooden structures smoldered in a number of locations. A quick recon showed only a handful villagers left.

Doc Evans yelled to gain Sgt. Levin's attention then pointed. Squatting in a doorframe with no building attached, an old woman motioned to the Americans, pointed to a young girl lying at her side. Brian found Dot, her face dirty and tear streaked, her body trembling. He examined her. She had numerous burns and likely a broken hip.

Sgt. Levin had his men post security.

Dot looked at him, her eyes and voice pleading. "All hurt everything. You fix."

He administered pain killer while Doc Evans started an IV. Brian cleaned and closed wounds on her arms, back, hips and scalp, all the while directing Doc Evans while he cleaned then sutured two lacerations in her legs.

They called a chopper which ferried the little one and two other wounded villagers to the medivac station. After checking the area just outside the village, Sgt. Levin decided no enemy remained so radioed that information to TOQ and Lt. Senna. They hiked back to day position which was five miles up a dusty road off Highway One.

An hour after they arrived, a Jeep, raising clouds of dust as it approached, stopped near the platoon. Two officers climbed out. Average height and husky, Colonel Nuvolari was fuming. He chewed on a cigar. The Col. pulled the soggy tobacco roll out of his teeth while walking up to the men. The battalion doctor, Capt. Herrmann, moved at his side.

Someone yelled, "Attention." The platoon jumped to their feet, stood at attention.

Hands on hips the colonel bellowed, "Where's the grunt who did the artery repair?"

Levin stepped forward, stood at attention. "That would be me, sir."

Lt. Senna stepped to Levin's side.

With hands on hips and speaking through clenched teeth, the Lt. Colonel sputtered, "How the fuck...in the field...nobody in their right mind except an absolute fucking expert...a many years experienced vascular expert, would attempt a repair like that."

"I know sir, but if I didn't, he'd a lost his foot."

"I'm aware, Sgt. Levin, I'm aware." The Lt. Colonel seethed while glaring at Brian. He chomped on his cigar for a minute, took a deep breath then asked, "Your experience?"

Brian sensed his platoon mates staring at him. "Five-year surgical residence in a big city hospital."

"But..."

"Started college at sixteen, med school at nineteen, sir."

The Lt. Colonel fumed, "What the fuck you doing out here, asshole? Do you have any idea how useful an experienced vascular surgeon...?"

Levin remained at attention and silent.

The veins at the Colonel's temples pulsed, his face purple. "Never fucking mind. For the last two months of your tour, you've been assigned to me...Dr. Levin."

Dr. Levin barked, "Yes, Sir."

Capt. Herrmann handed copies of his new orders to Brian and the platoon's Lt.

Levin gathered his gear, shook a few hands and climbed in the jeep. Reviewing his orders, he noted he'd been promoted.

"We'll have you up to speed and performing surgeries by noon tomorrow," Captain Hermann said.

Chapter 10

Late the next day, Captain Levin examined the next patient at the medivac station.

"Look at those railroad tracks!" James Ware said, remarking about the Captain's bars on Levin's collar. "You're a damn Captain?"

"Makes the patients feel more secure if they think I'm an officer." Brian removed the bandages from the wounds to Ware's upper arm and chest. "Who sewed this?"

"Doc Evans."

"Looks good."

James smirked. "Learned from an experienced surgeon, I hear."

"We're going to take some pictures and do a little work, Buddy. You're going to sleep shortly."

Ware tried to smile through his worry but exhibited fear. "I'll be okay, huh? Remember, that truck's waiting for me."

"You'll be back in the world before me and driving in no time." Brian pulled a piece of paper and a pen from his shirt pocket. "Here's my address and phone. Call me when you're home. We'll get together."

Brian performed the required surgery, then a few hours later, checked on James. The Montanan chatted to no one in particular but sounded as if he was talking to children. His boys, Brian assumed then headed to dinner.

Following his meal, he asked around and found Dot, who would be sent to a hospital ship for surgery on her hip the next day. She lay on a cot, an IV in her arm. He reviewed her chart. Brian put a chair next to her. Although groggy, she smiled when she saw him.

"Any pain?" he asked.

Dot shook her head.

"Tomorrow, you ride in another helicopter to a hospital ship. More doctors will repair Dot."

"Nurse she say, you not fix me in village, I die. You number one doc."

"Thank you."

She smiled, held out a hand. He gripped it, tears filled her eyes then slid down her cheeks.

"Scared?" Brian asked.

She nodded. "Big scared. You come with Dot? Go ship?"

He shook his head. "Sorry. Have to fix people here."

Dot appeared to think about his answer then asked, "You stay Dot this night?"

"I'll stay but you sleep."

The little one nodded, watched him for a few minutes then closed her eyes. He read and filled out reports. She woke a few times during the night, smiled when she saw him still at her side.

He helped move her to a stretcher the next day and walked her out to the chopper which would transport her to the hospital ship.

"My special patient," Brian yelled to the medic who would accompany her and the other wounded.

"No sweat, Captain," the medic replied with a grin. "I'll keep an eye on her, sir."

Dot raised her head slightly, smiled then gave him a little wave as the machine clawed its way into the air.

***

Two weeks later, the medical staff began a rugged week where they were short-staffed. Brian remembered his former infantry company was on a seven-day stand down. He requested Doc Martin Evans help.

"You follow what happened to Dot?" Martin asked while they ate lunch after four hours of surgery on the first day.

"She requires huge rehab after surgery on the hospital ship where they repaired much of her hip. Nothing like that in Vietnam, so they sent her to Ft. Sam in Houston. They'll transfer her for rehab to UTMB Galveston."

"Wouldn't she need someone, like family, to meet her?"

"Someone told officials she has family near Houston. Her grandmother will be heading over once she gets her paperwork squared away."

"She has money for that kind of travel?"

"Someone arranged it."

"You?"

Brian nodded. "Dot is my special patient."

"Where will the grandmother live?"

"Short bus trip from UTMB, but in Houston. My parents are heading down to Houston from Dallas to purchase a condo as we speak. They'll meet Dot when she arrives. I'll rent the condo to Dot's Grandmother when she's over there."

"Hell, I'm comfortable. How can I help?" Martin asked.

"Not sure."

"I've got family there. My sister would love to meet them and make sure they have what they need. Besides, Houston's my town. How about I give you half the money for the condo. Once I'm home, I can stay close and make sure things are okay."

"Out fucking standing," Brian said, shaking his buddy's hand.

The rumble of helicopters approaching reached their ears.

"Let's go," Brian said.

Both stood and raced out to the helipad.

For the balance of the week, Doc Evans received on the job training from surgical nurses, surgical assistants and surgeons.

Before he returned to his unit, Martin found Brian.

"Heading back, buddy," Martin said, extending his hand. "Learned a shit load this week and performed repairs on a shit load of soldiers...even a few civilians. Can't thank you enough for the experience."

"Thanks for all your help. It made a huge difference."

"For the first time in my life...for certain, I know what I want to do after the Army."

"Med school?"

"Yup."

"I have friends at UT where I received my training. If you'd consider attending there..."

"For sure, Buddy, I'll be in touch."

***

During and after a large battle in the A Shau Valley, the medivac station was swamped with casualties. Four days of surgery, the last twenty-seven hours' continuous, the intense concentration required by their work forced the medical staff to stay sharp and awake during the long hours. Their minds, still powered by caffeine and adrenaline, prevented sleep.

Alone now, Brian and a nurse sat side-by-side in camp chairs, outside her tent at two in the morning. His shirt opened, chest and belly shiny with sweat, they each held a glass of Bourbon. He used the edge of his hand to wipe his forehead. Rivulets of sweat ran down his face and onto his chest.

"Heard you're the asshole who didn't let the Army know you were an experienced surgeon," said surgical nurse Major Krista Downey. The front and back of her shirt also soaked in sweat, she was the head of the nursing staff and just short of ten years' experience.

Tired of trying to explain, Brian sighed then said, "Had other things to accomplish."

"Disgusting. You should be punished." She glanced at his muscular chest, noted the silver chain and Star of David. "You're Jewish."

He nodded. "You?"

"Baptist."

"Ever been to a Jewish service?"

"Couple times. Been to a Baptist?"

"Once."

Brian glanced up and down her figure. Even in Army fatigues, he could see the outline of a lovely body. He leaned over and gave her a long kiss. She pulled away. "You can't…I'm higher rank than you…"

"Well, excuse…"

"Damn it," she said, her cheeks blushing to the extent, their crimson appearance was evident even in the dim moonlight, "Been too long…speaking of religion," she said with an impish grin. "I've got a place where your bald monk can worship." They stood and she pulled him into her quarters.

"The heat and humidity…" he said.

"Make a guy's balls fill with desire. Apparently does things to a woman as well."

He nodded. They stripped and tumbled into her bed.

"We're using each other," Krista said after they'd finished.

"Or you can say we're sharing our bodies with a team member."

She laughed. "For little more than tension relief."

Brian considered her comment. "In a philosophic sense, please consider, it was more than that. Sharing our bodies reminds us we're still human, even in the midst of all this inhuman shit."

The major considered his thought then sounded pleased. "I...I like how that sounds."

They slept a few hours then showered.

"Someone special in your world?" she asked while they toweled off.

"Was," Brian said. "Unlikely we'll meet again. Great lady. Met during R&R. Opposites really. She's a country girl, raised on a sheep ranch...ah...station, she called it. I was raised the opposite. Near Dallas...tall buildings, great symphony, fabulous music scene, and all that in a great metropolitan area. You...someone special?"

"Major in the Infantry, light of my life. Also, career Army like me. Died seven months ago just north of Da Nang. Damn chopper went down due to mechanical problems. Came through here but he was too torn up..."

He rolled his shoulders, stretched forward and backwards. "Watched a helicopter go down once. Awful sight. All but one killed. Must have been tough on you to lose him like that."

They began dressing.

"I was back in the states when he died. Buried him near our home." She dropped her head, folded her hands as if reciting a prayer. "A blessed man who cared for me and understood my passion for military service, which goes back many generations in my family."

"How far?"

"Earliest I'm aware of, a nurse in the Civil War. One of the few female nurses in the medical corps back then. Name of Laura Hetherington. I have letters she wrote to family."

"Love to read them."

"When I'm home, I'll send you copies."

"That would be helpful."

"Because…"

"A book I'll be working on."

Both back in their uniforms, Krista took a long drink out of a canteen, peered at him with a questioning expression. "We'll go back to work…"

Cpt. Levin gave her arm a brief squeeze. "Like nothing happened."

She smiled. "Thank you."

A nurse yelled from outside the tent, "Major Downey, you're needed in the surgical recovery area."

"Be right there, Lieutenant," Krista said.

It was quiet for a bit then the same voice said, "Uh…Ah…ma'am…if you know where Captain Levin is, he's needed as well."

"Thank you, Lieutenant," Krista replied as she and Brian chuckled then walked to the triage area.

"Dr. Levin," a nurse called out, "this soldier is asking for you."

The soldier was being prepped for surgery.

Arnie Zalman appeared terror stricken but relieved the moment he saw Brian. He held up his undamaged left hand which his buddy shook with both hands.

"Levin, you're here. Bless the Lord. I shouldn't be so worried now."

"What the hell? You forget to duck?"

"Damn mortar round."

"Anyone else hurt?"

"Couple newbies. Both died. Couple other guys, minor stuff," Arnie took a deep breath, let it out slowly.

"We have a great medical team. You'll be up and around in no time."

"If you say so but I think my right arm and leg are in rough shape."

Keeping his expression stoic as he reviewed Arnie's injuries, Brian knew his platoon-mate's days participating in the sports he loved were over. "You're going to sleep. Talk to you in a few hours." He nodded to the team who wheeled Arnie into surgery.

Just prior to dinner, Brian visited his former squad mate.

"So, Dr. Levin, what's my prognosis?"

Brian grabbed a chair and sat at his buddy's side. He rubbed his face with his hands. "The broken bones will heal but there's nerve and muscle damage. I expect you'll be able to walk but running may be out of the question. Back in the states you'll have a multi-month recovery."

Arnie displayed a moment's sorrow then smiled. "That's a loss, but the Lord saved me. Don't know what for but…I'll have to find out." He smiled at Brian then added, "Bless the Lord, you'll find your purpose as well, although two nurses told me I was lucky you were the one working on me so maybe you've found yours."

"You need lots of rest. Are you in pain?"

"Not bad. But one thing. We were in a fire fight a couple days ago. I was on the machine gun. When we inspected the area, we found a family huddled together in a shack…Mom, Dad, kids. They'd been torn to hell. Bullet holes…my gun…depresses the hell out of me when I think how I destroyed that family. The kids must have been so frightened. Their parents died in a futile attempt to save them by laying on top of them."

"May not have been you…"

"7.62 rounds cause a hell of a lot more damage than 5.56…but I don't have to tell you that." Tears formed in his eyes. "There's a prayer book in my gear. Get it for me?"

Brian dug in his duffel then handed it to him. "Try not to think about what happened. Relax. Think of your wife. How happy she's going to be when you get home. Get some sleep. You'll be flown to Japan tomorrow. Not long after, back to a hospital in the states. Should be near your home."

After dinner Brian returned. He and Arnie recited a few prayers together.

He shook his friend's good hand. "You need rest. Take care, Arnie."

Arnie nodded but didn't let go of Brian's hand. "We'll get together some time…back in the world?"

"We will, Buddy. That's a promise."

The Brooklynite sighed, appeared to relax. "Stay safe," he said to his Texas friend.

***

The following month, Colonel Nuvolari invited Brian into his office.

Brian entered, saluted then sat in the chair the Colonel indicated. "Your surgical technique is excellent and your training ability with new surgeons and staff is peerless. I have several new surgeons arriving over the coming weeks. I would like you to extend in-country eight weeks to train them. This is strictly voluntary but if you do, you'll be discharged the moment you arrive home. No stateside deployment."

With only one week left in his twelve-month tour of Vietnam and already making plans on what he'd do when he returned, Brian didn't immediately reply.

The Colonel added, "The slot requires a Major. It kills me to do this, but you'll receive a promotion if you take the assignment."

Brian still didn't reply.

The Lt. Colonel fired his biggest weapon. "Our unit will remain at a high level of medical readiness, if those training the new team members are trained by our top people. The team continues to require your expertise, Captain Levin."

Brian remembered how effective our Air Force and Navy were during World War II because the best pilots returned home to train new pilots, leading to defeat of the German and Japanese Air Forces.

"I'll extend, sir," Levin said, dreading the fact he'd have to explain to his mother that he volunteered to remain an additional eight weeks in a war zone.

***

A week later and just after lunch, Colonel Nuvolari said, "I need a volunteer to head over to the staging area next door. An officer in supply had a shell from an M79 grenade launcher hit him. The round didn't explode."

Major Levin volunteered, as did Major Downey. Their Jeep was directed to an area in between two large tents, where they found soldiers stacking sandbags. The soldier with the grenade round imbedded in his side, on his back within the two-and-one-half foot high sandbagged area.

Brian checked the trembling soldier. "Don't move. Don't talk. I'm a surgeon and this is a surgical nurse. We're going to get that thing out and get you away from here."

"The round is between his skin and his rib cage," Brian said.

She nodded.

Brian injected pain killer. He used a scalpel to slowly expose the round. "Don't let it rotate," he reminded Krista as she steadied the shell. He continued to cut. The round free, staying low, she moved in slow motion, extending her hand beyond the wall of sand bags. Blood covered, the round began to slip. She dropped it, quickly withdrawing her hand. The explosion left them dusted them in sand.

"You okay?" Brian asked Krista, sat up then coughed and spit, wiped sand off his face, brushed it out of his hair.

"A bit shaken but okay."

She cleaned and he closed the soldier's wound.

"Am I gonna die?" the still trembling soldier asked.

Major Downey replied, "You will Lieutenant, but not today."

Other soldiers ran over and helped move the wounded man to a stretcher.

Brian put his hand on his right butt cheek. It felt wet.

He dropped the right side of his pants a few inches. "A scratch," Major Downey said as she cleaned the area then injected pain killer and used three stitches to close the wound. "You're cute butt is going to have a scar on it."

A brief jeep ride and they were back in the medical unit. Upon arrival, the Colonel approached. "You two take the rest of the day off."

Brian checked his watch, saw it was another two hours before supper. He walked to his hooch, laid down, figuring he'd sleep for an hour then read and do paperwork. Instead, Brian woke on time for breakfast the following day. He shook his head, laughed, and said to the empty tent, "Guess yesterday's little incident used more energy than I thought."

***

Following breakfast the same day, a newly arrived surgeon yelled, "Nurse, get your ass over here."

The Lieutenant rolled her eyes.

The new surgeon shouted, "I saw that, when I give an order, you move your fucking ass, not roll your eyes."

Major Levin took him aside, said in a calm voice, "You will treat the staff with respect and always consider those here have more experience than you."

The Captain seemed unimpressed, replied with a half-hearted, "Yes, Sir."

With fury in his expression, Brian bellowed with sufficient volume to rattle windows, "Or perhaps you'd like to use your medical education to disimpact bowels for the duration of your tour. I can arrange that. Speak in a disrespectful manner to staff of any rank and I promise, for the next year, you will find yourself up to your elbows in assholes. Is that understood?"

"Yes, Sir. Won't be a problem, Major," said the now, red-faced and trembling, new arrival.

Major Downey tried but couldn't conceal a grin. She mouthed, "Thank you, Major Levin."

At dinner that night, Brian said to Krista, "I was told you'll be discharged from the Army when you head home."

"Yes. Two days and a wakeup then on my way. Great ten years of service complete."

"Where will you go? What will you do?"

"Heading back to the family farm in Iowa. I'll take over the bookkeeping...inherit the place one day."

"If you're ever near Dallas..."

She gave him a warm smile. "I've got your address."

"You and I…"

"I understand," Krista said with a knowing grin. "Good friends who supported each other and saved many lives. Our friendship along with understanding each other's needs, made our work easier. Bless you for that."

"A few more weeks and I'll be heading home as well," Brian said. "I wonder how hard it will be to become a civilian again."

PART FOUR: SETH

Chapter 11

"The combat was bad enough, but the way we were treated when we came home was disgusting."
Richard Alan Schwartz, 101ˢᵗ Airborne Division, 2/327, Delta Company
(1975)

1971 March

He arrived at his North Texas acreage via taxi from Love Field, on a blustery, cool day. He paid the driver, and walked up the flagstone path to the front porch. Brian smiled and marveled that his wind chimes survived. He was certain they played a welcoming tune. Their sound warmed him as he unlocked the front door and dropped his duffel bag in the entry. Brian proceeded to the kitchen, put water in his coffee maker, and checked the fridge. He found a bottle of cream with a welcome-home note from his folks, plus eggs and butter. The veteran checked the freezer and said, "Thank you, Mom." He was certain it held enough food for the next three months.

Brian called his folks to let them know he was at home in Celina. His mother answered. "You're home!" she said, then began crying and handed the phone to his father. The combat veteran said he'd be over in a few hours. He filled the coffee maker, and sat at his kitchen table. While it perked, he thought of his buddies who were still at war. Brian wondered how Arnie's recovery was progressing and grinned when he thought of James Ware driving the monster sized mining truck then hoped James reintegration with his family would allow him to avoid talking to himself. His head bowed, he recited a prayer for the safety of the men and women he left behind. Upon reflection, he recited another for the sanity of men and women who witnessed or committed wartime horrors. He also prayed for those he couldn't save, and recited a prayer which asked that the family members of those who came home in a casket achieve a sense of peace.

In his office, Brian sipped a mug of coffee. He found a note from his father. It listed needed repairs around the property. From a roof leak in the detached garage to fences which needed mending, there was much to keep him occupied.

"A great idea," he thought. "It gives me simple, relatively mindless things to do while I adjust to civilian life."

He picked up a bottle of spray glass cleaner and a few rags then proceeded to the front porch. He sprayed and wiped each of the crystalline chimes.

The wind chimes increased in volume from a sudden gust, which reminded him of Andrea.

As if the wind chimes could hear, he said, "While I was half-way around the world, the memory of your sound, reminded me of home." He sighed. "Now you remind me of an Auburn-haired lady."

 "Blessed Andrea," he mumbled. His eyes filled with tears as he looked skyward and said, "Please, Lord, take care of that precious lady."

Brian decided to wear his dress uniform. He heated an iron and pressed out duffel-bag caused wrinkles. After polishing his shoes to a mirror gloss, he dressed in the uniform then entered the attached two car garage. He thought of the day he left home, wondering if that was the last time he'd see his Oldsmobile 442. Resplendent in gold with white stripes and a gold interior, he'd taken one look at this vehicle in the dealer's show room and knew it was for him.

"It represents who I am in an automotive form," He'd told his father at the time.

Brian looked at the other vehicle in the garage, a four-door pickup which had been recently cleaned and polished. He opened the Oldsmobile's door, slid behind the wheel, and twisted the key. The reassuring rumble and vibration of the four-hundred cubic inch engine coming to life made him grin. The sound assured him he was home, and not dreaming.

After a brief drive south to the town of Plano, Brian walked up to the front door of his parent's home. His father threw the door open, embraced his son then yelled to his wife. She came running, grabbed him and didn't let got for quite some time, crying quietly. They sat in the living room; his dad handed him a Scotch neat.

"What the hell?" his dad said. "When did you become a Major?"

"Long story," Brian said. He related the series of incidents which lead to his becoming an officer.

"What was it like to go from infantry to surgery?" his mother asked.

"Mentally different to use all one's energy to save rather than destroy life, but both were physically and mentally exhausting, at times like torture. You make a mistake in either endeavor and people die."

"Have you read about the anti-war demonstrations?" his mother asked.

"Saw it in newspapers at the airport in Washington State. I wondered if it was okay to wear my uniform once I arrived home."

"This is Texas," his Dad said. "Shouldn't be a problem here. When I came back to the States from North Africa, World War Two hadn't ended," his dad said, "I was given one week's leave to visit my folks in Chicago. When approaching a butcher shop on Milwaukee Avenue, wearing my uniform of course, I remember a grinning youngster running to open the door for me and the customers insisting I get served before them."

That evening, his father asleep, Brian talked to his mom.

"Dad went out to your place once a week to check on things," Brian's mother said. "I think he felt like he was closer to you when out there. If nothing else, he'd wash and polish your Oldsmobile and the pickup, take them for a run to ensure the batteries were up. Twice a month he'd fire up and run the John Deere to make sure it was ready for your return. The motorhome as well." She chuckled. "Even kept correct air pressure in the tires of your bicycle."

"Thought about you guys when I was over there."

"You wonder what your children think when they're so far away...if the values you taught them will help or hurt them...especially in a war zone."

"With Dad telling me so many stories from WWII, I had a pretty good idea what to expect. Even the harassment from the drill Sergeants during basic training didn't bother me because of what he'd said. Hell, I was mentally prepared. For other guys, the discipline chafed like ill-fitting shoes."

"Saturday night, the neighbors who watched you grow up, would like to come over and welcome you home. Also your Uncle Mike will be here. He can't wait to see you. If you remember, he was in the 101st Airborne Division during World War II."

"Great. I'm looking forward to seeing everyone."

"As far as your book is concerned," his mother said, "Remember, it wasn't only the men who felt they had a huge stake in the outcome of World War II, so did the women. While my home was here in Texas, I went to Georgia to be a coast watcher. I kept up correspondence with nine men besides my first husband. He was a navigator on a bomber, and as you are aware, died near the end of the war."

***

His third weekend home, Brian and his father painted the interior of the garage at his parent's home. The planned on selling the place and retiring to Apache Junction, Arizona. A large jet flew over, gear and flaps down, on its way to landing at Love Field in Dallas.

His father nodded toward the sound. "I was in still in North Africa when we heard the Germans had a plane that flew without a propeller. We laughed like crazy until fighter pilots told us they were faster than the P-38s and P-51s."

Brian said, "Makes me uncomfortable to think my friends continue to die on the other side of the globe and I'm out here painting."

"I understand," his father said. "When I was sent back to the states, six months before the war ended, I had the same feeling. Except for seeing so many men in uniform, I felt like I was far from being in harm's way."

"You're saying, I'm safe and my former team members are still fighting and dying."

"Precisely. But we were in the war until the end," his father said. "Although I was in the States to train new crews, I was anticipating orders to send me to the Pacific. Would have happened but the war ended."

They were quiet for a while, each lost in their own thoughts. The paint rollers making the only sounds.

Brian's father stopped painting, seemed lost in thought for a bit, then said, "A strange thing happened near the end of my time in North Africa. A lone JU-88 came over and began strafing our airfield. Rounds came close to me while I was running toward a bunker. A strange thought entered my mind.

I was angry with the pilot because I hadn't done anything to him and yet he was trying to kill me."

"Strange indeed but I've heard similar reactions from others," Brian said.

His father climbed off a ladder, opened a new can of paint, stirred it, climbed the ladder and returning to painting. He sighed then continued a previous thought. "Perhaps it's different emotionally to be in it to the end, as opposed to struggling to stay alive for twelve months. Also the guys we trained with initially were the guys we went to war with. We knew each other's strengths and weaknesses. Surely we were a cohesive team because of that." The World War II veteran concentrated on the work for a while as he placed masking tape on the edge of the ceiling. "Most of us came home with the same guys, except those who died. We were together for two weeks on ships arriving at ports on the east and west coasts, reviewing what we did, thinking of the friends we lost, missions we went on, talking about plans when we got home."

"A cohesive team from training to end of the war," Brian said. "Quite different."

"Another thing you might consider," his father said, "The Vietnam War doesn't have the all-out support of the public. That could be a problem for the soldiers returning home."

During cleanup, his father asked, "How's work at the hospital?"

"I've only been there a week and it will take a little time to adjust to their procedures but I have a great surgical team to work with. I work four, ten-hour days so have a three day weekend, interrupted by the occasional emergency if they get slammed in the Emergency Room. I'll have plenty of time to get the ranch in shape."

"For a family?"

Brian laughed. "Not yet. Want to enjoy being single for a while. My new position at the hospital and getting the place in shape are enough responsibility for now."

"You going to do any traveling?"

"Next weekend. I'll be visiting a couple friends near Houston. One's in medical school, the other in a rehabilitation center. I want to check on that condo. Thanks for buying it for us"

"Don't mention it. It's nice to see old friends. Are these friends you knew during the war?"

"Yes," Brian said. "Going to drive the motorhome down. I'll camp on Galveston Island."

"Beautiful location. You'll love it there."

***

"How's medical school?" Brian asked former medic and platoon mate Martin Evans. He'd just picked up Brian at the campground in Galveston.

"Frustrating at times but it ain't combat so I just keep plowing ahead," he said, while dodging early morning traffic. He was driving his Army buddy from his campground in Galveston to their jointly-owned condo.

"How are your folks and your girls?" Brian asked.

Martin smiled and chuckled. "Just like when I was growing up, my mom runs the household and my Dad, when he's not working, loves playing with the girls."

"Dot's grandmother?"

"I moved her into the condo a few days ago. She's a nervous wreck being in a new country and not speaking the language, but I found a Vietnamese couple who helped her get settled. They've taken her shopping and introduced the neighborhood and the bus system. I suspect she'll be relieved the minute she visits Dot."

"How's the little lady doing?"

"Her English skills are increasing by leaps and bounds. One of the rehab nurses is giving her lessons and written homework every day. You will be shocked at her English language skill."

"She knows her Grandmother is coming today?" Brian asked.

"Dot can't wait. They've spoken over the phone a few times since the old woman arrived. Dot's last day of residency at the rehab center is this Friday. She'll move in with her Grandmother then."

"I've managed papers for them, so they can stay in the States if they like."

Martin gave his friend a quizzical look. "That must have cost a pretty penny."

Brian shook his head. "Don't ask. I've never in my life, seen so many people with their hands out."

The old woman, waited in the lobby of her building. Dot's grandmother smiled the moment she recognized Brian. He walked her to the car and Martin drove them across town to the rehab center.

They knocked on the open door at the entrance to Dot's room. She sat a small table, wearing University of Texas emblazoned, orange sweat shirt, and sweat pants. Dot saw her visitors, then grabbed a cane and limped over to embrace each one of them. Brian left briefly to find extra chairs. Returning, he heard the relatives chatter away in Vietnamese.

Dot laughed hysterically, turned to Martin and Brian. "She said the most difficult part of her journey was the strange food."

The men laughed.

Brian asked if he could review her medical records. Dot nodded. Pouring over a thick file, he said. "Excellent progress."

Dot smiled. "Home to live with my Grandmother in three days."

The grandmother said something to Dot.

"Typical grandmother," Dot said with a giggle. "She has a job lined up at a bakery two blocks from her apartment. The people who helped her last night made some phone calls for her."

The former soldiers listened to more Vietnamese from Grandmother.

"She said she will be paying rent soon and will pay you back for the airplane ticket." Dot listened for a bit then laughed again. "Grandmother also said she knows where I will be starting school."

Martin asked, "Dot, any nightmares or concerns from the war?"

"Sometimes ugly dreams."

"I know a counselor you can talk to."

"How many days will you be here?" Dot asked Brian.

"Two more, then I have to head home for work."

***

Back in Celina, Brian shut the engine down on his John Deere Model 3020, and jumped off. He'd used the tractor with a sweeping attachment to clean the drive to his home. It was also used it for lawn care and gardening. The postman drove up in a two-door jeep then called to him.

"The address is a bit off but figured this might be for you, Dr. Levin. All the way from Australia."

The Vietnam vet thanked the postman, read the return address then ripped open the envelope.

Dearest Brian,

Thought I'd write and let you know; I'll be married this weekend. His name is Rodney and he's a kind man. Also a sheep farmer, so Dad likes him, and, as I'd hoped, I'll be a rancher's wife. Dad is doing well by the way. Sends his thanks. He's healed and back to his old curmudgeon self.

The feelings and emotions you and I discussed and experienced together, have made me a better person. I know we never finished numerous conversations but how can I ever thank you for our six days? Sorry, I couldn't tell you in person. Please know, you secured a place in my heart no one else will ever touch. I think of you whenever I hear my wind chimes.

Love Always,

Andrea

He slowly shook his head then reread the letter.

"Tough news, Dr. Levin?" the postman asked.

Brian forced a smile. "Happy news for a friend."

"You look like somebody ripped your heart out."

"I should be nothing but happy for my friend but...you know...life is friggin' crazy."

"Got that right," the postman said and climbed back in his jeep.

Brian held up the envelope and yelled, "Thanks for thinking of me."

A day later, he replied:

Andrea,

Thanks for the note. Congratulations on your marriage. If you visit the states, unlikely I know, you'll find me in Celina, Texas.

Yes, I'm a better person for having known you. Glad your father is doing well. Give him my best.
Love,
Brian Levin
PS. My wind chimes survived.

***

The commuter train rocked. Its side to side motion and clacking wheels, annoyed some but the rhythm of sound and motion, soothing to others. The sound of twisted metal and shattering glass filling the air, frightened Brian. The front end of the car he was riding in began climbing. The conveyance nearly vertical, he felt as if he was on a roller coaster, his weight pressing more on the back of the seat than the cushion below his legs. The car twisted like a pretzel, steel and aluminum groaning, screaming passengers tossed about. He was trapped in the wreckage. The passengers pitiful pleading for help ringing in his ears, but he couldn't move, his legs and arms trapped, he couldn't reach his medical bag. He saw injuries he knew would be easy to repair but if left unattended would result in blood loss and death. A young boy turned to him. An oriental face with a pen in his eye.

The alarm rang. Brian jumped out of bed. He stood there panting, his body trembling, sweat running down his brow. He banged his hand on the buzzing alarm clock to silence it.

Brian looked around his bedroom and heard his wind chimes. He said to the empty room, "Three months home...why would I have a nightmare like that?"

He took a hot shower to try and wash away the dream. Brian thought, *"Even though I spend numerous hours on my research, the war itself seems far away. Its horror, should be, receding in my memory."*

***

During early November of 1973, Brian received another letter from Andrea.

> *Dear Brian,*
> *We'll be visiting the U.S, the middle of this month.*
> *Would like to visit you. Is that okay?*
> *Andrea*

A huge smile spread across his face. Even the wind chimes seemed to play a happy tune. Brian ran to his office and replied in the affirmative along with a request for their itinerary.

He thought, *"It might be difficult, but I have to stay cool and remember she's married. I wonder if I should do anything special for their arrival. Perhaps I'll schedule a party so Andrea and Rodney can meet my friends? Jet lag could be taxing for them the first few days. It could be difficult with her husband if he knows how close I was to Andrea. Back in Oz, she was certain she never wanted to visit the states. I wonder what changed."* He thought of their time in Oz. *"Such sweet memories. I can't wait to see her."*

The phone rang bringing Brian back to his normal routine. A friend asked if he could provide extra plates for the dinner party he would be attending that night.

"Of course. I'll be there at seven."

Chapter 12

1973 November

Descending out of a leaden-gray sky through a light rain, typical for late November in Dallas, but adding to the already thick, humid air, the twin-engine jet flew approach in a nose up attitude; engines throttled back and flaps extended while its main landing gear appeared to reach for the earth like a steel legged Pterodactyl. A squeal and two puffs of smoke emanating from the tires announced its contact with terra-firma. Brian stood at the exit to the jet-way, watched the passengers disembark. Andrea, with a sullen expression, approached. A toddler in her left arm and a large handbag and diaper bag in the other. He expected her warm smile to lift his heart, but her expression was as gray as the sky.

"The pained expression of someone dreading their future?" he wondered.

"Welcome to Dallas," he said, his head on a swivel for her husband. He gave her a brief embrace then took her bags.

The toddler's radiant blue eyes examined him with a brief glance then rested his head on Andrea's shoulder. "Good to be here," she said in a tone of relief but without a smile. "At last. Seth can hardly hold his head up. We're exhausted. It was a long ride from Oz."

"Rodney?"

"Not with us."

"Where you staying?"

"Nowhere yet."

"Guest bedroom at my place…if that's okay."

She nodded.

With little conversation, they retrieved her bags. His black, full-sized, four-door pickup swallowed the trio and her six bags.

"How far away is your home?" she asked, as he eased onto the highway.

"Forty-minutes from here."

"I'll sleep."

She woke as the pickup bounced while he turned off the main road then drove up a long drive.

"Big place."

"Just over one-hundred acres. The state of Oklahoma, is a brief drive north of here."

A brick walled, two-story house came into view.

"Looks homey," she said.

"I grew up here. My folks bought it just as I entered my teens. Lots of wood trim inside...adds warmth."

"An expensive home."

"A bargain. The builder ran out of money before all the electric was in. The walls and floors not finished. My dad and I finished the wiring then he hired carpenters for the balance."

The pickup stopped under the covered portico which extended to the front door.

As she exited the truck, she pointed as the wind chimes sang in the light breeze as if announcing their pleasure at her arrival.

"Yes," he said with a smile, "The ones which sound like you."

She stopped briefly to listen, then displayed her first smile.

They entered the house; opposite the great room with its two-story window wall.

Andrea looked around. "Like you said, a warm interior."

Sleepy Seth yawned.

"I'll show you the guest room. He can sleep there," Brian offered.

She nodded.

Andrea carried the little one up a set of stairs. Brian indicated the room. She put the toddler in the middle of the bed, placed pillows on either side of him, and a wool blanket over him. When they returned to the family room, Andrea walked to and stared out the window wall.

"Great view," She said without looking at him.

"Tea?" he offered.

Andrea nodded, kicked off her shoes, plopped into the deep cushions of the couch across from the fireplace, and emitted a long sigh.

"An expensive trip from Oz," Brian said, as he handed her a mug of steaming brew.

Taking the mug in both hands she carefully sipped its contents. "Tastes like Billy tea."

"Yes. Enjoyed it in Oz. Found a place here that sold it."

"My father helped me get here. Something about buying rainbows." She yawned. "I'm going to join Seth for a while."

Four hours later, Andrea and Seth came down to the family room. Brian sat on the floor next to the little one, who crawled onto his lap.

Seth laughed and giggled while Brian held him over his head, encouraging him to put his arms out like an airplane.

"Seth has such brilliant blue eyes," he said.

"Just like his father," Andrea said.

Brian stood, put Seth on his left arm, and walked toward the window wall. He addressed the little one, "See the swimming pool and the pond behind it...won't be long and we'll see geese raising a gaggle of little ones, then skeins of ducks overhead and some evenings, in that tree line beyond the pond, listen to a parliament of..." Brian froze.

"Parliament did you say?" Andrea asked.

He slowly turned to face her.

She pulled her knees against her chest, wrapped her arms around them.

Seth's father stammered, "This guy...you mean...how old is he?" He stared at the little one, his own bright blue eyes returning his gaze. Seth smiled, the little one saying, "More airplane." He waved his arms then gripped and tugged on Brian's shirt collar.

The Aussie lady asked, "You said, parliament…?"

"Andrea, he's…?"

She took a deep breath, exhaled slowly, pulled her knees tighter against her chest, and nodded. "Yes. 7 March 1971. Thirty-three-months-old and he's our son."

His face bathed in incredulity, he stammered, "Oh…Ah…My God. Why didn't you let me know?"

"Not sure how, or if I should. Our six days seemed like a dream after a while…"

"I gave you my address. My phone."

Andrea shrugged. "We agreed there were good reasons not to stay in touch."

"But, a child?"

"I was angry with you. With myself…"

"Bit of a shock."

"Brian…"

"I need to be alone for a bit so I can get my head to stop spinning." Brian handed Seth to Andrea. The back door slammed as he left the house.

"Crap," he thought as he crossed the yard toward the garage through a light rain, his silver and blue motor home sitting on the apron. *"Just getting my head on straight and she brings me a child."* He shrugged and giggled. *"At least it's my child. I don't really know if that's good or bad."* Brian stopped next to his motorhome, kicked one of the tires, and patted its side. *"Sorry old girl. Don't know if it's practical to travel with a little one. I may have to store you for…hell, may have to sell you."* He turned back to the house. Seth stood at the base of the window wall wearing a

concerned expression while his little hand banged on the glass.

"If you're mine, little guy," Brian thought while waving at Seth, *"I'll take care of you."* Thinking of the fun he was having, he smiled and thought, *"Take care of you even if you're not mine."* He slowly shook his head. *"But your Mom...only knew her for six days...how do she and I build a relationship on that...if I stayed in Oz, would we have stayed together? Country Girl and City Boy. Not much chance of a happy ending with such opposites. And there was that story she started to tell me...she'd killed some people? Is she running away because the police are after her? Andrea seems remote...almost cold...especially in comparison to the woman I knew in Oz."*

After kicking the rear tires of the motor home, Brian entered the detached garage. Five vehicles, the beginning of a car and antique tractor collection lined one wall, the other wall setup for winter storage of his motor home. His just painted, 1935 John Deere tractor, resplendent in green and yellow held his attention. He walked over, ran his hand down the hood, made a mental note to check the tire pressure in the left rear then thought of Seth and smiled. *"Always imagined driving this tractor with a child on my lap. I have that little guy to support now...his mom as well. May not be able to keep my car collection. A sudden family...don't have a clue what the costs would be. What if she doesn't want me? Tough on Seth to start life traveling between two homes. Little guy doesn't deserve that. Not his fault if we can't make it."*

Brian spent time contemplating the changes he would have to make then walked back to the house. He kneeled in front of the fireplace, stacked a number of logs then flamed one end of a piece of resinous, pine heartwood to start them burning. Seth approached and kneeled at his side. Brian looked around, saw Andrea sitting on a rocker on the front porch. He ruffled Seth's hair, then stood and flopped onto the couch. The little one followed a few steps then ran over to, what his mother called, Seth's activity bag. He pulled out two books then returned to Brian who hoisted him onto his lap.

"The Happy Man and his Dump Truck," Brian said. "So, you like trucks." He read in an expressive voice, the little one giving him rapt attention and occasionally pointing to the illustrations. By the time the following story, "Scuffy the Tugboat," ended, Seth was curled up against his father, sound asleep.

Andrea walked back into the room then stood in front of the fireplace, holding out her hands to enjoy its warmth. "Comforting fire."

"You've been crying."

Eyes riveted on the dancing flames, she said, "Didn't know what to expect when I told you about Seth...didn't think you'd walk out."

"Needed to think. Sometimes it's best to leave me alone while I get my head on straight."

"I have money. We can get our own place."

"No."

"Might be best, until we work things out."

"Not necessary. Let me show you the guest room."

They walked upstairs, Brian carrying Seth. Andrea was greeted by a four-poster bed supported by debarked logs, a two-chair sitting area with a lamp and a wrought-iron legged table between them, a wood-burning fireplace and a large private bath.

"Seth takes to you."

"Andrea…" He reached out to hold her but she moved away.

She walked to and stared out a window. "I know, we barely know each other, and I've brought you a child you certainly didn't expect. We're a burden. Not fair to you."

"We have some decisions to make."

She nodded while he put the little one in bed.

They returned to the great room, sat at opposite ends of the couch, the tension between them forcing them apart like the similar ends of two magnets. The fireplace flashed yellow flames, providing pleasant warmth and a visual focus while their minds raced through the vagaries of their situation.

After a few minutes silence, Brian curled against the end of the couch. Without looking at her, he asked, "Rodney decided not to accompany you?"

"He divorced me."

"I'm sorry to hear that," Brian said. "I was shocked to receive the letter asking if you could visit. In Oz, you were against coming to the States because of the violence."

"If Seth thinks like you or me, it'll take a crazy dad like you to raise him."

A cold silence enveloped them. Only interrupted by an occasional pop or crack from the fireplace.

Andrea broke the quiet. "Out the guest room window, I could see a large garden with a tall fence."

"Fence keeps the deer out. This is a large property, not a sheep station but a country girl might find solace working the garden and working the other acreage…"

She stared at the fire as if she didn't hear him.

He continued, "We alternate clover, wheat, soy, and corn on the balance of the acreage. A neighbor tends it. I get a percentage."

"Thank you. I'll give it some thought."

"Drink?"

"White wine."

Brian left the room briefly, returned with two wine goblets, handed one to her. "Andrea," he said as he again curled tight against the end of the couch opposite her. "I'm Jewish, which is an important part of my life."

"I remembered. Took care of that; studied, dipped and everything, before he was born."

Shocked, he stared at her then mumbled, "Thank you."

Andrea glanced at him, replied with a brief smile.

Brian asked, "How'd you know we'd get together?"

She shrugged. "Didn't…but believed the man I knew during our six days would want to be involved in Seth's upbringing, if given the chance."

"How did you know whether I was alone…?"

"Didn't know."

"All the way from Oz…"

"I understood you might have someone significant in your life…but as long as you're involved in Seth's life…knew I'd be satisfied."

"We disagreed about some things…living in the US, for instance."

She pulled a blanket off the back of the couch, covered herself then tucked the blanket around her. Andrea said, "Argued about many things but we still felt an attachment to each other, except issues I couldn't talk about." She pulled her knees against her chest, wrapping the blanket tighter. Rocked a bit then said, "Your take on subjects we disagreed on?"

Brian sighed and shrugged. "Some things resolved. Others not so much, but we still had an excellent relationship." He shook his head, briefly glanced at her. "We each have issues. I still find things from the war upset me." He paused for a bit, staring at the fire then asked, "How did you and Rodney handle differences?"

"Poorly. With silence…for days at a time; nothing ever resolved. Eventually tore us apart. He wanted a rancher's life with a rancher's wife. I gave him neither. Wasn't fair of me to bring my "Sturm und Drang" into his life. Rodney knew Seth wasn't his. He eventually used that to divorce me. He was…" She cursed. "Mostly busy with the damn sheep anyway." She cursed again. "We never talked about our relationship like you and I did. He was tuned into the sheep but not me."

The flicker of the fireplace's yellow flames reflected in her eyes. "It's not fair of me to bring my problems into your life…but our son…"

"Deserves a mom and a dad."

Andrea leaned back, looked at the ceiling, closed her eyes; a brief smile on her lips. "Dad was right…" she mumbled without opening her eyes.

"About?"

She sat up straight. "Seth enjoys the way you play with him."

"I don't even have a proper bed for him…a child-sized bed and blankets…toys…little guys need toys…and books…always thought little ones need their own libraries…decorations, we'll have to decorate his room. And this place could use a feminine touch. So much to do…What fun we'll have."

"Brian, some conversation about us first."

He stood and walked to the phone. "I know who to call."

"Fine but we need to talk…"

He stopped, turned slightly toward her. "Yes, we'll talk, but meanwhile, he needs a bed, little kid stuff. We'll go shopping later. Great little book and toy store…not far."

"But…" Her serious expression maintained, she said, "Can we become friends such that you'll be comfortable living with Seth?"

He smiled. "We'll start like we did in Oz. Walks and sunsets."

"We had disagreements. Country Girl and City Boy."

"It will happen again."

"But then how…"

"No clue…" he said with a shrug, staring at the flames. "But we have Seth to motivate us."

She studied the dancing flames while a satisfied smile appeared on her lips. "Yes. For his sake."

He turned toward her. "Aussie lady, you look exhausted."

"Drained."

"Up to the guest room and relax."

As she plodded up the stairs, she heard him on the phone. "Hello Mrs. Stern. Brian Levin here. Need a child's bed with mattress, a highchair suitable for a three-year-old, and…yes sheets and blankets, please…one of those Pendleton Arrowhead blankets would be marvelous…deep blue? Excellent. Can you deliver them today? No? I'll have my pickup there within the hour."

***

That evening, he sat across from the fireplace, the sound of hickory logs cracking and popping, a book propped on his belly. A faded, oversized, sweatshirt, proclaiming a Jimi Hendrix concert, matched his faded, torn jeans. His bare feet propped on a wide ottoman which was covered in identical, oxblood colored leather as the couch he occupied. Andrea approached, unfolded a blanket, curled into a wide, thickly padded leather chair to Brian's left, tucking the blanket around her.

He looked up from his book. "You check on Seth?"

"He is snug as bug. His expression was glowing while he watched you assemble his bed and dresser. Thanks for those."

"I work four ten-hour days in the Emergency Room of a local hospital and I'm on call for mass casualties."

"So, three days off each week?"

"Yes, but I'm continuing my study of returning Vietnam Vets. I'll combine it with my notes from the war. Occupies most of my spare time but I complete most of the work here at home."

"Most of my fights with Rodney began because I tried to push him to be intellectual."

"Didn't become a problem for us."

"We were a together couple." She sighed and smiled. "If memory serves, we walked, danced, and worked on each other's concerns for all six days."

"Pressure to resolve things in a handful of days...no time to waste."

She slowly ran her fingers through her hair. "I'm here to find some peace."

"We're becoming friends again. We'll work things out from there."

She grinned. "I had a six-day love affair whose end was heart-wrenching. But even knowing the outcome, I would do it all over again."

"I'm glad. As far as Seth, it might be difficult living in the same house if we discover we don't love each other."

The wind picked up. His wind chimes began playing.

Andrea appeared warmed by their sound. "Your wind chimes are truly melodic. Sonorous, as you said." She twisted and turned to him. "But, seems like, I'd say, playing a sad tune right now."

"Sound full of joy to me..."

"Remember the wind chimes you put up for me in Oz? A constant reminder of us…how well we fit."

"Their sound must not have helped your relationship with Rodney."

Andrea folded her arms across her chest. "Their sweet melodies chastised me for settling for him…instead of finding you."

"Not good."

"I brought them from Oz."

"I'll mount them outside the guest room window," Brian said.

"I'd prefer if they were adjacent to your wind chimes, please. I want the sonorous tones your chimes create to combine with mine."

***

Six-thirty in the AM, a toddler's singing woke Brian as the little one greeted a new day. Seth walked up the hall to the master bedroom, stuck his head into the room and said, "Hi?"

"Morning Seth," Brian replied and jumped out of bed. The little one ran into the room, arms wide. The thirty-three-month-old smiled as he was lifted then tossed into the air. His Dad threw on a pair of cut-off shorts, and they proceeded to the kitchen where Brian placed him in a high-chair then peeled and mashed a banana which Seth ate with relish.

"Morning," Andrea said. "I'll put the kettle on."

"Fine," Brian said. "I made oatmeal before I turned in last night. You sleep okay?"

She nodded and filled the kettle, put it on a flame then watched him help Seth. Andrea seemed pleased as she observed their interaction. She gave the little one a small dish of oatmeal.

"Sunny with pleasant temps today," he said. "After breakfast, we should head out for a walk. Do some grocery shopping."

"And talk."

In town, they let Seth choose two, lifted, toy pickup trucks and a dinosaur, each item around five inches in length.

He held the dinosaur toward his father.

Brian enunciated slowly, "Triceratops."

Seth looked at the figure, then at his father, smiled and said, "Yes."

Andrea chose two educational toys and a game. On the street again, Brian greeted numerous friends. Most called him

Doc, a few Brian, but all of whom appeared shocked when he introduced his son.

After walking two blocks in silence, Andrea appeared anxious, not sure what to do with her hands.

Seth slept in the backpack-style carrier, his head resting on Brian's shoulder.

She noticed Seth sweating so loosened the blankets around the little one, her hands trembling. "You have friends…a life here. I've forced my way into your world. Just trying to be in a position to find some peace and I'm loaded with anxiety."

"Want to tell me why?"

Andria shook her head. She stared in the store fronts while they walked.

"Life forced you and I apart…now back together," Brian said.

"At a minimum to provide Seth with a father. Remember Mary Thompkins?"

"Your friend since childhood. I remember dancing with her. She was with that guy from the Cav…Michael, I think."

"They kept in touch after R&R. Live in Boston. He paid her way over. Married and happy as clams. Have twin girls and another on the way. He used his psych degree to obtain employment at a rehab center which counsels Vets."

"We should visit," Brian said. "I'll make reservations."

She gave him a brief smile. "Pain from the war bother you?"

"I replay certain events in my mind. Things I did, things I should have done. Keeps me awake some nights. The memories hurt, sometimes cause headaches, but not to a point they overwhelm me…not yet anyway."

Following lunch, they walked through a shopping mall, looking for wall decorations for Seth's room.

"Did you," Andrea asked, "think about me after R&R, when you went back to the war?"

"Had to concentrate on surviving. Little time to consider lost love. Although, I experienced an emotional letdown. I cried during an in-country R&R. Occurred three months after our six days. Sitting by myself on the sand, watching and listening to the surf rolling in from the South China Sea…thinking of you and me in Oz. As you said, it seemed like a dream. I sobbed like a baby. A couple of the guys asked if I was okay. I told them to leave me the hell alone."

"Why there and then?"

"Staring at the surf, realizing it was the same water which touched the beach at Bondi…I was overwhelmed with loneliness, plus anger and frustration at the damn war…probably sat there blubbering like a kid for a crazy amount of time."

She shook her head. "After we said goodbye…I was depressed for…don't remember how long. I was so angry at you."

"Angry?"

They stopped walking and faced each other. She continued, "For six day, even when we argued, it was like we were wrapped inside each other. The rest of the world be damned. I felt we could overcome anything as a couple. That was immature thinking on my part. Our six days together, so precious, and then you were gone. Angry? I was livid. Felt like you shoved a dagger in my heart."

"But then Rodney…"

"As time passed and I returned to my everyday existence, memory of our time fading, the relationship seemed apparitional. Gone like smoke up a chimney. I began convincing myself I'd be happy settling into a life like my mum and dad. Ended up, I was cruel to Rodney. Tried to push him into the person I imagined you were."

"Not fair."

"Not in the least. So, we fought...royal battles." She stopped and stared in the window of a kitchen supply store. "We had this huge argument. Screaming and calling each other terrible names...it was so mean of me...I ultimately screamed that Brian would understand."

"He knew about me?"

She nodded. "Rodney packed his things...left that night."

They began walking again. "I was alone again so focused all my energy on Seth for a number of months...signed divorce papers...argued with my father who insisted I contact you, tell you about our son. I ignored my feelings toward you, but, life forced me to agree. Seth needed his father."

They returned to the house, stored the items purchased, Brian put Seth down for a nap.

"Start a fire, please?" she asked.

He complied then sat on the couch opposite the fireplace, she on a chair to the side.

Staring at the dancing flames, her head resting on an arm of the chair, she asked, "Any chance we can discuss visiting Oz?"

"We can discuss anything."

"Would you consider it?"

"For a visit? Yes."

"Would love to have Seth at least see the sheep station."

"I'd be willing to take him."

She smiled. "Important item for me, kind of you to say."

Andrea stared at the fire. Brian read a novel. Only the cracks and pops from the fireplace provided sound for the next couple of hours

"You don't need me in your life," she said with a sigh and a smile.

"My decision, no? We still have issues to work out," Brian said.

"I know, but, your willingness to try, lets me know you'll do the right thing for Seth."

***

After Seth's nap, Brian and his son took the Olds 442 into town to visit a hardware store. Brian was examining a bright red, monster of a pipe wrench with a thirty-six-inch handle, Brian told his son, "Seth, this is a toy store for big boys." Along with the monster, he bought a six-incher for his son.

Back at the ranch, Andrea was in the house reading, Seth played with his new wrench inside the detatched garage. Brian began cutting and threading lengths of four-inch iron pipe. The little one stared at then pointed at the Motorhome. "Inside that one?"

"Sure buddy," his father replied then opened the door. The little one scrambled up the stairs, sat in the driver's seat then headed to the rear to explore.

He returned to his father's side as Brian completed threading a section of pipe, doping it and adding an elbow.

"We ride that one." Seth said, pointing at the motorhome.

"After I'm finished threading the pipe," his father replied.

The little one's face dropped. "Ride now, please."

Seth's expression defeated his father's resistance. "Let me wash my hands and we'll go."

The instant the big diesel engine roared to life, Seth's eyes went wide as a huge grin appeared. Both remained until the thirty-minute ride ended.

Brian returned to pipe work. Seth stayed at the wheel of the parked motorhome, happily making engine noises and regularly checking the mirrors as his father had.

Andrea called them for lunch.

Two days later and early on a cool but sunny day, Brian fired up the water heater for the pool. After lunch, he gave swimming lessons to Seth. His mother watched from the family room, a satisfied smile on her lips.

When a North Texas thunderstorm rattled the house, the frightened little one ran to his father.

Andrea grinned and said, "He feels secure with you. You'll be a rock for him."

Chapter 13

Gusty winds played an indeterminate melody on the wind chimes. Bundled in warm clothing on a cold, late December afternoon, Brian and Andrea shared the settee on the front porch. Seth napped in his father's lap.

"Then not your fault," Brian said.

"The woman driving the other vehicle was obviously drunk," Andrea said. "She reeked of beer…could barely stand. The police blamed her."

"Again, not…"

"If I was patient, not showing off, there was no damn reason to hurry. I could have made sure she was stopping. I mean, I knew she was coming."

"There is always something else which might have happened. It wasn't your fault if the other driver was drunk."

"I was conscious long enough to see my sister and her son were thrown out. I crawled out of the wreckage, hurt in lots of places. We didn't believe in seat belts." She shook her head and sighed. "We had this dumb idea, if we were in a burning car and the seat belt didn't release we'd burn alive…not realizing what crap that was. During the crash, I banged around the interior in a way that my feet and legs were injured, my face smashed against the dash more than once."

"Your sister-in-law and nephew?"

Her eyes tearing, she stared at the floor. "His skull fractured, that precious boy died in my arms soon after the accident…poor Jane run over by the other vehicle. It was crazy that the drivers survived."

"Your injuries?"

"All healed but left with a twisted face, pain in joints on occasion, a number of surgeries to achieve my current state. But still suffer devastating guilt and a brother who no longer talks to me."

"And you need…?"

"To work out the cruel, overwhelming, at times debilitating, guilt-caused, depression."

She folded her arms across her chest. "The sleepless nights, my mind in a fog, the difficulty dragging myself out of bed. Ultimately you then Seth's arrival forced me to accept what happened, and helped me heal to a degree."

"Ever talk to a professional?"

"I tried. They start with pills. I need a clear head. Not some damn drug induced fog. Dad encouraged me to find you. He was right. More importantly as it turns out, Seth needed to know his father."

"Finally." She took two deep breaths and let each out slowly. I've told you the story about the car crash." Andrea left her chair, cuddled against him. "There's a twist. When the other driver was so drunk she could barely stand, the police didn't consider I might be impaired."

Brian saw her eyes were filled with tears.

"Andrea...how drunk?"

"One beer, not drunk, but I'll never know for sure. I believed I could accelerate fast enough to get in front of the other car, when I didn't have a chance in hell." She shrugged. "I hit the throttle instead of waiting. The car accelerated maybe ten feet; I'd underestimated her speed. I heard the other car's tires screeching." She shivered at the memory and the cold. "Inside, please. I don't want Seth to catch a cold again."

Seth taking a nap, they sat on a small couch in his office. They clung to each other like lone survivors on a life raft. He kept kissing the top of her head as she cried.

"I made the reservations for the trip to Boston. We leave in four days."

"Thank you," Andrea said and kissed his lips. "Love to sleep with you tonight."

Slowly, as if she had the weight of the world on her shoulders, Andrea stood, put a hand on Brian's shoulder then said, "Going to walk around your property."

"I'll come with."

He moved to stand but she pushed down on his shoulder.

"Something else to tell you. Not sure how. Need time to think…"

"Andrea, tell me…"

"Time alone, please." She lifted his chin, kissed him then looked outside at a light mist on that cool, late December day. She changed into a rain resistant, insulated, and hooded jacket of his.

"Does the accident still depress you?"

"Among other things…yes."

Brian worked on his research for an hour then looked out a window.

The jacket's hood pulled over her head, her face not visible, shoulders drooped, hands in jacket pockets, Andrea plodded along as if her legs were leaden. A hand with a tissue occasionally moving toward her face, wiping away tears, he imagined.

***

"Hey," three-year-old Vera said to Andrea. "You talk Australian like my mom."

"Yea, she does," her twin sister Karen said.

They gathered around the dining room table at Mary and Michael's Boston home while Seth ran off to the play room with the twin girls.

"Back in Oz," Andrea asked, "you mentioned a brother."

"My folks," Michael said while shaking his head, "knew my brother drank himself to death. They learned a few days before I left for Nam. They worried about how I'd react so they didn't tell me. I found out when I came home. I was a basket case for a number of days but imagine how relived my folks were when I came home, well, came home in good shape."

"No problems?" Brian asked.

Michael thought for a while, then said, "You remember, I was a combat medic?"

Brian nodded.

"I had this nightmare, just after I came home and then a few months later. First dream, I was at the scene of a plane wreck. Lots of injured but I didn't know enough to help them. Second dream nearly identical but two buses collided resulting in many casualties. Same feeling of not knowing."

"Ever experience that feeling in Vietnam?"

"Heck yes. The whole damn year."

The two men walked to the family room bar to prepare drinks.

The men returned and each handed a drink to their partner. Mary turned to Andrea. "I owe you a lifetime of happiness," she said. "If you hadn't come with me to the dance club, I wouldn't have met Michael. We're madly in love, and work together like a bow and fiddle."

Andrea smiled. "I'm so happy for you. And, please remember, you've been a good and faithful friend since childhood."

"Do you see a future with Brian?"

Although listening to Michael, Brian was surprised to hear Andrea reply, "Not now. I'll tell you later."

When they said goodbye to their Boston friends, Mary seemed distraught at a level which surprised Brian.

***

Upon returning to Celina, and standing in his office, Brian noted Andrea seemed sullen, almost morose. "Andrea, we seem to be spending less time talking. It should be the opposite." They wrapped their arms around each other but then she pushed him away. She went to the guest room then returned carrying three expanding folders, laden with papers.

With tears welling up, she stood in front of him while he sat at his desk. She told him, "Brian, you suffered, and indeed still suffer, from your time as a soldier. You don't know how difficult it is to bring more pain into your life. I haven't been entirely honest about why I'm here. Some months ago, I was diagnosed with an inoperable brain tumor. I haven't got long to live. Like I feared in Oz..." Andrea stared at the floor then sighed, looked at him then continued, "My body could detect the end of the road approaching but my mind could only sense...not fully comprehend...but I knew our time would be limited."

His jaw dropped. "Andrea…"

Brian took a moment to compose himself, cleared his throat and said, "We have amazing specialists in Dallas and Houston."

"These are my records and scans. As it happens, I'm losing my fine motor skills and feel numbness at times, sharp pain at others." She handed him the folders, then plopped down on a couch.

He looked through them. "I'll make some calls. If nothing else, could be we can slow things down."

"No."

"Won't hurt to see if some medication or procedure..."

She folded her arms across her chest. "I'll go into hospice care. The thought of you having to feed me like a baby, change my diapers. Unacceptable."

"Andrea…"

The Aussie lady shook her head, said with determination, "Don't want you, or Seth, to remember me like that."

"As you wish." After spending the next hour reviewing her records, and finding it difficult to remain composed, he said, "I'd like you to see a friend of mine. I want him to review all this."

She nodded. "At the back of the third folder is a manila envelope. "It contains my will and Seth's birth certificate. You're listed as his father."

He moved to the couch and tried to hold her. Andrea pushed him away at first then threw her arms around him and sobbed.

An hour later, Andrea yawned and said, "I've love sleeping with you bit I'd like to sleep in Seth's room tonight."

"No problem," he said.

***

Up at five to prepare for work, Brian was dressing when he began reviewing what Andrea said during the last few weeks.

"I'm here to find some peace."

He buttoned his shirt, lifted the collar preparatory to putting on a tie.

"At a minimum to provide Seth with a father..."

He knotted the tie, centered it.

"Seth feels secure with you. You'll be a rock for him."

While placing a tie clip, he remembered his attempts to hold her. Even after he held her the night before, she insisted on sleeping near Seth.

He slipped into his shoes, tied them.

"The thought of you having to feed me and change my diapers...unacceptable."

His jaw dropped. Apprehension filled his mind.

Brian ran to Seth's room. She wasn't there. He noticed a hand-written note on Seth's dresser.

Heart pounding, Brian read:

Dearest Brian,

The pain is overwhelming and my motor skills are deserting me. I don't want you and Seth watching me die. Rather do it on my terms.

You and he have been the jewels of my life. I know you'll take care of him. One day, explain what happened to his mother and how much I love him and his blessed father.

If it suits you, please scatter my ashes on your ranch – within earshot of our wind chimes. The Lord bless you both.

All my love,

Andrea

Brian raced out of the house. As he neared the garage, he heard the engine of his antique pickup. He rotated the switch which opened the twelve-foot tall door installed for the motor home. When it had lifted a foot, he dropped to the ground and rolled under it. He tried to block the idea out of his mind but knew. He saw the old two-door pickup, a hose running from the exhaust to the interior, each end duct taped in place.

"No!" he screamed, ripping out the hose and yanking the door open, he pulled her to the garage floor. Andrea's skin cherry red, indicative of carbon monoxide poisoning. No breathing. No pulse. Eyes dilated and unresponsive to light. He crushed her lifeless boy against him. Sobbed for a while, laid her down then staggered out of the garage.

Seth, in his pajamas, appeared at the open kitchen door, paused briefly, yelled, "Daddy," and then began running to Brian. His father ran toward him and picked him up then held the young one in a way which prevented Seth from viewing the garage. He carried the little one into the house and placed him at the kitchen table, pouring cereal and milk for him.

"Stay here," Brian said.

"You crying," Seth said, then pointed at his father's tears.

He nodded, gave the little one a smile, squeezed his shoulder then, his body trembling, he walked to the phone in his office. Brian explained who he was, then asked that an ambulance be sent to his home to pick up a deceased woman located in the large garage beyond the house and would they please not use a siren.

Naturally, as night follows day, the wailing of the ambulance's siren along with that of the accompanying police car, signaled their impending arrival from miles away.

He waited inside, tried to hide what was happening from Seth until the ambulance raced out of the driveway. A policeman knocked at his front door.

Brian answered then asked if they could talk on his porch to avoid alarming Seth. The officer agreed then took notes as Brian explained Andrea's physical condition and anguished mental state.

"Just yesterday she gave me her medical records to review. Her motor skills were deserting her and she was in tremendous pain. She left a note." His legs getting weak, the policeman threw an arm around him and helped Brian to one of the rockers.

"Dr. Levin, did you think she was suicidal?"

Brian shook his head. Tears were running down his cheeks. "Yesterday, she'd agreed to see a friend. Thought we...had a plan." He put his face in his hands, cried quietly then wiped his eyes, took a deep breath and turned to the policeman. "Apparently she was the one with the plan."

"I'm sorry Doc. If I have more questions they can wait. Uh, you might want to check on the little guy, he's watching us."

Brian sat up straight, thanked the officer, and wiped his eyes. He walked to the front door, the wind chimes silent.

"Mommy?" Seth asked.

"Gone."

"Mommy come home?"

Brian shook his head. "No."

"You bring Mommy home. This house."

Brian scooped him up as the little one sobbed.

∗∗∗

Cried out, Seth slept.

Brian called Andrea's father. Andrea's brother answered in an anger filled voice. "So she offed herself. The bitch knew father died. Heart attack killed him a few days before she left. She talked some shit about finding peace."

"She suffered from a brain tumor."

"Don't send her back. Don't want any evidence she ever existed."

"I won't but, I'm taking care of Seth. One day he should meet the rest of his family."

"He's yours. You keep the little bastard. Don't you dare bring him back here. It would remind me how much I hate his mother for killing my wife and son. No telling what I'd do to him."

"The sheep station..."

"Have no use for it. Selling it. Never liked sheep. Dad left money in his will for me, Seth and Andrea. Won't be much but a solicitor will send it. I'll give him your number."

"I'll put the money away for the little one's education."

"One more thing."

"Sure."

"Never want to hear from you again, or that damn kid."

***

Mary, Michael and their daughters attended Andrea's funeral on a cool day in late December.

She stayed after her family headed home, sorting through her best friend's possessions, and setting aside most to give to charity. Brian assisted. Mary found a box of photos labeled for Seth and Brian; it contained photos of Seth, Andrea, Charles, the sheep station plus she and Brian during his R&R.

Seth was horrified when he realized evidence of Andrea was disappearing into boxes. Brian consoled the little one then helped him choose photos which he made into a collage of Andrea, Charles, himself, and Seth. He mounted it on the wall in the toddler's room. Seth was all smiles when he viewed it, the little one became subdued then sniffed twice and began to cry. Brian held his son then put him down for a nap.

Mary said, "Andrea was my best friend over the years. I'd like to stay in touch with you, get together sometimes, watch Andrea's son grow."

"Of course. I'd love that. You'll tell him of your childhood adventures with his mother. I'm certain Seth will appreciate your visits, as will I."

Brian and Seth struggled to adjust to life without Andrea. On the first sunny day following the funeral, the teary-eyed surgeon scattered Andrea's ashes on the broad lawn in front of the porch which supported the two sets of wind chimes. A gentle breeze spread the ashes and made the wind chimes sound as if they were in mourning.

Seth would appear fine then start crying and ask for his mother. This occurred while at home and at daycare. If Brian was nearby, he was the only one who could console him. Each day he seemed terrified when Brian left him at the door to his daycare classroom. Seth's teacher, Chana Goldberg, an attractive woman in her late-twenties, tried to placate the toddler with little success. His only smile occurred when his dad picked him up at the end of the day.

At daycare, a father, in discussion with his wife, made a disparaging remark about those, "dumb enough to become soldiers." Seth's father erupted in a verbal explosion of condemnation, thoroughly laced with profanity, which was heard in every corner of the building. Chana, seemed to want to befriend Brian She stood near him during the initial part of his tirade. She cringed at the volume and intensity of his anger, not to mention, the crudeness of his language. The teacher crossed to the farthest corner of the classroom. It took four weeks before she again attempted to befriend Brian. She invited Seth and him for a Sunday afternoon walk followed by dinner at her home.

He replied, "Thanks, Chana, but Seth takes all my time when I'm not working, plus my head isn't in a good place. Little things upset me and, unless it's Seth, I take it out on whoever's closest. Really not in an emotional state to have someone else in my life." Brian sighed. "I no longer have time for my research."

"I understand," Chana said.

"Actually, I know you have your own life but, I could use help with him when I'm called out on medical emergencies..."

She smiled. "I'm just a phone call and a short drive away."

PART FIVE: RACHEL

Chapter 14

*"The soldier above all other people, prays for peace, for they must suffer
and bear the deepest wounds and scars of war."*
Douglas MacArthur

A year passed with little change in Brian and Seth's routine
when Arnie Zalman called to invite Brian to join him and his
wife Shira, at a Thanksgiving celebration. They were meeting
in Dallas, at the home of Arnie's widowed cousin. The Levins
arrived at the seventh-floor condo in time for lunch on
Wednesday.

"Here he is," Arnie said with a broad grin while slapping
his Army buddy on the back and introducing Shira. "How's
the drive?"

"Less traffic then I expected so we're early. But Seth and I can walk around the block for a few minutes, if you'd prefer."

Through his laughter, Arnie said, "You're right on time for lunch."

Arnie's cousin entered the room carrying two tall glasses of iced tea. With a slim build and a height of four-foot-nine inches, the twenty-four-year-old was the definition of petite. Her medium length, raven black hair unkempt, she wore an oversized black sweatshirt, torn jeans and thick lensed, horn-rimmed glasses.

"Rachel, our guests have arrived. I want you to meet my Vietnam buddy, Brian Levin, and his son Seth. Brian, this is Rachel Moskowitz."

One glance at Brian, who was putting Seth on a booster-seat, and Rachel's eye's went wide, she gasped and brought a hand up to cover her mouth; in the process dropping one of the teas. Her cheeks blushing, she began apologizing as she ran out of the room.

"Sorry," Arnie said to his Army buddy, "she doesn't usually act like that when she meets my friends."

To the laughter of Arnie and his wife, Brian said, "Some soldiers have that effect on women." He then asked Arnie, "How are the injuries?"

"All healed but, as you predicted, have limited use of my right arm and leg."

"That's rough."

He shrugged. "I'm alive. More than many can say."

Rachel returned with a towel, broom and dust pan. Her hair brushed and no longer wearing her glasses.

"Let me help you with that," Brian said then began picking up the broken glass.

"Thank you," Rachel said, not looking at him, her voice sounding shaky.

"Have we met?" Brian asked, "Your voice..."

"I was raised and lived most of my life in Brooklyn. Moved here a couple years ago to run a pre-school program." She finally raised her face and looked at him.

The Texan found himself gazing into deep brown eyes which were so familiar it startled him. "Are you sure?"

"I've only lived here two years, and don't think we've met," Rachel said. She hurried away.

"Rachel's lived here," Arnie said, "since her husband was shot during a home invasion while we were in Vietnam. About the time you were on R&R. A long story but, you should know; she also experienced a miscarriage the same night."

"How far along?"

"Four weeks."

"That must have been difficult."

"She used to have this effervescent personality which could illuminate the sky at midnight. We don't see it anymore."

A short time later, Rachel reappeared wearing black slacks, the horn-rimmed glasses replaced by contacts, and wearing a tight fitting, bright shirt covered with splashes of pastel color; the combination emphasizing her substantial bust.

Both Arnie and his wife did double-takes at their now, neatly dressed, make-up, and lipstick-wearing cousin.

During lunch, Rachel sat next to Seth, Brian on the other side of him. Without being asked, she served the little one, cut his food into small pieces, and much to his father's amazement, made him laugh and giggle, plus wiped his hands and chin when necessary.

Rachel cleared her throat and asked, "So, Arnie said you were a soldier in Vietnam. Both infantry and as a surgeon."

Brian replied, "Primarily infantry, few months as a surgeon."

"My Great-aunt, was a surgeon in the Civil War. I have some of her letters and papers."

The doctor was surprised and stared at her for a moment, jaw dropped. "Please. We need to talk about her sometime."

Rachel smiled and nodded.

"How's the research for your book?" Arnie asked then turned to the others. "Brian was gathering information to write a book about combat and infantry, while we were in Vietnam."

"Little work since Andrea died," Brian said. "Work and Seth take up most of my time, although I've decided, the home front Vietnam vets returned to, needs to be researched and analyzed as we're coming home to an environment different from any other war. As a result, my book has changed into a research project on the psychological impact of war on combatants both during the war and afterward."

"My Great-Aunt was supposedly doing work in the area of war's impact on soldier's mental balance," Rachel said. "I have stacks of old papers of hers. Perhaps they might be relevant to your research"

"Beyond anything you can imagine, I'd love to review them."

Rachel smiled and nodded. "Of course."

A hand pounded the table. "I am sick and tired of war stories," Shira said. "Can't you people talk about anything else?"

"Sorry, Shira," Arnie said in a quiet voice then turned to his fellow Vet. "Sad to hear about Andrea."

"Nearly lost it, but time spent with this guy kept me from going over the edge."

"Does he attend day care?" Rachel asked, while slicing carrots for Seth.

"Yes, but since Andrea's death, the four, ten-hour days I work are difficult for the little guy. The other three days we do everything together. And I mean everything. He becomes anxious if I'm more than a few feet away. The days I'm home, he naps on the couch in my den while I fill out reports and such for work. I believe he does that so he sees me when he wakes up. I do a little research some evenings after he sleeps, but I'm mostly busy doing his clothes, cleaning, and meal prep."

"Poor fellow, he must miss his Mom." Rachel patted Seth then turned to Brian. "You're a good dad."

"Doubt it," Brian mumbled, but again, he found it difficult to look away from her deep brown eyes.

After the meal, they moved to her living room. Rachel suggested, "How about I play with Seth?"

Brian said, "You can try but he doesn't do well with strangers."

With a warm smile, she said, "Let me try."

Seth was riveted to his father's side as they sat on a couch.

Rachel left the room briefly then returned with a carton. "Through the years, if I saw toys that I believed my children would enjoy, I bought and stored them. I have none so it warms me to watch other's children enjoy these."

Out of the box, tumbled toy animals, cars, trucks, buildings and blocks of various colors, sizes, and shapes. Brian noted the carton was labeled, "Boys: pre-school."

Rachel sat crossed-legged on the floor, invited Seth to join her.

He looked up at his Dad who said, "Go."

The little one slid off his father's lap then kneeled at Rachel's side. He peered at the pile then began pulling little trucks out. Seth turned to his father and held up a small black pickup.

"Yes. Like our truck in Dallas," Brian said.

"He has great manual dexterity," Rachel said. She left the room briefly then returned with a package of interlocking logs.

"A new toy?" Brian said. "He has plenty with what you've brought out."

Sitting on the floor again, she tore open the wrapping. Rachel gave Brian a disarmingly warm smile. "If he'll enjoy them, why not?"

Seth became fascinated as Rachel stacked a few logs.

"Would you like to help me, Seth?" she asked.

Even when the toddler couldn't get the placement perfect and became frustrated, her patient demeanor and soft-spoken voice encouraged him to keep trying until four walls were complete and a plastic roof installed. Rachel congratulated him, Seth all smiles.

Rachel opened a board game called Chutes and Ladders. Within minutes, she had the three-year-old counting, and most pleased with, each of his moves around the board.

"It's his nap time," Brian said.

"You visit with Arnie. I'll get him ready for bed."

Surprised, he replied, "His things are in the little airline bag with the blue plastic on the handle."

Rachel chattered like a bird in spring time while taking care of Seth, which the little one adored.

Just when Brian was thinking it was taking too long, she returned, her expression one of satisfaction.

"Seth?"

"Asleep."

"You didn't have to..."

"Taught him a song then read a story and he was out like a light," she said with a pleased smile.

"Thank you for..."

Shaking her head and joining him on the couch, she interrupted, putting a hand on his shoulder and giving it a squeeze. "No. Thank you for letting me."

"No problem," he said, getting lost in those eyes again.

Shira handed mugs of tea to each.

"Rachel," Brian said, then paused to sip his tea, "you mentioned your great-aunt's research."

"It's scattered among my and my parent's belongings, much of it in storage. We can, if you like, retrieve them and at least organize her work."

Following the meal, Brian sat on the couch in Rachel's study adjacent to the kitchen. He noticed a historical novel concerning a female doctor and medicine during the Civil

War. He leafed through it. Shira and Rachel worked in the kitchen preparing dinner. Brian overheard Shira saying to Rachel, "You were raised Orthodox…there are a world of Orthodox men around you…you're flirting with him? He's not observant like your husband or Samuel."

"You don't know him."

"You do?"

"He makes me feel like…a pretty lady."

"A what? Pretty lady? He said he's never been to New York."

"Brian was kind to me and kept me going through lots of difficult times."

"She remembers!" Brian thought.

Shira's voice incredulous, she said, "What are you talking about? You said you hadn't met. Rachel, are you losing your mind?"

"He's a good man," Rachel said. She paused for a bit then added, "I owe him, big time. As far as Orthodox, I married an Orthodox man, kept a kosher kitchen and all the rest, but that was just too please Dov. I didn't do it for me." She ran a hand through her hair and sighed. "Not everyone who does those things for their husband feels as I did but, for many reasons, I felt contained and diminished."

***

Six-o'clock Thursday morning, Brian and Seth arrived at Rachel's home so the surgeon and Arnie could attend morning service. Seth was still wearing pajamas and asleep in his father's arms. Rachel put the little one on a couch, covered him with a brightly colored blanket. She turned to Brian while the former soldier was waiting for Arnie.

"Your prayer shawl?" she asked.

"I was so busy with Seth and thinking about packing his clothes. I forgot it at home."

She left the room briefly.

Upon return, Rachel said, "Take this." She handed Brian a pouch containing a prayer shawl. "It belonged to my father."

He held up a hand, palm out. "I couldn't," Brian said.

"Please. It would be an honor."

He accepted then opened the pouch and placed the prayer shawl over his shoulders. "Look okay?" Brian asked.

Wearing a broad smile, she stood on her toes and kissed his cheek.

"Thank you," Brian said, as he repacked the shawl. Arnie appeared and they headed out the door.

He and Arnie drove a few blocks then returned a couple hours later. They found Rachel dressing Seth and telling him about a Thanksgiving project they would create.

"Project for Thanksgiving..." he said, pulling up his pants then slipping his arms into the shirt she held for him. He turned to his father wearing a broad smile. "Seth and Rachel do Thanksgiving project."

"Excellent!" Brian said then thought, *"My son is in good hands. Seth reacts to Rachel like he did to his mother. Watching them interact, dare I say, warms me."*

Brian kept smiling during his and Arnie's workout at the gym each time he remembered Seth's expression while the little one dressed. Following the workout and back a Rachel's condo, they all gathered for lunch. Brian told them the story of the lady from Oz, her coming to Texas so he would take care of Seth, and ending her life.

"So sad," Rachel said, shaking her head. "But, bless the Lord, Andrea had you for a support system at the end. Certainly, that was comforting for her."

Brian stared at Rachel and thought, *This little lady is sharp as hell.*

"Sad she passed but a blessing you were there for her," Arnie said. "That was good of you."

"Thanks," Brian said.

Arnie thought for a while and said, "I'm not sure Brian was a support system."

"Arnie," Rachel asked, "How would you describe it?"

"It was just Brian. How can one person be a support system?"

"Not sure." Rachel turned to Brian then asked, "Did you have problems when you came home? Did you have anything which felt like a support system?"

Shira slammed the table. "More war stories. Do you ever move on?" Without waiting for a response, she left the room shaking her head.

Arnie shrugged. "She refuses to acknowledge the suffering."

"I experienced a couple nightmares," Brian said. "It was…nothing major. Once back home in Texas, I went for bike rides and fishing with my dad plus many hours with him while painting his home. We spent endless hours discussing military life and combat. He was a crew chief on a B-26 based in North Africa. My mom contributed her memories of World

War II on the home front. So yes. I had a support system when I arrived home."

"Anything else?" Rachel asked.

"I spent a lot of, one-on-one time talking to my Uncle Mike. He was a 101st Airborne and Battle of the Bulge veteran. We exchanged stories only few people outside of combat veterans would understand. Lots of identical horrors and suffering." Brian thought of some of the stories and shivered.

"Those discussions give credence to Rachel's idea of a support system," Arnie said.

"When you came home?" Brian asked Arnie.

"As for me," Arnie said, "I'm thankful I'm alive…and mostly intact. While in rehab, I had lots of Vets around me. What else would we talk about? Our war experiences. We also encouraged each other. Pushed each other to set goals. If someone was sad or down, someone put an arm around him or," Arnie laughed, "if he wasn't too bad, we'd joke with him until he smiled. We didn't think of them as a support system, just buddies with a common experience, and the common goal of adjusting to our disabilities." He stared out a window. "We did have group talks with counselors but for most of us, we grunts talked to each other about our concerns on how we'd reenter society. When Shira visited me at the rehab center, she refused to talk about what happened. In truth, never asked. She didn't want to know." Arnie's eyes now teary, he continued, "The feeling I got from her…like, this might sound crazy but…her behavior made me think she was jealous that I suffered and garnered attention for that." He shook his head. "Every day, I wake to a wounded body which reminds me of my military service. I'm thankful to those I served with, especially the ones who performed the medical treatment in the field and medivac station." He nodded at Brian.

"It was an honor," Brian said.

"And, I remember those we lost." He looked down, shook his head. "But my wife acts like the war was something I should somehow magically forget. Without doubt, my Vietnam experience is written in my mind with indelible ink. I believe my involvement in the war defines, to a large degree, who I am." He shrugged. "At least my mental state is balanced. Other guys I've met, not so much. Full of anger or depression, reliving horrors, and having trouble with relationships, not able to get a decent night's sleep." Arnie sighed. "Thank the Lord, none of that for me."

Silence enveloped the room and for a number of minutes, each person was lost in their own thoughts.

Brian sighed. "Both my uncle and my dad returned to the States in ships with the men they trained and served with. Took two weeks."

"Two weeks to begin rationalizing what happened," Rachel said.

Silence again filled the room.

Brian asked, "You think soldiers rationalize killing?"

"No way," Arnie said.

"Let me think about it," Rachel said. "Don't know of another mechanism."

Brian couldn't take his eyes off her.

"What?" she asked.

Incredulity in his voice, Brian said, "Your idea of a support system. After World War II, coming home for two weeks talking to the guys in your unit, then parades in your honor, an entire nation overflowing with gratitude for your sacrifice. Those events, perhaps, told the soldiers whatever they had to do or endure to win the war, was acceptable. Like me talking to my dad and uncle, but is rationalizing what happened?"

"More like a purification right..." she mumbled.

Brian's jaw dropped. He stared at the petite lady.

"Out of the question," Arnie said. "Killing someone is a terrible, life altering event. No one rationalizes away life altering events, a support system or otherwise."

"Not sure," Brian said in a quiet voice, stroking his chin, eyes riveted on the petite lady. "Rachel may be on to...amazing insight lady..."

"Doesn't make sense. Not logical," Arnie insisted while shaking his head.

Brian finally turned away from Rachel and addressed Arnie.

"Is your loss of ability to play sports painful?"

He shrugged. "It hurts. A part of my life gone forever, but I don't dwell on it. I teach weight training at the YMCA and I do my own workouts each morning." He laughed. "Lots of guys figure if a cripple like me can work hard, so can they."

"Religiously, he works out each morning," Rachel said.

Arnie held up a hand, "Except on the Sabbath."

The other two laughed.

"I think," Arnie said, "it would have bothered me more but I was so glad to be alive...I thanked the Lord for saving me and asked what I can do for Him."

"I remember our talk in the recovery area after your surgery. Your positive attitude...don't have research to show it, but in my experience, patients seem to heal faster with an upbeat attitude like yours, also those with a purpose or goal to achieve recover quicker. Logo Therapy, I believe it's called. Read a book by Viktor Frankl who developed the concept. He observed people in the concentration camps and determined those with a reason to stay alive, who had goals and future plans to achieve, managed the horrors better than those who didn't. He discussed a man whose goal was to continue some research he was working on. Ironic because all the work he completed before the war was, unknown to him, destroyed."

"My great-aunt," Rachel said, "in one of her papers, she mentioned attitude and its effect on healing."

"Where are those papers?" Brian said. "I'd love to read them."

"In boxes, in a storage unit I rent on the second floor."

"Oh, my Lord," Brian said. "Her work could be invaluable to my project. With your permission, let's spend Friday finding and organizing her research."

"Love to," Rachel said.

"I'll help," Arnie volunteered.

***

Following lunch, they worked in the kitchen while preparing Thanksgiving dinner. Rachel stood at the sink washing celery. Next to her, Brian cubed parsnips. She inadvertently bumped against him. He then purposely bumped her with his hips. She burst out laughing, then returned his action in kind. Brian wanted to ask a question about her great-aunt's papers but with Shira also in the kitchen decided not to.

They gathered at the Thanksgiving dinner table. It was laden with the results of multiple day's preparation and many hours of cooking.

Rachel, sitting at Brian's side, used both hands to straighten out his collar.

"Thank you," he said, amazed at the warmth he experienced from her simple gesture.

The assembled closed their eyes and bowed their heads as Arnie intoned, "We thank you Lord for allowing us to reach this day of Thanksgiving and the bounty before us. Please Lord, in your infinite mercy, see to it those still fighting in Vietnam come home safe and without injury. And those who've come home can heal and find peace within themselves" He looked up at Shira who was glaring at him. "And that this is the last year of the war."

In unison, they said, "Amen."

"Did you celebrate any holidays in Vietnam?" Rachel asked.

"Arnie and I attended Passover in Da Nang," Brian said. "I never liked gefilte fish but it was such a pleasant reminder of home, I ate extra."

"Could we have one meal without war stories?" Shira pleaded.

After a few minute's silence, Rachel said to Brian, "Arnie said you live on a ranch. Please tell me about it?"

***

Friday morning found Brian, Arnie, and Rachel working in Arnie's office with boxes of her Great-aunt's papers covering his desk, and couch, and much of the floor. Seth occupied himself in a corner playing with Rachel's toy collection.

"Should we organize by date or subject?" Rachel asked.

"Not sure. Safest to use date for now." He gazed at Rachel.

"What?" she asked.

He held up a few papers. "I've read these. Her intellect must have been up to the sky. And…the way she lays out her own feelings…such compassion. Your aunt, writes with clarity, I swear she's in the room talking to me…begging for answers to help soldiers…soldiers of any war… What was her full name?"

"Abbey Kaplan," Rachel said. "Doctor Abbey Kaplan."

Brian looked over the treasure trove of papers and letters. "If we get them organized by date today, we'll repack them and I'll study them at a later date."

"Perhaps," Rachel said, "we could also cross-index them by subject matter. I'll get file cards."

"Great thinking," Arnie said.

"Excellent," Brian said, returning Rachel's smile.

Mid-afternoon, still working on Abbey's papers, Arnie reminded them he invited local family members and community friends over for a Saturday evening gathering.

"Arnie," Rachel asked, trepidation in her voice, "did you invite Samuel?"

"He's part of our family."

"Who is?" Brian asked.

"After my husband died, I moved out here taking a new job. Knowing we had family around Dallas made the move easier," Rachel said, folding her arms across her chest. "Samuel's a distant cousin, not a blood relative, a financially successful man and a leader at his synagogue. But an unfeeling oaf in my opinion, most unlike Dov. We dated twice. We weren't even married yet and he tried to run my life. Wanted to make me quit college when I was taking my pre-school education classes so I could marry him, and become his full-time, at-home, wife. I wanted nothing more to do with him"

Shira reentered the room. Arnie patted the cushion next to him. She sat there, but with arms crossed and leaning away from him.

"Did you tell anyone?" Brian asked.

"Arrangements were made without consulting me."

"Your parents?"

Rachel nodded. "Everyone, parents included, believed, such a great match. They hoped to live long enough to attend my wedding but died within a few weeks of each other, a year after Dov's death."

"But you didn't agree with the match," Brian said.

"He's well known and respected." She sighed. "I'm nobody; expected to know my place, do what I'm told. Cousin Arnie was the only one who took my side." She smiled at him. Arnie nodded. "Finally, I told Samuel I wouldn't marry him."

"His reaction?"

"Not pleasant."

The surgeon glanced at Arnie who pantomimed being slapped.

Brian, with more anger in his voice than he intended, said, "Let me tell you. That wouldn't work with me."

Rachel rubbed her hands on the tops of her thighs. "No one else will ask me out."

"He hit you and people think you should still marry him?"

Rachel shrugged. "They believe I provoked him. If not for my cousin's support, I'd be married to the oaf by now."

"Even Arnie's paid a price," his wife Shira said.

"Little things," Arnie shrugged. "Rarely called for an *Aliyah*, never a Torah reading. Since I was a *Bar Mitzvah*, I was called to complete *minyanim*, you know, the ten needed for a prayer service. My shul is just across the street. It doesn't happen now."

"We don't always get what we want in life," Shira said, slowly shaking her head and giving disapproving looks to Rachel and Arnie.

"You and Seth join us at services tonight?" Rachel asked.

Brian nodded. "Love to."

***

Arnie, on Saturday morning, commented to Brian when they were alone in Rachel's study, "Have to say, I'm not sure if it's you or Seth, or maybe both of you but Rachel came out of her shell after you guys arrived. Haven't seen her like this since Dov passed."

Brian thought for a bit then said, "When she's around, maybe this is silly, but she makes me feel like I've reconnected with a long-lost friend." He shook his head. "No. Not reconnected." He gazed out a window for a bit then said, "When Andrea and I were together in Australia, she could take anxiety out of me with a simple touch or simply being near me. Rachel isn't Andrea but she accomplishes the same thing. I usually anxious and worry constantly how Seth is managing but when that little lady is nearby, when she does things and makes Seth laugh, I relax."

On Saturday evening, Rachel's apartment filled with family and friends, including a tall man with a full-face, neatly trimmed, black beard.

"Rachel, a word in private," the tall man said in a demanding tone.

She shook her head. "Samuel, there is nothing to talk about."

He grabbed the slim lady by the upper arm, pulled her into her office, and, despite her verbal protests, closed the door. Shouting could be heard plus the echo of a slap.

Brian charging across the room like an angry bull. He wore an expression which guaranteed someone was about to catch hell.

Dodging between guests while trying to reach him, Arnie yelled, "Easy Brian."

The door to the office exploded open. Rachel, one hand on her reddened cheek, tears running down her face; her tormentor's fingers digging into her shoulders.

"Leave her alone," Brian growled.

Samuel appraised Brian then gave him an expression of disgust as the veteran approached. "Get out little man, this is none of your affair. She's mine..."

"Brian," Rachel pleaded. "Don't..."

The big man released Rachel, then briefly smirking, swung a fist at Brian.

Rachel gasped.

Standing in the doorway, Arnie shook his head. "Oh hell. Shouldn't a done that."

Brian ducked the fist, in so doing, bent his knees then used his legs and upper body to smash a fist, like a pile driver, into the man's belly. While Samuel tried to regain his breath, the veteran jammed the big man against a wall. Brian shoved his hand under the knot of his tie, twisted it, shoved it to the side of his neck then used it to hoist Rachel's assailant such that if he wanted to breathe, he had to stand on his toes.

Again, Rachel pleaded, "Brian. Please. Don't. Not your concern."

Ignoring her, his expression dark, with fury in voice and demeanor, Brian put his face close to Samuel's and growled, "You sorry bastard, you listen to me. You ever touch her again, hell, you ever look at her again; I will find you and rip pieces off your mother fuckin' ass."

Samuel squeaked, "Someone...help."

"Doesn't need any help," Arnie said, shaking his head. "Has things under control." He blocked the doorway, preventing anyone else from entering although many crowded close to see what was happening.

Brian continued to growl. "No matter where or when...you see her, know I'm nearby. You got that asshole?"

"She's mine..."

The former Major bellowed in a voice which shook the walls, "Listen butt head," he twisted Samuel's tie. The big man's face getting red as he started choking. "You avoid her or I'll be on you like stink on shit. Got it?"

Samuel didn't have enough air to voice a response so just nodded.

Rachel put a hand on Brian's shoulder, "Please. Release him."

Brian complied, stepped back, glared at the tall man for a moment then turned to Rachel, his back to her nemesis.

Noting the many people watching, Samuel tried to recover some pride. The big man threw an arm around Brian's neck.

"Oh shit. Bad move," Arnie said.

Rachel's eyes went wide.

Brian bent forward then smashed the back of his head into the big man's face, breaking his nose. Samuel howled in pain, threw his hands up to his face while staggering backward, blood oozing between his fingers.

From a stance ready to inflict more damage and now wild-eyed, Brian shouted, "Try that again you fuckin' hockey puck and you'll leave through that window."

Rachel's eyes still wide, her hand in front of her mouth, she tried to conceal a grin.

Samuel appeared terrified, likely certain he was dealing with a crazy man…and just as likely remembering they were on the seventh floor. Trembling, he raised his blood covered hands in a gesture of surrender. He muttered, "Sorry."

Arnie crossed the room, grabbed Samuel, shoved him toward the door, saying, "Let's get that nose taken care of before he gets angry and loses his temper." He ushered the big man out of the room, closing the door on Rachel and Brian.

She turned to him with hands on hips, still trying but unable to contain her grin. "Hockey puck?" She giggled then tried to regain her composure. "The violence. Terrible. You should have found another way."

In a firm and measured voice, he replied, "Wrong. He hit you. The only currency he understands is violence. That's why I acted that way."

Rachel appeared incredulous. "Acted? Such anger...was an act?"

The Vietnam Vet's fury and anger evaporated, his body relaxed and his expression morphed into a warm smile. "In a violent confrontation, anger clouds one's judgement."

"Your expression, your body language, like you would kill him."

"I wanted him to believe that."

"I'm shocked. Your voice, your fury. An act?"

"Are you okay?"

"I...I am now, perhaps a bit overwhelmed. I have to admit when you...when the door flew open...your expression...I'm not sure what to say, but thank you."

He wiped a tear off her cheek. "Words not needed, pretty lady." He brushed a lock of hair out of Rachel's face.

Her expression radiant, she shrugged, then asked, "Pretty lady?"

Brian opened his arms.

Rachel shook her head. "It's not right. We haven't even been on a date."

Seth's dad stepped toward her then wrapped his arms around Rachel's slim figure.

She let him hold her, closed her eyes then leaned into him. Exhibiting a smile of utter satisfaction, Rachel put her arms around her rescuer, and held him tight.

Brian lifted her chin, kissed her lips one time briefly then a long kiss.

Rachel pushed away. "So, you're leaving in a couple hours."

He nodded. "A day of repairs around the ranch tomorrow. You should come up north to Celina. Seth and I would love to have you visit. I can arrange a hotel room for you."

Her face still radiant, she shrugged and said, "It's not easy to take time off from work and school, but," She tucked a lock of hair behind her ear. "Perhaps I could visit, next month, say, over the holiday break, maybe a long weekend? You could complete more of your research."

Brian nodded, smiled and said, "I'd love that. And so would Seth."

Chapter 15

1974 December

The following week, Brian received a call from former platoon mate, Scott Hendricks. Brian invited him out to the ranch for the weekend.

He arrived on a cool Saturday morning in early December. From the front porch, Brian and Seth saw him coming up the driveway driving a red with white cove, 1961 Corvette, its top down. The car's owner bringing a wide grin, a firm handshake, and a slap on the back for Brian. Shy Seth shook hands but stayed close to his father.

His hair still military short, the visitor talked to Seth but Brian noted his buddy kept reaching up to wipe his hands on the front of his jacket. Seth on the other hand, couldn't keep his eyes off the shiny Corvette.

"Nice car," Brian said.

They walked over to the roadster.

"My dad bought it new, gave it to me when I came home from the Army. Still runs great but not idling so well, needs a tune up. I call her Aunt Bea."

Brian looked at him with a questioning expression.

"Because she's reliable and like the Aunt Bea on that show, warm and inviting."

Brian chuckled. "Nice, but don't they take a lot of maintenance."

"Found a mechanic who knows the car. Regular maintenance and no problems. I love the darn thing. Even if it's freezing out, I put half the tonneau on and dial up the heat. Otherwise, top up, heat on, and snug as a bug in a rug."

Seth laughed and repeated, "Snug as a bug in a rug."

Scott rubbed his hands together, pulled the front of his jacket down.

"You on edge? Feel like a beer or something else to drink?" Brian asked.

"No. I'm good. A little wound up. Happens sometimes."

"How about a trip to the auto parts store, buy a tune-up kit and we'll install it."

Scott's eyes lit up. "Love the sound of that but you'll have to teach me."

"No sweat. Let's take my pickup."

Seth hesitated. The grownups eyed the little one.

"Coming?" Brian asked.

Seth pointed to the Vette. "I go that one."

The men laughed, promised him a ride after they finished shopping.

Upon return, Scott, with Seth all grins and belted in the passenger seat, drove the two-seater the quarter mile length of the driveway. Brian's former platoon mate kept the little V8 revved up and noisy by using only first and second gear. He made a U-turn at the end of the drive then followed it around the house. Brian waved him into the big garage then directed him to park on a lift adjacent to the work bench. The little one, enchanted with the sound of the car, kept trying to verbally duplicate it.

While installing a new set of points and distributor cap, Brian asked, "Tell me about the tension."

"Sometimes not so bad but other times, it's tough to concentrate on my work."

"Your work?"

"Professor at UT Dallas. Research and Teaching. Earned a Ph.D. in physics not long after my Army service."

"Nice. You have the summer off?"

"Sure do."

"You remember Doc Evans?"

Scott nodded. "Sure. Great guy. Would have clawed his way through the gates of hell to get to a wounded man."

"He's at UT Galveston med school."

"How's he doing?"

"Great but his wife abandoned him after he arrived home. She left him with two children."

"Bet that hurt. How does he manage med school?"

"His parents moved in."

"We should get together."

"I'll be visiting Houston the middle of next week if you're free. I'm taking the motorhome."

"Heck yea. I'm off for the summer. I'll go."

Brian removed engine tools from their storage box. Scott opened the packages of new parts and arranged them on the work bench. Brian started gapping the plugs, demonstrating on the first two then watching his platoon mate on the following six.

The surgeon gave his buddy a ratchet and socket then instructed him in its use to pull one of the old plugs.

Brian examined the first spark plug. "Excellent. Electrodes worn but plug is gray and no sign of oil."

Scott pulled the balance of the plugs.

The surgeon examined each one. He said, "Some of the guys in the platoon said you received a Dear John letter a few weeks before your R&R."

"The letter depressed the hell out of me at the time. I got nothing out of my R&R in Hawaii. I stayed in my room and watched TV." Scott shook his head then said, "but I managed to put it behind me when I returned Vietnam so I could concentrate on my job in the platoon. It was rougher when I came home and most of my friends had moved on."

"Define, moved on, please."

"They were married with kids and didn't have time for a single guy in their social circle. Even one with kids. Many were demonstrating against the war and didn't want anything to do with me as I'd been in the service."

Scott pulled the balance of the plugs and Brian examined them.

"Anything," Brian asked, "you believe is triggering your tension."

"An event before you joined the platoon. It didn't seem so bad when it happened, but the memory, it should be lessening with time but...sometimes hits me like it happened yesterday."

"Describe, please."

"Okay to discuss in front of Seth? A bloody story."

Brian glanced at Seth then said, "Nothing I've discussed so far has bothered him, so go ahead."

"Just another day in the jungle. Hot, humid, that damn rotting vegetation smell, we were hacking our way uphill through moderate under growth. Light rain falling, dark sky, visibility poor as what little light came from the sky was filtered by the canopy," he shook his head. "I was wearing my poncho, rain on my helmet sounding like it was striking a tin roof, my boots having a tough time getting purchase in the soft soil. I was number two in the column, about thirty of us in three squads. Had passed my rifle to the guy behind me. I held a machete in both hands to cut the occasional vine or widen the trail the point man was chopping. A guy in black pajamas seemed to jump up out of nowhere." Scott slowly shook his head then stared into the distance. "To this day, not sure where he came from, why I didn't see him sooner. Scared as hell and using both hands, I swung the machete with all my strength. Little thought of where I was aiming. I took his left arm off just below the shoulder." Scott took a long swig of his beer. "The guy stared at the severed arm, then was shot by somebody in the squad. He fell toward me. His bloody wound landing on my chest as he fell. Remember making a joke about that. On the ground, even in death, his eyes stared at me. Full of hate."

"Likely nothing else you could do."

"Never know. Does haunt me. Those eyes." He shuddered then wiped his hands on the front of his jacket.

"Wiping off blood?" Brian asked.

He nodded. "I noticed I do that when I'm tense." Scott put a plug in the engine, finger tight. "Just talking about it raises my blood pressure."

After getting the torque setting from the car's manual, Brian demonstrated how to use a torque wrench to tighten the plug. He noticed his son carefully observing what they were doing.

"Seth help?" the little one asked after all eight plugs and their leads were installed.

"Sure buddy," Scott said. He handed Seth a new air cleaner, removed the old one then hoisted the little one so he could place the filter in its holder.

"Good job," his father said.

"Thank you, Seth," Scott said.

The little one all smiles, he clapped for himself then said, "Yes. Seth help. Fix red car."

Brian re-checked the torque on all the fasteners, insured the ignition leads were tight then had Scott start the car. The engine's idle was velvety. He revved it a few times. The small-block, 283's cylinders fired as precise as a jazz drummer's sixteenth notes.

"Sounds great," Brian said.

"And thank you both," Scott said, shutting off the car and leaping out to shake Brian and Seth's hands.

"Clean up and lunch time," Brian said, holding out a hand to Seth.

They dined on hotdogs, cottage fries, and ice-cold bottles of Seth's favorite, root beer soda.

"A little mechanical work help the tension?" Brian asked as they cleaned dishes.

"Yea. It does. Takes my mind off other stuff."

Brian suggested chopping wood as a tension reliever.

The Corvette owner shook his head. "Describing my athletic ability would require orders of magnitude in the negative direction."

Brian laughed.

"Therefore," Scott continued, "swinging an ax? I'm sure I'd lose toes or worse."

"I'll teach you."

"Wouldn't work," he said with a grin. "In gym class during High School, we had to dribble a basketball half the distance of a basketball court. Every other bounce, the ball hit one of my feet. I'd retrieve the darn thing and kept trying. I'm so uncoordinated, it took me six-months and two clutches to achieve smooth shifting in my Vette."

They both chuckled.

"I have one of the bedrooms converted to a weight room," Brian said. "Or before that we can hike around the property. I have a number of trails cleared. That should kill some tension."

"Trails then weights. Sounds great," Scott said.

"Any romantic involvement?" Brian asked as they walked past the garage and entered a trail that followed the small creek which flowed through the acreage. Seth skipped and walked ahead of them, occasionally stopping to look for small fish in the stream. "Minnows!" the little one yelled while pointing.

The two men praised his find.

"No relationships that lasted." The professor shrugged. "I'm surrounded by bright people at the University, been on numerous dates, but just haven't clicked with any one."

A Great Blue Heron took off from the far bank of the stream.

Seth, eyes wide, pointed and said, "Bigger than me."

The buddies laughed and Brian ruffled his son's hair.

"You'll find someone," Brian said, trying to reassure Scott.

"Or not," Scott said with a wipe of his hand on the front of his jacket. "How about you?"

"Remember Arnie Zalman?"

"Sure. Great guy. Soon as you met him, you were his best friend."

"He invited me to his cousin's home in Dallas over Thanksgiving weekend. Rachel. Pretty lady. Perceptive, huge intellect, and great with Seth. Coming up here for a few days."

"Rachel come this house?" Seth asked.

"Two weeks, buddy," Brian replied.

Rachel arrived in Celina on a Friday at lunchtime, three weeks after Thanksgiving while her school was on break. Brian opened the front door, welcomed her then yelled to Seth. The little one ran into the room, saw their visitor then stopped next to Brian. Seth, wearing a shy smile, grabbed his father's leg.

His Dad gave him a little push and, arms open, he ran to Rachel.

She picked him up, gave him a warm embrace. Seth wrapped his arms around her neck for a few moments while she spun around. He said, "Hi Rachel."

"Hi Seth. Thank you for remembering my name."

Brian asked, "Long ride across town?" He stored her luggage in the front closet.

"Not much traffic."

"Would you like a drink?"

"Tea, please."

They proceeded to the kitchen. Seth pushed out of Rachel's arms, ran to his shelves of toys, removed a toy jeep then returned to Rachel.

"New Jeep," Seth said, holding up the five-inch toy.

"A new Jeep? How precious. Thank you for showing it to me." Seth glowed.

Brian nodded to Seth. "I have his lunch ready."

She put him in his chair, broke a hamburger into small pieces then served him cubed beets and corn plus a small glass of apple juice. "How's your research coming?"

He shook his head. "Still not much time between my surgical duties and being his only parent."

"Perhaps while I'm here..."

"That would be a blessing."

The adults ate spinach salad, tossed with red-wine vinaigrette and sliced almonds, plus chopped hard-boiled egg.

Rachel wiped the little one's chin. "Tonight is Tot-Shabbat at your synagogue. A special night for preschoolers. Going?"

"Hadn't planned on it, but if you'd enjoy that..."

She nodded. "One thing makes me nervous about living in Texas. Tornados."

"Not this time of year but we do get them. When we're done with lunch, I'll introduce our safe room."

His office was a high-ceilinged room with built-in bookshelves lining three walls, his desk centered in the room and piled with papers, books, and notebooks.

Proceeding to the shelves directly behind his desk, Brian removed three books exposing a keypad. Punching in a number, resulted in a deep metallic clunk. He pushed on a section of shelves. They pivoted into a small room with bunk beds attached to one wall and half a picnic table attached to the other. Directly opposite the opening, shelves of survival supplies, and radio gear.

He waved a hand around the room. "My…tornado-proof, safe room and survival shelter."

A rack of firearms on the back of the door caught her attention. "I've never fired a gun."

"If you need to, you grab the shotgun." He put his hand on it. "Just aim in the general direction of a bad guy and the noise alone may frighten him to death."

A chill went down her spine. "Don't want to think about that," she said then mumbled, "Don't think I could kill again."

Ignoring her last remark, he said, "If you're going to visit us any amount of time, with all these weapons in the house, you should learn to shoot."

Her eyes perused the variety of arms on display. "You'll teach me?"

"Beginner stuff only. I'll find a certified instructor. Too easy for me to leave out an important detail."

"I see survival supplies."

"Enough for one week over here," he said as he opened cupboards containing food and water. "Cabinet in back with supplies for an additional four weeks."

"Should I know the code to enter?"

"Within the next ten minutes, I'll change it to the number of your street address, a pound sign, followed by the number of this street address, followed by another pound sign and 1204."

"1204?"

"The date Maimonides, the famous philosopher, died."

His last words caused Rachel to smile. "We're going to have a delightful time. Would you take me grocery shopping?"

"Love to."

***

At synagogue that evening, Brian noted Rachel was shy when introduced to adults but her Pied-Piper ability with small children was most apparent. When the Rabbi asked children to join him at the front of the synagogue during the prayer over wine, Seth, urged by his father, refused as usual until Rachel held out her hand and said, "Let's go." She turned to another reluctant little one and held out her other hand. The shy little girl, looked at her mother who nodded then took Rachel's hand and the trio raced to the front with the other children.

Following dinner in the social hall, a number of preschoolers, many who knew her from the Jewish Community Center, gathered around Rachel then joined she and Seth in Sabbath oriented games and songs; all to the joy of the little ones and their parents.

On the ride home, he mentioned how she attracted the preschoolers.

She laughed. "The head of primary education asked if I was available to teach pre-school."

"You replied?"

"Already employed."

Back at the ranch, Brian smiled as Rachel read a book to Seth then put him in bed. She sat with Brian on the couch in front of the fireplace. Yellow flames from the crackling fire bathed them in a golden light; long shadows on the wall behind them made random leaps, guided by the flickering flames. The logs' cracks and pops echoed around the high-ceilinged room; providing a romantic soundtrack to the evening's mood.

"Wine?" he asked.

She smiled and nodded. "White please."

Brian half-filled two wine goblets, handed one to her then joined her on the couch. Brian noticed she seemed to avoid looking at him. She kept running a hand through her hair. He sipped his wine then studied the flames through his wine goblet. "You took a chance coming out here. We're little more than strangers."

"We'll be fine," she said, still not looking at him.

Staring at the flames, he said, "Rachel, we barely know each other."

"If half of what Arnie told me about you is true, we need each other and belong together."

"Because?"

While staring at the crackling fire, she twisted right and left, rolled her shoulders a few times, took a sip of her wine. Rachel brought the wine goblet to her lips, another small sip then a longer one. She sighed. "You have demons from the war…and I have ghosts from my past which torment me."

He marveled at the fire's dancing flames as they reflected in her deep brown eyes. "Want to discuss the ghosts?"

Rachel shook her head. "Not tonight."

"You seem anxious."

"A bit," blushing Rachel said without looking at him. She rubbed her hand on the top of her thigh. She cleared her throat, put a lock of hair behind her ear. "As I try not to drive on the Sabbath, would you mind if I stayed here tonight?"

"Your things?"

"Still in the front closet," she said, rolling her shoulders again.

"I'll put them in the guest room."

"Not yet. First I'd like to try something." She kept rubbing her hand on the top of her thigh.

"Rachel, you've seemed on edge since we left synagogue."

The slim lady stood, took his wine, placed both goblets on an end table, then sat on his lap, facing him. Rachel wrapped her arms around the veteran, leaned against him then rested her head on his shoulder. She engaged in a deep sigh as he wrapped his arms around her. "Anxiety?" she said then tightened her embrace. "What anxiety?" She kissed his lips.

The phone rang. Brian reached to the end table and picked up the receiver. "This is Dr. Levin." A pause to listen then, "Multiple injuries? State Trooper hurt? Be there in twenty minutes." She slid off his lap. He turned to Rachel after replacing the phone, "I'm sorry to run out on such a lovely evening, pretty lady." He walked to a dining room chair then slipped into his camo wind breaker.

"Please, not to worry." She reached for her wine, took a sip then said in a soft voice, "Little could make me happier than the man who thinks I'm a pretty lady, running off to heal someone."

"If he wakes, Seth might expect me..."

"We'll be fine."

He turned to leave then returned to her, put his hands on either side of her face. "Pretty lady…so special," and kissed her lips.

"Go," she whispered.

Brian ran out the door. The deep rumble of a loud, large displacement engine rumbled to life then tire squeal down the quarter-mile-long driveway, followed by the sound of a siren.

***

When Brian arrived home, Seth and Rachel were eating breakfast.

"How was it?" Rachel asked.

"Exhausting but everyone is at least stable." He sat at the counter next to Seth.

"Good news to start the day. Would you like to eat something?"

"Grabbed a snack around five this morning so all I need is a shower and sleep but would love a decaf coffee first. I'll be going back later today to check on my patients."

"Whatever you need to do. Seth and I have many Sabbath projects to accomplish today."

Seth stared at her. "Projects," the four-year-old said slowly, as if savoring the word then smiled at Rachel. "Do Sabbath projects."

"*Havdalah*, the end of Sabbath ceremony, at seven-thirty tonight if you can make it."

"I'll try..." Brow furrowed and lips tight, he worried she'd be disappointed if he wasn't there.

Likely sensing his emotion, she crossed the kitchen. Bending forward, Rachel placed a hand under his chin, tilted his head back and briefly kissed his lips. "Patient's need you. I understand."

She served him a steaming mug of coffee. He added cream and sipped the contents a few times.

"When you left last night, I heard the roar of a big engine then a siren?"

In as deep a voice as his almost four-year-old throat could manage, Seth rumbled an engine sound then said, "Four-Four-Two."

Brian laughed while giving his son's shoulder a squeeze. "I raced down the drive a police car met my Olds then led me to the Hospital."

"You always get a police escort?"

"If there is a car near the ranch, I do. I put a blue light on my dash and they clear the way. I'm going to grab some sleep then return to the hospital."

Seth met his father at the front door late that afternoon. He held up a four-inch by four-inch box made from Popsicle sticks and balsa wood. The little one sniffed it then handed the box to his father who also sniffed it. "Spice box," Brian said. "For *Havdalah*, then end of Sabbath celebration tonight."

Seth smiled and nodded.

As she approached from the kitchen, Rachel, flour up to her elbows, wiped her hands on her apron.

"The house smells wonderful."

"Italian dinner in two hours."

"Italian?"

Hands on hips, she said, "Why not? I grew up in New York. The menu for tonight is antipasto, eggplant, tomato, and egg tort, plus dill-poached salmon over linguini with Alfredo sauce, cannoli for desert."

"Wow. Do I smell bread?"

"Seth and I made baguettes. The last batch went in the oven a few minutes ago. Your son helped me mix the dough, then mixed the butter, parsley, garlic and chive mixture. He put your initials on the baguette he made for you. I made a dozen so I'll freeze most."

His eyes roamed the family room, his grin increasing. He noted the shelves were organized, books straightened, the rug vacuumed, the table in the dining room set. Not only had she cooked but she cleaned.

"Rachel," he said, taking his jacket off and about to place it on a chair.

She raised her eyebrows, nodded to the entry. Rachel found the cedar-wood coat rack he'd put in his office and didn't use; now moved to the entry.

He began to say something, stopped, then giggled while hanging his coat. "Sabbath today. You didn't have to clean...I'd have been glad to help."

"The Lord will forgive me for a little work and shopping on Sabbath. How are the patients?"

"Stable. Although one, an older man, is having chest pains so I may be called back depending on the results of his tests."

She walked up to him, kissed his lips then said, "I'm going to wash up then I'd appreciate a glass of white wine please."

"Yes, right away," he said. Leaving his emergency medical kit in the front closet, he hurried to comply.

Brian carried two wine goblets into the kitchen, handed one to her then sat on one of the tall chairs at the prep counter.

"I wanted to mention before dinner," Rachel said while slicing cheese for the antipasto. "You may want to give Arnie a call. Shira left him."

"What happened?" He sat on one of the tall chairs at the edge of the prep counter.

"According to Arnie she was sick of arguing with him. She needed her own space."

"Arguing? About what? Doesn't sound like Arnie." He stared out a window briefly then shook his head. "No. I don't think so. Maybe she's got someone else in her life." Brian sighed and shrugged. "Poor Arnie. Wonder how he's managing?"

She spent a minute placing pickled peppers in a small serving dish. "He cried. Arnie was certain she was his life partner. I would describe him as...crushed."

"Something else must be going on," Brian said.

"I'm going to wait a couple of weeks then call Shira. Get her side of things."

"Rachel, I know you're only here for one week, but any chance you could stay longer. We love having you here and I'm getting research done nearly every day."

She was quiet for a while, then tucked a lock of hair behind her ear and said, "You'll have to drive me to my condo tomorrow so I can get a few things."

"Perfect," he said.

Following dinner and after Seth was in bed, Brian completed a few hours' worth of notes on research he was exploring then approached Rachel. She was laying on the floor in front of the fireplace, reading a novel. He said, "Due to the emergency last night we missed an opportunity to perform the Sabbath good-deed."

"Ah yes, the Shabbat *mitzvah*." She became pensive then grinned and replied in a playful voice, "So we should do it twice tonight."

He laughed. Brian took her hands, pulled her to standing, kissed her lips and led her upstairs.

***

Three weeks later, early Sunday morning, Rachel was kneading bread. She asked, "How did last night's visit to the veteran's group go?"

"Disaster," Brian replied. He sat with elbows on the kitchen table, his head in his hands. "Mostly WWII and Korean era vets. Wanted nothing to do with Vietnam vets. I swear they think we're nothing but a bunch of hippies."

"Did you explain how they could help Vietnam vets?"

He shook his head his expression one of anger. "I tried. They didn't fucking listen. I swear they wished I hadn't shown up."

Brian stood and headed for the kitchen door.

"Where you going?"

"For a drive," he said.

"Your anger..."

"I know everyone wants to forget the war but we have to remember for the sake of the vets who are still suffering." His anger so intense, his body was shaking, his voice getting louder. "My work could help thousands and they didn't even want to hear what I had to say. I've no idea how to make them change their thinking. They didn't come home to the same environment."

"Change takes time," Rachel said as she crossed the room then moved between Brian and the door.

"I'm going for a drive."

She blocked his path. "Not like this you're not."

"I'm livid and need to get away for a while."

"Give me your keys."

"No way!" he shouted.

Rachel kept her voice calm but said in a firm tone. "Now. Give me your keys."

"You don't understand."

Eyes glaring, she said, "Too well, I understand." She held out her hand, palm up.

"Rachel..."

Speaking in a slow but firm manner, she insisted, "Give me the damn keys."

He glared at her, fury in his expression, his hands turning into fists. She returned his glare in kind. He slowly slipped his hand into his pocket, removed his keys and handed them to her.

"Thank you," she said. The petite lady dropped the keys in her apron pocket and returned to bread making. The entire house rattled as he slammed the back door.

Alone with his thoughts, Brian worked out his fury while splitting wood.

He thought, *"The damn idiots. These problems, which result in PTSD, have been around since Roman times. Without using that specific name, Marcus Aurelius noted the symptoms in his writings. So what the hell is wrong with Veterans from any war not wanting to know what my research demonstrates what we can do for veterans."*

He cursed and shook his head while his eyes teared up. *"Am I not explaining what my goal is?"* Brian left the wood pile, jogged for a half mile, then thought, *"This is some shit."* Brian shook his head then used his shoulders to wipe his tearing eyes. *"Maybe I should wait until there's another war...maybe then someone will listen."* He cursed again then mumbled, *"What a disgusting thought."* He took his anger out on the wood pile for the next hour.

Sweat covered even on that cool day, Brian returned to the house, found Rachel reading in the family room. He kissed her cheek and said, "Any normal woman wouldn't put up with my bat-shit craziness."

"If she cared about you as much as I do, she would."

He shook his head and sighed. "Pretty lady, you keep me sane."

***

"I'd planned to visit here for a few days, and it's been three weeks," Rachel said. They stood in the laundry room folding clothing. "I should head back to my place."

She glanced at Brian then out a window, admired the reddening, western sky as sundown approached.

"I understand," he said then kissed her lips.

"My life is on the other side of town."

Brian nodded as he put an arm around her. "I know."

She twisted away, stood up straight, folded her arms across her chest then pouted. "When we disagree, we argue like immature teenagers."

"True. Yet I've loved every minute you've been here."

"Why?"

"Even while at work this past few weeks, no matter how frustrated I became, knowing you'll be here to greet me kept me on an even keel. Even the staff at work have noticed."

"We both have separate working lives."

Brian smiled and said. "I love that Seth attends pre-school with you. Knowing you're keeping an eye one him, I don't worry how his day is going."

They carried the folded laundry upstairs then moved to the front porch, seated themselves on a settee, and watched the sunset.

They were quiet as each seemed lost in their own thoughts. The wind chimes played a gentle melody.

Brian broke the silence. "You should move in with us."

She shook her head. "Ridiculous. We've only been together for little more than a few weeks."

"Seth responds to you like he did to his birth mom."

"I doubt it."

"He's a happy child again."

She shook her head. "Little to do with me."

He kissed her cheek. "Everything to do with you. He's no longer riveted to my side."

Rachel shrugged. "We play a few children's games now and then."

He engaged in a deep sigh and showed her a warm smile. Brian intertwined his fingers with hers. "Inside you, you know we belong together. You feel it just like I do. The time between our Thanksgiving visit and you staying with us was awful for me...and I suspect the same for you."

"You don't know what I felt."

He smiled and said, "Tell me I'm wrong."

Rachel blushed, folded her arms across her chest, and turned away from him. "We've not been together long enough."

Brian shrugged and said, "You have your own life and you make wise decisions. If you don't wish to live with us, it will be sad but, we'll learn to live with that."

"You won't be angry with me if I decide not to stay?"

He shrugged. "Not a problem."

"It's too soon."

"Just one thing…" Brian said.

"What?"

He yelled for his son, who ran onto the porch. "Seth, Rachel has something to tell you."

The little one ran over to the settee, climbed up, sat on her lap then cuddled against her. His bright eyes looking up at her.

"Seth," she began, "I…" She opened her mouth as if to continue then stared at the three-year-old.

"Mommy Rachel tell Seth?" the little one asked then rested his head on her chest.

"I'm going…," she hesitated then turned to stare at the ocean of red clouds spreading across the Texas plains, the sun reduced to a pinpoint blaze. Rachel gave Seth a brief squeeze then kissed the top of his head. She took a deep breath, tucked a lock of hair behind her ear, "What would you think if I stayed here with you and your father?"

The little one became pensive, glanced at his father then turned back to Rachel. "You play Chutes and Ladders? Every day?"

Rachel laughed and said, "Of course." She leaned toward Brian and kissed his lips.

"I'll call the movers," Brian said. "What changed your mind?"

She shrugged then answered with a mischievous expression and voice. "Obviously, Seth understands where my future lies; with far better clarity than either one of us."

Chapter 16

1975 April

After sundown on a warm day in early April, Brian and Rachel moved to the patio to view planetary objects. Rachel had a pitcher of lemonade in one hand, two glasses in the other, and the day's newspaper.

"Brian, I could use a car to run around in while you're at work." She placed the items she carried on a small, round glass-topped table. Ice and liquid splashed into two frosty glasses as she poured a lemonade for each then handed one to Brian

"Thanks," he said and sipped the drink. "Take either of my cars." He peered through and adjusted the telescope.

She shook her head. "I don't like to drive stick-shift vehicles and your pick up is too big. I was thinking more of a family car."

"Pick something and I'll buy it for you."

Rachel stared at him briefly. "How much money are we talking about?"

"Doesn't matter. I earn good money. Whatever you like." He adjusted the telescope. "I have a good view of Saturn if you'd like to see it."

She rolled her shoulders and sighed. "We need to talk about something."

He looked up from the scope. "Anything."

Rachel plopped into one of the cushy patio chairs, tucking her legs under her.

"You have a cavalier attitude when it comes to spending money."

Brian stared at her. "Not sure what you're…"

"All I need is an old station wagon. Good enough to get to the store and pre-school."

"Old? I'll buy you a new one."

"I know you have money but the difference between new and old, you should give the difference to charity."

"I give to charity."

"When?"

"When someone approaches me and explains a need."

"Why do you wait?"

"Rachel, why is it necessary to discuss this? You need a car, pick one, and I'll buy it."

She folded her arms across her chest. "You've never asked me how I made a living in between my occasional bass guitar gigs. Didn't you ever wonder?"

"Not really. I assumed you lived with Arnie and Shira because it was cheap."

She shook her head, crossed her arms. "Wrong. Totally wrong. I was there for the moral support, and paid rent."

"But some of your work, sometimes months apart you said."

"That's right."

"As long as we're together money won't be a problem."

"My parents left me huge investments. Money isn't a problem but you're not careful with spending."

"You have money, I have money, why are we arguing about this?"

"News article today." Rachel held up the Dallas Morning News. "A number of veterans need appliances, wheelchairs, crutches, artificial limbs and the like."

"I didn't know."

"What are you going to do about that?"

"The VA will take care of them."

"Not all of them apparently."

Brian sounded exasperated. "Rachel, I have to admit, I'm baffled. What do you want me to do?"

"Buy me a small family vehicle. It will take me where I need to go and doesn't use much fuel."

"But I can get you a new station wagon or whatever..."

Her face red, apparent even in the darkness, she raised her voice, saying, "Find a way to buy appliances for your fellow vets with the money you'll save by buying what I'm asking for."

"I earn..." He turned away. Shook his head. Brian peered through his telescope while she sipped her lemonade. "You can see a number of Saturn's rings," he said.

"Brian..."

He straightened, said in an angry tone in a slow deliberate voice, "No. Not going to happen. You and Seth driving around in a small, lightweight vehicle…forget it. I want more steel around you two. I'll find a used Suburban."

"If I decide to buy one with my own money?"

He raised his voice. "Buy something I think isn't safe and I'll rip out its ignition." He glared at her, fury in his eyes. "Try me. No way in hell you're going to drive around in something small. I've performed surgery too many torn up passengers who were riding in small cars."

"Brian, you're shouting."

Fuming, he took a moment to calm down, stared at the pool for a while then said, "Sorry, but, forget it. Absolutely no small cars."

"Okay. Okay." She raised her hands in an expression of surrender. A deep sigh escaped her lips. "You buy me one of those Suburban things, but used, not new," Rachel's expression a frown, she twisted on her chair. "And I'll look into appliances for the veterans."

He nodded, turned back to the telescope.

"Also," Rachel said, "you mentioned your log cabin in Montana. Please tell me about it."

Brian pulled a cover over the telescope then moved to a patio chair. "I haven't been out there since shortly after I came home. I was thinking of putting it on the market."

"Describe please."

"A two-level log cabin with a nice interior which showcases the logs. I always imagined I go out with friends to fly fish and escape Texas' summer heat."

"Bedrooms?"

"Seven."

Eyes wide, Rachel spun her head in his direction. "Did you say seven?"

He nodded. "Yep. On Swan Lake, in Big Fork, near Kalispell, Montana. Located a short drive from Glacier National Park. Not far from Canada. Originally constructed to be a corporate retreat. Two story, set into a hill, on a couple acres. Big deck on the lake side which wraps around three sides of the house. Needs furniture, likely some repair, and a good cleaning."

"Dare I ask how many square feet?"

"Just under eight thousand."

Rachel's jaw dropped. "Eight thousand, that...that is not a cabin..."

"Well, it's built of stacked logs. Originally built to be a corporate retreat but never occupied so I bought it for a song. Just one bedroom, an office, and the kitchen partially furnished. And chairs and a table on the deck."

"When are we going?"

He considered her request, shrugged his shoulders, and said, "If you like, I can take off a few weeks around July Fourth."

Rachel nodded. "I'll start planning. You catch the news this morning?"

"The war is over. I should be happy but I'm more relieved than anything else. It looks like we left with our tail between our legs. Did we accomplish what we set out to do?" He stared at the tops of his shoes then answered his own question. "Don't think so. And we still have to deal with the Vets who continue to suffer."

"I can't say what was accomplished but I'm glad it's over."

Distant thunder rumbled. Rachel jumped.

"You okay?"

"Don't like rain," she reminded him as a few drops began falling.

"I'll finish packing up the telescope and meet you inside."

***

After a three- and one-half-day drive, during the last week of June, they arrived at the house in Montana.

"My Lord." Rachel gasped as the log home came into view. "Brian, this is gorgeous."

He parked the motorhome next to the house. Brian was pleased to see Rachel approach one of the debarked logs which held up the roof over the entrance and run her hand over it.

"You didn't tell me it would so elegant," she said while wearing a warm smile.

Brian unlocked the door, then stood aside to let Seth and Rachel enter. She marveled at the cedar wood floors and the exposed logs of the interior. Walking onto the deck off the main living space, the midday sunshine shimmered on a broad swath of Swan Lake which fronted the property. Mostly Douglas pines and a few Aspens waved in the light breeze. The petite lady turned back to view the interior. "But like you said, needs cleaning and furnishing. We should stay in the motor home until it's ready. I'm going to look for an interior decorator but find a cleaning service first. Can we do that?"

"The phone should be hooked up. I have to turn on the fifty-amp service for the coach and connect water and sewer just like at the campgrounds. Give me an hour and I'll get everything hooked up."

Seth stood on the deck as a small motorboat cruised past then wanted to know where their boat was so they could explore the lake.

His father said, "Help me with connecting the motorhome and we'll go shopping for a boat."

"Something I can enjoy, please," Rachel said. "It doesn't need the engine from Hades to get us around this small lake."

"Mom," Seth said, in the same tone she used when remonstrating him, "we need an engine that sounds like the 442." He thought for a bit then added, "Maybe two of them in case one breaks when we're way out on the water." He grabbed Brian's hand and they headed out the door.

Rachel said to the receding pair, "Like father, like son."

Wednesday morning, a cleaning crew arrived and a local decorator engaged with Rachel. The cleaning crew was instructed to begin in his office so Brian could move his research and notes from the motor home to the office.

On Friday evening, the home cleaned and mostly furnished, they enjoyed Sabbath dinner on the deck overlooking Swan Lake. Unlike the torrid summer temperatures of Texas, the temps were in the mid-seventies during the day and low fifties at night.

Rachel served a Greek salad, seared King Salmon, new potatoes, and asparagus, plus fresh, halved-cherries with cream for dessert.

After they finished eating, they moved to the family room with its stacked stone fireplace which divided the window wall, and view of the lake. Brian, with Seth's help, began stacking logs to build a fire then joined her on the couch.

Rachel said. "I was thinking you should tell me about Andrea. It might help me understand Seth."

"She suffered mental and physical wounds that happened before I met her. Andrea was in a car accident where her sister-in-law and nephew were killed. She was injured and experienced a difficult recovery. Andrea was driving and blamed herself for the deaths."

"Similar to a soldier who killed someone?"

He stood, considering her question then paced up and back, occasionally stopping to poke the logs in the fireplace, finally adding a few more.

"Brian?"

"Yes. I believe like a soldier, but the surrounding circumstances are different. From what I've learned, a traumatic event can cause mental damage which may increase in severity as time passes. I believe that happened to Andrea."

"Was the accident her fault?"

"The other driver was drunk but with more careful driving she felt she could have avoided the accident."

"The traumatic events you mentioned causing mental damage, why only in some people, not others."

His eyes left the fire, stared at her. "And there's the rub. No clue why. Although, there was a study which showed any soldier will suffer a mental breakdown after sixty days of constant contact with an enemy force."

"Did the accident's trauma cause Andrea to end her life?"

"I don't think so. She was depressed when she came here and arrived with plans to make sure Seth's Dad raised him, and end her life. I attributed the suicide to her illness, but the accident still weighed on her mental state. I suspect the combination pushed her over the edge..." He shrugged then walked to the bar and reached into a small fridge. Brian popped the top of a soda, poured some into a small glass for Seth then took a long sip from the can. He asked if she wanted one.

"I'm fine. How would you describe your relationship with Andrea?"

"During my R&R, like two metals slamming into each other at high velocity and high energy such that they meld together, become one."

"And when she came to Dallas?"

Brian sat next to her on the couch.

Seth stopped his play and watched them.

"Like two elements spinning around each other but unable to combine."

"Talking about Mommy Andrea?" Seth asked.

Brian nodded. "Your mother was a wonderful partner and mother."

Seth smiled and returned to building with his plastic blocks.

Rachel asked, "At the risk of being compared to elementary particles, dare I ask about you and me?"

"At times like two elements slamming into each other and releasing uncontrolled energy."

"Like when we disagree?"

He nodded, stood and walked to the fireplace, kneeled, then used a fire poker and tongs to rearrange the burning logs. "But at other times, like three elements combining and becoming greater than the sum of their individual characteristics."

She shook her head. "Three elements, greater than the sum. I can't imagine that," Rachel pulled a blanket over her.

"The way Seth responds to you. How often he expresses himself at the art center you created for him. A simple child-sized table and two chairs, a pile of blank paper and a bucket of crayons. The little guy is filled with boundless energy but spends many an hour quietly concentrating on a drawing. It would have never entered my mind to create an art center. And he adores you." Brian smiled as if remembering a pleasant memory. "The way you make me feel when you're close, the way I feel arriving home, much of the day's tension releasing as I motor up the driveway. The closer to the house, my smile growing, knowing you'll be there to welcome me." He poked the fire again then sat next to her.

Rachel was quiet for a bit then stammered, "You...I..." She pulled him close, threw her arms around him and kissed him then cuddled tight against him. "You and Seth. Put purpose in my life beyond my own needs."

"I'm happy to know that." He kissed her.

"I have an anniversary coming up, one which I dread. I'm hoping, it will be less severe this year because I'm here with you and our little guy."

"We should talk about that."

"I lost two people I dearly loved, in one evening."

"Tell me."

She opened the blanket to cover both of them. "I will. But don't have the energy tonight. Please, just hold me."

The moment he did, Seth ran to the couch and snuggled under the blanket, squeezing between them.

***

The following morning, Rachel entered Brian's office. "I was thinking of Arnie and Shira this morning. I Shira and asked about her and Arnie."

"She said...?"

She plopped into an overstuffed chair. "This...this is so strange. I'm not sure if I believe her."

"Tell me."

"She said they were at a Yankee's game. He began swearing and screaming at the players. After a few minute tirade, usher's came over and bodily lifted him out of his seat then carried him out of the stadium."

His jaw dropped. "We're taking about Arnie, right?"

"According to Shira, one usher asked that he keep the profanity down. Arnie called the guy a string of vile names. A group of ushers arrived and pulled him out of his seat. My cousin allegedly kicking and screaming. They bodily carried him out of the stadium. "

Shaking his head, Brian said, "Impossible. Not Arnie. Couldn't be. This is BS."

Rachel shrugged and left the office.

Still shaking his head, Brian returned to the work on his desk.

Twenty minutes later, Rachel returned. "I called New York and spoke to a longtime friend. She said she saw it on the evening news."

Brian shook his head, put his hands up palms out. "No. No. No. This is insanity. It must be a mistake. Arnie? NO way. Arnie wouldn't...on a bet he wouldn't..."

"She said he was arrested for disorderly conduct."

He opened his mouth as if to say something but just stared at Rachel.

She answered his unspoken question. "I have no clue what came over him."

***

Two days later, under a cloudless sky, the Montana sun warming them on a Sunday afternoon, Rachel, Brian and Seth hiked a trail in the Flathead National Forest. Seth ran ahead, searching for interesting rocks and watching for birds. Brian carried a camera with a zoom lens and a small backpack.

"Rachel, I must say, I love all you've done for us. From cooking to your insight on my research. Seth loves the way you engage with him. We love having you as part of our family, but what can I do for you?"

"Find a way to take time off from work for a week, go somewhere else and do your research so that your anger and frustration doesn't impinge on your family."

"Am I that bad?"

"At times."

"I'd love to, but I have things to work out in my own mind, that and the research result in anger which pushes people away."

"Arnie warned me, and I've seen it for myself. I'll help you, by taking care of this part of your world." She motioned, indicating Seth. "I'll make time to discuss anything you like, and tell you when your behavior is unacceptable." Rachel pointed to wood ducks paddling about in a nearby pond.

He stopped to take photos of them.

She smiled and took his hand as they began walking again. "I feel close. Family close to the two of you since our time at Arnie's."

"There must be something I can do for you..."

"If there is, I'll tell you."

"I worried because I'm not as religious as you are. That could be a problem. And we should talk about a more permanent arrangement."

She shook her head. "Not yet. Too soon. I can't think about marriage. Keeping my head on straight is enough for me to do without considering another marriage, and as for my religious involvement being deeper than yours, I knew before I moved in. We'll find ways to manage."

"I always have so much to do, attending services becomes a low priority. I fear that may damage our relationship."

Rachel stopped walking, grabbed his hands and held them up, spoke in a serious, near angry tone. "These hands repair people afflicted with terrible injuries. You torture your mind to understand what happens to soldiers in war in order to find ways to heal their mental state. You're a great father for Seth." She wrapped her arms around him and said in a quiet voice, "You found a plain and lonely girl and make her feel like a queen. You do these things every day. The Lord understands your absence."

He leaned forward, kissed her. "So much more than, a plain girl. But you're willing to give up being an observant Jew?"

"No, but my observance will in no way interfere with our relationship. I believe if I do things right, it will enhance what we have." In silence, they hiked past a small lake. Hooded Mergansers dove to find fish and crustaceans while chubby-cheeked, Green-winged Teal paddled about.

Again, Brian stopped for photographs.

"My entire life, I've prayed for an observant man to be my life's partner." Rachel giggled. "Instead the Lord sent you." She wrapped her arms around his arm as they continued walking.

"And...?" Brian said, then turned quickly to take a photo of a Bufflehead in flight.

Seth ran toward them then turned and began pointing at a gaggle of geese flying overhead in a large V formation.

Rachel praised his find. The little one smiled then proceeded back up the trail, alternately running and skipping. "Of course, the Lord was correct to send you," she continued. "I needed someone one who could grapple with and understand traumatic stress. Be a rock for me when needed, a good listener, and someone to reassure me I'm doing things right."

She paused when Seth returned to ask Brian questions concerning birds with webbed feet.

The little one listened intently to his father then ran ahead of them as they began walking again.

Rachel continued, "Besides, I'll bet we have differing views of leading an observant life. In a group discussion at synagogue, we were asked to imagine an observant Jew. Most people imagine a man who spends all his time praying and studying Torah. I immediately saw my Grandma Lena; a living example of how to live a Jewish life. She comported herself in a way such that each of her children and each of her grandchildren believed they were her favorite. She was a moral, kind, and giving person. One day, I hope I'll be remembered like her."

"Will you find a fulfilling life with us, far away from the musicians, family, and community you grew up with?"

"Before they returned to New York, Arnie talked about coming out again to visit us."

"Us? He assumed we'd be together?"

"Don't know if it's good or bad but Arnie said," Rachel giggled, "we deserve each other."

Brian laughed and put a new roll of film in his camera.

Seth ran up to show them a shiny rock.

"I'm needed here..." She laughed. "Even if it's to get excited over a rock."

They walked in silence for a while, Rachel's expression turning grim. She took a deep breath and said, "There are a couple events in my life you should know about." She stared at the horizon, took another deep breath. "I was molested when I was a child."

"Rachel..." he said.

She stopped walking then held up a hand. "Let me finish." The lady raised in Brooklyn stared in his eyes. "I've never told anyone, although I think Arnie and his parents suspected. For years, I tried to pretend it didn't happen. That's why I believed I could never have a successful relationship with anyone. The thought of having sex was so painful, I would never let a relationship become serious. One time I decided to do it with someone just to see. It was awful."

"But you were married..."

"I accepted an arranged marriage. I married because I wanted children and Dov seemed nice enough."

"Love?"

She looked down, shook her head. "I'm ashamed to say, not part of the equation."

"Sex?"

"We did it, of course. But I didn't enjoy it. I was, this is horrible to say, I was relieved when he was drafted." Rachel shivered. "Puffing and grunting, banging on my belly until he finished, then rolling over and snoring the night away."

"Then why, since you came to the ranch, we...?" He looked at her with a questioning expression then grinned. "Dare I mention the word rabbits?"

She laughed. "During Thanksgiving, when you held me, after I'd just seen how violent you could become, yet, holding you, was so right, and warmed me in a way, you made me feel safe."

They continued walking, this time holding hands.

Rachel shook her head. "It makes no sense. I always hated violence. Only one other time, during my adolescent years, I enjoyed someone holding, actually dancing, with our arms wrapped around each other. That was when I was fifteen."

She stared at him.

"What?" he asked.

Rachel kissed his cheek. "Sounds childish but, deep inside me, I was certain it would be different with you and you'd never hurt me."

"You couldn't possibly know that."

"The feeling I get when you smile at me, and even in the depths of our loudest arguments, I feel we're still a team, and we can work things out." She stopped to gaze at a skein of Ruddy Ducks floating in a pond. Rachel pointed to them. "So strange, ducks with a blue bill, and those are Avocets around the edges. I love this area. Beauty wherever you look." Again she kissed his cheek while Brian stopped to take numerous photos. "Thank you for driving us out here."

Walking again, she held one of his hands in both of hers. "Impolite to say, Dr. Levin, but my body aches for you. It has since you held me at Arnie's."

"But the abuse..."

"Never thought I'd tell anyone, but you, you're, I feel so close, we'll talk..." She nodded as if reassuring herself. "Arnie said I could share innermost feelings with you. He was right."

Brian wiped a tear off her cheek.

"Just holding hands...wonderful. You and Seth make me feel needed. That satisfies me. I have a purpose beyond my own needs and you provide space for me to be myself...do things my way. You and Seth regularly demonstrate how much you love me." Rachel held her head up, walked tall. "That's what Mr. Levin and Seth do for me. When people wanted to know what I wanted from life, I always told them, to be loved for who I am."

"We've been together for six months. Is it time to talk about marriage?"

She shook her head. "When I married the last time, I became a different person. What I wanted out of life no longer mattered. My life revolved around my husband's needs and wants. I felt boxed in. Diminished as a person. But for my music career, which I was allowed to pursue only because we needed the income, I was chained to the house."

"It wouldn't be that way for us."

"Our relationship is still new and I don't want to take a chance doing something which could damage that. What we have, is better than the majority of married couples I've met. Like I said, you took a plain girl and make her feel like a queen. As far as marriage, I feel happy and secure now but frightened, scared to death really, of anything which might damage that."

They walked in silence for a number of minutes.

She stopped, kissed him while they briefly embraced then wrapped her arms around his arm and they continued on the trail. "A beautiful day," she said. "We need to schedule more time out here. Let's plan on inviting friends at the same time next year. This could certainly be a peaceful retreat for your Army friends and their families. Love the mountains; this forest and its inhabitants are to die for. And we haven't even seen Glacier National Park yet."

"Certainly, we are surrounded by beauty. Perhaps we shouldn't discuss the abuse. We can save it for another day."

"Thank you, but..." She walked in silence for a number of minutes then said, "If I can get the story out, perhaps it will help me resolve the pain I still endure." Rachel took a deep breath and let it out slowly. "He lived in the basement of our building. The janitor. An older man."

"You were?"

"Six or seven." She took a deep breath and continued. "I remember a sudden downpour; I was playing on the sidewalk so I ran into the building but tripped just inside the door. I fell, started crying. He carried me to his basement apartment, put me on his lap, his hand down my pants. Many times, he invited me into his room to tell me a story, on his lap, with his hand between my legs. It happened again and again."

Shaking her body like a dog trying to dry its fur, Rachel tried to expunge the feeling of the old man's hands.

"After a number of years, my father eventually found out from my older sister who caught the old man with me on his lap and his hand down my pants."

"Did you talk to your parents?"

"I had no clue what to say. My parents never mentioned it, and like many abused children, I believed it was my fault."

"Is that why you become anxious during rainstorms?"

Rachel stopped walking, her eyes wide, jaw dropped, and staring straight ahead.

"I said..."

She slapped her forehead. "I heard you. I...never considered why, just never liked the rain. But maybe..." She appeared deep in thought as they began walking again. "Odd, but I never connected the two."

Rachel turned Brian toward her, pulled his lips down to hers for a long kiss then said, "Bless the Lord. He's given me someone who listens."

They continued walking. Clouds appeared, the wind picked up, and the temperature dropped. She zipped her jacket, called Seth over, pulled his jacket out of Brian's backpack and held it while he slipped his arms in.

Brian's expression became one of shock. He turned to her while Seth ran up the trail. "Wait. What sister? You've never mentioned a sister."

"Mirna was two years older. She left a note the day she turned eighteen and I haven't heard from her since. After she left, my parents grieved but never mentioned her again. Perhaps one day, I'll look for her."

"You said a couple of things in your life…your sister leaving one of them?"

"That was painful but wasn't one of the incidents I was talking about. I was referring to something I did which caused dreadful trauma to my mind…a life altering trauma caused by an act I committed. I came home one evening, to find an intruder in our bedroom. He'd tied my husband to a chair. He pointed a gun at him. I heard Dov curse the bastard. I approached the intruder from behind, plunged my survival knife into his kidney."

"No hesitation?"

"Lots, but only in my mind, the moment I saw that filth of a human being threatening my husband, my body took over as I had trained it during my self-defense class. It was as if I was watching someone else perform the deed."

"Knifing someone is personal."

"Personal enough, his smell, just like the sensation of the knife cutting through muscle and tissue, is written in my memory with letters chiseled in stone. The knife doesn't magically enter. You have to push it in. One's hand feels the sensation of slicing meat, the entire episode over in less than a second but I've replayed the memory so many times. For whatever reason, my mind forces me to replay the scene. Feeling the carpet under my bare feet as I approach, his raucous voice growling at Dov, his stink of sweat and anger, the sensation in my hand as the blade entered. His gun dropping out of his hand as he tried to reach the wound, he twisted toward me. Mouth agape, eyes bulging, he wore an expression showing terror and pain. Rapidly losing consciousness, he collapsed to his knees. My heart pounding, my ears ringing. I realized he'd fired his gun when I knifed him. Killing Dov." She stopped walking, her eyes filling with tears. "My poor husband stared at the hole in his chest, looked up at me with shock in his expression. Dov mouthed my name, his head falling to his chest. My husband's last sight of his wife, standing over a body oozing life, gripping a knife which dripped blood." Rachel hesitated, then looked up at Brian and said, "I miscarried that night."

Rachel buried her face in Brian's chest. He wrapped his arms around her and kept repeating, "I'm so sorry." She cried quietly.

The little one ran up and asked, "Why Mommy Rachel is crying?"

She wiped her eyes with the back of her hands then reached for the little's one hand. "A sad memory. But if you hold my hand, I'll be happy again."

Seth grinned and skipped as they walked. The little one mumbled, "Make Mommy happy."

Rachel wiped her eyes again. "I know the wind chimes are personal to you and Andrea, but, through Seth, I feel close to her. Like sister close. As if she's still part of our family. When we're back in Celina, would you mind adding a set of wind chimes for me?"

"Brilliant idea. You find a set you enjoy and I'll hang them with the others."

"Enough about me," Rachel said. "What does Brian want from life?"

"To finish the research and use it to improve the lives of soldiers and their families."

"Anything else?"

"Be an excellent father to Seth and spend the rest of my life with you."

She pulled his lips down to hers for a long kiss.

"Thank you, pretty lady." Brian said, "Have you heard, there are rumors in Washington the Vietnam War will end soon?"

PART SIX: WAR'S AFTERMATH

Chapter 17

Dear Sgt. Levin,

So the Vietnam War has finally ended. I was thinking of you so thought I'd write. I'm on a one-week vacation with my wife. Visiting the French Quarter in New Orleans again. Good times musically and superb eats down here. The children stayed with relatives. No business calls, no children needing our attention. Lots of time to think…and remember…resulting in this letter.

In my own mind, my thoughts run to cold wet nights, exhaustion from weeks of inadequate sleep, rarely a hot meal and the personal responsibility for causing death and maiming. Also, sadness for wounded we couldn't save. However, the memory of the friends I made, warms me like a bowl of gumbo on a cold night.

Personally, I wanted to serve my country and stop the communists. While I did accomplish the first, the second goal hasn't happened. Makes me wonder if we really accomplished anything. Your thoughts? Sad to think so many died and we didn't achieve the goals the country set out to achieve.

Must mention Savanah, a lady from Baton Rouge. As you likely remember, started corresponding as pen pals and exchanged letters for the duration of my tour. Agreed we'd meet when I got home. Didn't imagine events in Vietnam would affect our relationship...

***

Ten o'clock sharp, the bus pulled up to the pharmacy and general store of the tiny, South Louisiana town. Coming to a halt, the air brakes releasing a blast of air that generated a barrel-sized dust cloud that floated across the street on that, hot and humid, mid-August day of 1971. Once a bustling town which served the local farm community, it was bypassed by the interstate ten years prior, its population dwindling ever since. Across the street, Paul Slidell, dressed in denim overalls but wearing a sleeveless plaid shirt, leaned against a lamp post and watched a single passenger disembark. Released by the Army a week earlier, his hair was still military short, he waited with his hands in the pockets of his overalls, twisted the toe of his boot in the dirt.

A woman of average height with curly black hair, wide hips and small bust, descended from the bus preceded by the driver. She waved a paper fan at her red, sweat covered face, used the back of the hand which held the fan to wipe damp hair out of her face, her other hand tightly gripping a leather bag. Her sandaled feet on the dusty road, she glanced about then proceeded to the open cargo door of the bus, gave the driver a few coins then collected her single suitcase.

Paul crossed the street. "Miss Savanah Stewart?" Paul said in a nervous voice.

"I am, sir. Whom am I addressing?"

"Paul Slidell, at your service."

"A pleasure to meet you, Mr. Slidell."

The door of the bus slammed closed; its engine moaned as it pulled away from the bus stop.

"An honor to meet the woman whose correspondence provided a link to home while I prowled the mountains and lowlands of Vietnam plus raised my spirits during my recovery from the wound in my hip."

They shook hands. He took her bag. They walked to his two-door pickup. He opened the front door for her, placed her bag in the back.

He fired up the pickup, backed into the street, and proceeded toward his home. She angled the wing vent so it would direct as much air as possible onto her. Savanah asked, "You recovered from your Army service? No nightmares or stuff?"

"Just got home. Nothing yet."

After a minute's silence, she said, "On one hand I feel like I know you but on the other, I sense we're strangers who've just met."

"If you'll pardon my disagreeing, I felt your pain when you received the news that your brother, Robert was Missing In

Action…and know your concern was evident, and appreciated, when I got wounded. Makes us more than strangers…"

She smiled. "I'm pleased you feel that way. Any one in your platoon MIA?"

"A few died, a few torn up but no MIAs. Your folks managing?"

"No. Inconsolable would describe their emotional state. They had plans how he'd take over the family business…" Savanah crossed her arms across her chest said in a bitter voice, "They wouldn't think of giving it to me. Actually feel, like they wish I was the one who'd gone MIA. I'm glad to get away from them for a while."

"Tell me about your brother."

"We were close. Fraternal twins, as it happens. Have four other brothers and sisters but they're quite a bit younger than us." She thought for a bit, smiled, then added, "We did all kind of things together growing up. From fishing to hunting, we were a good pair. I was as good a shot as he was."

Looking sheepish, he said, "I was nervous waiting for you to arrive."

She giggled. "Me too."

"How your folks feel about you coming out to spend time with someone you never met?"

"Angry."

"Because?"

She giggled. "Won't have their scullery maid around."

"Is that why you're here, Miss Stewart?"

"Certainly not. In your letters…got the sense you're lonely…that you didn't have much to come back to…being an orphan and all." She stared out the side window for a bit then said, "Kinda' lonely myself. I was hoping I might be the one you might enjoy spending time with."

"You read me right. Don't make friends easy." He twisted on his seat. "Want to thank you for all those letters. Meant the world to me…hearing from you every couple weeks…that kept me sane." He stopped at a light. "Have to tell you, that box of sugar cookies you sent at Christmas time…I shared them with my squad. For a few minutes, we all had a taste of home."

She smiled. "My pleasure."

"Have some things for us to do…if you'd like."

"Such as?"

"Blue Grass festival over in Edwards at the fairgrounds tomorrow."

"Love Blue Grass."

"I remember," he said. "How about lunch?"

"Fine. Where?"

"My place. Have gumbo simmering on the stove since a couple hours ago. Just need to add the shrimp, heat 'em through."

She smiled.

He turned off the highway, drove on pavement for a while then followed a dirt road for two miles then proceeded up a gravel covered driveway. He parked in front of a small home. Kudzu covered most of the house. Old, stately trees dominated the property, Spanish moss hung from them. Four wooden steps up from the yard, a long, deep porch wrapped around the front. Two rocking chairs with a small, glass-topped, table between them, one rocker well used, the other new. Paul unlocked the front door, pushed it open, and held the screen door for her.

"I'll put your case in the second bedroom…was my office but I cleared it out for you. Had a professional cleaning outfit go through the entire house yesterday. I bought new linens for the bed in there."

"Thoughtful of you."

They moved to the kitchen…the table set for two. He poured wine then opened the refrigerator, removed a tray of oysters on a bed of ice from the refrigerator.

"Shucked 'em fifteen minutes ago, just before I left to pick you up," he said.

Following the oysters, he served bowls of gumbo.

"My Cajun neighbor's recipe," he said. "Hope you like it."

She tried it. "I detect crab, chicken…no…smoked chicken, shrimp, andouille…and trinity."

A proud grin crossed his face. "Yes, ma'am."

"Spiced just enough for me."

After the meal Savanah, insisted on doing the cleanup.

When she'd finished he offered to take her on a walk around his property.

They spent the afternoon roaming his land and discussing their family history and each of their likes and dislikes.

"This was just an old swamp property," he said. "My grandfather bought it in the 1920's. Thought when I came home from the Army, I'd hire myself out as a fishing guide, and do some mud-bug farming. I was home on leave before I was to fly to Vietnam when this fella stops by, says they want to drill for oil on my land. Tells me I get a percentage of what they pump out."

"A lucrative proposition."

"Ain't gonna be no millionaire but I don't need much so I've been taking courses in finance and learning how to manage my oil money in stocks and bonds."

She prepared Etouffee for dinner with mud bugs and trinity. Savanah asked if she could put flowers in the flower boxes which lined the front porch.

"Sure," he said, reaching for his wallet.

"Don't need but a couple dollars."

He gave her a questioning expression. "Plants cost more than that."

"I planned to buy seed. Be cheaper that way."

Paul drove her to a garden center. Returning to the house, they prepped two flower beds and planted the seeds.

They slept together that night, but Paul didn't have a sense of closeness with Savanah. He felt like she did it with him more out of a sense of duty rather than attraction.

"I know what a soldier needs when he returns home," she said at breakfast the following day.

Following three days together, Paul couldn't get rid of the feeling, everything she did came out of a sense of duty rather than affection for him.

He found Savanah on the porch in the middle of the night, engaged in conversation with her MIA brother. Savanah reviewed what she and Paul did as if she wanted her brother's approval.

The following morning, she suggested Paul meet her family, learn about their hardware business, and consider taking over running it from her father.

His hands moved to his hips and his brow furrowed, he said. "In other words, replace your brother."

"Please. Listen to me." she said, her hands gripping his arm and her voice pleading, "Robert. Please. The family needs you."

He stared at her. Savanah's hand came up to cover her mouth when she realized she'd addressed him with her brother's name.

Paul swore. "I think you should get your things and I'll buy you a bus ticket home."

He put her things in his pickup and drove to the bus station.

After watching her bus disappear down the road, Paul climbed into his pickup, used the back of his hands to wipe tears from his eyes. He muttered, "Seemed too good to be true, and turns out it was."

***

Things have gotten better for me, buddy...but became much worse before they improved.
My wife is calling me. We have a reservation at Antoine's in the French quarter. Look out, Huîtres en coquille à la Rockefeller, here I come!
Take Care and I'll write again.
No Slack, Paul

***

After a long day of surgery, Brain motored home in his 442. A policewoman waved him down. A patrol car was in front of a small bungalow, its red light still rotating, and a second patrol car sat in the driveway. Brian pulled his 442 to the side of the road, just beyond the police vehicle, cranked his window down. The policewoman ran to his car then indicated a forlorn looking man sitting on the front steps of his house.

"Hey, Doc. Hope you don't mind. I recognized your car." She nodded toward the house as Brian exited his car. "Guy up there is Benton Willis. Vietnam Veteran. Picked up on drug possession a couple times. Must a' took some pills or something, slurring his speech something terrible. Won't tell us what he's high on," the policewoman shook her head. "Couple patrolmen are searching the house, haven't found anything. Paramedics on the way. Any chance you could talk to him?"

The surgeon said, "If we don't know what he took, they might not be able to do much for him at the ER."

Brian approached the desolate looking man, sat next to him. Trembling and teary, a scruffy black beard ringed the man's face. He wore a torn tee shirt and jeans plus jungle combat boots. He was thin, had an overall slovenly appearance. From his smell, Brian surmised, it must have been weeks since he'd bathed.

"I'm Doctor Levin, Benton. You need to tell me what you swallowed," Brian said.

"I let them down. I's their sergeant, and let them down. Shrapnel from an RPG tore half my foot off. Couldn't get around to direct fire. Couldn't be a proper leader."

"You must have been in terrible pain, but you need…"

"Our medic wrapped it. The guys kept me still, said I'd bleed out if I didn't, but I wanted to keep shooting and directing fire, calling in Arty. But they wouldn't let me." He wiped a tear with his shoulder. "One of my guys killed and three torn up worse than me, all cause I couldn't lead."

"You don't know that."

"Wouldn't let me lead. Chopper came."

"Benton, I want to help you but you need to tell me what you took."

"Still under fire, they loaded me on that chopper. I screamed, ordered them not to take me."

"Benton, listen to me..."

"The memory of that day, rips holes in my mind. The sight of my men, torn to hell."

"Did you take pills or inject something?"

The forlorn man shook his head, tears running down his cheeks, oblivious to Brian. "If I was leading, not fucked up, I could a' prevented that. Didn't lose nobody while I was their squad leader, until then."

"Benton, what did you take? Pills? Medication? Something else?"

His head lolled sideways as he said, "Don't matter. Won't bring my men back, won't fix 'em. They deserved better."

"Your men wouldn't want you to die. Tell me what you took."

Benton didn't hear. He stared at Brian for a few seconds. "Doc, they wouldn't let me direct fire, talk to Arty."

His slurred his last words such that they were barely intelligible, Brian nodded to the paramedics who'd just arrived. They loaded the distraught veteran on a gurney. Brian held Benton's hand until the gurney was placed in the ambulance, the distraught soldier's hand becoming limp."

Brian shook his head, walked back to his car.

"Will he make it, Doc?" the policewoman asked as the ambulance's siren wailed into the distance.

He shrugged. "Not sure. Poor bastard. I tried but don't think he heard me. No clue if he'll make it."

"Had something similar happen over in Aubrey last month." The officer shook her head. "You think there'll be more of this?"

"Don't know, but for some, I'm finding the memories get more painful over time." He removed a card from his pocket. "Certainly, there could be more of this. Call me if you think I can help. Anytime, day or night."

"Sure thing, Doc. And thanks for trying."

***

"He died?" Rachel asked. She lay on the floor in the family room in front of a crackling, warm fire. Seth played at the art center.

Brian nodded then rubbed his temples. "I called the ER. Dead on arrival. His heart stopped as the ambulance arrived. They tried to revive him but without knowing what he swallowed or injected there was little they could do. I tried to talk to him while we waited for the paramedics. Case of extreme guilt because he felt he let his squad down."

"Did you ever feel the same way?"

"Conflict in my mind at times because I could have used my medical knowledge to be a surgeon instead of a grunt. Although I started out to write a novel, I now believe the notes I made when I was over there, will allow me to write a research paper which will help more soldiers than my surgical talent." He stood, rubbed his face with both hands then walked over to a window, briefly stared at the full moon. "One time, in the jungle, I had a bout with heat exhaustion, my guys let me sleep through the night instead of waking me for my turn at guard duty. Felt guilty over that for weeks. Still think about it."

"Why? You were sick."

"I let my squad mates down. Besides his own heavy pack, James Ware carried my seventy pounds of gear to our night position. Felt awful that I couldn't carry my own gear."

"At the risk of repeating myself, you were ill."

"A squad is a family. Each member like a link in a chain. We depend on each other and each must carry their own load. Sick or not."

"But if you were wounded?"

"Someone else has to take care of you which causes another link in the chain to weaken. When we lost our sniper, I took his place. He was a much better shot than I was. His shooting could have taken out targets at longer range, lessening the enemy's opportunity to kill our guys." Brian shook his head, rubbed his temples. "That poor guy today. I pray he's at peace now. Guilt like his seems to magnify over time, which in his case was debilitating, and defeated his desire to live."

"You didn't have combat every day."

"True. Numerous weeks in between action, could be mind numbing with so little to do but patrol. But there's always that tension that combat could occur at any moment and any location. Remember, we didn't have front lines. The need to be mentally ready for combat twenty-four hours a day is physically and mentally exhausting. That's why I so appreciated a relation who sent me paperbacks every few weeks, and my Mom sent me a medical journal each month." He began rubbing his temples again. "I should make notes on today's incident.

"After Seth sleeps tonight, I need to tell you about a milestone event in my life," Rachel said with a coquettish expression

.

Chapter 18

Seth asleep, Brian sat on the floor while reading, his back against the couch where Rachel read a novel. She closed the book then stared at the flames in the fireplace. "It's nearly bedtime but before we sleep, I want to tell you how I experienced our first meeting." She slid off the couch and sat across his lap, rested her head on his shoulder.

He smiled and tightened his embrace. "You do remember!"

With a broad smile, she nodded and kissed him. "So, I was a freshman in high school. Attended a distant relative's wedding in the, far from Brooklyn, city of Houston. Over one-hundred-fifty guests. There was a dance at the reception. Back then, I wore thick glasses, like the ends of a soda bottle and had a figure with all the curves of an airplane runway. Guys and girls roughly my age, about thirty of us, gathered in a group to one side of the dance floor. Between songs, one boy told another to ask me for a dance. Instead of asking, he made fun of my glasses, said he wouldn't dance with someone who had four eyes. Everyone who heard him laughed. I wanted a hole to open and swallow me. My eyes filled with tears. I'm certain my face was beet red. I was mortified."

She rubbed her nose against Brian's cheek.

"Then, like magic, out of the crowd a college guy approached, offered me his hand. In a southern drawl he asked me to dance. I was in shock. This guy, not tall but big boned, broad at the shoulders and hips, and piercing blue eyes. I considered he might be making fun of me. I didn't move."

"Rachel..."

"Please," she said, putting a finger on his lips. "Let me finish. He grabbed my hand, his fingers intertwining with mine, guided me onto the dance floor, and we danced to a number of fast songs. In between songs, we talked like old friends…every time I looked at him, he showed me this warm smile. A cha-cha played, I barely knew how, but he led in a way which made it easy. Told me I was a natural. A slow tune began. I'll never forget it. Henry Mancini's Dreamsville. He didn't even inquire if I'd slow dance with him. Just pulled me against him." Rachel laughed. "I distinctly remember offering no resistance. My father didn't approve. The moment the college guy's arms were around me, my father stood. I gave Papa what he later referred to as, the look. Not pleased, he sat down anyway." Rachel sighed, kissed Brian. "The warmth and emotions the guy filled me with... Another dance and he brought me an iced tea. We sat at a table, talked like no one else was there, and shared wedding cake. Conversation so easy with him. He wanted to know all about me, like my goals for college and, of all things, we talked about Maimonides, the medieval Sephardic philosopher. Then more dancing, another slow tune, more conversation."

She kissed his cheek, cuddled against him then continued.

"The older guy told me, 'Thank you, for providing such a memorable evening, pretty lady.'" She sighed and traced the outline of Brian's jaw with her finger while saying, "Not that being called pretty lady is a special name but, he said it in a way which made me feel special. I shook my head. Not pretty, I told him."

"Your smile, he told me, it warms me. He then reached up, and with a gentle motion, used both hands to remove my glasses, folded them and put them in his shirt pocket."

"He said...And your deep brown eyes, I could get lost in those. Yes. Pretty lady you are."

Rachel kissed Brian's lips.

She sighed, "Late that night, the music ended as did the magic of our first meeting. You put your hands on my shoulders, your lips brushed mine, a brief goodbye and you walked away."

The petite lady kissed him again. "After that, whenever I felt I'd never have a partner, I'd remember the man who said I was a pretty lady. That memory helped me through numerous sad times. I prayed another man like him would enter my life." She kissed his cheek. "Never in my wildest dreams would I have imagined the same guy would show up again. When Arnie came home from Vietnam, he told us stories about his friend Brian and what they accomplished in the military. I fantasized that it might be the same Brian. A soldier, a surgeon, a best friend to my cousin, but dared not believe it. And then you were there. Even called me pretty lady again."

"I'm amazed you remember in such detail. A long time ago and you were so young..."

"Not a major event for you, but for a plain girl from Brooklyn who felt she had few prospects, who couldn't even get a guy to ask her for a lousy dance, a life-changing event."

"I didn't even tell you my name."

"True. I heard someone call you Brian but no last name."

He enjoyed the warmth of her body, eyes closed, massaged her back muscles, the week's concerns leaving him. Brian shook his head, saying, "At the reception, I was furious with myself, falling for someone I couldn't ask out because you were so much younger than me, but..."

"Falling for her...?"

"How about intrigued? Fascinated? Drawn to, and the scent of apple blossoms. Crazy but when we danced close...I remember the sweet fragrance of apple blossoms."

She laughed. "Apple blossom perfume. Only thing I could afford." Rachel kissed him. "Tell me. Why did you ask me to dance? Dozens of girls there, better looking and older than me."

"During dinner, this young girl, sitting at a nearby table, gave an intellectual discourse on Maimonides, how much of his work attempted to bridge Judaism and philosophy. When those at her table asked complex questions, her learned replies reminded me of the time I watched the Mississippi river as it rounded a bend near Memphis, Tennessee. Strong and steady with huge energy hidden beneath its surface. Did I want to meet her? I was drawn to the petite lady like iron to a magnet."

"For real?"

"You were, and are, good looking, but it was your thoughts and the way you expressed them that attracted me."

A satisfied smile crossed Rachel's lips. "Who would believe, Maimonides died in 1204 and seven-hundred years later, he brought you to me." Her fingers caressed his cheek. "Did you recognize me when you arrived at Arnie's?"

"I did but assumed you didn't remember me. Within minutes, though, we were talking like old friends. And I believe my son somehow sensed we had a connection. Only a matter of minutes and Seth was secure around you."

"Which pleased me no end."

"Since Andrea died, you're the first person he's comfortable with besides me."

"You held me one time at my condo."

"Yes, following my...discussion with Samuel."

"Discussion?" Rachel laughed. "You can't imagine how I felt, your arms around me again." She kissed his cheek. "A combination of relief, warmth, and gratitude. A terrible event but resolved a huge problem in my life. He never came near me again."

"I worry problems from my war experience will surface and push us apart."

Rachel sighed. "We're two torn and tattered souls. Putting together a relationship is like fitting the pieces of a jigsaw puzzle." She kissed him then giggled. "Speaking of pieces that fit, and based on what I'm sitting on, I think it's time for bed."

He laughed and nodded.

***

Three weeks later, late Sunday morning in the big garage, Brian wore coveralls with the sleeves folded above the elbows. Dirt and grease covered his forearms and hands, plus he had a few streaks of dirt on his face. He had just installed new V-belts on the 442. Seth just outside the big door, played on a jungle gym.

Rachel approached, took a stool from the workbench, placed it near the front of the car, and sat down. "How's the maintenance going?" Her expression one of unease, she rubbed the tops of her thighs, often running a hand through her hair.

A quick glance at her and while checking the tension on the belts said, "Going good. New plugs and leads, chassis greased, changed oil and filters. Checked the brake pads, have another six months at least before they need replacing. Still need to grease a few parts but enough for today, I have to reattach the battery negative cable and I'll finish the rest tomorrow." His head and upper body still under the hood, he glanced at her. "What's wrong?"

She took a deep breath. "I may be unable to conceive. We remain together, Seth may never have a brother or sister." Rachel stared at the ground. "It's the anniversary of three deaths today. I miscarried at four weeks, the same night I caused two deaths. It took a number of days in the hospital to get my strength back, almost a year and a half to get my mind near an even keel."

Brian straightened and closed the car's hood. "Arnie mentioned the miscarriage." He picked up a rag from the top of the car's radiator and began wiping his hands and forearms. "It doesn't mean it will happen again."

"But the odds are higher it will. I'm not a soldier. I don't know if I can endure the loss of another child." She twisted on the stool. "We had names picked out. A room prepared, a crib and baby supplies. I gave it all away."

He popped the snaps down the front of his coveralls then pulled them off his shoulders, stepped out of them, and stuffed them into a black plastic bag. "You may not be a soldier, but you have a soldier to support you." Brian moved to a sink. Rachel followed. He opened a large can, took a handful of skin cleaner then scrubbed his face, hands and forearms. A few minutes of work with a nail brush followed. He finished washing with bar soap then pulled a clean towel off a shelf above the bench.

Rachel, now teary, brushed a few strands of hair out of her face. "It was like the nightmare that never ends. Except for women who've gone through the same thing, most people in my life didn't understand my loss, they treated me like my child never existed and thought I should be happy and jolly like nothing happened. They wanted me to just forget about my baby like he never existed. It was so painful."

Brian moved to her side.

She buried her face in his chest as he wrapped his arms around her. "He was real to me from the moment I knew I was pregnant. I was his Mother, who let him down."

"I wasn't around so can't tell you what happened, but my medical knowledge and experience have taught me that it's rarely something the mother did. We don't know why but it happens. You didn't let him down."

"I loved him. He grew inside me. I felt him moving, listened to his heartbeat. I experienced a tragic evening. In one seven-hour period, I killed someone, caused my husband's death, and the same evening lost my child."

"Traumatic events may result in a miscarriage."

Hands on hips, she spat out her words. "Miscarriage. What a terrible, non-descriptive word. It doesn't begin to describe the depression's crushing embrace inflicted on a Mother when she loses a child."

"What can we do for you?"

"Staying close is enough for now."

He put his hands on either side of her face, kissed her lips.

She wrapped her arms around him. "Being out here, far from the locations of Dov's and my son's deaths, is wearing especially today. It's like..." She paused to run a hand through her hair. "Like I'm on an emotional hike but it's always uphill and gets steeper over time. Negative emotion weighing me down and take the next step." She stared at the floor.

Brian raised her chin, wiped a tear off her cheek, and kissed her. "Miscarriages happen all the time, but no one wants to talk about them. Perhaps you could get together with women who've experienced similar loss. Exchange thoughts and ideas. My understanding is, someone loses a child during pregnancy and no one wishes to discuss the event. As you said, you felt him move, heard his heartbeat. I would imagine others feel the same. You could write an editorial in our local paper with a brief discussion of your own experience. Give our phone number and see if anyone would like to get together."

"If more than a couple people showed up, someone should be present to lead the group."

He pointed at her. "You, pretty lady, would be perfect."

"I don't have a clue how to do that."

"I'll talk to a psychologist I know at the hospital, get some ideas."

She still appeared apprehensive.

Brian added. "You could meet with her. If you wish, I'll help lead the first meeting. If you think it will help, use my name, state that I'll be there."

Rachel spent a number of hours writing an article which Brian edited and made suggestions to improve the clarity of a few points.

Within hours of the article's publication in the local journal, with its suggestion for a gathering, it began raining phone calls. Intermittent showers at first then a deluge. Each caller wanting to know when and where the group was meeting.

Rachel held up the newspaper and pointed at the article. "Struck a chord."

Brian shook his head. "I wonder how close this trauma is to the PTSD which a soldier experiences?"

"Come to the meeting and find out." She smiled at him and kissed his cheek. "One more thing we'll need."

"Tell me."

Evidencing a serious expression, she said, "Numerous boxes of tissues to wipe teary eyes."

Chapter 19

On the designated Sunday afternoon, the meeting of those who'd experienced miscarriages was scheduled for two o'clock. By one-forty-five, the circular drive in front of the house was filled and Brian was directing cars to park in back. A diverse group of women arrived, young and old alike, most carried homemade baked goods to share.

To Rachel's surprise, Chana Goldberg and Brian entered together. Both stood at the doorway and observed the crowded family room. They approached Rachel then Chana announced, "I had a miscarriage at age twenty-two during my fifth week. I've never talked about it. To anyone."

Rachel gave her a brief embrace. "I'm glad you had the courage to come."

"When I got out of my car, I'm sure I appeared scared to death. Poor Brian rushed over to check on me." Brian laughed. "In truth, I was considering getting back in my car but, I hope you don't mind, he embraced me then walked me inside."

The petite lady smiled at Chana. "I don't mind. I'm just glad you're here."

The tall women sighed, shook her head. "It took more energy than you can imagine. As recently as an hour ago, I had decided not to attend."

Brian said, "I hope you're in a place where you can share your experience."

"No." She raised her hands, palms forward while shaking her head and taking a step back. "Definitely not. Listening to others will do for today."

As the attendees approached the house, a light breeze rattled the leaves of the liveoaks. Their sound combined with the wind chimes, thereby providing a warm and welcoming audio for the arriving guests.

The ladies gathered in the family room, the fireplace's flames and crackling logs providing a convivial environment. Chattering among themselves, they were seated on furniture, folding chairs, bean bag chairs, and pillows on the floor.

Brian introduced himself and Rachel. They welcomed everyone to their home then began the meeting with a prayer. "Please Lord, help each us achieve a modicum of peace through shared discussion and fellowship."

Rachel asked for a volunteer to detail her experience, fully expecting she would have to share her personal journey first to get the others talking. Rachel looked around the room.

One hand went up.

"I'll share mine," a petite, white-haired, and rosy cheeked woman said.

Rachel nodded and indicated she should stand.

With the help of a cane, the woman stood, glanced around at the group.

"I'm Majella Clark. I was born in Galway, Ireland, 84 years ago in the year 1890. My family came to the states when I was ten. We settled in Dallas. I've lived here all my life. My second husband passed two years ago. I married the first when I was 16. I experienced a number of miscarriages. In those days, a miscarriage was blamed on the mother. I wasted thousands of hours wracking my mind attempting to divine what I did wrong. My first husband divorced me as he didn't want to be childless. Those were the darkest days of my life. People stared at me as if I killed my own children. No one, and I mean no one, would talk to me about what happened. I felt shunned and shamed." Majella stopped talking to look over her audience. "Eventually, a woman I worked with at a textile mill befriended me. She'd miscarried then suffered the same as me. Only one person out of the hundreds I knew, was willing to talk to me about the loss of my child. Like a beacon of light, Kiana guided me on a path out of the depths of my depression." She paused to pull a handkerchief from her sleeve and wiped her eyes. "Like a child lost in a dark wood, she took my hand, guided me out." Majella took a deep breath and smiled. "I believed I'd never have children, but she introduced me to her brother. He married me even though we believed we'd never have children but, bless the Lord, we brought six healthy children into the world. After the first four, I did have two additional miscarriages before the last two healthy births."

"The additional miscarriages, please tell us about those," Rachel suggested.

"Tragic, of course, but I had my other children to occupy me. My oldest daughter stepped up when I became depressed following the miscarriages. She did her best to engage me in conversation, and made sure I was busy so didn't dwell on the loss. And my second husband didn't belittle me as the first one did. He reminded me I was a good mother and my children needed me. Benjamin constantly reminded me that we married to share a life as a couple, not only for the purpose of having children."

"Your friend?" Rachel asked.

"Kiana passed twelve years ago. Lives with the angels, I'm certain."

"In your opinion, how did she help?"

"I'm not a professional but, looking back, she acknowledged that there had been a living being in me. That was important as it validated the feelings that I was a mother."

"Do you believe you would have been more upbeat, avoided depression possibly, if you had strong support from your family?" one woman asked.

"In those days, people didn't talk about some things. Miscarriages were one of them."

"We should know better today," a second women said. Most nodded agreement.

"But still, with all the medical knowledge we have today, it continues to be painful," Rachel said. "Thank you for sharing your story with us, Majella."

After two more women voiced their experiences, she announced a break. She and Brian brought out tea and soft drinks.

Brian leaned toward Rachel and whispered, "At least two of the speakers are showing signs of PTSD."

"At the end of the meeting, I'll mention you have cards of a therapist."

Following the break, Rachel called on Chana Goldberg to detail her experience.

The thin woman shook her head and wouldn't stand until Majella, who sat near her, took her hand then said in a quiet voice, "You're surrounded by friends, dear. We'd love to hear from you."

Trembling, Chana stood and spoke while staring at the fire. "Even with my mighty college degree and all the books I read about a miscarriage not being the mother's fault, to this day, buried deep inside me, there exists guilt which is my constant companion. I lost my child four years ago."

"Did you have support from those around you?" Rachel asked.

Chana closed her eyes, sighed while shaking her head, finally looking at the others. "I tend to be withdrawn. I would do anything to avoid painful situations. I couldn't voice my shame let alone initiate a conversation, until today," A nervous smile crossed her lips. "Y'all are the first to know."

A few people clapped, many smiled encouragement.

"Did the child's father know?" Rachel asked.

Chana's eyes tearing, she swallowed hard. The woman next to her held up a box of tissues. Chana thanked her, lifted a tissue, and dabbed at her eyes before continuing. "I'm ashamed to say," she paused to take a deep breath, "I had a number of partners during a night of drunken revelry. No clue who the father was. Losing my child, and the way I became pregnant, was a shameful, devastating experience which I kept to myself. It has inhibited my behavior in a myriad of ways. I believe it has prevented me from staying in relationships with men."

"In what way?" Rachel asked.

"I'm an honest person, so eventually I'd have to tell an intended life partner what I did. The thought of that overwhelmed me, causing me to find a reason to end any promising relationship."

"Thank you, Chana," Rachel said. "I encourage you and everyone else to make a new friend today. What could be better than a new friend who understands what we've all been through?"

Another women detailed her experience then Rachel spoke. "The same night I lost my child, my husband, who was home safe after surviving a year in Vietnam as an infantry soldier, was shot and killed. I entered a deep depression. Even my choice in clothing reflected my somber mood. The days immediately following were little remembered. The trauma so great, I experienced short term memory loss. I loved, and still love Noah like every mother who was able to hold their child in her arms. As others have stated, I was his mother from the moment I was aware I was pregnant."

She wiped her eyes with the backs of her hands before continuing. "I withdrew from many activities, considered giving up on my lifetime goal of becoming a pre-school teacher."

"How did you get over your sadness?" a woman asked.

"Four years after that tragic event, and still trapped in a deep depression, a man with a three-year-old son entered my life. Suddenly, two people needed me. I refused to allow the depression to overwhelm me as my new responsibilities kept me focused on using my energy to help raise that child, and making a home for him and his father. The times when my depression was close to overwhelming, their love lifted me." She turned and smiled at Brain as she spoke. "They will never understand how close I was to throwing my life away." Rachel turned back to face the group. "But I suspect many of you will."

Many heads nodded agreement.

Rachel continued after looking around the room at the diverse group. "I know my behavior is still inhibited by the loss of my child. My mood darkens every year on the anniversary of Noah's death."

She gazed around the room at faces which understood and felt her pain. The thin lady wiped her eyes. "Before you leave today, please make a new friend. Call that friend during the week, get together, and talk. For anyone interested, my husband has cards from a therapist he recommends." Rachel took a deep breath and her expression brightened. "There's still tea and coffee. And please, help me finish the pastry!"

"When are we meeting again?" a woman called out.

Rachel appeared surprised then replied, "How does the second Sunday, same time, next month sound?"

Many checked appointment books, wrote notes to save the date.

Three women approached Rachel. "I'm Anne Rubin, this is Tory Benson, and you know Majella. We propose the four of us, if you'd join us, and anyone else who is interested, should meet next Sunday at the same time to organize in a more formal manner, work out leadership, publicity, outreach and whatever else we can think of."

"A steering committee," Rachel said.

"Precisely," Majella said, while the others nodded.

"Ladies, I'll have tea and coffee ready at two next Sunday."

Rachel announced their intention and an invitation to the other attendees.

Chana remained to help with cleanup. She walked the room, emptying trash cans of tissue into a black plastic bag. Brian removed the folding chairs to the garage.

Willow-figured Chana approached Rachel and said, "A weight has been lifted. For the first time in years, I feel...this is what healing must be like, but I still have a long road ahead of me." Chana took both of Rachel's hands in hers. "Having you as a friend is a blessing."

She embraced Rachel who said, "Steering committee meeting for this group next Sunday same time."

"I'm not a leader."

"Neither am I, but we need ideas. You're a head full of brains. You should be here to give us your thoughts and ideas."

Chana shook her head, took a bag of garbage outside. Upon re-entering the house, she announced, "Next week...I'll be here."

The willowy lady headed home wearing a broad smile.

Rachel entered his office and sat in front of Brian's desk.

He was reviewing the notes he'd made during the meeting. "Successful first get together," he said without looking up from his work.

"It was. Next time, you need to disappear."

Eyes wide and jaw dropped, he said, "What? Hell no. These experiences will help my research."

Rachel shook her head. "Having a man in the room, especially one making notes, was inhibiting to some of the women."

"Did they say anything?"

"No, but I could see it. Particularly those close to you. They appeared anxious."

"This was my idea."

"An excellent idea but you won't be visible during the next meeting."

His voice getting loud, he said, "I'm a doctor...doing research. They should understand and accept my presence."

"You were the doctor who caused anxiety. And as a doctor, you are a man not a god. Sometimes you forget."

His face turned beet red as he attempted to control his boiling emotion.

Rachel expected a verbal explosion but instead he swore once then stormed away. Brian drummed for an hour then returned to tell her he would do as she asked.

"By the way," Brian said, "short term memory loss is a symptom of PTSD."

"What are others?"

"Let me get my list." He dug through a drawer and removed a notebook. Flipping it open he said, "According to the Mayo clinic, post-traumatic stress disorder symptoms may start within one month of a traumatic event, but sometimes symptoms may not appear until years after the occurrence. These symptoms cause significant problems in social or work situations and in relationships. They can also interfere with an individual's ability to go about normal daily tasks."

Rachel picked up a pen and legal pad then began taking notes.

Brian searched through papers on his desk, picked up a report then told her, "PTSD symptoms are generally grouped into four types: intrusive memories, avoidance behavior, negative changes in thinking and mood, and lastly, changes in physical and emotional reactions. Symptoms can vary over time and may not be consistent from person to person. More specifically the first type, intrusive memories, are those which may include memories of some traumatic event which repeat, flashbacks of the event, nightmares based on the event, or emotional or physical reactions to reminders of trauma."

He flipped through a few pages then continued. "Avoidance behavior, as is its name describes is avoidance of memories, such as, locations of activities, or people are a remainder of a traumatic event. With negative changes, one or more of the following may occur: negative feelings, such as a general feeling of hopelessness or memory problems like memory loss concerning details of a triggering event. In addition, difficulty maintaining relationships, feeling separated from family and friends, a lack of interest in activities enjoyed prior to the onset of symptoms, problems experiencing positive emotions, or feeling numb. A few or many of these may take place and are perceived as negative changes."

"Give me a minute to finish my note on the last one," Rachel said, writing furiously.

Brian paused until she indicated she was ready then began reading again. "The last group consists of symptoms of changes in physical and emotional reactions (also called arousal symptoms) such as, being easily startled or frightened, always being mentally alert for danger when there is little threat. Self-destructive behavior, such as drinking too excess or driving too fast, problems sleeping, trouble concentrating, feeling irritable demonstrated through aggressive behavior or angry outbursts may also be symptoms. In addition, all-consuming guilt or shame."

"Are some symptoms more obvious than others?"

"They can vary in intensity. More PTSD symptoms may express themselves when the individual is stressed, or when he encounters reminders of what the traumatic event caused them to experience. Examples might be loud noises similar to those experienced in combat, which may cause an individual to feel like they are back in combat. Hearing or seeing a traumatic event may trigger a reaction where one may feel overwhelmed by the memory of his own traumatic event." He paused for a bit, looked up at her then said, "You realize when I use the word he, I'm also referring to women, or children."

She nodded, wrote a few more notes. "I understand. I'll make a poster listing the symptoms. You will please, get me an easel so I can put it up at the next meeting along with the number of a therapist."

***

They returned to the ranch after Friday night services. Brian held sleeping Seth in one arm. Walking up the few stairs to the front porch, Rachel said, "This is a bit embarrassing, but I've wanted to ask...you've had a number of partners..."

"Yes, but..." He unlocked the front door, stood aside so she could enter first.

"Brian, do I take care of you...please you when we..."

"Absolutely."

"You're not just saying..."

"Let me put Seth to bed."

"I'll put the kettle on."

He returned, took a mug of tea from Rachel's hand then sat next to her on the front porch. A panoply of stars filled the sky while a raucous rhythm section of night time insects provided audio accompaniment.

Brian said, "There's a strange component to sex. When you're close to someone up here," he tapped his forehead, "the sex is fantastic. I can't tell you why but I know it's true."

"So..."

He put an arm around her. "Yes, pretty lady. You take care of me." Brian evidenced a broad grin. The veteran nodded then giggled. "Oh, my Lord you do."

A contented smile appeared on Rachel's lips. "Thank you. I needed to know that."

"And you enjoy what I do?" Brian asked.

She thought for a bit then, blushing and unable to look directly at him, replied, "Once, a friend told me her husband takes her there. When you and I...well...I know where her husband takes her, and it's a great place."

"Excellent."

Brian noticed Rachel kept crossing and uncrossing her legs plus rubbing her hand son the tops of her thighs. "Something wrong?" he asked.

"I have news," she replied, while using one hand to straighten her collar.

"Tell me," he said.

"In a minute," she said. Rachel stared at the stars then straightened her collar again.

Rachel sipped his tea then shivered. "The temperature's dropping. Perhaps we should go in."

They stood.

Rachel smiled. "I love how Seth helps the other children at pre-school."

"Is that the news?"

"He'll be a great brother."

"Some future day, I'm sure that will be true."

Rachel cleared her throat, then said in a nervous voice, "Actually, in a little less than nine months."

Brian picked her up then spun her around while giving her a long kiss.

"Easy," she said.

"You nervous about another miscarriage?" he asked.

She nodded and said, "Terrified."

"Whatever happens we'll manage."

"It could be a struggle."

"In case you haven't noticed, I was made for struggle. We've supported each other no matter what the problem since you moved out here. Pretty lady that will not change." He held her against him.

Rachel slipped her arms around him and rested her head against his chest. "I know." She sighed, then stared at the stars. "Thank you, Lord. I know."

***

Brian, Rachel, and Arnie, who was out for a week-long visit, gathered in front of the fireplace in Brian's office.

From behind his desk he said to Arnie, "Couple incidents from the war have been coming up lately."

"The exploded head our first night in combat?" Arnie said. "That one still bothers me...like it was yesterday."

"The guy I killed with the pen," Brian said.

"That was bad I imagine. Glad I didn't see it...didn't watch the guy die."

Brian shrugged. "Not so bad at the time. Not enough time to bring my rifle to bare, so used the pen." He stared at his lap. "In truth, I felt happy that I stopped him but I felt guilty afterward. Then felt worse due to the way people in the market, as well as my platoon mates, looked at me."

"In what way?" Rachel asked.

"Like I committed an act of atrocity that a normal human being wouldn't do."

"It was bad for those who saw the guy on the ground in death tremors," Arnie said.

"A pen?" Rachel asked.

"I jammed it through his eye and into his brain."

"Describe what led up to the incident," Rachel said, rubbing her hands on her thighs.

Brian watched her reaction as he talked. "I stopped to write a note in a marketplace. For whatever reason, the eight of us, generally in pairs, had spread out and most were negotiating purchases. Dressed like every day Vietnamese, these, we think, three guys were just wandering the market about thirty feet apart. They, simultaneously, pulled out frags...fragmentation grenades. The idea being, to toss them toward the Americans who were scattered around the quarter block square, market area. Also insuring many of the venders who were selling items to the G.I.'s, were also killed. One guy was next to me." Brian took a deep breath, noted Rachel paying rapt attention to his description but still rubbing her hands on her thighs. He took another sip of his drink before continuing. "My rifle was between my knees so I could write a note. I didn't have time to bring it up. Fastest thing I could do was the pen."

Rachel shuddered. "Why did you feel you faced a deadly threat? You didn't know what he was going to do."

"I saw the frag...hand grenade...come out of his pocket. He was about to pull the pin."

"I see," Rachel said, rubbing her chin and appearing deep in thought.

"One of the thrown frags came in my direction," Arnie said. "We were on the other side of the market."

"Your reaction?" Rachel asked.

"Used my M16 like a bat, sending the frag toward the edge of the market...where it exploded, killing a villager and wounding many. The third grenade had a bad fuse, it went off just out of the enemy soldier's hand, killing him and injuring a number close by. None of us were hurt."

"Our radio man began yelling," Brian leaned back, sipped his drink. "We had to get back to day position immediately. Lots of folks hurt and we were ordered away."

"You must have felt terrible," Rachel said.

"Orders are orders," Brian said with a shrug. "You follow them, or people die."

"But just leaving the wounded..." Rachel said. She shook her head in disbelief.

"In the military," Arnie said, "you must believe, leadership has an overall view, therefore, know what needs to happen."

"Leaving the wounded..." Rachel said, continuing to shake her head, "Don't know if I could have done that."

"When we arrived at day position, we could hear helicopters in the distance," Arnie said, "we were told to gather our gear as they would be arriving to transport us to the Central Highlands to support other troops. Within ten minutes we were many miles away."

They were quiet for a while, sipping their drinks, each lost in their own thoughts.

"You mentioned another incident?" Arnie asked Brian. "Something horrible?"

"Scott Hendricks-remember?"

Arnie nodded, sipped his drink. "Yea. You and I weren't in-country yet. He used a machete to chop a guy's arm off."

"I talked to him recently. He lives in Dallas and told me it didn't bother him at the time. When it happened, Scott laughed about the blood spurting out of the guy's wound landing on his chest, but now he's been having nightmares. Something about the guy's eyes staring at him."

Quiet enveloped the room for a few minutes.

"That's enough war discussion for now," Arnie said with a yawn. He stood. "Night all." The Brooklynite headed for the guest room.

"Are you having nightmares about the killing with the pen?" Rachel asked after they were alone.

"Not so much a nightmare but reliving it in other ways."

"Like?" Rachel asked.

"At the baseball game with Arnie three days ago, someone in front of us stood, slowly turned to look our way. As he rotated his head, I became apprehensive that he would have a pen sticking out of his eye." He stretched his shoulders, forward then back. "I was going to do some research that night but was afraid I'd read something which would trigger a nightmare."

Rachel crossed her arms. "I remember that night. You got angry with me over something I thought was trivial. We had words then you drummed for an hour."

He nodded and kissed her cheek. "Sorry. Tough to get a grip at times. Gets so damn frustrating. Even had thoughts of dropping the whole research project."

In a firm tone, Rachel said, "Bullshit. I won't allow you to let down your fellow vets because of your frustration."

"Frustrated? I can't get people to even discuss my findings. Of course I'm frustrated."

Shaking a finger at him, she remonstrated in a loud voice, "This will continue to be a multi-year project. Get used to it. I'm in this for the long haul, which is also how you should be thinking."

Brian held his hands up in a gesture of surrender. "Just said it came to mind. I'm not dropping anything."

"Good," Rachel said, then asked, "Did you talk to Arnie about getting hauled out of Yankee stadium?"

He shrugged. "Said it was blown out of proportion. Laughed and said he downed too many beers."

"That's odd. As far as I can remember, he doesn't drink beer."

PART SEVEN: AUNT ABBEY AND WAR VICTIMS

Chapter 20

1975 January

"Rachel, this is a treasure trove of information on the mental state of Civil War Soldiers; both during and after the war."

Brian spread the papers out in his office, arranging them chronologically. Stopping to review many of them.

"My aunt's papers...useful then?" Rachel asked. Seated in a rocker, she looked up from the, care-of-newborns, book she was reading.

"Oh my Lord, more useful than you can imagine...heck, more than I hoped for. My final research will have to list her as a contributor." He rifled through a number of papers then held one up. "Consider this letter. Not war related but a demonstration of the depth of her thinking. She acknowledges differences between the closeness of women to nature and, as she describes, the desire of men to bend nature."

Rachel tilted her head and asked, "Does she give an example?"

"She mentions a sylvan scene at the edge of a lake. Aunt Abbey loved watching a flock of geese bob in the water then describes one taking off. She then discusses a man adjacent to her viewing the same thing, but he wonders what it would take to make a flying machine which could carry a man."

Rachel rubbed her chin, twisted slightly then folded her hands over her, thirty-five-week, swollen belly. "Interesting..."

"Also, she mentions women are reminded they are child bearers on a monthly basis from their teen years on, which could make them feel closer to nature than men. Aunt Abbey felt this was something she should take into account when treating women with mental concerns."

Brian was lost in reading and note taking for the next four hours.

"Rachel," Brian said as he and Seth joined her at the kitchen table for lunch, "Abbey discusses being part of a team making it more likely for a soldier to engage in killing."

"Because..."

"Not wanting to let down your fellow soldiers."

"Example, please," Rachel said.

Brian thought for a bit then said, "I suspect crew served weapons, those who loaded and fired cannon in Aunt Abbey's day, tank crews, artillery, sniper teams, and machine gun crews, in our day. Each a team and depending on each other. I certain she's correct." He ate quietly for a while. "The research I've done would explain the success of the Greek and Roman phalanx occurred for the same reason."

Rachel looked up with a questioning expression.

"The phalanx was a group of soldiers working in unison but with different weapons such as various types of spears or bows, and lead by men holding shields. They depended on each other to complete their mission."

Brian said, "It's like...Dr. Kaplan is talking to me. Her voice coming through time as clear as can be. She must have been possessed of extreme intellect and sense of compassion, not to mention sense of drive. Her analysis of the soldiers, not to mention analyzing herself, must have been painful. And she knew she didn't have answers but thought we might one day so her observations are written for future use."

"After spending a number of years as a surgeon during the war," Rachel asked, "surviving what must have been traumatic horrors, what motivated her to work on this?"

"Can only tell you why I did the same. But words like dedication, compassion, commitment, and curiosity, surely describe her."

"And what motivates you, Brian Levin?"

"Before I joined the Army, writing a book about combat. But then older friends returning from Vietnam suffered terrible depression, although we'd likely call it PTSD now."

"And now?"

"The burning desire to understand the psychological impact of war on a soldier, as well as his society. I'm coming to believe, the need to understand and take corrective action in regards to combat and returning soldiers is greater than ever."

Brian put logs in the fire place and started them burning.

"I was thinking," Rachel said, "about your research showing many men in combat are reluctant to shoot their fellow human beings. Consider, please, animals of the same species don't kill each other. Like males competing for mates, their combat rarely results in a death."

Brian stared at her, jaw dropped.

"What's wrong?" she asked.

"You are a genius," he said, bent toward her, planted a long kiss on her lips then returned to his desk chair, writing a flurry of notes.

Rachel left the room briefly then returned with tea and slices of cheese cake.

"Thank you," he said then sipped the tea. He ate a few bites, stared out the office's windows briefly, rubbed his chin then said, "I just remembered a WWII story my Dad told me. My father was a crew chief on a B-26, twin engine, bomber. He flew on many of the missions his aircraft went on. On one mission a waist gunner was wounded. Dad placed bandages on the man then took his place at the fifty-caliber machine gun. Thirty minutes later he spotted a lone fighter approaching. Dad fired a few bursts from the gun, putting tracers over the fighter's canopy. The enemy aircraft immediately banked away then headed for the tree tops."

Rachel queried, "And that is significant because...?"

Brian rubbed his chin for a bit while formulating an answer. "If you're good enough to put tracers near an approaching plane's canopy, you're good enough to hit and destroy that plane."

"But why didn't he..."

"Never thought to ask. But your observation that animals rarely kill their own kind may explain many stories of front line troops I've read who were reluctant to engage the enemy."

"What about those who fought in fighter aircraft?" Rachel asked.

"Among American fighter pilots during WWII, ten-percent of the pilots accounted for ninety-percent of the kills."

Rachel nodded while stating, "Which corresponds to Marshal's estimate of only ten to fifteen-percent of combat soldiers engaging the enemy." She engaged in quiet reflection for a few minutes then asked. "How did you feel toward the enemy soldiers?"

"Feeling ranged from dislike to indifference when I was over there."

"And now..."

"Strange but I feel a sense of brotherhood. The brotherhood of those who have fought a lethal struggle at their country's behest."

"Thought of a name for our child?" Brian asked.

"Tradition says we name after a relative who has passed."

"Such as..."

"If a boy, William, after your grandfather, if a girl, Abbey after my Great-aunt."

"William or Abbey...love those names." He came around the desk and kissed her.

***

A month later, Brian rushed into the family room late one evening. Rachel was just hanging up the phone. He exclaimed, "I have to tell you what I discovered in Aunt Abbey's papers. She discusses war fatigue in terms of a boxer, who can only take so many blows...but in a soldier's case, blows to their mental state."

"Love to discuss it in few days," Rachel said, standing then arching her back.

"Why?"

"Abbey or William is arriving tonight. Chana will be here in five minutes to baby-sit Seth."

Chana arrived, obviously more anxious than Rachel, assisted Brian in getting her friend out of the house and into the Olds.

A noisy car ride and seven hours later, those in the delivery room were treated to the sight and sound of a battle-hardened combat soldier dancing with his newborn, Abbey Louise Levin, while singing Leslie Gore's, "Sunshine, lollipops, and roses, everything that's wonderful is what I feel when we're together..." followed by numerous choruses of the Beach Boys', "I Can Hear Music."

***

Brian entered the bedroom they had converted into a nursery, where Rachel, seated on a rocking chair, was nursing two-month-old, Abbey. Seth played at her feet.

"But I thought when I have a sister," Seth complained, "she would play with me. Abbey just eats and sleeps." He giggled. "And poops her diapers."

"She'll be able to play with you but needs to grow first," Rachel told him.

Disappointed, Seth went back to building with his construction blocks. Brian plopped into a chair.

"What's wrong?" Rachel asked Brian, seeing his concerned expression.

"I've mentioned a platoon mate, James Ware. Donna, his wife, called. She's worried about his mental state. Wants me to visit."

"We'll all go. She might need support as well."

"Abbey?"

"Will help."

"A newborn? How?"

"Go. Pack. But first, please put a small suitcase in Seth's room."

***

Mid-morning, a light snow was falling at the Ware home in Butte, Montana. Having arrived the night before and staying at a hotel, the Levin family met James, his boys Mitchel and Corey, ages ten and eight, plus wife Donna.

"Tea or coffee?" Donna asked Rachel who held Abbey.

"Decaf coffee would be marvelous," she said then followed Donna into the kitchen. James' wife gave the boys soft drinks then sent them to a spare bedroom which had been converted into a playroom.

James invited Brian into their living room, motioned his former platoon mate to sit on a small couch in front of a crackling fire which glowed from the base of a large stone facade. He moved to a bar, opened a small fridge and removed two beers, popped the caps off, handed one to Brian then sat on a dark leather covered, recliner.

After conversation between the Army buddies on how things were in general, James said he hated driving the mining truck. "The trucks are slow, only an occasional turn or dumping the load to break the monotony." He slowly shook his head. "The diesel engine drones and drones. I hate it." He rocked his upper body slowly side to side. "I can hear the fucking thing even when I'm not at work."

"Thought you enjoyed it...that you would enjoy driving it after our Army service."

James shook his head. "No longer." He sat then slouched on his recliner, extending the footrest. He took a long sip of beer. "I got a radio in the cab, can even play eight tracks, but that damn low pitch droning goes through everything…some days like a jack hammer in my head, and there's nothing to think about except what I did to those people, them kids…wow, it hurts. Somehow, I gotta get this shit outta' my mind." He violently shook his head.

"How was your arrival home?" Brian asked.

"Met by a crowd at the LA airport carrying signs against the war. Was spat on." James stood, walked over to the fireplace then used a fire poker to move the logs, which caused their flames to brighten. Bits of glowing ash shot up the chimney. "Should a slugged the long-haired, little shit but was so shocked, I didn't do anything. A cop grabbed him.

Hauled him away" He was quiet for a while, sipped his beer then said, "What we did, it was okay when we were over there. We was following orders, so it was okay, right?" James shook his head, stared at the fire. "But the people we killed…they should leave me alone. Not tell me their names and shit."

Brian's jaw dropped; shocked the memories were talking to James; a certain sign of psychosis. "James, we need to get you some help."

James continued as if he hadn't heard. "You was a sniper. You watched 'em die through your scope. Don't it just burn your insides? I mean, can't ya' still see 'em go down?"

"A few…but this is what happens in a war. It's what's expected of a soldier."

Brian motioned for James to sit in a chair opposite him. He waited until he had James undivided attention. "Life…it's like…heading out on a march with an emotional rucksack on your back." He paused to choose his words. "Sometimes it's uphill…sometimes downhill…the rucksack heavier or lighter…but each day you begin by lifting the rucksack, no matter what it weighs then keep moving forward."

"Forward? I'm trying man…but the stench of the jungle, the scent of the market place, my body starts to shiver when I think of shooting them two kids…when we was scattered along that trail, hiding behind trees and shit, shooting at them kids. All that crap is holding me back, weighing me down."

"Buddy, I agree it was a terrible situation we were in…but remember, they were shooting at us."

"Yea, and they're dead and we're okay."

"If we didn't return fire, they may have killed us…and we didn't know we killed kids until it was over."

James shuddered. "That one kid, Vo, keeps asking me…why him? Why his family had to suffer but not mine. Hell, he's the same age as my Mitchel. He had a family picture in his back pocket just like I carried." James stood, walked up to the fireplace, stared at the flames, poked the logs for a bit then asked, "You remember, don't you? That family photo Vo had?"

"Sorry, I have no memory of that. How do you know his name?"

"He told me. I know 'em all. They all been telling me their names and shit."

"When?"

The truck driver's face contorted as if in he was in pain. "When I see them, in agony, twisting and turning in the dirt, like they're trying to escape from death's embrace…but they know it's coming…they stared at me…their eyes dark, full of hate."

In a voice which strained to remain calm, Brian said, "They were over one-hundred yards away. Even with the illumination rounds, you couldn't have seen that they were kids. They were dead by the time we approached and learned those two were maybe ten or twelve-years-old." Brian shook his head. "James, I'm worried you're imagining more than actually occurred."

"No man. This shit happened. I can see it. I can feel it. I can smell it. It's as real as you and me sitting here."

"I'm going to make a few calls. You need to talk to someone."

"You?"

"Not qualified. Muscle and tissue, I know how to repair, but someone else has to get the demons out of your mind."

James stood and walked to the fireplace, said in a subdued voice while he poked at the burning logs, "Ain't no demons." He put the fire poker in its stand then shook his head. "They're kids I killed."

***

"My back is sore. Would you mind holding Abbey?" Rachel said to Donna after they'd finish cleanup following lunch.

Seated on a rocker in their living room, Donna took the bright-eyed infant in her arms. A warm smile and radiant expression accompanied the song Donna sang to her. The tiny one waved her arms and made cute vocalizations which brought an even broader smile to Donna's face. She sang another song then turned to Rachel. "Isn't taking care of these tiny one's the most precious gift God gives us?"

"It certainly is."

Donna smiled, rocked the little one who returned her smile in kind.

"Like to tell me about your concerns in regards to James?" Rachel asked.

"Voices. He's hearing voices, and I'm afraid he's listening to them as if they're real. At times, he argues with them."

"Do you feel he's dangerous or might become dangerous?"

"Just concerned that his mental health is less than normal, but what if it gets worse? I lay in bed at night worrying, having a tough time sleeping. For the most part the boys haven't noticed."

"Brian knows of a number of veteran's groups and is involved with the VA. He'll know who to contact if he believes that's necessary."

"Mitchel found James arguing with one of his imaginary...what should I call them? Friends?"

"Was your son frightened?

"Concerned would be a better description. He told his father that there wasn't anyone in the room. James smiled, said he was talking to a memory."

Abbey began yawning after a third song, Donna placed her in the crib James put up for the tiny one's visit, and tucked a blanket around her.

***

"I left a phone number for a VA counselor," Brian said to Rachel on the flight home.

"Donna seems overwhelmed by his behavior."

"Perhaps she should see a counselor as well."

Brian checked his son who was fast asleep. "A while ago, you mentioned you had another life experience I should know about. Seth's asleep...might be a good time to tell me."

Rachel nodded. "My sister Mirna, sixteen at the time, and I were watching television, my parents gone to Florida for a week, a noise at the back of the house startled us, we ran to her room. She told me to hide in her closet once it was apparent strangers had broken into the house. Mirna piled dirty clothes on me. She slid under her bed, where they found her. I listened while four men abused her, peaked out at one point, saw them. The police found three, who my sister and I identified, and some years later, as I've told you, killed the fourth, who was trying to find and kill me."

"What effect did this have on you?"

"I took a self-defense course and began carrying a knife in my purse."

"Mirna left home because?"

"The note she left for my parents, only saw it once, indicated they wouldn't talk to her about the incident. They acted like nothing happened. Poor Mirna, and my poor folks. They didn't have a clue what to do with their two abused daughters."

"Know where she went?"

"A friend of hers said she took a bus to California." She thought for a while and said, "Not sure how, but, one day, I'd love to find her."

"I received a second letter from my platoon buddy who lives near Baton Rouge," Brian said. "On my dresser if you'd like to read it."

Chapter 21

Dear Sgt. Levin,

You remember I liked to sing Gospel music? My church choir was invited, along with other Baptist congregations, to sing at a gospel music festival in a huge church in Shreveport, La. I drove up there on a Saturday morning. You might remember, my home is near Baton Rouge, so about a three-and-a-half hour drive. Probably one-hundred of us attended, began practice after lunch that same day. Saw a lady about our age who looked familiar but put her out of my mind to concentrate on my singing. Saturday night, a few locals and I ate dinner at a funky little blues bar. We performed during the service on Sunday morning.

You know that bible passage that instructs us to bring a joyful noise before the lord? We fulfilled that verse by providing a melodic and energy filled performance. We rocked that old building to its foundation. The church members provided an outdoor buffet. Proceeding down the food line, filling my plate with turnip greens, okra, fried green tomatoes, and other southern delicacies. That lady I'd seen, seemed to be moving with me but stayed a few feet away. I spied a couple hams at the end of the buffet table; brown sugar coated and prickly with cloves so I didn't pay her much attention...

***

His plate, a mound of southern deliciousness, Paul looked for a place to sit.

"Excuse me sir, but are you Paul Slidell?"

Surprised at the question from the bright eyed, slim woman who now stood at his side, he answered, "Yes, ma'am."

"From Baton Rouge?"

"Have we met?"

"Ever rescue a girl from a burning building?"

"Candice!"

She grabbed his hand. Walking with a slight limp, Candice pulled him between a number of tables to an opening among the tall sycamore trees where her family members occupied three, lined up, picnic tables.

"Y'all hush," Candice yelled. She waited until she had their attention. "Y'all know the story of how I was rescued from a collapsed, burning building. How I was holding on to a soldier's shirt?" Dropping Paul's hand, she gripped his shirt. "I'm holding his shirt again."

A man of average height but stocky, leaped to his feet and ran around the table, shook Paul's hand then gave him a hug. Candice introduced her father, Thomas.

"An honor to meet the man who saved my daughter's life. And a fellow 101st Airborne veteran as well."

Overwhelmed, Paul said in a modest voice, "Just a soldier doing what needed to be done, Mr. Thomas."

Teary-eyed, Candice's mom embraced Paul for so long he began to feel embarrassed. Her husband finally pulled her away, saying, "Let the boy sit and eat, Anna."

Paul took a seat at the end of the picnic table opposite Candice's parents. She asked what he'd like to drink, returned with a tart lemonade then sat next to him, actually against him. He moved to make room for her. She leaned toward him, whispered with a giggle, "Come back here."

He chuckled, moved so their hips and shoulders were touching again.

"What outfit?" her father asked.

"2/327, Delta Company," Brian replied.

With pride in his voice and wearing a broad grin, Thomas said, "I went into Normandy with the 2/327 battalion on D-day, Charlie Company. Glider unit back then."

"They referred to us as Airmobile because we rode around in helicopters."

Paul and her father began trading war stories, both serious and hilarious.

When they were finished eating, Candice took him down the trio of tables introducing him to family members which included three cousins, two of whom served in Vietnam with the Marines and one who served with the Navy. Everyone was dressed in their Sunday best with the exception of a frumpy and disheveled women who appeared to be in her early-thirties.

"My cousin Nora," Candice said. She lives with and takes care of her invalid parents." Paul extended his hand and, with a quick glance, the frumpy woman met his hand with a limp grip and a weak smile. Ironically, she would become one of the most important people in his life.

He also met ten-year-old Betsy, whose parent's died in an airplane crash so she lived with her grandparents.

The couple sat again. Candice' father turned to his wife, said, "Mother..." She nodded and said, "Of course."

"We'd be honored son," Thomas said, "if you'd spend the afternoon at our home, and stay for dinner. We have a spare room you can sleep in at our place tonight so's you don't have to drive home in the dark." He motioned down the line of tables. "Most of the family comes over for Sunday dinner and we watch sports if there's a game on. Even those two Marines are invited." Most joined Thomas' laughter.

"Sounds great," Paul said.

Candice rode with Paul in his pickup, directed him to a modest craftsman home which was filled with family. After an hour of talking with Thomas, the two marines, and the sailor about their military service, Candice asked, "Would you like to go for a walk?"

"Love to."

They started toward the door. Betsy approached, her hands on her hips. "Aunt Candice, the boys are being mean. Can I go with you?"

Candice glanced at Paul who said, "Of course, young lady. Let's go."

Sporting a huge grin, Betsy grabbed their hands and led them outside.

A brisk breeze accompanied the trio as they followed a sidewalk to a small park, conversation between the two adults consisted of what they'd done since coming home which included many months of rehabilitation for Candice.

"I'm living with my grandparents because my parents died," Betsy explained. "That makes me an orphan."

Paul explained he was an orphan as well.

"I'm surprised a lovely woman like yourself is still single," Paul said to Candice.

With a twinkle in her eye, she replied, "When people asked, I always told them I hadn't found the right guy."

They returned to her home to watch the late afternoon football game. Betsy climbed onto his lap. "You got rough skin on your face. How did that happen?"

"Got too close to a fire."

"Did it hurt?"

"I was busy at the time so didn't think about it."

"Aunt Candice has skin like that on her arms."

"Same fire burned both of us," Candice said then kissed the scar on Paul's cheek, pulled his arm around her, and cuddled close.

***

Being an orphan, I didn't have family to welcome me home. No one excited to see me, no one to share stories with. Didn't realize how sad that was. How the lack of family made it tougher to get over the bad stuff I witnessed or took part in. The point I'm trying to make is, I had no pride in my military service after I came home. All the negative news coverage, the demonstrations against the war, the anti-military rhetoric, all of it depressed me. But with Candice's family, between Thomas and the other's joy at meeting a fellow vet...well...her family wasn't just proud of me because I rescued their daughter...but proud that I served my country. Every time her dad greeted me with our 2/327 battalion moto, "No slack," the words reminded me to be proud of my unit. The closer I felt to her family, and without saying the words, they made me feel my participation in the war was appreciated. I started to feel good about myself and my service...and damn proud I was part of the 101st. Candice and I married after three months of dating We brought Betsy to live with us, and we had a son...but the war wasn't finished with us.

I'll write again when I have time.
No Slack,
Paul

***

Three weeks after their visit to Butte, Montana, teary eyed, and with deep sorrow written in her expression, Rachel entered Brian's office. "Donna called."

He looked up from his typewriter. "James?"

"Killed himself early this morning."

"Ah shit." Brian used both hands to cover his face, his head dropping to his chest, his eyes tearing. "Don't need this."

"I'm so sorry. He died in the parking lot of a police station. Seems he planned it so his family wouldn't be the ones to find his body." She walked up to him, putting a hand on his shoulder.

"Oh hell. Donna and the kids must be a wreck." He leaned forward, his elbows on his desk, his head in his hands. Without looking up asked, "Funeral?"

"Day after tomorrow."

"His parents?"

"Devastated. Lost their only child."

"Her parents?"

"Trying to get to Montana from Chile."

"I need to call Arnie."

Brian's eyes filled with tears, he stood, and Rachel embraced him.

He pushed her away. "After I call, I'm going to drum."

For the next hour, Brian punished his drum set with a steady tattoo of anger, frustration and sorrow.

Oddly, his wind chimes were silent. He returned to his office, slumped back in his chair. Rachel entered with tea and cookies.

Brian rubbed his face. "I wonder if he went for help."

"She said he did."

"It didn't work or was too late."

"Donna said he left a sealed letter for you."

He took a sip of tea, his eyes again filling with tears. Brian leaned back in his chair, stared at the ceiling then said, "I dread going to his funeral. My research keeps me sufficiently depressed, rubs my emotions raw. I need some time to deal with this. A few days would be good..."

In a stern voice, Rachel said, "Your fellow platoon mate...you guys arrived in-country together, served together. You will..."

He shook his head. "You don't understand. We had a memorial service for one of the guys in Vietnam. It was awful. One of the guys read a few bible passages, how our buddy had moved on to a better place. I pray that happened but couldn't wonder what the Lord thinks of those of us who hunt and kill our fellow man. Not to mention what he thinks of the ones who send us to do the killing. Tom McKenzie, nice kid, hadn't been in-country but a few weeks, a land mine tore him apart. Swore I'd never go to one of those again because the depression lasted for days and days. I could barely think straight, maybe we just show up at the funeral then come right home."

"We leave late this afternoon. I booked a flight. We'll also be there the day after the funeral. Donna will need help and support. If she wants, I'll stay longer."

"Rachel, please," Brian pleaded, "the depression I experienced was so painful, let's discuss..."

She interrupted. "We can discuss all you wish but pack first."

"Please, listen..."

Now with hands on hips, she remonstrated him in an angry voice. "I'll listen for as long as you like but Donna and her family will need our support. I'm going. That's the least I can do for her…for certain, you will accompany Seth, Abbey, and me. And you will begin planning what you will say to Donna and her children."

Dread of the depression which would accompany him, at and after the funeral, overwhelmed him. He slouched in his desk chair, closed his eyes for a while then rubbed his face with both hands. "Shit." Brian opened his eyes, approached his wife, and kissed her forehead. "I'll likely need your help with what to say."

For the balance of the day, Brian heard the wind chimes play a mournful tune.

***

At they walked up the steps of the church in Butte, Montana, Rachel asked Brian, "Arnie going to make it?"

"East coast is snowed in. Couldn't get a flight."

She cursed. "I know he wanted to be here."

They entered and saw Donna, who waved them to her side.

Following a brief service, Brian helped carry James' coffin to his grave through a heavy snowstorm on a blustery morning.

He thought, "The last thing I'll do for him." Brian's feet crunched through many inches of snow.

As a preacher droned on at graveside, Brian stood stiffly, Donna and her boys on one side of him, then Seth and Rachel who held Abbey. Tears streaming down his face, Brian silently lectured his friend who could no longer hear him. *"Not like this, man. All the shit we survived…to end like this…you…your family…all deserve better…all of us who went where our government sent us, we did our best to serve, not to end up like this after making it home."*

The snowstorm intensified. He raised his collar to keep the snow off his neck, then thought he heard the deep tones of his wind chimes, but realized it was church bells; their sound further depressing his mood.

The graveside service ended. The Levin family traveled to the Ware home. Donna and Rachel put out food for those who came to offer their condolences. After the majority of mourners left, Donna sent her children to the play room with Seth, approached Brian, and handed him a sealed envelope. Brian's name on the front, inside a message scrawled in an unsteady hand.

> *Brian,*
> *Sorry. I wasn't strong enough to pick up my ruck one more time. It's weighed down with the eleven, with what I did to them…it's just too damn heavy. How did I deserve to live and they didn't? I'm not smart enough to explain to Donna why I'm doing this. I'm depending on you one last time. I know you'll do that for me.*
> *Thanks.*
> *No Slack,*
> *James*

He turned to Donna. "This is addressed to me. You should read it but…sit down first."

She sat on a dining room chair, Rachel standing behind her with her hand on the widow's shoulder, Abbey in her other arm. James' wife took a deep breath, unfolded and read the letter, glanced at Brian then read it again. "What the hell is a ruck? What eleven?"

"The ruck is a kind of backpack. He's using it as a metaphor. He believed he killed eleven people. That memory haunted him and became more difficult over time, like a backpack with an increasing load."

"Get this away from me," Donna said in an angry tone. She threw the letter at Brian and folded her arms across her chest. "Why not ask for help? Why couldn't he tell me? He never once talked about killing…is there something I should have done so that he would have discussed this? My father was in the Marines during WWII. Didn't come home with…all this shit…at least I don't think he did." She stared at Brian. "Maybe it was me…what was I supposed to do?"

In a firm voice, Brian intoned, "No. It has nothing to do with you. Many soldiers aren't able to discuss what happened, even with loved ones."

She stared at her friends then said in a pleading voice, "I need him. The kids need their father."

Brian said, "And you feel guilty you're angry with him."

Donna appeared surprised at his comment. "He's dead. I've no right to be angry with him."

He shook his head. "Seen it before. Anger is a normal reaction."

Donna's face became red. She spoke with fury in her voice, "Angry? Fucking livid!"

Her teeth clenched and her hands tightened into fists, Donna stood. She spat out, "Anger? How about hate? At him for leaving us, at the God dammed government who sent him there; for no good purpose I might add. Lastly, hatred of those who should have known what would happen but didn't protect him."

"If I find answers…"

She interrupted. "Why him? He was a good dad and husband. Did he consider what he was doing to us? How do I explain to the boys?"

"I can refer you to counselors…"

Donna continued as if she didn't hear him. "It's like I didn't know him. One evening, the boys and I are rolling on the floor laughing at his antics. The following morning, he rips my heart out. How do you explain that?"

"It's the nature of his illness."

Donna's tears running down her cheek, her mind filled with righteous anger, her body shaking. "The bastard abandoned us."

Rachel put an arm around Donna, who was now crying hysterically, and helped her to her bedroom.

The boys returned at hearing their mother's cries.

They turned to Brian. Ten-year-old Mitchel asked, "Were you at that place that messed up my Dad?"

"I was."

"Are you messed up?"

"Not like your dad."

Through her closed bedroom door, Donna's sobs provided an audio back drop to the boy's sadness.

Young Corey stated, "Mom is crying lots."

Brian checked the weather, which was no longer snowing. He suggested he, Seth, and the brothers, head outside for a walk. He helped Seth into his jacket, boots, and gloves. The four-some walked in silence but for their footsteps crunching the snow; only interrupted by James younger son Corey's occasional sniff and random dry leaves blowing across their path. In the sky to the west, dark clouds gathered, as if in sympathy with their grief. Donna and James' youngest finally stopped walking and began sobbing. Brian picked up Corey, who rested his head on his shoulder. After a few minutes, Corey cried out for the moment, was put back on his feet and the foursome began walking again, Corey holding Brian's hand.

Another half-block of silence and occasional downy snowflakes began to fall.

Mitchel asked, "Dr. Levin, if I get to be a soldier, will I do what my dad did…you know…when I come home?"

Brian sighed and shook his head. "We'll talk before you go, and when you come home."

"Does this happen to a lot of soldiers," Corey asked.

"Not a lot but too many, especially after the Vietnam war."

"But you said you did the same stuff as my Dad. You seem okay."

"We don't know why some manage and others don't."

Mitchel asked, "Did me and Corey do something bad?"

Brian spun toward him, used his free hand to firmly grip Mitchel's shoulder then spoke in a forceful manner. "Absolutely not. No way. Your father loved everything about you boys. You are wonderful children. Both your parents told me that. Your father suffered from an illness which is not your fault. Is that clear?"

The boys nodded.

Within minutes the weather changed from occasional feathery plumes to a squall with flakes the size of golf balls. Visibility decreased to half a block. The foursome slapped accumulated snow off their clothing.

"We should head back to the house," Brian said.

Two days later as the Levin family was about to head out the door for the airport, Rachel said to Donna, "Call me. Daily. More if you need."

"My folks will be here tomorrow," Donna said. "That should help."

Standing at the door, Donna was trying to speak but the words caught in her throat. Instead the widow embraced each of them. She took a deep breath to try to get control then told Rachel, "Don't know how I'd a made it if you weren't here. Bless you."

***

Their airliner gathered speed then lifted off the runway on its return flight to Dallas.

Brian said, "That was awful."

"Could be happening all across the country," Rachel said.

"The three of us who came in-country together believed, if we survived our one-year assignment, we'd stay in touch and grow old together. Now the first of us who made it home is gone." His eyes filled with tears. "We all had the same expectation. Make it through one year in Vietnam then back to a regular life. Once back, I was certain we could work out anything…James, his family…didn't deserve this."

"Maybe the information your research provides will find answers."

Brian covered his face with his hands, cried quietly.

Seth glanced at Rachel, asked, "Why Daddy cry?"

"Because his friend James died."

"Gone like Mommy Andrea?"

She nodded. "Yes."

The little one stared at his father, patted his arm then cuddled against him.

"Thought I heard the wind chimes at graveside," Brian said.

Rachel shrugged her shoulders and said, "Didn't hear anything but crying. I have a strong connection to Donna. And I feel like I just abandoned her."

Chapter 22

1976

Donna and her boys visited Texas for two weeks during mid-summer, one year and four months after James passed.

Upon their arrival at the ranch, Rachel mentioned, it appeared Donna had lost weight.

"I exercise to lose tension, avoid taking my anger out on my boys. Side benefit is being fit and losing twenty pounds."

Brian, Seth, and Rachel, who carried eighteen-month-old Abbey, helped them store their things; Donna in the guest bedroom and the boys sharing bunk beds in Seth's room. Donna noticed luggage in one of the other bedrooms.

Brian explained, "My buddy Scott is here for the weekend. We were in the same platoon in Vietnam." He addressed the boys, "Gentlemen, if you put on swimsuits, we can head out to the pool."

Standing in front of a large smoker, a slim man of average height, wore a BBQ cook's apron, insulated gloves, a swimming suit and tennis shoes. He opened the unit. A cloud of hickory smoke billowed toward the heavens. Scott Hendricks hung sausages below racks of lamb in the vertical section of the smoker. Two full-sized briskets had been in the horizontal end of the smoker since well before dawn.

"Scott Hendricks, this is Donna Ware, and her boys, Mitchel and Corey."

"Pleased to meet you," he said, removing an insulated glove before shaking hands with her and each of the boys.

"Scott's also staying with us for the weekend to attend our party tomorrow night and review some of my research on Sunday."

"Nice," Donna said, smiling at Scott.

"I love smoking meats," Brian told them, "but Scott is an expert. He arrived last night to season everything then was up at four this morning."

"Have to get up early to smoke brisket," Scott said.

"They'll be in the smoker for...?" Donna asked.

"Sixteen hours," Scott replied.

"That's dedication," Donna said.

"Have to do this," Scott said while motioning at the smoker, "or people would think I only have one accomplishment in this world." '

The others laughed.

"What's the other?" Donna asked.

"Physics. I'm a professor at UT Dallas."

"Swimming boys?" Brian said, then guided the younger ones to the pool.

After a brief conversation with Donna, Scott took off his cooking gear, dove in the pool where he and Brian played games with the three boys.

***

Rachel put sunscreen on Abbey. She and Donna relaxed in chaise lounge chairs situated in the shallow end of the pool, enjoyed iced tea and occasionally reached into the pool to splash water onto their bodies.

The boy's joyous peals of laughter filled the air as the men took turns letting them jump off their shoulders.

Donna, speaking in a wistful manner, said, "That's what they sounded like when James played with them."

"His absence...," Rachel said.

"Left a Grand Canyon sized hole in my heart." She took a long sip of tea while watching her boys frolic in the pool. "A hole in three hearts really."

"It's been a year and a few months since James died, how are you managing?"

"I've rearranged my life to try and cover things James would take care of, leaving no time for me to relax. Had some terrible days when I couldn't stop crying. Hard for the boys to understand how empty and alone I feel. But, it's like...in Montana when the weather is below zero for multiple weeks, the cold, gradually soaks into everything, cars freeze in garages, pipes freeze, gets more difficult to clear roads. You can't seem to find the right combination of clothing to keep out the chill. Substitute loneliness for cold, and that's how I feel. Every part of my life would be improved if I wasn't so lonely."

"Your friends?"

"They try and include me when they can but it's not the same as a partner. I get sick or overwhelmed with daily chores and there's no one to give me a break."

"Your folks?"

"Have a happy life in Chile where my dad teaches."

After another sip of tea, Donna watched Corey try to perform a flip off Scott's shoulders, laughed then asked, "Scott have a love interest in his life?"

"None that I know of."

"Seems nice. Great with the boys."

"Been a good friend to Brian. You ready to move on?"

"Not sure." She took a long sip of her iced tea; laughed as Mitchel attempted a back flip off Brian's shoulders which turned into a belly flop.

"They're having so much fun. I haven't heard my boy's voices like that since James died." As more screams and laughter echoed around the pool from the men and three boys, she added, "My boys deserve to have fun like that."

***

"Lunch is ready," Brian heard Rachel announce after she and Donna put a lovely spread on the poolside picnic table.

"Dry off and put your shirts on," the surgeon said to the Ware boys and Seth as they scrambled out of the pool.

"Be right there," Scott said. "Have to check temps, possibly add wood to the fire."

"I want to learn what you're doing," Donna said, hurrying after him.

"That Scott guy must really be funny," Mitchel said to Brian as they toweled off.

"Why do you think so?" Brian asked.

"Mom doesn't laugh much at home but she's laughing like crazy around him."

"I heard her tell Mrs. Levin, he's got a cute butt," younger brother Corey said. He shrugged. "Don't know why she'd even notice."

After a brief rest following lunch, the boys returned to the pool with Brian and Scott. As they could barely hold their heads up during dinner, they were in bed shortly after.

The four adults gathered outside on the patio adjacent to the pool deck, seated in director chairs around a fire pit. Abbey slept in a portable crib between Rachel and Donna. Brian used a lighter to start a row of Tiki lights burning as well as a few logs. The four friends were illuminated by the lights and the glow of flames in the fire pit. Scott filled mugs of beer from a keg for Donna, himself, and Brian, but served Rachel a white wine.

"You served with Brian?" Donna asked Scott.

He nodded. "About six months. Came home just before he went on R&R. I understand you lost your husband after he came home. I remember James. A good man. My condolences."

"Thank you," Donna said.

"While you were in combat," Rachel said, "if you don't mind me asking, I was told you received a Dear John letter from your fiancé. How did that make you feel?"

Scott stared at the fire pit then said, "Her letters went from love to hate in six months. I wrote her that I wanted to meet in Hawaii for my R&R...I thought we still had a chance to work things out. She replied with crap about my being a baby killer, a butcher...hated me...never wanted to see me again. My mother contacted her to find out what happened. She gave my mother a bunch of crap for raising a baby killer."

"Your reaction while you were still in Vietnam?" Donna asked. "If this is too personal..."

"No. It's good to talk...especially with folks who've suffered because of the damn war." He took a long sip of his beer, swallowed hard. "I was so shocked. Kept thinking it couldn't have happened. I walked around like a zombie for days...felt numb, couldn't sleep...kept reviewing our relationship, wondered what I did wrong, first anger then depressed for weeks, was sent to the rear for a while where they gave me some pills, which didn't do shit other than fog up my head, as soon as the pills wore off, I felt the same." He took another swig of beer, wiped his mouth with the back of his hand.

"And when you came home?" Rachel asked.

"Really, until I was back in the world, and after a number of sorrow-filled months, I realized it was the environment at home that caused her to turn on me. All her friends were taking part in anti-war demonstrations. The slanted news coverage encouraging them, the politicians and celebrities who were so vocal against the war, thousands in the streets, all hating the military." He thought for a while then added, "When I tried to contact her, she accused me of being like the National Guard soldiers who shot the students at Kent State."

"That must have been painful," Donna said.

Scott nodded. "You can't imagine, depressed for months." He stared at Donna for a bit then added, "On the other hand, some of us, or our loved ones, suffered worse pain."

Donna whispered, "Thank you."

"The guardsmen at Kent State killed four people, wounded eight and permanently paralyzed one," Brian said.

"Tragic," Rachel said.

"Why do you think it happened?" Brian asked his fellow vet.

"My expertise is in Physics but," Scott said after another swig of beer, "it does occur to me, if the guardsmen believed they were outnumbered, facing an angry, hostile crowd, who were two-thousand strong, if I remember correctly. Someone felt their life was in danger and pulled the trigger."

Silence enveloped the foursome as they considered Scott's ideas, the silence only broken by an occasional pop from the fire pit. They sipped their drinks, stared at the fire or gazed skyward at the canopy of sparkling stars in the North Texas sky.

"But they were unarmed college students, little more than children..." Rachel said.

Brian said, "And they were similarly aged, National Guard soldiers who'd never been in combat."

"If a large group of individuals" Donna said, "an angry, two thousand strong mob really, they were shouting epithets, calling you baby killers, throwing rocks at you..."

"I'd be scared," Rachel said.

"Enough to kill someone?" Scott asked, emptying his beer mug and staring at the others.

"The soldiers wore gas masks and had fixed bayonets. Shoot at college students? Have to be awfully scared," Rachel said.

"Not sure what I'd do," Donna said.

Rachel asked Scott, "Another?" He nodded. She refilled his beer mug.

"As the Vietnam War became more unpopular at home," Brian said. "I suspect there was a record set for the most "Dear John" letters being sent to soldiers."

In an angry tone, Scott mumbled, "Don't remember killing any babies."

Rachel glanced at Brian who returned her glance and mouthed, "I do." She shook her head.

"So how are soldiers enabled to kill?" Rachel asked.

"They must be trained. If S. L. A. Marshall's numbers are to be believed, only ten to fifteen percent of soldiers actually engaged the enemy during WWII and most previous wars. This increased to forty to fifty percent during the Korean War and ninety-five percent in the Vietnam War."

"Why the increase?" Rachel asked.

"During training, we used realistic, pop-up targets and were taught to react by reflex instead of taking our time and carefully aiming at a bullseye target. In addition, you received immediate feedback if you hit the target."

"What have you learned about soldiers committing atrocities?" Donna asked.

"They happen through a combination of conditioning, pressure of leadership, and of being part of a team."

"So you're saying, with the right conditioning, anyone will commit atrocities," Rachel said.

"My Lord, I hope not," Brian said while shaking his head.

"How do people deny that atrocity can or has happened?" Donna asked.

He walked up and back a few times then responded, "I suspect they say to themselves, because we are good people, we aren't evil, therefore evil doesn't exist."

Scott remarked, "During an evil event so atrocious, it put 100 million people in slave-labor camps, rivaling Auschwitz and Buchenwald, Soviet Marxists killed more peasants, workers, and even fellow communists than all the capitalist governments since the beginning of time, and acted like it was justified to achieve their socialist goals."

"And yet," Rachel said, folding her arms across her chest, "good people at the time it happened...and today, still deny this happened."

"So imagine a good person of German heritage," Scott said, "reads the history of the Holocaust. Must he deny, people just like himself, his own ancestors, perpetrated such a horror? If not, how can he live with himself?"

Donna said, "If you denigrate a population to the level of animals, as the National Socialists did with Jews and non-Aryans, then killing them may become an easier task."

"Perhaps that's why soldiers," Scott said, "make up degrading names for the enemy they face." He shook his head then added, "But I've always felt there is a brotherhood among soldiers, each of us doing what we feel is necessary for our respective nations."

The foursome stared at the fire in silence, each contemplating the concepts each expressed.

"Let's get off this depressing subject," Scott said.

"Tell us what you're doing in physics," Rachel said in a cheery voice.

The next few hours were spent discussing non-war related topics.

Brian yawned.

"We're going to bed," Rachel said. She and Brian bid goodnight to the other couple and proceeded to the master bedroom.

"They hit it off," Brian said.

"Both have been grievously wounded," Rachel said. "Healing together, could give them a strong foundation to build a relationship on."

***

On Saturday afternoon, the three boys played in the pool while Brian kept an eye on them. Scott and Donna filled canteens, a couple of plastic bags with trail mix then set out on a hike around the ranch.

Two hours before dinner, former medic but now doctor, Martin Evans arrived. He introduced his two daughters, Michelle, age eight and Janine, age five. The five-year-old seemed visually out of place with her red hair and green eyes.

Brian greeted his former squad mate with a strong handshake and a slap on the back.

He called Seth. After introducing him to Martin's girls, Seth invited them to the art center and playroom where Donna's boys played. The young trio hurried away.

Until the little ones left, Brian couldn't seem to take his eyes off Janine.

"She's not mine," Martin said.

"Sorry..."

"No need. I don't make an issue of it, but my wife became pregnant while I was overseas. I came home to a newborn, who she abandoned. I'm listed as the father on the birth certificate but was overseas when she became pregnant."

"Does Janine know?"

"Haven't told her. When she's older, I'll discuss it with her."

"Ready for your residency?" Brian asked Martin.

"Can't wait to get started. Thanks for the recommendation."

"We're putting the squad back together," Martin joked as he spotted Scott.

"Guys, I want you to meet someone," Brian said as he saw Krista Downey enter the backyard.

Brian briefly embraced Ms. Downey. He addressed the others. "Krista was a surgical nurse when I was a surgeon in Vietnam. She and her team of nurses were like a flock of medical angels, tending to the needs of the wounded. Scott asked for drink orders.

"Thought you'd returned to farming," Brian said to Krista after Scott handed her a glass of Chablis. They sat around a glass topped table under the extended eave of the house which shaded them from the intense, summer, Texas sun.

"Farming didn't hold me, kept feeling a need to help our fellow vets, so many troubled. Finished a master's degree in psych and applied to the VA, ended up here in Dallas."

"Compassionate Lady," Martin said. "Bet your patients appreciate you."

"Krista," Brian said, "Martin just completed medical school and is about to begin his ER residency at the hospital where I work."

"Before I forget," Krista said to Brian, "I have those letters from Laura Hetherington, the Civil War nurse, in my car. Front seat." She handed him the keys to her vehicle.

He retrieved them, stored them in his office, returned with a broad smile, and presented a hand written letter to Krista.

"You need to read this," he said. "This is from Rachel's Great-Great-aunt Abbey, written to her mother."

April 11, 1885
Boston, Mass

Dear Mother,
Blessed Laura Hetherington (formerly Grafton) and her family arrived today. Just as during the war, when I referred to her as a medical angel, Laura is full of energy and motivated to begin our new task. She will help me with my inspection of the asylum. As another medically trained individual, she will help me evaluate the living conditions and together we will make recommendations to alleviate the suffering of those poor souls living in, what she accurately described as, retched, squalid, and inhuman conditions. Of course,

Talia Warshawsky, Kaylee Gershom, Margaret Herzog and the Lombardi sisters will accompany us.

Speaking of retched conditions, Laura is aware and, as am I, horrified at the suffering of workers in factories. We'll gather with others who harbor like-minded concern and begin, hopefully, a movement which will be a force for change.

If only women could vote. The politicians couldn't shut us out and would have to listen to us. We could achieve change so much sooner. I've read women in Texas are organizing to that end. I am making an effort to contact them.

Laura has agreed to review my notes on veterans who suffer mental problems from their war time soldiering. She's written down some of her own observations, which we will discuss.

Much to accomplish but with strong, motivated friends, we ladies will set goals and work hard to achieve them.

Looking forward with great anticipation to your arrival next month. Your grandchildren inquire daily, how long until your arrival.

Love, Abbey

Krista opened her mouth to say something but instead, read the letter a second time. She turned to Rachel. "This is a treasure. Your Aunt, if her last name is Kaplan, is mentioned in a number of Laura Hetherington's letters that she sent to her parents during and after the Civil War."

"Kaplan it was. Brian has verified dates and unit assignments which prove they worked together," Rachel said.

"The other woman?"

"No clue," Rachel said. "But I've made identifying them my personal research project. A college friend who lives in Boston has relatives named Lombardi. I expect to hear from her shortly." After additional guests arrived, she invited everyone to the buffet line for dinner.

Before dessert, Krista told Brian and Martin. "I have a patient in one of my support groups. He has PTSD."

"Combat soldier?" Martin asked.

"No. A truck driver."

"Strange," Brian said, rubbing his chin.

They filled plates, sat in a group around the patio.

"I'm discovering more and more support personnel suffering just like the combat vets," Krista said.

"Support personnel? Why?" Martin asked.

"Just speculating, but unlike WWII, where, say, a truck driver might take supplies to the front line but went back to a relatively safe rear area; rear meaning behind the front lines and away from combat, a trucker carrying war supplies in Vietnam was never safe as there were no front lines. The truck driver I mentioned carried an M16 and a combat load of magazines in his truck, he was ambushed a couple times, saw one of his helpers ripped in half by a grenade."

"We should get together," Brian said. "Like to meet him if possible. Love to attend some of your group meetings."

Krista nodded. "Rachel told me her theory on support systems. I believe the idea has merit. It should be explored. Have another patient I'm counseling who spent his year in

Vietnam as a company clerk never in combat, has all the signs of PTSD but not diagnosed yet. I'll bring some notes on soldiers with and without support systems when they arrive home, nothing to ID them, just notes on their condition."

"Excellent," Brian said.

Brian smiled when he saw Janine and Seth walking around his antique John Deere, his son likely pointing out features then helping her climb up to the driver's seat and pointing out the controls and gauges.

Krista turned to Martin. "I remember Brian requested your help at the medivac station."

He laughed. "He did. You and I worked on a number of casualties. While Brian was a grunt, we didn't know he was a surgeon, some of us speculated but until they pulled him out, we weren't sure."

"You're following in his footsteps?"

"Not exactly. He's a vascular and surgical specialist. My interest is the emergency room."

Krista peered over the top edge of her glasses, smiled and said, "If memory serves, you worked with us during a week when we were short-handed."

"Our company was given a one-week stand-down. A time to relax, blow off a little steam," Martin said. "Brian heard and sent for me." He chuckled and shook his head. "Instead of relaxing for a week, I memorized tons of new procedures and placed more stitches than a mattress seamstress." The others laughed. "In that short time, I helped more soldiers than I could count."

Krista sipped her wine and shook her head. "I remember those seven days. We got caught with incomplete staffing."

She gave him a warm smile. "You worked long hours. Your help was much appreciated."

"Thank you," Evans said, nodding and returning her warm smile. "By the end of the week, Brian even had me close for him a few times. Unsure about my future before then but my work as a team member in the medivac unit convinced me my future was in medicine and specifically the Emergency Room."

"And," Brian said, "imagine how reassuring it is, knowing I have a battle-hardened doctor to depend on in our ER."

Krista said, "I only knew Brian as a surgeon. He utilized an amazing economy of motion, could work for long hours, picked up new techniques in a micro-second, and, like lightening, communicate his knowledge to new medical staff."

"Please, Please, Krista," Rachel pleaded. "Don't talk like that in front of him. Sometimes he forgets he's just a man."

The group laughed.

"In fact," Rachel continued, "A friend recently visited heaven. He saw a surgeon with the initials BL on his scrubs. My friend said to St. Peter, "So, you have Brian Levin performing surgery up here. St. Peter replied, That's not Brian Levin. That's God. He just thinks he's Brian Levin."

The adults were convulsed with laughter.

Krista finished her wine. Martin asked if she'd like another. She nodded. He took other drink orders then he and Brian headed to the bar.

When they returned with their drinks, Krista thanked Martin and said, "Tell me about your family."

"Michele and Janine. My wife left us one week after I came home, just after Janine was born. I haven't seen her since."

"Must have been rough on the little ones."

"The older one mostly. The little one too young to know what was going on. I was busy with medical school so couldn't' dwell on her abandoning us. My parents moved in to help. The children have adjusted to a degree, but being kids, still wonder if they did something to cause her to leave."

"Was your Vietnam service a problem for your wife?"

"May never know. She was like a stranger when I returned home. First hint things weren't right occurred when she refused to meet me in Hawaii for my R&R. Turns out she was three months pregnant. One day after Janine's birth, she left the hospital and disappeared. I found evidence she was abusing drugs. After her delivery, Janine went through a terrible withdrawal."

Rachel turned to the former nurse. "What was the most difficult thing about being a nurse in the Army?"

Krista took a deep breath then said, "Not showing emotion when walking up to a young man who lost a leg or similar grave injury, insisting he take his medications when he only wanted to die. What I really wanted to do was cry with him and hold him. And the other thing, smiling at men I knew had no chance of surviving, holding their hands until they drew their last breath, and then going to another patient and pretending nothing happened. That was heart wrenching." She picked up a napkin and blotted her tears.

"Don't know if I'd have the strength to do that," Rachel said, while putting a hand on Krista's shoulder.

Martin's children came running up. He introduced Janine and Michelle to Krista. Michelle said to their father, "Mr.

Hendricks said we can go for a hike with him, Seth, Corey, and Mitchel, if our dad comes with us."

Janine said, "Please Dad."

"It's still light outside," Michelle pleaded.

"There are beautiful trails around this property," he said to Krista. "Join us for a walk?"

She nodded. "Good timing. I was tired of sitting. Let's go."

***

Donna talked to Rachel after the evening's event while they washed and stored kitchenware. "Scott's nothing like James, who I adored, but I get a vibe from Scott like I did from James, which makes me feel, I'm not sure how to describe it."

"Good or bad vibe?"

"I've been so damn lonely since I lost James. Just having someone to hold hands with would be a blessing."

"How was the hike this morning?"

"We discussed a myriad of topics. Scott and I share values around religion and family. I find it easy to talk to Scott because he can talk about his feelings. I know where his head is at, and he listens carefully when I discuss what I feel."

"All good things, I would think."

"I was telling him about James suicide, its impact on the boys and me. I cried. He held me. My Lord that felt great." Donna shook her head. "Impossible relationship. He's sophisticated, an intellectual giant, and I'm a high school graduate, and a full-time housewife. Spent all my life in mining country. Scott's spent his entire life living near downtown

Dallas, and since Vietnam, surrounded by academics." She seemed to organize her thoughts as she hoisted a stack of dishes then put them on a shelf. "The year he started college; I was pregnant with Mitchel. Makes me sad but our backgrounds are as if we're from opposite parts of the galaxy..."

"And yet he's attached himself to you like a flea on a hound dog."

Donna laughed then became serious, turned to Rachel. "He makes me, only known him for a couple days, is it sappy to say, I feel better when he's near me?"

"Not sappy at all."

"Do you have feelings like that toward Brian, when you met as adults?"

Rachel thought for a bit while she dried a platter, placed it on the counter then, with one hand on her hip, faced Donna. "So, he's this amazing surgeon who's smart as hell. My intellectual accomplishments consist of a handful of community college classes in pre-school education and psychology. But after getting to know Brian for a few days during Thanksgiving, I came up here to visit for a week." She giggled. "And haven't left."

***

Early Sunday morning, Scott and Donna left for church before the children were awake.

While serving breakfast to the boys, Brian whispered to Rachel, "The way they were touching this morning, I'll bet they spent the night together."

371

She laughed. "No wonder they went to church."

Brian chuckled.

"It's too cool for the pool today," Rachel said, glancing outside at the cloudy day. "Have other plans for the boys?"

"I called our neighbor to the north, Fred Wayne," Brian said. "He told me I could hitch up a team to his old freight wagon. I'll take the boys around our ranch, start teaching them how to take care of horses and handle a team."

"They'll love that."

Lunch time saw the boys bragging to their parents and Scott about two horses named Daisy and Dolly.

"They pulled us all over Texas," Seth exclaimed. "And I got to hold the reins. I learned how to watch the traces to see if they were pulling equally."

"We shoveled horse poop out of their stalls and put fresh straw down," Mitchel said.

"And we gave them water and we put out feed for them," Corey added.

Following lunch, Brian and Scott worked cleaning the grills of the smoker. Brian said, "I have the research I'd like you to review in my office."

Brian scraped burnt food off a grill with a brass wire brush. "You and Donna?" he asked his buddy.

"Usually I'm wound up tight as a drum. That woman talks to me and the tension...like...fades. Not sure how to describe it, but, she, I'd say she has a window into my mind. When I see you getting tense, the way Rachel takes care of you, Donna does that for me."

"Stay together and you'd have two teenage sons, not an easy task."

"If that's the price of having Donna around, not a problem, and truthfully, I'm enjoying the hell out of those boys."

Brian scraped two additional mesh grills then put them back in the smoker. "Your and Donna's backgrounds, so different."

"At the University," Scott said, "I'm surrounded by folks with IQ's up to the sky. Donna has an IQ up to the sky when it comes to me. Since the war, no one's come close to understanding, let alone helping me deal with my tension, until her. While surrounded by the, less than real, world of academia, a woman like Donna could help keep me stay grounded." Scott smiled then said, "Like to read your research."

Brian and he moved to Brian's office.

After reading for a few hours and making notes, Scott read a paper, written by a researcher, concerning a combat soldier, who, while on R&R with his wife in Hawaii, consumed copious amounts of alcohol. Driving around while inebriated, they were involved in a car accident where his wife became a paraplegic. He was so overwhelmed with guilt, he couldn't function. Shortly after returning to his unit in Vietnam, the man was given a medical discharge from the Army. The researcher wrote, it's important to consider, he never drank before his service in Vietnam."

Rachel and Donna entered the room.

"Poor guy." Scott said, his eyes tearing. "Attempted suicide when he returned home. The pain of what he did in combat combined with his wife's injuries; pain just piled on top of pain I suspect. At one point I was so distraught, that could have been me."

"Thoughts of suicide?" Brian asked

"Thank the Lord, I had my physics to keep my mind occupied. Talking to my Dad, a Marine in WWII, helped, until he died. At times, still get depressed to a point where it's tough to get out of bed."

"About your fiancé?" Rachel asked.

"Plus things I did in the war." Scott wiped his eyes then his chest.

"Why don't we drive into town for a coffee and then some window shopping?" Donna said, resting a hand on Scott's shoulder.

He nodded.

"I'll keep an eye on the boys," Rachel said, while feeding Abbey.

Donna mouthed a thank you.

As Scott and Donna walked to his car, Rachel noted Donna kept a hand on his shoulder.

Upon their return, Brian and Scott plus the boys drove to the hardware store to buy parts for repairs around the ranch.

Donna and Rachel brought books out to the patio. They read and sipped iced tea while Abbey slept in a nearby crib.

Donna said, "Scott isn't working this summer. Any chance he could stay here for the rest of the week so we can spend more time getting to know each other...with your and Brian's permission, of course."

"Scott agreed?"

"He'd love to. We'd have to drive to his apartment on the other side of Dallas to get additional clothing."

"Go," Rachel said.

"Brian won't mind?"

"He'll be happy for both of you, as am I."

***

"I could listen to music like that every day for the rest of my life," Donna said after the four adults attended a concert at the Dallas Symphony Orchestra where they listened to an evening of Mozart.

"Saturday afternoon," Brian said, "there is a children's concert. They're performing 'The Sorcerer's Apprentice' plus Prokofiev's 'Peter and the Wolf.' Seth's never heard either one. After the concert the children are allowed on stage to examine the instruments up close."

Rachel glanced at Donna who nodded. Rachel said, "Let's plan on it. We should phone Martin and tell him of our plans. See if he can bring Michelle and Janine. Maybe Krista can join us as well. "

***

The following Saturday morning, Donna and Rachel each wearing swimsuits and wide-brimmed straw hats sat at a small round table on the patio watching the boys, Brian and Scott, frolic in the pool. They shared a large pitcher of iced tea while relaxing under a warm Texas sun.

Donna reported to Rachel, "As Scott stated, we feel like Humpty-Dumpty except..." She took a sip of tea.

"Except what?"

"The war caused Scott and me to suffer a great fall but, unlike all the king's horses and all the king's men, our relationship is, a piece at a time, putting us back together again."

Rachel laughed, reached across the table and squeezed Donna's arm. "You feel you have a future with him?"

Donna hesitated, then said, "We've spent little more than a week together, but yesterday, just for fun, we checked out homes in Plano and engaged in a huge disagreement about private vs. public school, but, ultimately, and without malice, simply agreed to disagree."

"Wonderful but why Plano?"

"Scott said they have one of the best school districts for the boys and not far from where he works."

"Houses down here are going to be more expensive than in mining country, and college professors don't earn huge sums."

"He's been offered a position by some instruments company here in Dallas. They want him to research digital signal something or other. Scott asked my advice on whether he should take the job. He told me the kind of money they offered him. I didn't believe it until he showed me the written offer. It included stock options as well."

"A good amount?"

Donna picked up her tea, added sugar, swirled it, took a long drink then reached for the pitcher and while adding more tea, said with a grin, "You know I rarely use profanity but, when I saw the amount of money, the words, holy shit, fell out of my mouth."

The two women laughed.

"The houses we inspected," Donna continued, "more than adequate for our family, would have mortgage payments a fraction of his salary. Scott demonstrated we'd have money left over to set aside for the kid's education and a nice retirement."

"He's thinking of a future as a family..."

"Don't get me wrong. I'd like this guy money or no money, but..."

"As my Great-Grandmother Rebecca said, it's not that I want my children to be rich...but it would certainly help pay the bills."

Donna laughed. "That I can understand."

"Sounds like he's willing to make a commitment to you and your boys."

"Even said he'd sell his little car. Get a family vehicle."

Rachel, astonishment in her voice, said, "Sell his beloved Corvette?"

Donna nodded. "Also, Corey is bright as can be. He gave rapt attention to Scott when he was using a candle and two tennis balls to describe an eclipse plus planetary orbital motion. When Scott wrote down the equations of planetary motion, my younger son wanted to know how to use them and asked if he could keep the paper with the equations. Could be a good influence to have a man with a Ph.D. in physics in our home."

"I'd love to have you living nearby."

"Would make leaving mining country easier knowing I have a close friend a short drive away."

"Have you talked about having more children?"

"He said he'd be happy with my two but, knowing we can afford to educate them, I'd like at least two more."

Rachel eyed Donna for a bit. "But you still seem hesitant."

"We both have demons. It will take time to destroy them, may not be able to destroy them but, please Lord, at least adjust to them. That could be painful, a drain on each other's emotions."

"Might be easier to manage those demons as a couple."

Donna giggled. "That's what Scott said."

"Time to get the kids ready for the concert."

***

On Sunday, the two families and Scott met Krista, Martin and his two girls, at the Dallas Zoo. After two hours of walking, including twenty minutes admiring and feeding the giraffes, they stopped for lunch at the Serengeti Grill.

They ate at a large round table.

Mitchel asked Scott. "You were in that war like my dad and Dr. Levin. Did it mess you up?"

"Yes, but not as bad as your father."

"When you get upset because of the war," Corey asked, "What do you do?"

"Until I met your Mom, feel sad for lots of days."

"And now?" Mitchel asked.

"I stay close to your mom, we talk, and she helps me get over the sadness."

Rachel raised an eyebrow at Donna who appeared pleased with his response.

"Mom laughs a lot when you're around," Mitchel said, "but, you're different from my Dad."

"Your father," Scott said, "could drive a truck as big as a house. I couldn't do that to save my life. Heck, I have trouble staying upright on a bicycle."

The younger ones laughed hysterically.

"Can the kids lead around the next part of the zoo?" Seth asked.

Brian looked at the adults who nodded. "As long as you stay together, I don't see a problem."

The children were leading the way around the northern half of the zoo with the adults in a group not far behind.

Krista said, "Friends, I need your help."

"Of course," Rachel said, while Donna and Brian nodded.

"I find myself in an uncomfortable position. As I spend more time with Martin and his girls, I find solace in my relationship with Martin, but his girls, have questions about girl things."

"You're concerned because?" Brian asked.

"All of my adult life, I've interfaced with soldiers; grown men and women. I've led them, trained them, repaired them, gave them orders, laughed, cried, and mourned with them." Krista took a deep breath, took a moment to consider her next statement, grinned and said, "Never once, did one of them ask how to talk to boys or explain why boys are so mean."

The others joined her laughter.

"On a more serious note, Michelle needs someone to explain about love and sex."

"Her father..." Donna suggested.

Martin said, "I've asked Krista...I feel it will easier for the girls to hear from a woman."

"I have boys so it's lessons from a different perspective for me," Donna said.

Krista said, "I'm most familiar with the physiological aspects but Michelle needs to learn about the emotional side, what she should expect from a partner. I know what I want from a partner but never put those needs into words."

They walked in silence for a bit then Krista continued. "I'm also concerned about the emotional damage their mother's desertion may cause in the future. Like PTSD, in some cases not showing up for years. I need to prepare them for that possibility." They stopped to admire a row of pink-topped pampas grass. "Ultimately, I'll have to explain to them when casual sex is allowable. Inside me, I understand when I need a man. How do I get that across to a 13-year old?"

"May I suggest, they don't need all the information at once," Brian said. "When a specific concern comes up, address it then."

"When they have confidence in the information you're providing," Rachel said, "I believe they'll ask more questions."

***

A week later and after Donna and her boys returned to Wyoming, a surprise visitor arrived at the front door of the Levin home.

"Just in time for lunch, Cousin," Rachel said to Arnie.

He was all grins as he embraced Rachel who guided him out to the pool area.

"Arnie? What the hell?" Brian said, climbing out of the pool and giving his buddy a wet handshake.

"Rachel thought it would be fun to surprise you."

"Good to see you. Come. Sit by the pool. Have to keep an eye on Seth and his friends."

Rachel handed him a Nehi grape soda.

"You remembered my favorite...thanks," Arnie said with a giggle.

"I saw the soda but didn't imagine it was for you." Brian said with a laugh then became serious. "Sad that Shira wants a divorce."

Arnie shrugged. "She's happier without me so...we're finishing the divorce paperwork and I'm moving on with my life. Rachel's set up an interview for me at the Jewish Day School in Richardson."

"As?"

"Education director."

"That's only thirty minutes from here."

"Great opportunity if it happens."

"Where are you staying?"

"Have a room near the airport paid for by the folks where I'll be interviewing."

Rachel, setting up for lunch on the pool deck, heard a car arriving, glanced at it then called to her cousin. She waved him to her side. Together, they walked across the pool deck to greet the new arrival. "Chana Goldberg, this is my cousin Arnie Zalman."

"Pleased to meet you," Arnie said, trying not to stare at her tall, thin, willowy figure.

"Hello," Chana said in a shy voice.

Rachel told her cousin, "Chana is the director of pre-school education at our synagogue." She guided them to the shaded table where lunch would be served.

"Something to drink?" Brian asked. "Iced tea, soda?"

"Iced tea would be fine," Chana said.

"Same for me," Arnie said.

Rachel called to Seth and his friends as lunch was ready.

While they toweled off, Chana suggested she and Rachel take the children to the amusement park in Carrollton.

As the children cheered, Arnie volunteered, "I'll help."

Upon return, the children related their experiences at the park while the four adults prepared dinner.

That evening, Arnie built a cozy fire in the family room fireplace where he and Chana continued conversing past midnight.

The following day, Rachel said to Brian, "I invited Arnie out but he's spending the day with Chana. They're visiting the Botanic Garden in Dallas then attending a Ranger's baseball game."

"The way they talked last night, they seemed comfortable with each other. I heard him telling her war stories; how he was injured."

"Please Lord, I pray they'll be a successful couple. She's dying for a family. Arnie is dying for children and hates living by himself."

"She's a gentle soul and he's a sensitive guy. Does he know about her miscarriage?"

"I told him. I honestly believe it doesn't matter to him. He'd gladly adopt, and since the group meetings, Chana said she's more comfortable with what happened."

"She's one caring lady. Hopefully, his war experience won't upset her as it did Shira."

Rachel appraised him with a questioning expression. "You and Chana..."

"Acquaintances, nothing more. Not my type. When I'd get upset, in other words, loud, she'd cringe, and try to find a place to hide."

***

Late the following day, Rachel, looking concerned, talked to Brian after the children were asleep. "I had a discussion with the woman who took my place at pre-school today when I picked up Abbey. One of the boys has tendencies to bully the smaller boys and the girls. After one of Abbey's friends was knocked to the floor, our daughter gathered four of her friends and, in the words of the substitute, they taught him a lesson he won't soon forget. I've spoken to her but would appreciate if you did as well."

"Sure. I'll talk to her."

"But first, get that proud-father grin, off your face."

Brian nodded but couldn't contain his grin.

"Another thing," Rachel said. "Have a talk with Seth. He was with me when I picked up Abbey. When he learned what happened, his face appeared just like yours did when you had your discussion with Samuel. I had to grab and drag our son out of the room. If I wasn't close enough to stop Seth, that bully would have suffered..." She put her hands on her hips. "Brian Levin, this is not funny. You must teach our son and daughter when violence is justified. Which means rarely!"

"Okay, Okay. I'll talk to both."

"Thank you. I've been meaning to ask, have you received another letter from Paul Slidell?"

"Arrived yesterday. It's on my desk."

***

Dear Sgt. Levin,

Hope you and the family are doing well. Nora and the kids are spending the day at a waterpark so I have time to get this story finished.

Learned of James Ware's passing. If you're in touch with his family, tell them I said he was a good friend, a good soldier, and will be missed by all of us who knew him. When I'd remember him, I'd imagine James driving that huge truck…his ever-present grin warming all who knew him. Can't imagine the depth of pain he suffered such that he took his own life. How are his family handling his death? I regularly say a prayer for him and his family…that they all find a sense of peace.

Last thing I mentioned in my last letter was the Vietnam War messing with me again.

It started in the middle of the week when we heard Candice's mother was going to the hospital for surgery, would be at the hospital for a few days then bed-ridden at home for a few more. We decided it might be a good idea for my wife, with our son Kevin, to drive up to Shreveport to stay with her folks to help out during this time. After a quarter hour's driving on the Interstate, a Vietnam veteran, high on heroin and according to his doctor, suffering from PTSD, collapsed at the wheel of his pickup truck. He drove across the median and slammed into Candice's car. The doctor said she died instantly. My son wasn't expected to live, having received a skull fracture and numerous broken bones. He was put into what they called a medically induced coma. I'm not sure why but you probably do.

When I arrived at the hospital, the docs told me it was unlikely he'd survive the next twenty-four hours, but the little guy passed that mark then survived another day and another. After a number of days, his condition improved to the point where the doctors ended the induced coma.

Remember that frumpy, chubby woman named Nora I told you about. She was living alone as her parents had passed. She called me the day after the accident, offered to come to Baton Rouge to stay with Betsy and take care of funeral arrangements while I stayed at the hospital with Kevin. I told her it would be a blessing...

***

"You have one tough son," the doctor told Paul, two weeks after the accident. "He's awake and alert. Ate a huge lunch. Another week or so and you'll likely be able to take him home."

Paul tried to thank the doctors but couldn't as sobs filled his throat. After regaining his composure, he called home to tell Betsy and Nora.

When he returned to the house for a shower and a change of clothes, the frumpy lady offered to stay with Paul until Kevin came home and afterward remain to help Kevin with his daily physical therapy.

"That would be most kind of you, Nora," Paul told her with a brief embrace. He noted her choice in clothing had changed, actually appeared stylish.

Nora stayed in the guest room. After Paul brought Kevin home, the adults would find a sitter and go to a movie or dinner on Saturday night. She got up every morning to exercise with Paul then both prepared breakfast for the children followed by physical therapy for Kevin. When he decided to begin running, Nora did that as well. Like a key in a lock, Nora fit into their lives.

Six months after Candice's death, Paul passed a park near his home. A woman played with two children. He was admiring the woman's lovely body then needed to jerk the steering wheel to stay on the road because he realized he was staring at...Nora. Paul performed a rapid U-turn, stopped in a parking space near them. As he walked over he remembered the first time he saw her. "Frumpy and chubby, no longer," he mumbled as he admired her curves.

Betsy ran to him and yelled, "Hi, Dad. Come push me on the swings."

While he did, he began reminiscing about Nora and what she'd done for him and the children. From housekeeping to guiding, teaching Betsy, plus six months of daily physical therapy with Kevin, his home was a place where Paul loved to live and work.

The following Saturday morning he drove to a florist and brought home flowers.

"What's that for?" Nora asked when he arrived home.

"It's our six-month anniversary," Paul replied. "Find a sitter. I have reservations at a great place in Baton Rouge so we can celebrate."

"We're just friends, you don't need to do anything special."

"You're more than a friend." He pulled her close, wrapped his arms around her, and kissed her lips. "I have a complete family again, woven from the yarn of your love."

Her expression radiant, Nora said, "Thank you. Those are the kindest words..."

"The children and I adore you. You've made this pile of wood into a home again. Never thought I'd want to get close to someone after Candice died because I felt like I'd been crushed. I never considered I'd find someone to fill the hole in my heart, but you, Nora Taylor, we belong together. Marry me?"

Tears filling her eyes and her throat tight, she nodded and whispered, "I'd love to."

***

We married up in Shreveport...same church where I married Candice. Nora asked me to put up two more flag poles so I can fly the 101st and POW/MIA flags on either side of Old Glory.

I'm still close to Candice's family, especially her parents. We're having them and some cousins down for Thanksgiving.

My work is paying good money. We're thinking of driving over to Texas next spring. We'd love to meet your family. Nora loves to tent camp but I'd like a shower every day so we may buy a camping trailer which we'll tow with my pickup. Do you have room so we can camp at your ranch?

One more thing. Nora is pregnant with twins...should arrive mid-March.

Hope to hear from you soon. Be well.
No Slack, Buddy.
Paul

***

The Levin family took the motorhome to a campground along the Gulf in Galveston, Texas.

They'd decided on a fish dinner. The family entered a small fish market adjacent to a fishing-boat lined canal near downtown Galveston. Just caught that morning, shrimp, red snapper, grouper, crab and other local delicacies were displayed on ice.

A young woman with a mischievous smile, yelled from behind the counter. "Sorry. No bread today."

Brian spun and stared at the familiar face. She ran around the counter and embraced him.

Brian introduced his wife and two children.

Dot introduced her uncle and his family.

"Where's your grandmother?" Brian asked.

"She's not here today but she will be happy you came to our market." She addressed Seth and Abbey. "My name is...Dot. Your father found me, burned, with broken bones and bleeding. I was dying. He gave me something for the pain, bandaged my wounds then sent me to a medivac station where they operated on me. After the surgery, he stayed up all night with me, reassuring me, a frightened ten-year-old, until I was moved to a hospital ship the next day." She stopped to wipe a tear off her face. "Your father saved my life, and arranged for me to be sent to Galveston for rehabilitation."

The children turned to their father, who said, "That's what doctor's do," paused for a bit then asked Dot, "And you? In school?"

"Of course."

"Boy friend?"

She giggled. "No! My grandmother warned me, threatened really, if I have time for a boyfriend, I can come to the market every day and clean fish."

They laughed.

Rachel asked, "Favorite class?"

"I live for Chemistry. My college major will be chemistry."

Brian gave her his card. "If you're in Dallas, we'd be pleased to welcome you to our home."

Rachel addressed Dot's uncle, "I'd like four Red Snapper filets, please."

He chose four fat fish, weighed then fileted and wrapped them in plastic film.

Dot whispered something to her uncle in Vietnamese.

He laughed, handed the fish to Dot who placed the filets in a bag along with crushed ice. She handed the bag to Rachel saying, "Souvenir you."

"I don't understand," Rachel said with a questioning expression.

"No..." Brian said.

Her uncle said with a bowed head, "You save my niece, so free fish for you today."

"Thank you." Brian said.

"You welcome," the uncle said. "And thank you for saving my precious niece."

"We're at a campground in Jamaica Beach," Rachel said to Dot. "Perhaps you and your family could join us for dinner Saturday night."

"An honor," the uncle said.

***

Rachel appeared puzzled on late Saturday afternoon as she finished cleaning a few utensils in the motorhome. She asked Brian, "How did the grandmother have the money to buy a fishing boat for her son? I was under the impression they left with nothing."

'They're here now. You can ask." Brian said, as he opened the door to the motorhome.

With Dot translating, Rachel asked her grandmother how she managed to get to Houston.

"An American bought me a plane ticket to Houston," Dot said as she translated for her grandmother. "He arranged all the paperwork. Then he and a friend bought an apartment which they rented to me. The apartment was near the hospital where Dot received her rehabilitation. I took a job in a bakery. Saved money and paid back the Americans then asked them for a loan to buy a fishing boat when my son arrived."

Rachel glanced at Brian. "You?

He nodded. "And Martin Evans."

"Why did the military bring Dot to Houston?"

"I said she had family in Texas. I believed she'd have the best care at a hospital in Galveston. Also close enough, either Martin or I could check on her."

"You trained there?"

Brian nodded. "Med school and surgical residency."

"But she doesn't have family..."

"I lied and said she was my child."

Rachel stared at him with a questioning expression.

He smiled and shook his head. "She's not."

They enjoyed further conversation. Brian noted Dot seemed fascinated with Abbey. She also taught Seth a Vietnamese children's song.

The evening ended with promises that the families would visit again.

***

Back in Celina, Brian looked up from his work as Arnie, now married to Chana, entered his office. Chana and Rachel, wearing expressions of concern, engaged in whispered conversation just outside the office door.

"Thought you were going to a ball game," Brian said.

Arnie, rubbed his red eyes, used his shoulder to wipe a tear off his cheek, his appearance was that of a man who was saddened and angry, like a man who was struggling to keep his emotions in check. Brian motioned to the couch. The Brooklynite plopped down then said, "Chana thinks I should talk to you."

"About?"

"There was this traffic accident, a station wagon, overloaded with kids going to a little league game, ran a red light...got slammed by a moving van, three or four cars collided into the first two." He twisted on the couch, kept crossing and uncrossing his arms and legs while he talked. "Kids got tossed out of the station wagon. I left my car with my first aid kit, ran up to the first injured kid I saw, knelt at his side. He's moaning, pleading for help. His left leg from the knee down...looked like it went through a meat grinder, his right lower leg one way...his foot the other...the foot attached to his leg by a thread of muscle. I felt light headed. The Army taught me what to do, watched you plenty of times...my first aid kit next to me. I was ready, but instead of helping the poor kid...I stood, walked a few steps and started vomiting. I wretched my guts out. People who were trying to help me, asked if I was in one of the broken cars. I glanced back at the little boy...other people were using my first aid kit to help him, but I couldn't help. A kid and, Lord forgive me, I couldn't help him. I staggered back to our car, told Chana she needed to drive me home. Instead she drove me out here. She insisted I talk to you."

Chana entered the room sat next to Arnie and tried to put an arm around him. He shoved her arm away.

"If you were there," Arnie said to Brian, "you'd a taken care of him. Taken care of most of 'em, I'll bet. But me..." His eyes filled with tears.

"Not everyone can do..."

In an angry tone he said, "Hell, man. You think I didn't notice? When you needed someone to help you with bloody injuries, you never once asked me."

"Some people..."

His voice now one of rage, Arnie shouted, "That damn kid needed my help today and I couldn't. If you'd asked me to help during the war, I'd a gotten over my nausea. But no." He shook his head. "Not the great surgeon. He wouldn't ask someone he thought was nothing but a scumbag for assistance."

"Arnie, I never..."

Brian's former squad mate waved a hand of dismissal then interrupted saying, "Remember the day you jammed a pen in that poor guy's eye? Didn't see it personally, but got sick just hearing about it. What a fucking loser I am."

"Treating bloody injuries is not something everyone can do."

The Brooklynite shook his head, saying, "Don't give me that crap. I'm a man...I was in combat. I should have been able but, if people, like you, didn't immediately assume I wasn't capable then given me a chance to get over my problem...I could a helped that kid today." He crossed his arms. "But no..."

"Arnie people are different..."

"Sure," his voice raising enough to rattle the windows. "You could be up to your elbows in intestines, the smell of warm blood, the stink of shit from torn guts...you ignored all that and worked to save them, and Zalman is off to the side puking his guts out." He shook his head. "Nobody offers to help me. You must have thought I was nothing but a damn loser. The genius surgeon is fucking right as usual. It's clear. To him, I'm not much of a man..."

"I didn't say anything of the kind."

Chana tried to get his attention then, red-faced, left the room. "You think, when you left the platoon, they asked Arnie Zalman to become the squad leader? Hell no. Ten months in-country and was never even asked to be a team leader. Did you, my good friend, recommend me? Of course not. They took someone who'd been in-country half the time I was, and they did that because he could do most of the shit you did, that I...wasn't trained to do. Me. Your buddy you came in-country with. I wasn't worth training."

"You had a different upbringing, you're a different person."

Arnie twisted on the couch and swore. There was fury in his voice and visage. "A kid. Laying on the pavement, bleeding out. I knew what to do but couldn't. Do you know how painful that is? Shit. Maybe you don't. I still see it today. Still experience the horror. Heads exploding into red mist, body parts torn off by artillery shells, men cut down like stalks of wheat, and you, you just kept shooting, not letting the suffering affect you. Allowing other people do what they could for the wounded until the firefight ended. Lord almighty, how could you? All your knowledge, your ability to repair grievous injuries, and you kept shooting. Talking on the radio directing arty which tore the hell out of people. Body parts flying everywhere with each explosion. Atrocious suffering in all directions. But, but you…I'd give anything to be able to do that medical stuff, and yet, damn you, you chose…I mean…you made a conscious decision, not to help."

"I had responsibilities as a soldier and squad leader…"

Arnie stood, walked to Brian's desk, hands on the desktop leaning toward him. The Brooklynite's body trembled as he yelled, "A trained…god-damned surgeon. What were you doing? Slumming with us grunts? Out to prove your manhood or some shit? After you left, everybody wanted to know why…your precious damn research you told me. What bullshit." He shook his head, then stood straight, placed his hands on his hips, and continued shouting, "And don't think I haven't heard, nobody wants to read your precious research. How many of our friends died so that you could complete, that fucking, waste of time, bullshit research?"

"Arnie, calm down."

The Brooklynite ignored him, didn't move, he just glared at Brian.

Brian stood. "I'm sorry you feel…I'll leave you alone…You need to calm down, then we can talk. I'll be outside." He left the room then discovered Rachel was listening just beyond the door.

They walked to the front porch, sat together on the glider. She put a hand on Brian's shoulder. "He didn't mean what he said."

"Bullshit." Brian sighed. "He absolutely did." He stared at the horizon. "Chana?"

"Left."

Brian sighed and said, "I've never seen him like that."

"My cousin is frustrated because of what happened today. The accident shoved in his face what he perceives as his inadequacies."

"He blamed me. Why all of a sudden? The entire time I've known him, I never heard him carry on like that."

"His anger is from his inability to follow in your footsteps and Shira walking out. He took his frustration out on you."

"It has to be more than that." Brian shook his head, turned to Rachel and said, "And he's right you know."

"Concerning?"

"He wasn't a leader. Arnie wouldn't or couldn't do the things necessary to become one. Not everyone can become a leader. Followers are important. And no, I didn't ask him to help with medical stuff because I'd seen how he, well, he'd get sick when he saw bloody injuries. He never took on responsibility, never tried to be a leader. I couldn't recommend him." He stared at the ground, glanced at Rachel then said, "Lots of guys couldn't handle the bloody stuff. Not a big deal. We each did what we could."

"Was he the only one who felt that way about you?"

"I suspect many of the guys believed I was wacko to be a grunt instead of a surgeon. But when they got hurt, they were glad I was around." He glanced at the wind chimes which were silent. "And he's right about the research. After months of phone calls and letters, I can't get anyone interested in my work."

"The war just ended. It will take time before people are willing to consider in an objective manner what occured. May have to wait until those in charge retire."

"All that anger. I wonder how long Arnie's suppressed how he felt about me."

Rachel shook her head, cuddled close, pulled his arm around her. "You'll see. He'll apologize and it will be like old times."

"No. Something's changed. He meant what he said. It will never be the same." He thought for a while, sighed and shook his head.

A sudden puff of wind blew across them, also animating the wind chimes, which played an anxious melody.

Brian continued, "When we meet again, every vile word he said today will be echoing in my mind."

Arnie walked out of the house, noticed Chana's car was absent, said in a subdued voice, "I need a ride."

"I'll drive you," Rachel said.

Head down, with a grim expression and not looking at Brian, Arnie offered his hand, said in barely audible voice, "Sorry. I didn't mean that stuff. Don't know what came over me."

"Don't mention it, old buddy." Brian stood and shook his hand. He watched as they got into her car, headed down the drive.

Upon her return, she found Brian reading on the porch.

Rachel sat next to him and said, "He was silent during the ride. But such anger in your office. Never heard him carry on like that."

"Believed I had a lifetime friend. No longer."

"Not true, and like you said to Arnie, people are different."

He kissed her cheek. "He's my good buddy since Vietnam. I feel like I'm missing something. His behavior was such a radical change..."

They stared at each other for a moment, both with expressions transitioning from confusion to certainty. They shouted in unison, "PTSD."

Rachel said, "That list of PTSD symptoms accurately describes his behavior."

Brian nodded. "The accident they witnessed reminded him of traumatic events in Vietnam. That's why it came on so suddenly. His behavior was manic in my office but surely depressed as he left. A definite sign of PTSD. The car accident and its casualties was the trigger..."

"I'll call Chana."

"Arnie needs to see a therapist as soon as possible. I know a therapist for Chana as well. If they're going to stay together, I predict they'll both need help."

"So sad. The war's impact on Arnie is tragic." Rachel shook her head. "Will your research do anything for people like Arnie?"

"In the short run no. But for future combat trauma, my research could yield huge dividends. Speaking of my research, I had a talk with the executive board at the hospital. They want to establish a department to perform research and asked me to manage it. The position requires a Ph.D. in medicine. The board is willing to give me a paid, one year sabbatical to complete a Ph.D. in medicine. This will allow me to finish my research, put it in thesis form, get it peer reviewed and get it published. I talked to Scott Hendricks and he thinks my research would have wide distribution if I completed the

Ph.D. and used my research to form my thesis. He's willing to use his background to assist me as well."

"This could be a huge time commitment," Rachel said.

"I'm willing to put in the time. All I have to do is think about guys struggling like Arnie and the effort will worthwhile."

"At last. I'm so happy for you." She stood and kissed her husband. "By the way, everyone I've talked to about getting together this summer in Montana around July Fourth has confirmed."

Chapter 23

1978

At dinner on Saturday, the first night at the log home in Bigfork, Montana, everyone sat around two long tables. The children were chattering away at one end near the window wall.

"Welcome everyone," Brian told the assembled. "So glad you've come out here."

"We've hired a naturalist," Rachel announced, "to take the children on an all-day Tuesday tour of the forests and lakes around here. We're renting two vans. Chana and Arnie will accompany that group. Any else interested, is welcome to take part in the tour. Just let us know. On Wednesday, we're organizing a trip to Glacier National Park."

Donna said, "We may be in far north Montana but the towns around here have great shopping and excellent eateries. I've made a list which I'll distribute."

"I've found fly fishing guides," Paul Slidell announced, "for those so inclined. Let me know if you're interested and we'll organize when and where. If you're a beginner and want to learn to cast a fly, I'll be lakeside tomorrow morning after breakfast."

"Tomorrow afternoon," Brian announced, "Donna's son Mitchel, plus Paul, and I are going to teach canoeing skills to the grade schoolers and anyone else who wishes to learn."

Seth yelled, "Yes," then high-fived with Vera, Corey, and Janine.

"Chana, Mary, Nora, and I," Donna said, "have volunteered to keep the tiny ones busy with age appropriate activities."

"I found a square dance caller for Saturday night," Scott said.

A cheer went up.

"Nora, Betsy, Mary, Donna and I have planned themed meals," Rachel said. "We have a plan for the week, including; Copper River Salmon night, Louisiana Creole night..."

Paul and Nora's son Kevin yelled, "Yes!" and threw a fist in the air.

The group laughed then Rachel continued, "New York style Italian evening, plus an Australian evening and a traditional Jewish Sabbath meal on Friday. Scott bought a smoker so Texas BBQ will occupy Saturday night's meal which will take place before our square dance. We'll be clearing out this room for the dance."

Brian whispered to Seth, "Anyone who goes home hungry after this week, it's their own fault."

Seth giggled, nodded then repeated Brian's remark to Janine who also giggled.

"For breakfast and lunches, just let us know how many people will be here," Rachel said.

"For those interested," Brian said. "I have copies of my research thesis in my office. Anyone interested, please read and I'd like your impressions."

Nora asked, "How is the research coming?"

"Distribution and getting people's attention was a nightmare. My solution was adding a Ph.D. to my M.D. All my work has been peer reviewed and published in medical journals. I received my Ph.D. a month ago."

The grownups congratulated him.

"Also, working on my current research inspired ideas for other areas which need investigation but are more cross disciplinary. One involves the structures of various toxic bacterium like anthrax. I have another doctor who will assist us. Martin Evans just finished his Emergency Room residency and is working full time at my hospital," Brian said. "He's volunteered to assist me managing the research department by proposing projects to improve our knowledge of toxic bacterium. We also found a physicist to work with us." He nodded toward Scott Hendricks. "Tomorrow morning, we'll have our first planning meeting."

Paul Slidell asked. "My expertise is finance. Any way I can help?"

"Not sure," Brian said with a questioning expression. "We've been thinking about setting up a lab but we're not sure of the best way to pay for it. Please join us in my office tomorrow morning at nine."

"Has anyone found any other vets from our platoon?" Paul asked.

"Lt. Senna," Martin said. "He lives in Omaha. Said he couldn't make it this year but asked to be included if we get together again. The Lt. said he knows SSgt. Touhy is living in Tucson, Arizona. I couldn't locate him but will keep trying after I get home."

"I'll be visiting Tucson next month on business," Paul said. "Let me try and find him."

"I found Mark Acorn," Brian said. "If anyone remembers him, he awoke in the middle of the night then starting shooting for no reason."

"Good guy," Scott said. "From California, if I remember."

Brian continued, "He's in the VA hospital in San Diego, living in a Psych ward. He experienced what I was told was a nervous breakdown and never recovered."

"So sad," Donna said.

"Also," Brian said. He seemed to hesitate for a moment then said, "I found David Trout. Lives in Seattle now. Hoped he and his family would join us. Gave him a call. He cursed at me, accused me of committing a war crime and said he still experienced nightmares about the killing in the market place and never wanted to hear from me again."

"That's rough on both of you," Paul said, He then turned to Martin and asked, "What was it like when you came home?"

"I was so busy in med school," Martin said, "I didn't have a moment to think about the war. When I finally had a break, some war events came to mind and troubled me, but I was so proud of the work I did as a medic and my week at the medivac center, I believe those positive memories overwhelmed the negative thoughts from the war. In fact, looking back, my brief time in the medivac unit is remembered in great detail...like it was more than seven days."

Brian asked. "It had that big an impact on your emotions?"

"I'm certain it did," Martin said. "But please consider, after the war, my thousands of hours studying didn't allow me television or newspaper time for a few years so the negative news had little impact on me."

Paul shook his head. "The worst for me was when I'd see enemy troops close enough to see their eyes. Easier to shoot the enemy at a longer range."

Martin said, "If one believes, as I do, eyes are a window to the soul, it is easier to kill someone at a distance as you don't have to look into their soul as you take their life."

"True," Scott said while nodding his head. "So true."

"Before we begin eating," Brian said as he stood and raised his tumbler of Scotch, "I'd like everyone to take a moment, and raise our glasses to a great soldier, friend, father, and husband, James Ware."

Donna mouth a thank you to Brian.

"I can't wait to get out and fly fish," Scott said.

"Scheduled for Tuesday," Brian said. "I've been looking forward the entire spring to getting out here to fish."

***

On a cool and clear Tuesday morning, Brian gazed to the east from the bow of a three-man drift boat that floated down the Flathead River. The rising sun, was just peaking over the mountain tops. From his viewpoint, the sun was filtered through an Aspen whose leaves were turning golden. The deep green sides of the valley, resplendent with Aspen and Pine trees, were now flecked with gold as the first of the Aspen's leaves transformed into autumnal hues. Gentle bird song filled their ears and cool, pine scented, mountain air filled their nostrils.

Four drift boats contained a fisherman at each end and a guide in the center seat. The guide advised them on their technique and where to cast. The guide also used oars to position the craft as it drifted. The boats were separated by roughly fifty yards. Brian and Scott, Martin and Paul, Rachel and Mary, plus Donna and Krista, cast dry flies onto the shimmering cold river, whose headwaters came from the glacier melt of Glacier National Park and the Bob Marshal Wilderness.

After a cast along the shore, Scott slowly brought in his line then asked Brian, "Arnie seems quiet. Stays apart from the group."

"He's not the same guy we knew. Arnie exploded at me earlier this spring after viewing the carnage resulting from a car accident."

"Hard to imagine Arnie exploding for any reason," Scott said.

"Wasn't pretty," Brian said. "Classic case of PTSD with a delayed trigger. Can happen months or even years later. Happy and jolly then symptoms ranging from manic-depression, anger, rage, and nightmares. The VA has Arnie visiting a therapist twice a week."

"He's gained a tremendous amount of weight," Scott said.

"It is the damn medications he's on. I'm working with his therapist to find another combination."

"How is Chana?"

"She's seeing a therapist every couple weeks for counseling. Gives her a chance to vent and understand why Arnie is suffering."

"Chana seems so quiet and reserved." Scott cast again, his line making an arc behind his head then lay across the top of the water. "I'm surprised she stayed."

"She's with him for now, but I fear for their future."

Scott shook his head. "Not fair to her. Sad the war would place such a heavy burden on such a gentle lady. Must take huge energy to accommodate his needs...in addition to their child."

"How are things now that you've published your research?"

"I've lectured at a few universities. You were right. My research is being circulated. Now I need to find a way to achieve changes based on the research."

***

Wednesday afternoon, most of the men and children plus Donna and Chana were out hiking in Glacier National Park while Krista, Nora, Betsy, Mary, Brian, and Rachel prepared the evening meal.

"Michael couldn't come out?" Krista asked Mary.

"Big project to present at work. This is the first time we've been apart since I moved from Oz," Mary said. "We didn't want the children to miss this event. An excellent chance to meet the people and their children who, if you consider how our lives intertwined, the war brought together."

"Martin is still super occupied in the Emergency Room, even with his residency completed," Krista said as she sliced and chopped carrots, "but since our wedding, he somehow manages to find time for the children and me plus volunteers at the VA two mornings a month. The nurses out there call him Mr. Patience because he sits next to the vets and smiles at the same stories week after week like he's just hearing them for the first time...which is exactly what those unfortunates need. Michele accompanies him occasionally. I predict a future in medicine for her." Krista scooped up the carrots, put them in a bowl then began slicing celery. She shook her head and smiled. "Martin is five years younger but treats me like a treasure. He dedicated a wall at our home for photographs and memorabilia of our military service, which means mostly pictures and awards of mine. Because of my nursing experience, I can appreciate and understand his trials and tribulations in the ER. He's told me our discussions help him keep his head on straight. And the girls have started calling me Mom. Michelle might be more excited than I am over this pregnancy." She turned to Rachel. "I created an art center at home like you have and she regularly spends time drawing pictures to put in the nursery."

"And Janine?" Rachel asked.

"She has a thing about Seth," Krista said.

"I've noticed. It's rather cute."

"More than cute," Krista said. "During yesterday's hike in the Flathead Forest, Janine was getting upset and loud over, what should have been, a minor incident. It seems to happen more and more often lately. Martin and I tried get her to calm down. She didn't until Seth, in a loud voice which sounded just like Major Levin when he needed someone's undivided attention, yelled, 'Cut the crap, Janine.'"

Jaw dropped and standing straight, Brian stopped fileting the salmon he was preparing then said in a voice tinged with disappointment, "I'm sorry he talked to her like that."

Mary said, while staring at Brian over the tops of her glasses, "Likely someone at home talks to Seth like that when he gets carried away."

Rachel nodded and gave Brian a disparaging look. She turned to Krista. "I am so sorry he used language like that."

Janine's new mom shook her head. "Don't be. Seth's words had an instant effect. Janine even apologized...to him, of course." She scooped chopped celery into a large soup pot then added the carrots. "In my wildest dreams as a parent, never would have said...cut the crap."

The others laughed with her.

Krista began dicing turnips and said, "Martin told me, the next time she acts out, we'll get Seth on the phone." While the others laughed, she became pensive for a bit, then said, "Martin and I and the girls, we struggle at times like most families, but overall we manage." She opened a package of fresh cranberries and dumped them in a sauce pan of boiling water along with orange zest, honey, a quarter teaspoon of clove, and a dash of cinnamon. "At times, our respective war experiences can depress one or both of us. Martin gets depressed thinking of things he could have done for the wounded if he had a little more knowledge. I look back and wonder if my training and leadership skills couldn't have been better. At times, I feel sad, depressed really, thinking of the wounded who died while we worked on them...but the blessing in our relationship is, thank you Lord, we're a family and solve problems as a family."

"That's what works at our home," Mary said.

"Same in Louisiana," Nora added. "Although, I do worry at times because I'm the third mother in Betsy's life..."

Betsy interrupted, "For certain, Nora loves us as if she was our birth mother."

Nora mouthed a thank you.

"I'm happy for you," Rachel gazed at the ladies, smiled and said, "Happy for y'all."

"Careful," Krista said, peering over her glasses at Rachel. "You're beginning to talk like a Texan."

Rachel giggled and said, "I find spending time with those of you who married veterans reassuring. I don't feel alone when memories of traumatic experiences occur because I know I can call one of you."

"I agree," Krista said, nodding her head. "I'll make up a list of everyone's phone numbers and distribute them."

Brian said, "The kids are returning from their canoe lessons."

Cory, Mary's oldest child Vera, plus Seth and Janine approached Rachel while she worked in the kitchen.

"Mrs. Kaplan," Janine said, "We, us four, think this place is missing wind chimes."

"I love their sound," Vera said. "But we think brass tubes would be better for this place."

"More of a forest kind of sound," Seth said. He turned to Corey who nodded agreement.

"What does the sound of wind chimes create?" Rachel asked.

"They remind us to be happy," Janine replied.

"Yea...happy," Seth agreed.

Rachel smiled and said, "Tomorrow, first thing, we'll go shopping for a set but you have make a hanger for them and help me decide where to hang them." She smiled at the group then asked, "Where's Karen?"

Vera shrugged and said, "Always hanging around Mitchel. Doesn't have time for us."

"Mr. Slidell is taking them out to learn some birding stuff," Corey said.

The young foursome headed outside, busy debating about and searching for, an appropriate location.

***

Late Thursday evening, Krista entered Brian's Montana office. "Dr. Levin, when you have a chance, I would like to talk to you about a war experience..."

"Now would be a good time." He motioned her to a chair facing his desk.

"Can we keep this discussion between us?"

"Of course." He closed the office door.

Krista twisted on the chair then cleared her throat. "The day you responded to the request for help, to aid the man with the unexploded shell adjacent to his chest, I volunteered to accompany you thinking it would be like any other surgical procedure. Afterward, I didn't sleep for two days as the gravity of the danger I put myself in registered." She again twisted on her chair then ran a hand through her hair. "Lately, I've had dreams where I hear an explosion then see my body torn like so many of the injured we treated." She gazed around the office for a bit then said, "I imagine the situation we were in was more like combat for you. Similar to other battle engagements you experienced. Something you knew how to handle, in an emotional sense."

He nodded and said, "It was."

Krista twisted on her chair again, pushed her hands into her lap then added, "Therefore you understood working under the pressure of possible imminent death. The grenade could have exploded at any moment. Killed or maimed both of us."

"We were careful, it didn't detonate, and we survived."

"What if something happens with the girls and we are in a similar position? Will I, without considering the danger, put myself, along with members of my family, in a life-threatening situation? What if the grenade explodes the next time?"

"I know a great counselor."

Krista shook her head. "No. I need to understand why I didn't consider the danger beforehand. I'd like to schedule a session with you weekly, starting next month, after we return to Texas so I can work through my actions and emotions."

"I'm not..."

She interrupted. "Martin and I agree. You were there. You'll understand better than anyone else. I've done enough counseling to know, working through my emotions with someone who's been there, gone through similar or identical situations, is the best thing I can do for myself, if you'll agree."

"Let's try. If it helps, we'll continue, otherwise..."

Krista nodded. "Certainly. I'll go elsewhere."

"I'm free Fridays. Early morning would be best."

Showing a sense of relief, Krista said, "I'll adjust my schedule to accommodate that."

"Good. Anything else?"

She hesitated, rubbed her chin then said, "One more item, please."

Brian nodded. "Of course."

"Instead of flying back to Dallas, Michelle and I are flying to Iowa to spend two weeks with my family."

"Nice," Brian said with a smile and a nod.

"Michelle understands my need for alone time to gather my thoughts and work out stress. I'll get her a library card and she'll have a delightful week of reading and my mother is going to teach her knitting. Michelle is looking forward to our trip to continue learning various farming skills and we'll be there on time to help with canning again this year."

"Martin and Janine?"

"Martin back to work but Janine, this is a big ask, but, could she stay at your home? I know you'll be working but Rachel and Seth have the ability to understand and cope with her needs. Two weeks in an environment like that could be good for her."

"Martin?"

"Agrees. More often than I'm comfortable with, Janine is all guns forward and firing, which can make me crazy, but doesn't faze Rachel, or your son. In fact, Martin referred to him as Janine's barometer. Seth knows when a storm is coming; recognizes when she's loaded with excess energy. Your little guy matches her energy and they engage in a physical activity like running, chasing a Frisbee, or, I've just learned, wrestle."

Brian's eyebrows went up. "Wrestle?" he said in a voice loaded with incredulity.

She nodded. "Like two little boys. It's supposed to be a secret between them but they didn't know I was watching one time...so strange...although similar in size, he's much stronger but uses his strength to allow her to burn off energy until she's had enough."

"And then?"

"They play like any five-year-old children. After the bout I witnessed, they moved to the art center for more than an hour. In silence, Janine created drawings of birds they'd seen in the Flathead Forest, while Seth drew a detailed picture of the Motorhome with a jeep attached, driving up a mountain; this place and Swan Lake in the distance. Following which the duo hauled a four step ladder out of the garage and taped their art to the wall of the playroom, then walked along the lake looking for minnows and water striders."

"I'll talk to Rachel, but I'm sure she'll agree."

With a sly grin, Krista said, "I shouldn't be surprised your wife can handle Janine's energy...I mean..." She giggled. "She handles you."

Brian burst out laughing.

Krista thought for a bit then added. "I'm concerned that Janine learn control of her emotions at this age. When she's old enough, we'll explain how her mother abandoned her. That could be traumatic. We don't know how she'll react."

Brian's expression changed to one of sadness. "The damn war. Janine wasn't any part of it but may suffer years after it ended." He sighed. "The war's impact was so cruel. So wide reaching."

***

Early the following morning, Brian, Rachel and Chana, sat on the deck, looking out on Swan Lake. Puffy clouds dotted the blue sky. A cool gust of wind blew across them, the leaves of the nearby Aspens rattled.

Chana wrapped a second blanket around her little one, who was sound asleep.

Brian asked. "What has it been like, living with Arnie since the onset of his PTSD symptoms?"

"The manic-depression scared and confused me, as does his sudden dislike of activities he enjoyed previously. We haven't been to a baseball game since the accident which seemed to have triggered his PTSD. He's been seeing the psychiatrist Brian recommended. For me, I have biweekly sessions with a therapist, which has helped. Understanding what caused his outbreaks and discussions of how to engage with him when he seems to be another person are useful but in don't make things easier."

Rachel said, "You're aware his behavior may change at any time, even with the meds?"

"My therapist mentioned. I need to watch for that and get him to his psychiatrist when it happens."

Brian asked, "What about his work?"

"They gave him a month off to straighten his head out. He's returned without a problem but one of the teachers is a close friend of mine and she let me know his behavior is not the same. Not bad but not the same."

Rachel asked, "This is none of my business but...did you ever consider leaving?"

Chana looked around to make sure no one else could hear. "Please, keep this to yourselves...I'm trying to be patient, but, the mood swings will be the death of me. If it doesn't improve, this is not the person I married. Certainly, not the person I want raising my child."

"Where is he?" Brian asked.

"Out for a drive."

The phone rang. While listening, Brian cursed then stared at Chana. He hung up the phone, closed his eyes, and shook his head.

"Who was it?" Rachel asked.

"The medical center in town." He looked at Chana. "Arnie tried to kill himself. He's in intensive care now but the ER doc said they expect him to live."

Chana turned pale.

"How did they know to call here?"

"ER doc knows me. I guess Arnie mentioned my name."

Chapter 24

"It is foolish and wrong to mourn the men who died. Rather we should thank God that such men lived."
General George S. Patton

June 1980

Sitting on the pool deck back in Texas, they sipped coffee early one morning in late September, it was still tee shirts and shorts weather. Brian said to Rachel, "I'm going to the garden center today to pick up bulbs. I believe a row in front of the porch would look pretty."

"Plants? So low tech. It seems so…not you…to have an interest in them."

"Relaxes me to work with them. Andrea taught me that when we visited her father's sheep station. Simple so doesn't take much thinking. She believed plants brought peace to tortured souls. After months of concentrating on the suffering of my fellow soldiers, flora brings peace and balance to my world…like she did and now you do."

"Thank you, but…I bring peace and balance?"

"Rachel, you and our children mean the world to me."

He placed his hands on either side of her face and kissed her.

"Pretty lady, will you marry me?"

"Rachel tilted her head slightly and asked, 'Why now?'"

"Because both our heads are in a place where I don't envision past trauma rearing its ugly head and pushing us apart."

"I agree," Rachel said in a quiet voice, grasping his hand.

"Besides, three sets of wind chimes are telling me, we belong together."

She laughed, "They talk to you now?"

"Rachel…"

She teased with a lilting tone in her voice, "We have a disagreement…you end up drumming or splitting wood for an hour."

Brian caressed her cheek. "How many times do I return…tell you how wise you are?"

"About as often as I let my partner know how pleased I am to be part of his life." She smiled and kissed his cheek, her expression radiating satisfaction. "Of course, I'll marry you."

***

Eight months later, in June of 1980, Brian, Rachel, and Donna were sitting around the kitchen table at the Levin's Texas ranch planning that year's July Fourth gathering at the Montana log home.

While they talked, Brian helped Abbey prepare slides for the five-year-old's microscope. As she finished each slide, the young one examined it under the optic then made a drawing of what she'd observed.

Abbey pointed to the microscope then said to Donna, "This used to be Dad's but he gave it to me so I can see things that are itty-bitty small."

"May I have one of the drawings?" Donna asked.

"Sure you can," Abbey said.

Rachel said, "Everyone is coming out to Montana again, except Arnie. Mary told me Michael will join us this year."

"How's Arnie?" Donna asked.

"Recovering but has a ways to go," Brian said. "So sad. He did so much to keep everyone's spirits up while we were in combat. As soon as you met him you thought you were his best friend."

"Poor, Chana," Donna said "The Vietnam War's impact is so far reaching. I wonder what will happen to the children of the Veterans who have difficulty coming to terms with their involvement in the war." Donna shook her head then added, "On a brighter note, I talked to Krista earlier this week. I swear, she and Martin were made for each other. Michelle fits with them but problems continue with Janine."

"We have her out for the weekend once a month. She and I are close, feel like she's family."

Brian said Abbey, "Just one drop of dye on that one."

Abbey used an eye dropper, centered it over the slide, added one drop of the dye then placed a cover slip over it.

"Excellent, Abbey," Brian said.

Donna addressed the five-year-old. "Do you and Janine play together?"

The five-year-old turned to her and said, "Sometimes she helps me with drawings but doesn't like my microscope." Abbey shrugged. "Dad or Mom have to help me with some slides but mostly I can make my own because I'm five-years-old now."

"Excellent," Donna said with a grin.

"Janine pretty much ignores her," Rachel said. "Which doesn't bother Abbey who has her own sense of direction. But Janine and Seth engage like brother and sister."

"Square dance again this year? Everyone loved that," Donna said.

Rachel laughed, patted her belly. "As I'll be in my ninth month in early July, I won't be joining in but definitely put that on the schedule."

Her friend laughed, became wistful and said, "I pray the children will remember these gatherings and remain close as they enter adulthood." Donna made some notes on the activity planning chart then said, "Did I tell you, since last year's Montana get together, Corey and Mary's daughter Vera, have been writing? Scott bought a computer from Radio Shack, and is teaching Corey how to use it. Apparently, Vera's dad bought one as well."

"I bought one," Brian said, "based on Scott's recommendation. We spent an entire day together setting it up and running programs."

"A relative of Brian, Michael Levin, is about Cory's age and is communicating and exchanging instructions with him..." Donna shrugged, "...and they've never met, never even talked on the phone."

Abbey showed a drawing to Donna. "That's a tree leaf. You can have this drawing. See all the cells?"

"Good work, Abbey," she said and gave her a brief hug. "Please put your name on that one and I'll put it up in our family room."

"Good drawing, Abbey," Rachel said, then gave her daughter's shoulder a squeeze and then turned to Donna. "Seth is communicating with Michael over our computer so my son is learning about the little machine as well. Brian had our computer hooked up to a computer at UT. That computer can talk to the computer at Scott's work and a computer at Brian's hospital."

"Scott is super pleased that Cory is consumed with doing things with that little box. As our computer is connected to his office, he works from home one day a week, spends all day on that machine, his attention riveted to the screen."

Wearing an expression of shock, Rachel said, "They pay him while he works from home?"

Donna nodded.

Rachel giggled. "Where can I get one of those jobs?"

The trio laughed.

"Not sure if I mentioned," Rachel said, "I received another call from my sister Mirna. She and her daughter are visiting for a week, the last week in August."

"What joy!"

"I was shocked when she called back in May. We stayed on the phone for two hours. She's had a difficult life since she left home. Her daughter sounds like a bitter person, lacking any sense of direction."

"Could be a rough week," Donna said.

"That's what Brian thinks. I'm hoping for the best. I haven't seen her in so long..."

The phone rang. Brian answered then set it to speaker so he could continue to help Abbey.

The caller said, "I'm Colonel Bruce Clark calling from the Pentagon. I'm trying to reach Major Brian Levin."

With a look of surprise, Brian answered. "This is Major Levin. What can I do for you?"

"You served with the 101st Airborne Division in 1970 and authored research we've been reviewing. We're assembling a discussion group. We were hoping to schedule a time when you would be available to meet a group of us at Fort Sam near Houston to review and discuss your work. We were thinking the third week of August."

Rachel's expression was one of shock and joy.

Donna's eyes went wide. She smiled and punched the air.

The colonel continued, "There are some procedures we're thinking of implementing but wish to have your input."

"I'll...I'll..." Brian steeled himself and cleared his throat. "I'll arrange to clear my calendar and schedule time to meet with your group. Let me have your number, Colonel."

He wrote it down then thanked the colonel for calling. Rachel turned to Donna. The friends embraced.

"Finally," Brian said then embraced Rachel.

"Thank the Lord," Donna said. "About time."

***

The five were bathed in the golden glow of a North Texas sunrise. Three sets of wind chimes painted rainbows across the porch.

Rachel sat in a glider, her face radiant, Andrea in her arms, Abbey on her father's lap, Seth sitting between his parents, reading to his sisters.

Brian thanked the Lord for putting Rachel in his life. A wind chime chorus sounded. *"I know,"* he thought, as if answering their sonorous voice. *"When I was in need, first Andrea, and then Rachel, lifted me....and became the wind chimes of my life."* He considered his tremendous good fortune then remembered his fellow vets. *"Please Lord, if you've got time, I know lots of troubled vets who could use wind chimes in their lives..."*

~~~The End~~~

If you enjoyed my novel, please leave a review on the website from which you purchased it. Reviews help Indie Authors like myself to become known to more readers, ranked with book sites, and earn an income. Thank you!

Author's Notes:

I studied Lt. Col. Dave Grossman's book, *On Killing, The Psychological Cost of Learning to Kill in War and Society*. Anyone wishing to understand the psychological impact of war on soldiers and society, must read Grossman's book. This author also details the Vietnam War experience, and why it was unique. He explains in precise detail how much of the violence in our society is due to our electronic devices and media. According to his analysis, we are training large segments of our children to become violent and accepting of violence to a degree unknown to previous generations.

For military field and hospital procedures, I studied Emergency War Surgery produced by the Department of the Army, third edition. The medical procedures depicted in this novel are for fictional purposes only.

About the Author

Richard is a 101st Airborne Division Vietnam veteran. After an education in mathematics, 17-years in manufacturing engineering, then 22-years as a software engineer, Richard embarked on a career in writing. He has written American Journeys, a series of historical fiction novels set in 1847 – 1865. Expertly researched the series details a family's struggles during the Great Irish Famine, emigration from Ireland to Boston, and their journey across the United States. Abbey is introduced as a little girl in Volume One of American Journeys, a teen in Volume Two, and she becomes Dr. Abby Kaplan, a surgeon during the Civil War in Volume Three.

Being a lifelong learner, Richard loves pursuing the research for his historical fiction. It is frequently accomplished while RV traveling with his wife, Carolynn, to libraries, museums, and historical sites around the country. Having a career that is portable permits traveling to many spectacular areas of the United States. It also provides opportunities to visit our adult children, grandchildren, other relatives, and friends

ALSO BY RICHARD ALAN

Have you read them all?

Additional detailed blurbs and purchasing information available on villagedrummerfiction.com/books

In the American Journeys Series

American Journeys from Ireland to the United States (1847–1854) Previously titled American Journeys: From Ireland to the Pacific Northwest (1847–1900) Book 1

A cruel famine. A fight for survival. Can a voyage across the sea bring new life? After so much death, this young immigrant will do anything to start her new life. If you like courageous heroines, richly-detailed settings, and stories of relentless determination, then you'll love Richard Alan's poignant tale.

American Journeys: The Pacific Northwest and the Oregon Trail (1854 – 1880) Previously titled *American Journeys: From Ireland to the Pacific Northwest (1847–1900) Book 2*

Their dreams carried them this far, but what happens when the next generation doesn't share the same vision? A new generation. A dangerous town. Can an immigrant family make room for new traditions? If you like multi-generational sagas, beautifully-wrought settings, and stories of the human experience, then you'll love Richard Alan's rugged tale.

A Female Doctor in the Civil War

Virginia Field Hospital, 1862. Abbey Kaplan will do whatever it takes to become a doctor. As a surgical assistant, her first major test is tolerating her chauvinistic male associates. But when her inaugural posting lands her smack in the middle of a Civil War field hospital, proving herself isn't about pride—it's a matter of life or death. If you like brave heroines, authentic settings, and stories that bring the past to life, then you'll love Richard Alan's stunning saga.

Although this book is the 3rd in the American Journeys Series, it can be read as a stand-alone.

~~~~~

Sign up for the Village Drummer Fiction Newsletter (villagedrummerfiction.com/newsletter) to be notified when new books, discounts, and author appearances are available
~~~~~